MESS - MEND

YANKEES IN PETROGRAD

MARIETTA SHAGINIAN

INTRODUCED & TRANSLATED
BY
SAMUEL D. CIORAN

ARDIS, ANN ARBOR

Copyright © 1991 by Ardis Publishers
All rights reserved under International and
Pan-American Copyright Conventions
Printed in the United States of America

Book design by Ross Teasley
Jacket design by Ross Teasley based on
original designs by A. Rodchenko.

Translated from the original Russian

Ardis Publishers
2901 Heatherway
Ann Arbor, Michigan 48104

Library of Congress Cataloging-in-Publication Data

Shaginian, Marietta Sergeevna, 1888-1982.
[Mess-mend. English]

Mess-mend, the Yankee in Petrograd / Marietta Shaginian ;
translated by Samuel D. Cioran.
p.   cm.
Translation of: Mess-mend, ili IAnki v Petrograde.
ISBN 0-88233-971-0
I. Title.
PG 3476.S437M413 1991
891.73'42–dc20   90-35869
                    CIP

CONTENTS

Translator's Introduction
    Marietta Shaginian's *Mess-Mend: Yankees in Petrograd*   *7*

Mess-Mend: Yankees in Petrograd
    Jim Dollar, His Life and Work: Introductory Essay   *27*
    Prologue   *32*
    Chapters 1-58   *34*
    Epilogue   *267*

Marietta Shaginian's
Mess-Mend:
Yankees in Petrograd

A cheerful blue-eyed, red-bearded giant of a man, in a work-apron, a pipe clenched in his teeth, was working away full steam with a wood plane and brushing the beads of sweat from his face. His curly blond hair was clinging to his forehead, his apron was fluttering like a sail, the wood shavings were flying with a whistling sound in all directions... He held his handiwork up to the light, admired it, pulled his pipe out and began to sing under his breath:

With wooden lathe and plane and glue,
We promise husbands fine for you,
From workers' hands and craftsmen's too,
Our daughters come like pretty things.

Go forth on guard where foes do dwell,
In banks and belle-étages as well.
Return from there to tattle-tell
About their regal lords and kings.

The rest of the workshop laid down their tools and gathered around the blue-eyed giant, and, in a single voice, took up the tune:

On kulaks' carts so richly laden,
Upon the general's mighty gun,
On all the rich man's source of fun,
Our trademark travels through the land.

For all our fathers' calloused pains,
For all our want and bitter chains,
Avenge yourselves in labor plain,
Creating marvels with your worker's hand.

The blond giant moved away, his song grew more and more indistinct, the large bearded face with even blond eye-brows over a cheerful gaze faded little by little—and he was gone, he had to rally the striking telegraph operators...

"Who is that man?" a curly, fair-haired stranger asked, as he gazed after the disappearing giant. "Who the devil is that?"

Indeed, who is this blue-eyed, bearded, handsome giant of a man? Is he a 19th Century Russian worker-revolutionary out of some unpublished piece of fiction by Maxim Gorky? Or is he possibly some little-known version of the New Soviet Man, the worker-hero of a five-year plan novel? No, he is neither one nor the other. His co-workers reveal his identity to a gaping-mouthed stranger:

> "And where do you come from if you don't know him?" was to be heard on all sides. "Just remember, and don't go passing it on any farther! That's Michael Thingsmaster, from the wood-working factory in Middletown. He's a wood-turner, a carpenter, a cabinet-maker—anything you want, he can be it: Mike's the smartest one of all our fellow-workers in America!"

Michael Thingsmaster. As his name suggests, he is a master of all things. In order to protect the interests of workers everywhere, to make them masters of their own destinies, to prevent future cataclysmic wars, to check the rapacious greed of capitalism and the lust for power of fascism, Michael Thingsmaster has created a secret international alliance of workers called "Mess-Mend", whose trademark is a microscopic double "m" stamped on the manufactured products of the workers' labor. As the name of the secret alliance suggests, they have shouldered the responsibility of mending the mess created in the world by capitalism and fascism.

The theory of proletarian supremacy over capitalism is simply put by Thingsmaster to his co-workers:

> Just think, never before has it occurred to anyone that we are stronger than anyone else, richer, happier; the homes in the cities, the furniture of those homes, people's clothing, bread, the printed book, machines, tools, utensils, weapons, ships, cannons, sausages, beer, shackles, steamers, railway cars, railway tracks—we're the ones that make them and no one else... I say to myself: Mike Thingsmaster, aren't you the father of all these beautiful little things... Aren't they really all my own children? I make them with my own two hands, I know them, I love them and I say to them: "Aha, my children, you are going forth into alien quarters to do your service; you, my wardrobe, will stand in some bloodsucker's nook; you, bed, will groan beneath the libertine; my fancy little case, you will guard some she-spider's diamonds—so take care, my little ones, don't forget your father! Go there with caution, as my faithful helpers..." Thingsmaster stretched to his full height and swept the crowd with his eyes. "That's right, fellows, go ahead and inspire things with the magic of resistance. Difficult? Nothing of the sort! Locks, the strongest and most cunning of our artifices, go ahead and make them open up from our touch alone! Make doors listen and then report to us, make mirrors recollect what they've seen, make walls collapse, ceilings cave in, roofs lift off like lids. The master of things is the one who makes them, whereas the slave of things is the one who merely uses them!

Such, then, is the theoretical backbone of international "Mess-Mendism." In the suspenseful and adventure-packed first novel of her trilogy, *Mess Mend, ili Yanki v Petrograde*, (1923), Marietta Shaginian will pit the master-craftsman and master proletarian sleuth, Michael Thingsmaster, against a villainous cabal of international capitalists and fascists, led by the American multi-millionaire, Jack Kressling, and his diabolical elusive henchman, Gregorio Cice. Dedicated to the overthrow of Communism and the ascendancy of capitalism and autocratic rule throughout the world, Kressling and his international co-conspirators are plotting to overthrow the fledgling Soviet regime by a mass assassination of the Soviet hierarchy. Waiting in the wings are the Russian White Guardists who will then reinstate the Russian Monarchy and give Kressling unlimited and lucrative business concessions throughout Russia. It is the self-assumed responsibility of Michael Thingsmaster and the workers of the "Mess-Mend" alliance to become international proletarian detectives, ferret out the details of the plot, thwart the assassination attempt and bring the fascist criminals to justice. With help from very unlikely quarters they manage to succeed in everything except catching all of the villains. Naturally, this state of affairs enables Shaginian to resurrect the criminals for two further showdowns in the successive novels, *Laurie Lane, Metalworker* (1924) and *The Road to Baghdad* (1925).

Shaginian's novel of international intrigue was immensely popular with its Soviet readership in the mid-1920's, although it suffered badly at the hands of hard-nosed Marxist critics in those years. Nonetheless, most of the official Soviet publications give Shaginian credit for creating the first, and one of the most successful, "anti-fascist, propaganda, satirico-fantastic novels" in Soviet literature. Several questions arise. For the overtly propagandistic purpose of promoting the Workers' International, why did a Soviet writer elect to resort to the patently bourgeois form of the detective novel? And why create her proletarian Sherlock Holmes out of a member of the American, and not the Russian, working classes? A search for the answer to this curiosity leads us into the seemingly different worlds of literary experimentation, popular cinematic art and Soviet political propaganda in the early 1920's.

A number of literary works began appearing in the early years after the Revolution which portrayed serious political, ideological and social questions in a "satirico-fantastic" or "fantastic-adventurous" form. The best known authors of serious Soviet adventure fiction were Ilya Ehrenburg with his *Extraordinary Adventures of Julio Juarenito* and *Cartel D. E.;* and Alexey Tolstoy's *Engineer Garin's Death Ray* and *Aelita*. Of course, Yevgeny Zamyatin's science fiction novel *We* and Mikhail Bulgakov's novellas *The Fatal Eggs* and *Heart of a Dog* must be included in this category. However, such competent and serious authors as these represented but the refined tip of the proverbial iceberg, four-fifths of which concealed a massive interest in escapist literature both in pre-revolutionary and post-revolutionary Russia. Within this larger category of adventure fiction, the detective novel was especially popular with a vast readership. It would perhaps be accurate, if somewhat cynical, to suggest that, volume-wise, more Russians read the exotic adventures depicted in the novels of Jules Verne and Pierre Benoit, were more conversant with the investigative abilities of Sherlock Holmes, Nat Pinkerton and Nick Carter, than perhaps with the poetic delights of Pushkin and the literary artistry of Tolstoy. In all due respect to the greats of Russian literature, it must be acknowledged that Dostoevsky, at least, recognized the allurement exercised by crime and desperate criminal minds on a popular readership. A formidable deluge of what came to be known as *Pinkertonovshchina*, or simply "detective fiction," flooded pre-revolutionary book markets in Russia and spilled over into the 1920's. We can trace the derivation of the name *Pinkertonovshchina* to the American detective, Nat Pinkerton, a hero of literally countless tales of detective derring-do that appeared in English, French, German, Italian, Russian, Polish and even the Turkic languages at the turn of the century. Nat Pinkerton was supposedly based on the true-life cases of the flamboyant chief of America's first investigative organization, Allan Pinkerton. But also included under *Pinkertonovshchina* were the no less indomitable talents of another American sleuth, Nick Carter, subject of more than 2,000 stories by dozens of authors both in the 19th and 20th centuries (and for those who haunt tatty second-hand paperback emporia, a familiar name hogging space on the shelves and obviously still going strong). And, naturally, the triumvirate of international crime detection was completed by Sherlock Holmes, both in the authentic versions of Arthur Conan Doyle, as well as innumerable spurious editions, even including such an unlikely but popular Russian title as *Sherlock Holmes in Simbirsk*.

Where respectable pre-revolutionary authors had to content themselves with editions of four or five thousand, Nat Pinkerton, Nick Carter and Sherlock Holmes commanded stupendous editions of anywhere from sixty thousand to two hundred thousand. Book publishers were obviously aware of the fact that, contrary to the prejudices of common morality, crime really did pay. Serious drama had to compete, on a lower level, of course, with theatrical performances of the exploits of Sherlock Holmes and Nat Pinkerton apprehending diabolical foes. And in the Petersburg Zoo-Park there were regular performances of so-

TRANSLATOR'S INTRODUCTION

called *feerii-balety* or "fairy-tale ballets" depicting unsophisticated versions of *Pinkertonovshchina*.

Pinkertonovshchina's only serious contender in pre-revolutionary Russia for the light entertainment market was pornography, also sold on street-corners and at disreputable kiosks. One early Soviet critic gave a somewhat sour, but ironic view, not only of the different clientele served by these two despicable forms of escapist literature, but of the mutual exclusiveness of each:

> *Pinkertonovshchina* performed its function of escapism from the revolution together with pornographic literature. But while standing cheek-by-jowl, *Pinkertonovshchina* and pornographic literature served different readers. The average price of a thin pornographic book was not lower than one rouble, while an issue about detectives cost five to seven kopecks. It was typical that pornographic elements were absent in the stories about detectives.

The moral seems simple. You only get what you pay for. Those who could afford it, were able to enjoy the ultimate criminal delight of pornography. The less fortunate had to be content with mere murder and mayhem. And thus, Russia borrowed the concept of the inexpensive French criminal novel-feuilleton, the English "Penny-Dreadful" or "Newgate Novel" and the American "Dime Thriller", and created its own immensely popular literature of cheap thrills and adventures.

With the coming of the Revolution, one might have expected this brand of *Pinkertonovshchina*, with its cheap villains, unconvincing heroes, unlikely situations and torturous plots that severely tested the elasticity of the reader's imagination, to be buried together with other outmoded forms of bourgeois culture. Yet, a renewed interest in and a firm initiative on its behalf arose out of three very unlikely quarters: the literary polemics of the Serapion Brotherhood, the influx of Western movies, and the direct appeal of Nikolai Bukharin, whom Lenin considered to be the Communist Party's most talented theoretician.

Soon after the Revolution, a spirited discussion arose in certain literary circles of young experimental writer-critics about the disregard accorded the "sujet", or plot development, in Russian literature. Victor Shklovsky pointed out this characteristic neglect in Russian literature: "Plot construction has never occupied a strong position in Russian literature..." Others were even more outspoken in their criticism of the typical inability of Russian writers to create an interesting and cohesive development of the plot line. Valentin Kaverin, a member of the Serapion Brotherhood, in commenting on Zamyatin's *Islanders*, wrote "...the plot, which in Russia has never enjoyed any great significance, even now languishes in the shadows or plays a subordinate role." Mikhail Slonimsky, another Serapion, added his voice to Kaverin's, complaining that "It's been a long while since Russian literature has spoiled us with plot constructions... The disregard for plot is a tradition in its own right that began in the 1860's."

The most vehement critic, however, of poorly constructed and boring plots, was a third Serapion, Lev Lunts. In a slightly hysterical article, first delivered as a speech, entitled "Na Zapad" (1922), Lunts enjoined his fellow-Serapions to "Go West" in order to study the means and methods for instilling a fresh excitement and suspense into lifeless literary creations. The trouble with Russian literature, according to Lunts, was its overly serious and ponderous nature:

> For ages there has existed in the West a kind of literary creation which from our Russian point of view is frivolous, if not harmful. This is the so-called literature of exploits and adventures. In Russia it has been grudgingly tolerated for children. You can't do anything with children: they read "The World of Adventure" and the Soikin series of Cooper, Dumas and Stevenson, but they refuse to read the literary supplement to the journal *Niva*. Well, after all, they are silly and "don't understand". Later, when they become grown-ups and have grown wiser, they are instructed by the teachers of Russian literature, they are enlightened. And so, with bitter regret, they hide Haggard and Conan Doyle in their bookcases. It's not proper for them to read such child's play; instead, there awaits them the terribly boring, but terribly serious Gleb Uspensky. This is the literature for adults. But how often—admit it, you enlightened progressive and you bald adherent of "serious" creations—how often have you mournfully daydreamed about Dumas' dogeared books; books which in view of your respectability are forbidden to you! And with what pleasure you reread him, sitting in the train, concealing the cover so that your neighbor (also a respectable citizen) would not smile contemptuously on seeing that you read dime-store novels instead of Chernyshevsky?

The solution to this lamentable set of circumstances is simple, yet demanding, according to Lunts, namely, **PLOT!**: "That which the West considers classic we have termed dime-store novel drivel and child's play. Plot! The ability to handle a complex intrigue, to tie and untie knots, to twine and untwine them—this is acquired by many years of painstaking work, this is created by a continuous and excellent culture."

Lunts was certainly not advocating the creation of an adventure literature purely of cheap thrills, of sheer escapism. He was advocating, instead, the need to skillfully create a genuinely intriguing, fascinating and romantic literature wherein complex and masterfully composed plots would thrill the readers. Precisely the kind of adventure and detective fiction with which such consummate western writers as Arthur Conan Doyle, Rider Haggard, Alexander Dumas and Robert Louis Stevenson had held a vast Russian reading audience spell-bound.

TRANSLATOR'S INTRODUCTION

The early Soviet-style thriller or adventure novel also fell under the sway of the tremendously popular entertainment of the silent film. Many of the early silent films that Russians had the opportunity to view were, predictably enough, sensational thrillers. They revealed a silent but gripping world of vicarious thrills, spills and chills that had audiences literally on the edges of their seats. Film producers were just as aware in the early years of this century, as they are nowadays, that they had to create an aura of imaginative sensationalism and horror to achieve box-office successes. The detective film was very much a preferred genre for this very reason. For example, literally dozens of Sherlock Holmes silent films were produced in England, France and Germany and found their way into Russia. Usually, these films were "serials", consisting of 8, 9 or more reels shown on successive occasions. A vast repertoire of films based on the stories of Edgar Allan Poe— some depicting Poe himself, others faithful reproductions of his stories, and many that may as well have been made on the moon for all the resemblance they had to the original—also appeared in Russia before and after the Revolution: "The Raven" (1912); "The Pit and the Pendulum" (1913); "Murders in the Rue Morgue" (1914) and so forth. In fact, the Russians even made a number of their own thriller films, including "The Isle of Oblivion" (1917), based on a story by Edgar Allan Poe.

It would take more space than we have to go on listing the incredible influx of such adventure films into Russia before and after the Revolution. The Soviets themselves made a number of excellent thriller serials for cinema audiences. Perhaps the most famous of all was Kuleshov's "The Adventures of Mr. West in the Land of the Soviets" (1922). By a curious coincidence, one of the leading actors in that film and an understudy of Kuleshov's, was Boris Barnet, who a few years later made a serial film based on Shaginian's *Mess-Mend*. The year that Shaginian began her *Mess-Mend* trilogy, 1923, was the year of unmatched box-office smashes for two European films in Russia. The first was the film version of Pierre Benoit's "Atlantis". The plot of this extraordinary novel concerned the search for and discovery of the long-lost Atlantis in the Sahara Desert, of all places, where an incredibly beautiful, exotic and very rapacious Queen holds sway over her secret kingdom and rapidly runs through lovers, whom she has abducted from the outside world, at the rate of one per month. The other success was "Sodom and Gomorrha", an early version of our contemporary "shake-and-bake" films, replete with disastrous earthquakes and fiery infernos.

What was the reason for the popularity of such films of crime and adventure? The usual ones that apply today and hardly require belaboring: the enjoyment of vicarious thrills and the romantic escapism. Entertainment, pure and simple. But there was another interesting facet to the world of the cinema in the 1920's.

From the writings of a great number of critics, it was obvious that film was having a significant influence on the concept of the novel. Many innovative students of literature, such as Victor Shklovsky, saw the possibility for absorbing cinematic techniques into various literary genres. The terse, episodic nature of cinematic art appealed to him and many others who saw artistic techniques revealed in a new and fascinating way. The action was rapid, the intrigue was quickly laid bare, character development was pared to the bone, and superfluous material was quickly skimmed away. The camera worked for startling angles and dramatic effects with the utmost economy of time and artistic material. The novelty and the freshness of the medium made many writers look at their own literary craft in a new and startling fashion. Marietta Shaginian was not the only writer who frankly admitted that she was striving for the same effective techniques in her writing as she saw disclosed in the cinema.

Independent and indirect support of the general principles proposed by Lev Lunts and the influential world of cinematic entertainment came from a very unlikely quarter in 1923: the hierarchy of the Communist Party. No lesser a personage than Nikolai Bukharin, member of the Politburo, editor of *Pravda*, and a leading theoretician for the Communist Party, issued an appeal on the pages of the party newspaper *Pravda*, for the creation of a *krasnyi Pinkerton* or Red Pinkerton: "It's not such a bad idea for us to have our very own red Pinkerton," he wrote. While Bukharin's appeal was no doubt prompted more for reasons of literary propaganda than general literary innovation, nonetheless, it did its part in provoking an exuberant and popular stream of Soviet-style detective fiction during the next few years. This is not to say that, in general, the rest of the Party hierarchy, and the hard-core of Soviet Marxist criticism, were by any means enamored of Bukharin's appeal. Far from it! Lunacharsky, for one, thought that this tendency in contemporary literature, which he associated very much with Ilya Ehrenburg, was frivolous and unproductive. And the critics of the leading tendentious journals in the 1920's generally supported the view of the minister for education and enlightenment. An article which appeared in *Pechat' i Revolyutsiya* in 1925 was typical of this negative attitude towards the more fanciful results of Bukharin's appeal:

> When comrade Bukharin spoke about a red Pinkerton, he never meant to suggest by this some mythological story of non-existent death-rays and a legendary revolution in America. This is hardly what the contemporary Soviet reader requires. The artistic

portrayal of the USSR on the upswing and not some contrived plot out of the life of America, the traditional place of action for all the old adventure novels—this is the task of a Red Pinkerton.

One can well understand the apprehension of critics when one realizes the threatened and precarious international position of Soviet Russia in 1923. It hardly seemed the appropriate moment for a proletarian Nat Pinkerton or the working man's Sherlock Holmes to make a frivolous appearance. But with his good humor, his freshness of outlook and his sense of the value of propagandistic satire, Bukharin must have felt that it would be profitable to capitalize on the prevalent reading tastes of the masses. If they were going to read "junk fiction" or escapist literature, at least let it be Soviet in content and capable of both entertainment and propaganda (after all, why should the bourgeois and capitalists have all the entertaining fiction?)

The first Soviet author to respond to this triple challenge from Lev Lunts, contemporary cinema and Nikolai Bukharin, was a most unlikely choice: Marietta Shaginian.

Born in 1888 in Moscow of middle-class Russian and Russianized Armenian parents, Marietta Shaginian presents the western reader with the curious, but familiar, and not always flattering, spectacle of a Russian author whose creativity has successfully spanned the pre- and post-revolutionary eras. The same arduous journey from night into day that destroyed, crushed or maimed so many other early experimental writers, apparently left Shaginian completely unscathed, indeed, caused her to flourish. From a pre-revolutionary zealot of religious idealism, Shaginian became, with apparent ease, a post-revolutionary zealot of Marxist-Leninism. Her first major literary tendency grew out of her association with the "Fellow-Travelers" in the 1920's, particularly with the Serapion Brotherhood. After the Revolution she embarked on a series of novels that ranged from realistic and sympathetic portrayals of the Revolution and Russia in the throes of change, to imaginative, innovative and very self-conscious experimentation with novelistic techniques. The same zeal which had led her first to religious idealism and then to literary experimentation, eventually induced her to be among the first to take up the call to arms for *Sovzakaz* and Five-Year-Plan literature. With her customary fervent involvement, Shaginian spent several years on the construction site of a hydro-electric station in Armenia at Dzorages, documenting, experiencing first-hand and writing her novel *HydroCentral* (1929) which has since become one of the standard classics of Socialist Realism. Shaginian's work became generally lackluster and pedestrian after the 1920's when she devoted herself increasingly to a journalistic and biographical approach in literature. She wrote a Marxist-Leninist interpretation of Goethe, an extensive sociological study of Armenia, a biography about the young Lenin and dozens of journalistic essays that were more sociological than literary.

In October of 1923, on the wings of inspiration and with innovative skill hitherto unsuspected in her, Marietta Shaginian set out to create the "krasnyi Pinkerton" demanded by Bukharin and to heed the literary advice of those like Lev Lunts who were concerned with the surfeit of poorly constructed intrigues in Russian literature. Before she finished, she managed to create one of the most intricate and amusing parodies in Russian literature: *Mess-Mend, ili Yanki v Petrograde.* Not only did she expertly parody practically every recognizable device of the detective thriller, but she managed at the same time to mount a polemic with the pessimistic worker novels of Upton Sinclair that were so popular in Russia just before and after the Revolution. The result was a fresh form of lively and entertaining propaganda: the first proletarian novel of international intrigue and detection. Instead of depicting the miserable lives of a proletarian class crushed, exploited and manipulated by the capitalists, Shaginian immediately sets a tone of cheerful and determined resistance in the prologue to *Mess-Mend* when Mike Thingsmaster addresses a worker's rally:

> Fellows, Upton Sinclair is a wonderful writer, but he's not for us! Let him torment the Industrialist's liver and serve as a reference book for agitators. But give us the kind of literature that will make us feel like the masters of our own lives... It's no good for you and me to constantly see our reflection in the tearful figures of various wretched [Jimmie] Higginses and to imagine ourselves as the wretched, enslaved and vanquished. In fact, we won't get very far that way. Give us instead a book that will make bold spirits out of us!

This cheerful attitude of international proletarian resistance greatly impressed Nikolai Bukharin when he read the manuscript of Shaginian's book and obviously provided the kind of militant *krasnaya Pinkertonovshchina* that he apparently desired.

When Shaginian's book began to appear late in 1923, no one suspected who the genuine author was. This was due to an elaborate literary subterfuge. The novel was offered in the traditional format of adventure literature: a serial issue, every two weeks, of the next "adventurous episode" in the tale. The issues were inexpensive, paperbound, and bore a sensational, colorful cover depicting a suspenseful moment in that particular issue (the covers were artistically done by Rodchenko and Stepanova). To promote Shaginian's idea of a spoof of the entire genre of detective fiction, the author's real name did not appear on the successive issues. Instead, she created an utterly fictitious author, Jim Dollar, for whom a detailed biography was provided in the first issue. Supposedly an orphan, Jim Dollar had a proletarian upbringing in the American school of hard knocks, sleeping under bridges and working in the factories of bloodsucking capitalists. But as it turns out, he was the abandoned child of some anonymous American millionaire who leaves him all his wealth. Jim Dollar uses this wealth to help his former proletarian comrades, and to write propagandistic novels such as *Mess-Mend* which he forces the large and indifferent American capitalist presses to publish by paying three times the value of the entire edition (a kind of proletarian capitalism, if you will). Shaginian's spoof was supported by none other than the prestigious head of the State Publishing House (Gozizdat), Nikolai Meshcheryakov, who wrote an introduction that supported the authorship of *Mess-Mend* by the unknown American author, Jim Dollar.

A final satiric touch was added by the inclusion of a portrait of Jim Dollar, wearing a fez, and looking very much like a masculine portrait of Shaginian herself. Few people suspected who the author was for some time. Many thought that it was either Ilya Ehrenburg or Alexei Tolstoy. In fact, there were even those who thought that Nikolai Bukharin himself was the real author and had concealed his identity behind this elaborate ruse. Only in 1926 did it become common knowledge, when a serial movie was made of *Mess-Mend*, that Shaginian was, indeed, solely responsible for all three novels in the series.

With amazing ingenuity Shaginian was able to incorporate all the traditional devices of thriller-fiction into her novel: purloined letters; secret passages concealed in walls, subterranean tunnels and even the heating and plumbing systems of buildings; two-way mirrors with hidden photographic equipment; mysterious strangers; secret potions and diabolical poisons; an insane asylum where the villainous Gregorio Cice incarcerates his hapless victims in hellish conditions; murder by drowning, poison, stoning, stabbing, shifting walls, giant meat-grinding machines; the use of supernatural and occult powers; hypnosis, secret amulets and mysterious, wonder-working devices; the art of self-disguise rendered absurd through the doubling and even tripling of disguises in a single person (at one point in the novel, there are no fewer than six characters in disguises confronting one another). In short, Shaginian created a veritable pot-pourri of every typical thriller within the confines of a single book. And yet she managed to carry the parody even further in her ironic treatment of characters and situations. To the traditionally facile and uncomplicated relationships usually encountered in cheaper versions of *Pinkertonovshchina,* she gives an additional twist with her parody of deviant sexual psychology: Mike Thingsmaster prefers his shaggy dog, Beauty, to any female companionship; young Arthur Morlender, a self-avowed misogynist, is insanely jealous of his father's avowed attachment to the mysterious Elizabeth Wesson; the corpulent Dr. Lepsius wears female jewelry; Grace Notabit, an American Senator's tomboy daughter, falls madly in love with a scandalous masked lady; Grace's old school-friend, and niece of Elizabeth Wesson, has more than the strong hint of a moustache on her upper lip and speaks in a disconcertingly masculine bass voice; Bob Druck, the self-fancied sleuth, lives in the protective custody of his doting mother. Moreover, when one examines the vehicle whereby all the clues to the mystery are assembled, the parody is carried from merely sublime levels to the ridiculous: all the primary clues for the solution are held entirely in the hands, or more appropriately, the paws, claws, talons, hoofs and flippers of a misdirected hutch of prize rabbits, a dead tomcat that chases from its nest a thieving crow that stole an important letter, the same crow that loses its valuable burden while on a migration westward across America, a dog that mysteriously arrives in Soviet Russia bearing another important letter, a walrus that travels half-way round the world with a secret message in a bottle in its stomach, and a rebellious donkey that delivers a strange Russian emigrant to a farm in the American Mid-West. Yet, Shaginian manages to assemble this disparate menagerie at the remote Illinois farm of Attorney General Milky by some plausible yet incredible stretch of the imagination!

While creating an entertaining send-up of detective fiction, Shaginian nevertheless succeeded in combating the ineffectual passivism of the workers' novels of Upton Sinclair, in particular, the prototype of Jimmie Higgins. In her novel, the workers are extremely well-organized, they are cheerful, they are determined to be masters of their own destinies and they succeed in thwarting the evil designs of international capitalism. Strong, humorous, thoughtful and inventive, they are a good match for the Jack Kresslings of this world. Through thrilling plot and counterplot, romantic intrigue and counter-intrigue, they nullify the attempts of international capitalism to subjugate them and break their spirit.

In Soviet Russia, the novel was so popular among the general readership and appealed so highly to some members of the hierarchy like Nikolai Bukharin and Nikolai Meshcheryakov, that Shaginian was induced to write two sequels: *Laurie Lane, Metalworker* (1924) and *The Road to Baghdad* (1925). But these were not as successful nor quite as inspired as the first novel. They lacked the light and imaginative touch of *Yankees in Petrograd* and the intrigues became even more torturously twisted and confusing. The parody of detective fiction threatened to take over completely, often resulting in bewildering and heavy-handed contrivance. In *The Road to Baghdad*, for instance, no fewer than five distinct groups of spies and private detectives are chasing one another nose-to-tail. Sexual parody became even more desperate: a Rumanian prince by the name of Gonorescu operates a spy facility disguised as a brothel; a syphilitic and wanton capitalist, dressed as an English vicar, has a "Turkish mistress" who turns out to be a male acrobat and tightrope walker; Grace Notabit, the "virgin wife" of Westinghouse, seduces the metalworker Laurie Lane who is dressed as a woman. Moreover, Soviet critics remained uninspired by Shaginian's imaginative plots and humorous parodies. Critics from the major Soviet journals ganged up on the hapless Shaginian. One of the leading Marxist literary critics, Gabor Lelevich, gave her work the disparaging title of *Mess-Mendovshchina* and called it "cheap and anti-revolutionary fiction that was assuming threatening proportions." And Lelevich perceived a very ominous aspect to this kind of literature that failed to give credit to the proper authorities: "And here, instead of a class struggle among people, we have a struggle for things. And here we find depicted the so-called proletarian revolution but nothing is even mentioned about either the Communist International or the Communist Party, just as though they didn't even exist... Disguise it as you may, there's no way you can transform *Mess-Mendovshchina* into revolutionary literature... It's time to initiate a serious struggle with *Mess-Mendovshchina!*"

However, the criticism that stung Shaginian most painfully was that of a reviewer for *Russkiy sovremennik* who accused "Jim Dollar" of concentrating only on the development of the intrigue without any commitment to the portrayal of contemporary reality and events. In succeeding years, Shaginian often defended her work against this charge. She claimed that all of the inspiration for *Mess-Mend* came directly from contemporary reality, that the events and situations described formed the very atmosphere of the times they were living through in the early 1920's. All one had to do was to read the pages of *Pravda* 1922 to 1925, as she avidly did, to realize where much of the material was gleaned. There was more than ample evidence of the fact that big business and fascism were joining hands throughout the world to crush the proletarian movement. Mussolini had seized power in Italy and the Italian communist party was being viciously persecuted. In Germany Hitler had become a household name after his attempt to gain power. The threat of another disastrous world war was in the air as the French marched in and occupied the Ruhr. Nations argued over German war reparations and Lord Curzon was menacing Soviet Russia with intervention.

Clearly, Shaginian was able to gain the inspiration for writing the *Mess-Mend* trilogy directly from current events printed in the newspapers and the menacing international situation being promoted by an apparent alliance between capitalism and fascism. Needless to say, she did not give a verbatim report on those events, but her novels did certainly capture the atmosphere of international intrigue that was rampant in the 1920's.

There were several very important facts which militated against the Soviet critics accepting Shaginian's brand of *krasnaya Pinkertonovshchina*. Her novels were far too "international" rather than "Russian" in content and in spirit. Few Russians appear in any of the three novels, and when they do, only episodically and two-dimensionally. And as is frequently the case with this type of literature, the villains, by reason of their evil genius, are usually more fascinating than the upright and predictable heroes. Parody of literary devices and genres, indeed, even satirization of international capitalism devoid of a firm and serious Soviet footing, was simply a superfluous literature in the eyes of most critics. And, the affiliation of Nikolai Bukharin's name with *krasnaya Pinkertonovshchina* would ultimately prove to be a handicap rather than a benefit when Bukharin fell victim to the Stalinist purges in the 1930's.

Another serious stumbling-block to this type of adventure literature was the fact that many critics firmly associated it with decadent and bourgeois Western culture. After all, it had to be admitted that the vast percentage of *Pinkertonovshchina* that had appeared in pre-revolutionary Russia and was still appearing after the Revolution, was authored by so-called bourgeois authors. In a very detailed and knowledgeable article written by P. Kaletsky on *Pinkerstonovshchina* for the official *Literaturnaya entsiklopediya* in 1934, there is no mistaking the deep mistrust of Soviet Marxist critics over this type of literature:

> A revolutionary literature of adventure cannot be created according to the outmoded cliches of *Pinkertonovshchina* which is a weapon for bourgeois ascendency over the remainder of the petty bourgeois masses and aimed at their demoralization... Seducing the readers with the incredible effectiveness and action of its hero, who is far removed from any psychological complexity, [*Pinkertonovshchina*] envelopes the detective and policeman standing on guard for bourgeois law and order in an aura of glory and heroism. The ideological function of *Pinkertonovshchina* is the protection of the bourgeois order, it is an extreme form of propaganda for imperialistic tendencies.

For interest's sake, the more recent *Kratkaya literaturnaya entsiklopediya* (1962-75), reiterates many of the same ideas as the first *Literaturnaya entsiklopediya*, but omits the rabid mistrust of such literature, simply referring the reader back to the 1934 article by Kaletsky for a fuller discussion of *Pinkertonovshchina.*

Finally, it seems as though Russians still have difficulty in overcoming certain literary prejudices, just as Lev Lunts claimed in his article "Go West!" Literature of the fantastic, literature of intrigue, literature of adventure—these genres belong manifestly to the category of *zheleznodorozhnaya literatura*, or light entertainment for long trips and dentists' offices, unworthy of serious consideration. For them, the literature of adventure is still viewed primarily as detskaya literatura or "children's literature." This curious fact is borne out by the case history of Shaginian's *Mess-Mend* itself. All three novels were published in full for the last time in Shaginian's collected works in 1931-35. Only the first novel of the trilogy, *The Yankees in Petrograd* has been republished since, and not until 1956, when it appeared in *Biblioteka priklyucheniy i nauchnoy fantastiki* under the auspices of the State Publishing House for Children's Literature. That publication was reissued in 1960 by the same publishing house. Since 1956, two editions have appeared of Shaginian's collected works (1956-58 and 1971-73). While all her other works, including the pre-revolutionary ones, have been reprinted in those two editions, only *Yankees in Petrograd* have survived of the original *Mess-Mend* trilogy. Moreover, for the 1956 edition Shaginian was requested "to rewrite" and "correct" certain inadequacies that had cropped up in the original 1923 edition.

Samuel D. Cioran
McMaster University

Eight of ten covers by Alexander Rodchenko for the *Mess-Mend* series, 1924.

MESS - MEND: YANKEES IN PETROGRAD

JIMMY DOLLAR, HIS LIFE AND WORK

INTRODUCTORY ESSAY

On a March morning of 1888 a well-dressed man with a new-born baby came running up to the porter with badge No. 701 in one of the New York train stations.

"Porter, your number? Fine, take the baby, but carefully, damn it, if you want to make a dollar... Wait for me over there, by the bus stop, I'm in a hurry to look for a woman..."

Having said that, the stranger plunged into the crowd. Badge No. 701 carefully carried the baby to the bus platform, waited for ten minutes, then half an hour, then an hour. The baby began to cry. The porter became frightened—maybe the child had been dumped on him. When no one appeared after two hours and there was no sign of the stranger in the station, the porter said to himself bitterly: "There's your dollar for you"—and set off with the baby for the district police station.

Along the way a thought occurred to him. The child was handsomely dressed, in monogrammed baby clothes. Suppose something has happened to the stranger but then he suddenly misses the baby, comes searching for the porter by his number, and is enraged to learn that the child is at the police station. Wouldn't it be better to keep the child with him at home and in the meanwhile look for the stranger?

He took him home and turned him over to his wife. The child proved to be a marvellous little boy. His linen was monogrammed with "J.D." Since the porter was called James, as a joke he called the boy "Jim Dollar" a few times—and that name was forever fated to become attached to the lost creature and subsequently earned him a widespread reputation.

The parents of the baby did not show up. The porter adopted him. He grew up as an ordinary city kid and spent all his time on the street until badge No. 701 passed away. Following him, his wife died as well, leaving Jimmy Dollar the badge from his foster father and a brief history of his adoption.

For about a year and a half Jim led a vagrant's life. He slept under a bridge and on roofs, fed himself together with the dogs on the city's scraps. "My sense of smell was perfected during these years," he related in his brief autobiography, "I learned that every city, every street and every yard had its own smell."

Once he caught sight of a cart with large shipping crates in front of a tavern, crawled into one of them, closed himself in with the lid and fell asleep. He was awakened by a jolting. Following that a brilliant electric light spilled over him. A tall spinster in hair curlers was standing over the carton and examining him with compressed lips. He leapt out of the carton, intending to slip away.

"I suppose that I've paid for the carton with good money," said the spinster.

"You don't believe, ma'am, that you've bought me together with the carton?" Jim exclaimed in horror.

"Indeed, I do," replied the implacable spinster, "after all I only take things by weight."

The wretched Jim had no knowledge of the law. He sincerely believed the spinster and remained in her service for a good twelve years.

Those were the gloomiest years of his life. The spinster exploited the boy, forcing him to work even on Sundays. By fits and starts he learned to read and write. When he had turned nineteen, she suddenly presented him with a bicycle. After a short time had elapsed she again made another present to him—a dozen ties. Jim was seized with a strange presentiment: had the spinster gotten the idea of making him marry her? No sooner had he formulated this presentiment in his mind than an inborn love of freedom flared up within him. He hopped on his bicycle and was gone.

Jim was free. He was once again on the streets of New York. But here he was made to suffer the full burden of his lack of rights: what matters freedom when you don't have a crust of bread? Wandering through the factory district of New York, somehow or other he got himself into a match factory and became a worker. Two circumstances proved to have a deep influence on him: his first strike and his first introduction to the cinema.

The strike, as he subsequently wrote, taught him "the ability to defend himself with his back turned to the enemy," whereas the cinema led him to the theory of the "urban novel" that numbers so many adherents at the present time.

Returning from the cinema where he had seen a primitive drama from Parisian life with a noble Apache and a courtesan, Jim Dollar began to imitate the cinema like a madman for his comrades at work.

He collected a fistful of young people around himself, composed plays, performed them during the lunch break right there in the factory, using the equipment and machines for his acrobatic tricks. To this period belong the first sketches of two of his beloved heroes, the metal-worker Laurie, and the "tamer of things," Michael Thingsmaster (Mike-the-Magician of his much later novels). At night he would feverishly devour textbooks, attempting "to comprehend that liaison of prescribed notions which is customarily called education."* Refusing no type of work whatsoever, he made his way from one industrial center of America to another, periodically returning, nonetheless, to the old match factory where his friends and acquaintances remained.

That very same factory, or more precisely, the circle of matchworkers grouped around him, became acquainted with Jim Dollar's first literary experiment, the scenario of a large cinematic novel which he had conceived and drafted in the course of twelve hours. Here, incidentally, there came to light that fateful peculiarity of Dollar's which was to hinder his career as a novelist for a long while. By first gaining access to the significance of the fable through a visual image (not in a book, but on the cinema screen), Dollar would immediately sketch his heroes on the borders of the manuscript and insert hither and yon into the text drawings which served as illustrations. Like the majority of gifted people, Jim espied his talent not at all wherein it truly lay, but rather in what was by far his weakest area. Thus, in the depths of his heart he considered himself to be a born sketch-artist. But all the while, Jim Dollar's drawings were worse than bad,—they were illiterate and hapless.

His first cinematic novel (subsequently destroyed by the author) was greeted with an ecstatic outburst in the matchmakers' circle. Encouraged by his friends, Dollar made his way to the enormous New York publisher "Prix-Fixe-Book" and presented his manuscript. The editor, barely looking at his drawings, rolled the manuscript up into a tube and immediately returned it to the young author without saying a word.

"Go back to your wallpaper store, young man," the pitiless editor replied.

Jim shrugged and worked feverishly for the following two years on new scenarios, garnishing them abundantly with drawings. But despite all his efforts, the very same fate lay in store for them. No one knows what would have happened to our novelist if all at once he had not heard an insane pounding at his door.

"Jim!" roared the matchworker Rolls, flying into the tiny room with a newspaper in his hands. "Take a look here, you son-of-a-gun!"

---

*<i>New York Herald</i>, No. 381, "The Autobiography of Dollar."

In the classified section there stood in bold print:

URGENTLY, EARNESTLY, IMPERATIVELY we are seeking the former PORTER BADGE No. 701 for the benefit of his very own, and to him entrusted, INFANT. Wall Street No. 92.

With the newspaper in his hand, Dollar ran off to the indicated address. He was already dreaming about his newly-found parents, brothers and sisters. A fat notary emerged to greet him and upon examination of his documents and after a thorough interrogation of Jim, put him in possession of a solid enough inheritance without raising the veil over the mystery of his origins with a single word.

Dollar was sullen; he took no joy in his unexpected riches. However strange it may have been, he did not even leave the match factory and for the first half-year did not even touch the money.

But then the editor of "Prix-Fixe-Book" received a new manuscript scribbled over the amusing drawings. He glanced behind his back—to see whether there was a fire in the fireplace—and was in the midst of dispatching the ill-fated paper thence. But a letter fell out of the manuscript and in the letter Jim Dollar had written that he was offering the publishing firm a sum that would reimburse thrice over the amount of any loss from the publication of his novel. The editor shrugged and unravelled the manuscript. In a minute's time he had forgotten about everything in the world; the telephone rang twice, the secretary came and went, the typist coughed away—but he read on. The following day he said to Jim:

"We're buying your novel. But one condition: toss out the drawings."

"I'll buy the entire edition from you in advance and give it back to you in total with the condition that you print the drawings," replied Jim.

The negotiations continued for ten days. Finally "Prix-Fixe-Book" agreed to the publication of Dollar's first book.

In all probability, our readers know that the book was sold out in the first eight days and is presently appearing in the twenty-second edition.

It was not without a veiled sigh that the editor somehow brought himself to say to Jim Dollar:

"You're an excellent writer, Jim. But, by God, you do have one shortcoming.. Don't be angry with me, but you're completely overestimating yourself as an artist."

It was the first time that Dollar had heard any hint of the worthlessness of his drawings. It stung him, he blushed and replied haughtily:

"Even if it is a shortcoming, then it's one that I share with a certain Goethe."

Unfortunately he did not cease to cover his novels with drawings making their reproduction an unalterable condition with every editor. We are offering our readers under the general title of "Mess-Mend" a series of Jim Dollar's novels which achieved the greatest popularity for him and at the same time provoked all possible administrative persecutions, including the withdrawal of the first novel of this series, "The Yankees in Petrograd," which had been inspired by the Russian October Revolution.

In order to clarify for oneself the character of Dollar as a novelist, one must be reminded that his traditions are linked to the cinema and not to literature. He never studied bookish technique. He studied only in the cinema. His entire novelistic baggage is predicated on that. Although an American himself and a native of New York, he offers us nothing that resembles the real New York. The designation of streets, the localities, the factories, the everyday features—all of this is quite fantastic and in Dollar's novels a conditional, "screen-like" world is unravelled before our eyes. It's as though he were saying that the cinema was a kind of Esperanto for all of humanity. It is in this general "conditional" language that Dollar's novels are written. If Jim Dollar describes his own American reality in a fantastic fashion, then one can well imagine how far removed from reality are the descriptions mentioned in his novels of Soviet Russia and other countries which he never laid eyes on during his life. But a profound admiration and delight with the Great October Revolution leads him through all these eccentricities to a genuine feeling of the reality of the new world being created in the Land of the Soviets.

1923 M. S.

PROLOGUE

"Fellows, Upton Sinclair is a wonderful writer, but he's not for us! Let him torment the industrialist's liver and serve as a reference book for agitators. But give us the kind of literature that will make us feel like the masters of our lives. Just think, never before has it occurred to anyone that we are stronger than anyone else, richer, happier; the homes in the cities, the furniture of those homes, people's clothing, bread, the printed book, machines, instruments, utensils, weapons, ships, cannons, sausages, beer, shackles, steamers, railway cars, railway tracks—we're the ones that make them and no one else. All we have to do is lower our hands—and things will disappear, they'll become antiquarian rarities. It's no good for you and me to constantly see our reflection in the tearful figures of various miserable Higginses and to imagine ourselves as the wretched, enslaved and vanquished. In fact, we won't get very far that way. Give us instead a book that will make bold spirits of us!"

Speaking thus, an enormous man in a blue shirt tossed away a scruffy brochure and leapt down from the speaker's table into the jaded and pale-looking crowd that had been listening attentively to him. The action was taking place in Sweaton, at Rockefeller's metalworks. The metalworkers were on strike for the second week. But it had not been strikers alone who had come to hear the extraordinary orator. The hall, which had been supplied by the local library as an assembly place, was packed. Inside there were cautious country lads—the hired hands from local farms; telegraph operators and despatchers from the Sweaton station; a multitude of fellows from nearby factories and plants; and even the young metalworker, Laurie Lane, who had surreptitiously made his way here from Jack Kressling's "Secret Works."

"You're spinning tall tales, Mike," the yellow-faced pitworker, Carlo, shouted at the orator's back.

"Tall tales? Come over to our factory and take a look with your own eyes. I say to myself: Mike Thingsmaster, aren't you the father of all these beautiful little things? Aren't you the one who makes wood into decorative patterns like paper tissue? Don't your wooden panels twitter more tenderly than the birdies as you lay bare the language of wood and the kind of tracings whose existence no schoolteachers of drawing ever suspected? Mirrored cabinets for grand ladies, the cunning visages of doors that are always facing in your direction, decorative cases, writing desks, solid beds, secret boxes—are these really not all my own children? I make them with my own hands, I know them, I love and say to them:

Aha, my children, you are going forth into alien quarters to do your service; you, my wardrobe, will stand in some bloodsucker's nook; you, bed, will creak beneath the libertine; you, my fancy little case, will guard some she-spider's diamonds—so take care, my little ones, don't forget your father! Go there with caution, as my faithful helpers..." Thingsmaster stretched to his full height and swept the crowd with his eyes. "That's right, fellows. Go ahead and inspire things with the magic of resistance. Difficult? Nothing of the sort! Locks, the strongest and most cunning of our artifices, make them open up from our touch alone! Make doors listen and then inform us, make mirrors recollect, make walls conceal secret passages, make floors collapse, ceilings cave in, roofs lift off like lids. The master of things is the one who makes them, whereas the slave of things is the one who simply uses them!"

"That way we'd have to know more than an engineer," an old worker interposed. "An ignorant person can't invent anything new, Mike, he just makes what he's shown and that's that."

"You're wrong! Fall in love with your work and your eyes will become opened. Just take a look at these bands of metal. They really do breathe, they work, they have their own spectrum, they radiate forth for man even though they're invisible to the enemy. You ought to know how they operate, you've been exposed to them for dozens of years. Study every metal, become impregnated with it, exploit it— and then let it slip into the world with your secret instructions and fulfill, fulfill, fulfill..."

...Thingsmaster was moving away, his speech became more and more muffled, the large bearded face with blond even eyebrows over a cheerful gaze faded little by little—he was gone, he had to rally the striking telegraph operators in Roven-Square, he was already far away...

"Who was that?" excitedly asked the curly blond-haired Laurie Lane, a metalworker from the "Secret Works," as he gazed after the disappearing orator. "Who the devil was that?"

"And where do you come from if you don't know him?" was to be heard from all sides. But the elderly and slow-moving Willings, of whom it was known that he filled his pipe and moved in obvious imitation of Mike Thingsmaster and even attempted to let his beard grow in precisely the same manner, pronounced in a didactic voice:

"Just remember and don't pass it on any farther! That's Michael Thingsmaster, from the woodworking factory in Middletown. He's a wood-turner, a carpenter, a cabinetmaker—anything you want: he's the smartest of our brethren in America!"

CHAPTER 1
JACK KRESSLING LEARNS THE NEWS

The little town of Middletown wallowed among the high black smoke stacks which surrounded it on all sides and which had long since banished all semblance of greenery from its center. On its eastern boundary, gleaming with bright windows, stood the buildings of Kressling's wood-working factory. Every five minutes freight trains from the southeastern mainline, nine-tenths of whose stocks belonged to Jack Kressling, arrived at the railway station. To the south and the north the city was being squeezed in by the pipeworks, the boilerworks, and the various mechanical, hydroturbine and automobile factories of Kressling's. And to the west, behind the steel sheets of a high enclosure, was Kressling's relatively small, but extraordinarily important and highly expensive, "Secret Works."

A pathological love of publicity and a strange nervous restlessness which gnawed away at the billionaire Kressling day and night, would not allow him to make his "Secret Works" so secret that no one would suspect anything of it. On the contrary, the entire American press knew that mysteries were being constructed there at his personal expense. They wrote about unusual experiments which were being conducted at these works, about its connection with far-off mines whose whereabouts, to be sure, could not be specified, yet at the same time mention was made of a former French concession in Russia and about the fact that the Russian Revolution had had a strong effect on this concession; they wrote about a secret mine which had apparently been discovered by Kressling and which promised to make him the master of the world; they wrote, and there was a great deal they did not write, about Jack Kressling himself, the most interesting billionaire in the family of American financial magnates.

Jack Kressling was a bachelor. He was forty years old. He was tall, lean, solid and well-built, clean-shaven, grey-eyed, his hair stylishly arranged on his imposingly shaped head, cut short and heavily pomaded, its ash-grey color a guarantee for dozens of years of that indeterminate condition which is rendered familiar in the phrase "young for his age." Contrary to the habit of American billionaires of knowing nothing and learning nothing, of being unable to distinguish Dante from Kant and the poet Coleridge from porridge, Jack Kressling had finished Oxford in his youth, read the Greek poets in the original, even published a work of many years' effort under the title of "Capital as The Substratum Of

Psycho-Energy." Even if it were not for his persistent, almost maniacal enthusiasm for politics, and the suspicious beauty of his personal secretary, he would have been the most eligible groom for the daughters of America's first "two hundred families."

But even more than about Jack Kressling, even more than about his hundreds of plants and factories, the newspapers wrote about Kressling's right-hand man, the chief engineer of his enormous industrial economy, the director of the "Secret Works" and the world-famous inventor, Mr. Jeremy Morlender. It had in fact been Morlender who had found out about the mysterious mine; he was the one who was doing something at the "Secret Works" that promised Kressling mastery over the world; he was the one who had built the magical villa of "Ephemerides" for his "boss" in Middletown's surroundings; and he had been the one, as the papers wrote, who shared Kressling's hatred for the Russian Revolution and Russia. The fact that the engineer Morlender had left for Eastern Europe a month before on a special mission for Jack Kressling, was apparent from the newspapers. But no one in America, including Morlender's own son, Arthur, knew as yet that Jeremy Morlender had already returned from his secret journey.

He had arrived on Kressling's private plane, landing on the wide asphalt roof of one of the secondary buildings of the villa "Ephemerides." By way of moving staircases he had descended and then mounted to Kressling's private office and was now sitting good-humoredly in front of him, having placed beneath the overhead fan his energetic, tanned and prominent face which he had braced beforehand with the scent of gilley-flower and jasmine. While the fan hummed, dispensing its fragrant odor together with the cool air, Jack Kressling was pacing impatiently back and forth about the room, casting sidelong glances at his lieutenant. Something in the face and extremely strained silence of Jeremy Morlender was obviously making the billionaire feel nervous.

"Well," he began, stopping in front of the inventor and tapping his foot, "Let's have it!"

"Well, Jack," Jeremy Morlender responded in the same tone, "I'll give it to you straightaway!"

Kressling's round, grey eyes, encircled by yellow rims, like a bird's, fastened on the engineer.

"You are probably going to be amazed by what I'm going to tell you," Morlender began. "You know that I've put all my inventiveness at your service. I never bargained with you, I never worried about an equal share and that sort of thing. After all, we even studied together, you did philology, I did physics. You were ten years younger than me. But I got the chance to study late in life, and you caught up with me. Do you remember our first conversation on the steamer *Accordance*, when the two of us, me the son of a simple American, you the billionaire, were returning to the States?"

"What's all this foreword for?"

"At that time you explained to me the basic ideas of your remarkable book, and from that moment I became your man, Jack! 'Capital accumulates human energy', you said. I must confess that I understood nothing at that time. You set about explaining: a squirrel drags into his hole nuts which he can't eat right away; the ant lays up stores for the winter. Everything on earth puts aside stores: a leaf does it in the nodules of chlorophyll; a clam in a pearl; a stone in a mine; water in lime; the sun in coal; oil and peat-moss. And man, too, has learned to store up supplies of energy for himself, he has learned how to accumulate electricity. 'But what can accumulate, can collect for storing man's own energy?' you asked, and then answered yourself: 'Human energy is accumulated by capital'. At that time I did not understand entirely and in my confusion asked you to explain in greater detail..."

"And I did explain to you!" Kressling exclaimed impatiently. "I explained and you understood. A person can store up capital... And what is capital if not the hidden opportunity for audacity, willfulness, passion, power! You keep it in the bank, but money in the bank is the pearl growing in the shell of your unbounded opportunities to manifest yourself in the world! You convert money into stocks, but stocks are the storage tower of all the passions welling up inside a person. Millions of impoverished geniuses have died without making themselves known to mankind because they were impoverished. Whereas I, a capitalist, can deploy my will, my talents, I can thunder throughout the entire world, I can purchase anything I wish, influence any development, any movement in the world, I can create, I can destroy, I can..."

"Wait!" exclaimed Morlender. "Now I can understand what you ment. Capital extends our power and will beyond the boundaries of the most powerful human desire, it lengthens our arms by thousands of miles, strengthens our muscles up to the elemental force of an earthquake,—isn't that it? I'm saying it in your words. I was gripped by them. I repeated them all my life. The growth of accumulated human energy in the billions of Jack Kressling! And when I left for Russia, you once again admonished me, Jack... You advised me to look into the basis of the Soviet economy. When we capitalists cast gold on to the ground, you said, it springs forth in gold that is three, four, ten, twenty times greater than what was cast, and the personal opportunities of its master grow together with that gold. But the communists have killed capital, they have killed these human opportunities. No matter how much they cast, the same amount remains. Capital doesn't grow! Their human energy is a day-by-day thing, it can't be stored up, like the life-span of a butterfly: for a single, brief working day, no longer than the length of the human arm,—do you remember? I'm repeating it exactly, I'm practically quoting you. So listen now, Jack..." Morlender stopped.

"Go ahead" said Kressling in a strange voice. The engineer did not notice the tone of his voice. Nor did he notice the cold, bird-like immobility of the billionaire's eyes fixed on him. He was caught up in his own thoughts which had occupied him during the entire journey in the airplane.

"So listen, now, dear Jack, you were wrong, and so was I. I spent a month in the land of the Bolsheviks. According to your instructions I travelled from one end of that country to the other in the hope of regaining the concession of your friend, Montmorency, by some legal means. I studied every other possible way as well. I examined all the loopholes. I studied the people... Jack, don't delude yourself! Their creative opportunities are far greater than ours! So what if money doesn't grow from dead money there, nonetheless factories are springing up, bridges, machines, roads, canals, stations! So what if they don't have any capital, or as you call it, the 'substratum of psychic energy'. All the same they do have that very same energy—and in an unlimited quantity! Even in that energy of theirs they still have the same multiplying "x," that germinating fungus which is fostered through money and forces the growth of capitalism in our country. Do you know what kind of fungus this is, Jack?"

Morlender leaned almost imperceptibly in the direction of the motionless Kressling. He stretched out his hand to his sharp knees. And he began to speak in a friendly, confidential fashion, pronouncing aloud his secret thoughts:

"Wouldn't it be better for us to forget about our plan, eh? On the way I was thinking... Accumulated energy, the substratum—you're right there. Only, here'ss the problem: whose, Jack, whose energy is being accumulated in capital, of whose energy is it the substratum? The fact is that it isn't yours, Jack, but it belongs to these same masses who right here in Middletown, and there, in every state, are working for you. And if that's so, what meaning can all your personal resources have? The Bolsheviks, every single one of them, every single worker in their country, they have more of these personal resources than you and I; this germinating fungus, the growth of industrial power, in their country it's increasing together with their own energy."

Jack Kressling burst into laughter. It was a sharp laughter, with a shrill tone on the upper notes, and while he laughed, Kressling kept his head lowered so that his partner would not notice the bizarre hysterical fury flaring up in his eyes. His foot was searching imperceptibly beneath the desk and when it found what it was looking for, it pressed the pedal on the extreme left.

In response to the touch on the pedal the door immediately opened part way and a woman of extraordinary beauty, with fiery red hair, her face a dark-olive complexion and striking like a tropical flower, glanced into the room.

"Come in, Mrs. Wesson," Jack Kressling spoke. "As always, you're right on time! Morlender, what you're saying is smart. It should be given some thought. We'll think it over together. Meanwhile, let's have a smoke and discuss what to do to replace Montmorency's concession." Mrs. Wesson slipped silently into the room. With a snake-like movement she opened the door to a wall cabinet that was trimmed in mother-of-pearl, pulled out a bottle, glasses and a seltzer flask. A box exuding the aroma of tobacco, lay on the table. Morlender reached out his hand for a cigar.

"By the way, where are your drafts, old buddy? You know what I mean, those ones..." asked Kressling suddenly as though he had remembered something urgent.

"In Kraft's safe," Morlender replied in surprise, as he lit up his Havana and puffed on it with pleasure.

"Everything's at Kraft's. Before I left, as you yourself know full well, I turned over to him our technical calculations, the model, the formulae... My last will and testament I even managed... managed..."

He suddenly stopped. Once again, twisting his tongue, sleepily, as though he were marking off the letters, he drawled: "ma-na-ge...," and let his head drop onto his chest.

"He's fallen asleep," declared Jack Kressling, arising and looking his secretary in the eye. "He's become dangerous. We have to hide him and keep him in a safe place. They've indoctrinated him! They've indoctrinated my engineer! A will— damn it! Elizabeth, in the meanwhile we'll make you his legal widow... Remember this: you are secretly married to him. He left you his sketches according to his will. And quickly, quickly, all of this will have to be taken care of in the next two or three days!

CHAPTER 2
ARTHUR MORLENDER MEETS HIS FATHER

On a May morning, an automobile was streaking at an insane speed along Riverside Drive.

A young man, all in white, sitting beside a thoughtful fat man, was practically shouting in his ear as he struggled with the noise of the street and the wind:

"Don't try to calm me, Doctor. All the same I'm upset, upset!"

The fat man shrugged:

"If I were you I wouldn't make a mountain out of a molehill. Mr. Jeremy is too clever a person, Arthur, to let anything happen to him."

"But the telegram, the telegram, Lepsius! How can you explain that it came from some strangers? How can you explain that it came not to me but to Kressling's secretary, that velvety Mrs. Wesson who reminds me of a cobra!"

"A very beautiful cobra!" the doctor interjected as he winked.

"To hell with her!" Arthur sputtered. "You know how friendly father and I are—we can even read each other's thoughts from our faces, like two comrades, and not a father and a son. How is it possible to accept the fact that he instructed someone to telegraph about his arrival to Wesson's address and not to our own, not to me, not to me... What does it mean, what's behind all this?"

"Wesson's address is after all Kressling's address, Arthur. And Kressling is the boss. Anything could have prevented Mr. Morlender from sending the despatch in person. He knew that you would be notified immediately from the head office, just as, in fact, you were."

"So they did notify me... Someone else's repulsive, purring voice on the telephone, the indecently familiar tone,—what does she mean calling me 'Arthur'? Why 'Arthur'? 'Dear Arthur'—how dare she call me dear! 'Father is arriving tomorrow on the *Torpedo*... a despatch from Captain Gregoire...' And you're still trying to convince me not to be upset! Why did she say "father' and not 'your father'? Who is she anyway, this Mrs. Wesson?"

"Mr. Jeremy never mentioned this horrible woman to you before?" asked the fat man. And when his neighbor shook his head abruptly, he shrugged imperceptibly. The doctor had heard a few things. Jeremy Morlender, who had been a widow for fifteen years, was a man of rare health and a warrior's stoutness... Rumors had been circulating that he had been intimate with some secretary there. Perhaps it was this same Wesson. The son alone, as was always the case, knew nothing about his own father's affairs.

Stop! The chauffeur turned the steering-wheel sharply and braked. The automobile came to a stop. Before them, all laid out in the brilliant gleam of the sun, was the Hudson which had poured out of a thousand canals and creeks. Along the embankment were countless steamers, sparkling in a colorful profusion of flags, white smokestacks and cabin portholes. A multitude of small white craft were ploughing up the bay in all directions.

"The *Torpedo* has already come alongside," said the chauffeur, turning to Arthur Morlender and the doctor." You'll have to hurry if you want to get there when they lower the landing ramp."

The young Morlender leapt out of the automobile and helped his neighbor. The fat man crawled out puffing. This was the famous doctor Lepsius, an old friend of the Morlender family. His small, piercing, parrot-like eyes were screened by spectacles, his upper lip was noticeably shorter than the lower, whereas the lower was shorter than his chin, so that taken all together it created the impression of a handy staircase with three distinct steps leading from the bottom directly upwards to just below the nose itself.

As far as the young man was concerned, he was a pleasant young man; one of those for whom there exists a great demand in the cinema and in novels. He was agile, sure of himself, handsome, well-built, well-dressed and, apparently, he did not suffer from a lack of introspection. His blond hair was combed straight and closely cut, which did not prevent it from winding into thick curls on the back of his neck. Incidentally, there was a certain something gleaming in his eyes that made this stage idol not altogether ordinary. Mister Charles Dickens, pointing to this strange gleam, would have remarked to his reader that here lay concealed some ominous feature of the character. But Mister Dickens and I employ different devices for characterization.

And thus, both climbed down and hastened to mix with the crowd of New Yorkers casting glances at the newly arrived steamer.

The *Torpedo*, an enormous ocean-going steamer belonging to the partnership of Douglas and Burley, was an entire city in itself with an internal self-government, storage, radio, military-engineering division, newspaper, sick-bay, theater, intrigues and family dramas.

The ramp was lowered, the passengers began to disembark. There were placid Yankees returning from distant travel with pipes in their mouths and newspapers under their arms just as though the day before they had still been sitting in the New York "Business Club." There were sick people who could hardly stretch their limbs, beautiful women looking for gold in America, gamblers, worldwide adventurers and crooks.

"Strange!" Doctor Lepsius muttered through his teeth as he removed his hat and bowed deeply to some red-faced military type. "Strange, General Gibgeld in New York!"

His whisper was interrupted by Arthur's exclamation:

"Viscount! How unexpected!" And the young man moved swiftly towards the handsome brown-haired man who was a permanent client of Kressling's office and who was limping along while he supported himself on the arm of an attendant. "Do you know where my father is?"

"Viscount Montmorency!" muttered Lepsius, again removing his hat and bowing, although no one took any notice of him. "It's getting stranger by the minute. What brings them to New York at such a time!"

Meanwhile, the crowd which was pouring off the ramp separated them and for a moment Lepsius lost Arthur from view. The weather had taken a sharp turn. The colors had faded, just as though ink had spread over everything. Clouds scudded across the sky, the waters of the Hudson turned a dirty, yellowish-grey color, flecked here and there with a white band of foam. The seagulls were crying along the bank as they took flight *en masse* right beside the quay. The embankment grew deserted, the passengers dispersed.

"Where is old Morlender?" the doctor asked himself, peering in all directions. At that very moment he caught sight of Arthur who had turned pale and had his eyes rivetted on a single spot.

Down the empty ramp there now descended a strange procession. Several men dressed in black were slowly carrying a zinc coffin covered with a piece of black velvet. Beside them, pressing a handkerchief to her face, walked a woman in deep mourning, shapely, red-haired and despite the color of her hair, dark-olive in complexion. She appeared to be crushed by grief.

"What does it mean?" Arthur whispered. "Why is Wesson here... and where is my father?"

The procession moved on. Elizabeth Wesson, raising her eyes, caught sight of the young Morlender, raised her hands slightly and took several steps in his direction.

"Arthur, my dearest, be brave!" she pronounced with great dignity.

The young man staggered back from her, seizing the railing of the ramp. As though in a trance, he stared and stared at the slowly approaching coffin.

"Be brave, my child!" Mrs. Wesson uttered in a velvety whisper once more right beside his ear.

"Where's father?" the young Morlender shouted.

"Yes, Arthur, he's here, Jeremy is here, in this coffin. He was killed in Russia."

Mrs. Elizabeth uttered this in a trembling voice, covered her face with her hands and began to weep.

The woeful profession proceeded on its way. Lepsius took hold of the stumbling Arthur and led him to the automobile. The embankment had become deserted, from the sky a fine rain began to beat down like the rapid fingers of a qualified typist.

Spitting, out in the middle of the rain, two sailors from the *Torpedo* were making for the docks, their shirts unbuttoned. They had not yet had the chance but were now determined to have a few drinks. Both had rings in their ears, and their teeth were sparkling like pearls.

"It's true, Dip, you're lying, sure you are. Admit it to a friend!"

"Shut up, Dan, if you were in my situation, maybe you wouldn't be talking so freely. Maybe you'd bite your tongue."

"If you want to keep quiet, then we shouldn't be going to this place, buddy!"

"But only rum will drown the words of that dame. You yourself heard her: he was killed in Russia. Killed in Russia! But that coffin was loaded on board in my presence, while I was on watch, in the dead of night in Halifax. That's a good one, ten years I've been sailing and never once did they make a detour to go into Halifax! I've gotta drown it in rum..."

The rest was lost in the corridor downstairs, in the cellar of the *Oceania*: "hot food and strong drinks—especially for sailors." You and I, reader, shouldn't go down there for anything, particularly since someone else, vague and unmemorable in appearance, with coarse cat's whiskers and a large Adam's apple, with weak dangling hands all swollen at the joints as though from gout, had followed the two sailors down there.

CHAPTER 3
DOCTOR LEPSIUS ALL BY HIMSELF

With rapid steps that did not correspond either to his age or his corpulence, Doctor Lepsius climbed the steps to his home on the second floor. He occupied a dwelling that was more than modest. The rooms were free of furniture, the windows were curtainless, the floors without carpets. Only the dining room with a fireplace and a small bedroom appeared to be habitable. Incidentally, behind Doctor Lepsius' house there was another structure where no one was permitted to enter, with the exception of his mulatto servant and the nurses. This was the private clinic of Lepsius where he conducted his secret experiments.

As he climbed the stairs, the doctor appeared to be excited. All three steps leading up to his nose were dancing as he muttered to himself:

"A convention, a real convention. What the devil has brought them all together here in New York? But so much the better, so much the better! How opportune for you, my dear Lepsius, just when your discovery is beginning to require some additional specimens for verification... Toby! Toby!"

A mulatto with protruding lips and small, monkey-like arms, slipped in from a neighboring room. Lepsius handed him his hat and cane, sat down in an armchair and remained motionless for several moments. Toby stood like a statue, staring at the floor.

"Toby," he said, finally, in a soft voice, "what is his Highness Bugas up to?"

"He's eating badly, cursing. He won't go off to his gymnastics for anything, even though I threatened to complain to you."

"Wouldn't go, you say?"

"No he wouldn't, master."

"Hm-hm. And did you try hanging a bottle from above?"

"I did everything as you ordered."

"Well, let's go and pay him a visit. By the way, Toby, please send the chauffeurr with my card to this address here."

Lepsius wrote several words on the envelope and handed them over to the mulatto. Thereupon he opened the cabinet, took a small bottle with dark contents, dropped it into his side pocket and began slowly to descend the stairs, but this time the inside ones leading to the rear portion of the house. A moment later Toby caught up to him once more. They passed several empty and gloomy rooms with traces of dust and cobwebs on the wallpaper and then by way of a small door they emerged into an inner courtyard. It was covered over with asphalt. The high stone walls to the right and the left concealed it completely from passers-by on the street. Nowhere was there a bench or a flower pot, as though this were not a yard in the central quarter of New York, but a stone hole in a prison. In about a hundred paces they arrived at a low concrete structure that resembled an automobile garage. A door with a steel shackle was locked with a heavy lock. Lepsius had barely inserted the key into the keyhole when from the direction of the main house someone's voice resounded. Lepsius turned around nervously:

"Who's there?"

"Doctor, you're wanted," screeched the housekeeper in a white cap, all red as a beet. "You're wanted, you're wanted, you're wanted!"

Miss Small, the doctor's housekeeper, was a bit deaf:;a very insignificant quality in a woman who isn't deprived of the use of her tongue.

"Who-o?" Lepsius cried, drawing out the sounds.

"Alright!" replied Miss Small, nodding her head forcefully. Immediately someone, poorly dressed, quickly made his way across the courtyard towards Lepsius.

"Damn that fool!" the doctor cursed to himself. "You keep her so that she won't overhear anything, but then she goes and plays dirty tricks on you from the other direction." "Who are you, what do you want?" These words concerned the approaching stranger.

"Doctor, help a sick man, an awfully sick man," said the stranger, barely pausing for breath.

Lepsius gazed at the speaker through his round spectacles:

"What's the matter with your sick man?"

"He... something heavy fell on him. A fracture, internal bleeding, in short, pretty bad."

"Alright, I'll come in a quarter of an hour. Leave your address."

"No, not in a quarter of an hour. Come right now!"

Doctor Lepsius raised his eyebrows and smiled. This rarely happened with him. He indicated the door to the clinic with his eyes to the mulatto, handed him the key and set off after the insistent stranger. Only now did he look him over properly. He was a short, Jewish-looking person, with shoulder-blades that worked under his shirt, with slightly swollen joints in his hands. His eyes were sunken, wan, grieving like those of a hardcase drunkard who had been forced into sobriety for a while. Beneath his nose were sparse, coarse cat's whiskers, a large Adam's apple bobbed up and down on his neck.

"There you see, just across the street," he confirmed feverishly for the doctor as they drew near a very high skyscraper of the commercial variety. "There it is, we don't need a cab..." It was obvious that he was bothered by every step taken by the doctor and he would gladly have lent his own feet for this purpose.

Doctor Lepsius began to wonder. Before him was a branch of the Credit Bank of Mexico that had nothing to do with living quarters.

"Where are you dragging me?" he blurted out. "This is an office and a bank. Everything is closed. How could the sick man be here!"

"At the doorman's," replied the stranger, quickly opening the side door and ushering the doctor into a small, bright room in the basement.

The sick man was indeed to be found here. He was an enormous man, who apparently had just been brought here on a stretcher and hurriedly thrown directly onto the floor. He was covered with a sheet. Two people were bent over him: a grey-headed, important-looking man in the ceremonial uniform of the doorman of a bank, and an old woman, wizened, small, sharp-nosed, sobbing violently.

The stranger quickly removed the sheet from the wounded man and shoved the doctor towards him. The man on the floor was literally crushed. His chest was badly caved in and smashed, the ribs were broken, his stomach slit as though from the pressure of a giant, round paper press which had left whole only the head and the extremities. He was fading.

"I can't do anything here," the doctor pronounced breathlessly, gazing in bewilderment at the dying man, "he's already in his death agony, to his great good fortune."

"What! Then you believe that it's impossible to force him to speak?" cried the stranger in the most genuine despair, so it seemed to Lepsius. "He won't pronounce another word even if he regains consciousness, eh?" He was looking at the doctor with beseeching eyes.

"No," replied the doctor, "he won't regain consciousness, he is dying, in fact, he's dead. Is he a relative of yours?"

But to his amazement, the stranger had quickly turned and ran out of the room without even waiting to hear the question. The old people bending over the corpse were weeping. Lepsius realized only now that the casualty was a sailor. On the sleeve of his blue jacket was embroidery with an anchor and in large print, *Torpedo*.

The doctor shuddered involuntarily. He touched the shoulder of the weeping old woman.

"Tell me, dear, who is this poor wretch?"

"My son, my little boy, Cut-throat Dip, that's what they called him on the ship... Oi-oi, sir, what a day this has been! We were expecting him from overseas, and instead of that we ended up with him from underneath a stone... The ocean never touched him, the dear, but here in the city, right in broad daylight... ai-ai-ai!"

"How did it happen?"

"They told us that he was coming from a tavern when a piece of flagstone broke loose from the viaduct up above and crushed him like an insect. And he never opened his mouth, they brought him here and he never cried out."

"But who brought him here, that man who just left?"

"Sailors and the police brought him. The other one, sir, is a stranger to us. He must have taken pity on us out of the goodness of his heart. He took it upon himself to go for a doctor and was worried all the while as to whether Dip, our dear little son, would have something final to say... Really, if you know him, then please tell him thanks from us old folks."

"Yes, indeed, but now the coroner must be summoned," replied Lepsius and left the doorman's room.

"Strange," he said to himself, "a multitude of oddities on the same day. The *Torpedo* arrives and brings a political cast of characters with it; oddity number one. A deceased Morlender is delivered to us on the very same *Torpedo*; oddity number two. And finally this sailor from the *Torpedo*, who died not just from any old cause, but from a stone that flew off a viaduct. And the strangest thing of all: this unknown person, just a simple worker judging from his looks, who must urgently learn, if you please, whether the crushed sailor will be able to talk. If I had more free time I would take up these oddities in my spare time, mull them over with a pipe. But now..."

Now Doctor Lepsius had his own oddity; number five. And it was quite evident that it had crowded out all the others.

Arriving in his bedroom and turning on the electricity, the doctor discarded his jacket with a sigh of relief. The mulatto unlaced his shoes and put on his embroidered Turkish slippers.

"Has the chauffeur returned?" asked the doctor.

Silently the mulatto handed him an envelope. "General Gibgeld requests Doctor Lepsius to pay him a visit between 7:00 p.m. and 8:00 p.m..."

The doctor raised a plump arm with a wristband to his glasses. A delicate woman's watch, with an enormous, pea-sized diamond, indicated 6:45 p.m.

"Damn it all, no rest and no peace. His Highness Bugas XXXI will once again have to wait well into the night for his little bottle. Toby, try to entertain him with tales of some sort so that he won't fall asleep before my return."

The doctor sat for half an hour, his feet stretched out towards the grate of the cold fireplace. He was resting silently, efficiently, with concentration, the way a sportsman or athlete does before performing. He breathed first through the one, then through the other nostril, methodically closing each nostril with his fingers. He was not thinking. He wiped his temples with eau-de-cologne, first the one, then the other side, using a fragrant Arabian oil. But then the half-hour was almost up. The vacant expression on his face became once more sharply attentive, crafty. The large glasses were gleaming cheerfully. The slippers were kicked off, once more into his jacket, shoes, hat, everything in order, his briefcase in hand, billfold and pipe into his inside pocket,—Doctor Lepsius had been refreshed, he was ready for a new expedition that would, perhaps, furnish him with facts, small and large, and with test subjects for something whose nature we cannot even begin to surmise— all the more so because the mulatto Toby calmly allowed the doctor's instruction to enter one ear and pass out the other, had two or three wee glasses on the sly and then lay down to sleep on the cold mat in the half-empty room without giving any further thought to paying the mysterious Bugas a visit.

CHAPTER 4
WHICH BEGINS WITH INTERJECTIONS

"Ai, ai!"

"Oh, Lord!"

"O-oi! Oi, mercy me, mercy us!"

The faithful servants greeted Jeremy Morlender's body with these kinds of exclamations. The old negress, Polly, his nurse, who had reared Massah Jeremy and Master Arthur, was the only one not weeping—and this was all the more remarkable because she especially had loved the elder Morlender with a genuine love. Wide-eyed and unblinking she gazed upon the zinc coffin, fingering a grayish stone talisman in her hands. No wonder the butler could not refrain from saying something to her—to be sure, in a respectful fashion—because the negresses in the kitchen were rather afraid:

"What's the matter with you, Polly, doesn't it mean anything to you?"

"Fool," Polly replied calmly and did not shed even the slightest little tear.

Upstairs in the boudoir of Arthur's deceased mother, to his greatest amazement and wrath, Mrs. Elizabeth Wesson had for some reason established herself.

Mastering his grief and hatred, Arthur Morlender climbed the stairs with determined steps.

He had not been in this room for almost five years. It had been locked up long ago, and from the street for all those years it had been impossible to see through the heavy, lowered blinds over the windows. To Arthur's amazement, instead of the stuffy odor of carpets and silks, instead of the faded lacquer and moth-eaten upholstery, everything in this old, neglected room had been renovated and spruced up. There were cheerful, bright curtains on the windows; the present furniture did not resemble in the least the former which had stood there for fifteen years; green plants were in flower boxes; a handsome writing desk and bookcase with the latest publications. No one, beside the elder Morlender, had had access to this room; the key always hung on his watch chain together with other pendants. It was clear that Jeremy Morlender himself had prepared the room for its new inhabitant. As though responding to these thoughts, Elizabeth Wesson raised her beautiful head and looked at Arthur:

"As you can see, your father was expecting me. He responded so attentively to my simple taste! The only pity is that he never forewarned his son about our marriage."

Taking a sheet of paper folded in four out of her handbag, she held it out to Morlender:

"Have a look, Arthur, it's our marriage certificate. It's difficult for me to talk about it at this moment, but it's even more difficult to see your amazement and distrust. Despite all the strength and firmness of Jeremy's character, despite all of his passionate love for me, he apparently could not make up his mind to tell you about your stepmother."

She sighed and hung her head. Delicate tears slipped down her cheeks. Nothing in this beautiful and bereaved woman who held herself so wondrously calm, suggested either an impostor or adventuress. And yet Arthur Morlender was choking with hatred. It had been a blow—a blow to his heart, to his vanity, to his esteem for his father. Even his grief had seemed to be poisoned by a fair dose of vinegar and pepper. From her beauty right down to her velvety voice—every feature, every movement of this woman aroused a fit of rage in him that was akin to seasickness.

"I came here to say that I am moving out of this house," he uttered in such a hissing tone of voice which he himself did not even recognize as his own. "But before leaving here, I am determined to hear the details of my father's death of which you are apparently better informed than I."

Elizabeth Wesson rose. Something sparkled responsively in her blue-tinged dark eyes with narrow pupils almost like dots:

"I wished for peace with Jeremy's son," she began slowly, "I was prepared to offer him hospitality and a portion of the means which have been left to me because, Mr. Morlender Junior, your father has willed this house to me, as well as all his savings and the plans for his invention... But in the face of such an unseemly tone..."

"The plans for his invention!" exclaimed Arthur.

"Yes, the plans for his invention, together with the house and his savings. Do you want to see the will? Should I show it to you just as I showed you the marriage certificate?"

"My father's will is kept at Lawyer Kraft's!"

"Jeremy wrote a new one in Russia. The captain of the *Torpedo* passed it on to me together with the deceased's personal effects."

Kraft was the long-time lawyer for the Morlender family. Arthur rushed to the telephone stand. While his fingers were automatically dialing the number, he was thinking, thinking, trying to comprehend his father's behavior. Hypnosis? Treachery? A criminal act?

"Hello! Eight, one, zero, five, one, zero, five. Give me Kraft the lawyer. What?... But when? Just now? My God, my God!"

He put the receiver down and turned to the woman:

"He has just been brought home with a smashed skull. His chauffeur was drunk and wrecked the car!"

The new Mrs. Morlender did not react to this with an excess of grief; she hardly knew Kraft. But Arthur was so crushed that for a moment he felt utterly weak: his father's best friend! One could even say—his one and only friend! He had known him like the back of his hand...

A servant entered and announced Dr. Lepsius' arrival. Arthur rushed to meet him.

The doctor walked without haste. His face reflected a sorrow befitting the occasion.

"Dear Mister Arthur, I have been summoned to General Gibgeld, but along the way I decided to look in on you... Mrs. Wesson, I did not manage to greet you this morning."

"Mrs. Morlender," she gently corrected Lepsius.

"I'm happy to see you, doctor," Arthur interrupted her, "I beg you to read father's new will together with me."

"New will? Jeremy Morlender, insofar as I recall, wrote one just before his departure for Russia."

"But he wrote a second one there..." Arthur's stepmother interjected, and tears appeared once more in her eyes.

She stood up, unlocked a case standing in front of her on the table and handed Arthur a packet where Morlender's will had been written on official paper with the observance of all the formalities.

Arthur and Lepsius put their heads close together and read it through almost simultaneously. It was a strange document which had been composed in a pathetic tone. It said that the danger of communism was threatening the entire world. For that reason, he, Jeremy Morlender, in the event of his death, was bequeathing his last invention to the holy war against the communists. As the custodian of his plans he was naming his dear wife, Elizabeth, Wesson by her first marriage. All his possessions and the house in New York he was unconditionally bequeathing to her inasmuch as his son, Arthur, was now at the age where he could provide for himself. There then followed the signature of Morlender and two witnesses. Lepsius grasped the contents of the will in a single glance and exclaimed involuntarily:

"But where is Kraft? This must, before all else, be shown to Kraft."

"He's dead."

"Dead?"

"An automobile accident," Arthur's stepmother interjected.

Lepsius bit his lower lip. Something was on the verge of slipping off his tongue but was cleverly grabbed by the tail and tucked away back into the depths of the doctor's taciturn memory.

"Yes," he said, "you are ruined, Arthur."

"Everything that belongs to me, I give to his servants," Mrs. Morlender said drily, "everything except, of course, the plans which have been bequeathed for a sacred purpose. I am convinced that Jeremy composed this will while under the impression of what he had seen in Russia. He was an observant and sharp-witted person; and perhaps, for reasons of what he did see, the communists killed him."

She uttered these words so simply and convincingly that Arthur's thoughts immediately took a different direction.

"I swear I will take revenge on the murderers!" he exclaimed, involuntarily investing these words with everything that he had been undergoing during the past few hours. "I will take revenge or I will not return alive, just like my father!"

Lepsius looked at him for a few moments, then he took his hat.

"Arthur, I wish you success with all my heart," he uttered slowly.

He kissed the widow's hand and moved towards the door, maintaining all the while the same ingenuously bereaved expression on his face.

But on the staircase his face changed instantly. A lamplighter ran up the three steps towards his nose, peeked at him under the lenses of his spectacles and thrust a lighted match in there. Lepsius' eyes were positively aflame, like a street gas-lamp, as he muttered to himself beneath his nose:

"Either I am a fool and a blindman, or that is not Morlender's signature!"

He came out on the street where an automobile was waiting for him a few steps away, but then he was forced to halt. Someone's black, thin hand had seized him by the cane. An old woman's voice spoke:

"Massah Lepsius, Massah Lepsius!"

"Is that you, Polly? What do you want?"

"You're an important man, Massah Lepsius! Lots of folk will listen to you..."

"But what's the matter?"

"Black Polly is telling you: order them to open up Massah Morlender's coffin, order them to do it!"

"What's gotten into your head, Polly?"

But the negress had already disappeared. Lepsius looked about on all sides, waited a short while, and then quickly got into the automobile, ordering the chauffeur to drive to the "Patrician." He thought about nothing along the way. Doctor Lepsius had a rule: never to think about anything during brief moments of rest.

CHAPTER 5
THE HOTEL *PATRICIAN*

I must tell you that the owner of the *Patrician*, a rich Armenian from Diarbekir, by the name of Setto, had but one weakness: he did not drink, did not smoke, was not unfaithful to his wife, but he was powerless to resist his passion for renovation. It must have been that Setto's distant ancestors were stonemasons. Every spring, with the departure of foreigners from his hotel, Setto would begin to renovate everything, from top to bottom. He reupholstered the furniture, plastered, painted, refaced the veneered doors, retinned, scraped, cleaned, oiled and redid the ornamental designs. It was tantamount to a fever of ninety-eight degrees. Regardless of what you might have done with him, he would unfailingly organize renovations on the entire street, causing the New York dogs to start sneezing.

Many might have said this sounded plebeian and did not accord at all with the title of the hotel. They were right. But the man from Diarbekir had nothing to do with it: he never wanted to have a hotel, he never wanted to call it the *Patrician* and he never wanted to designate it for an illustrious clientele. It all came about in a fateful way. When Setto and his wife and children, together with a large supply of cabinetmaker's tools, as well as Armenian embroideries, were emigrating from Diarbekir to America, the ship bumped into a floating mine and the majority of passengers drowned. Among the casualties bobbing about in the water was a man with epaulettes that were as heavy as horseshoes, brilliant as the sun and all worked with gold braid. Growing heavy under their weight he was about to drown when suddenly he raised his eyes, caught sight of an entire squadron of large yellow, round pumpkins above him. They were floating, and hanging on to them, as though everything were perfectly normal, their legs tucked up, swam the entire family of the man from Diarbekir, exchanging all the while calm remarks on the topic of the weather.

"Save me!" the drowning man shouted to them.

Setto stared fixedly at his wife. She nodded her head and uttered in Armenian:

"Save a person once over and God will save you twice over."

"That's a good profit," replied Setto and tossed the stranger a pair of magnificent empty pumpkins. The stranger—a former president of one of the miniature republics who had just been banished by his nation,— clutched gratefully at the pumpkins and floated on, blessing his fate. Thus they drifted for three days, reinforcing themselves with mouthfuls of rum and a mixture of "Nestle" powder which the man from Diarbekir kept in a tin box on his chest. It was in fact during these hours of their sea-going existence that the nearly drowned man promised to build a magnificent hotel for his saviour in New York, but on one unalterable condition: that the hotel accept only crowned ex-heads of state, ex-ministers and ex-generals and that it would be named, in honor of this noble clientele, the *Patrician*. The man from Diarbekir agreed. They were picked up on the fourth day and just imagine Setto's amazement when his travelling companion from the sea kept his promise. This was how Setto from Diarbekir became the owner of the hotel *Patrician*.

He zealously fulfilled the condition. Not a single ordinary mortal, not a single honorable worker had the right to remain in his hotel. On the other hand any "former" personage—a fleeing president or an overthrown prince, whose entire possessions consisted only of his silver braid, not to mention the purely operatic army of troops which had been beaten somewhere and consisting of innumerable persons wishing to do battle on hire, had unrestricted entry to the *Patrician*. The wretched man from Diarbekir made very little money from his hotel. He earned his living on the side through business deals. It frequently happened that the illustrious guests would ask him for a loan. This he bore with patience and without grumbling. Only once did his wife hear a word of anger from him: coming into her room he suddenly took the icon depicting the saint, Sister Shushanik, and turned it face to the wall.

"What are you doing, you wretch!" his wife exclaimed.

"Let them up there learn the squaring of accounts and two-faced book-keeping," Setto replied, "I was expecting a hundred from God for the fifty I invested, but instead of that he forces me to save illustrious refugees not once, but eighty-thousandfold!"

So then, with the onslaught of spring, this same Setto had once again made up his mind to devote himself in his spare time to his passion and set to work on the renovations. "The Workers Union for Repair Work Throughout the City of New York" received an urgent order from him and immediately dispatched to him an army of qualified painters, roofers, plasterers, wallpaper hangers, plumbers, sewer-workers and chimney-sweeps.

They had only just set about work when to the genuine rage of Setto an automobile delivered two illustrious gentlemen to the *Patrician*: General Gibgeld and Viscount de Montmorency.

As though for spite, the rooms which had been designated for them were in the midst of renovation.

"It doesn't matter," said the elderly carpenter who was fixing the locks in No. 2 A-B, "don't go wracking your brains. Let them move in and I'll finish up while they're here. There's no more than an hour's work at the most here."

And while the illustrious gentlemen were sitting at the table d'hôte, the carpenter, as promised, made his way with all his tools to the apartments on the mezzanine which bore the fanciful numeration of 2 A-B and which consisted of a suite of large, regal rooms with absolutely all the luxuries right down to the self-contained interurban telephone station and post-office department.

Closing the door tightly behind him, Willings the carpenter first of all set his box of tools on the floor and then packed his pipe and lit up exactly the way Michael Thingsmaster would have done it. Puffing once or twice on it, instead of beginning his repairs, to my very own amazement, he made a little jump. Then he stopped and listened—not a sound. Then Willings made yet another pirouette, pressing with his heels on some spot that began to move, was lifted up and set on its edge across the room, revealing a dark hole leading downwards.

"Mend-mess!" the carpenter send in a whisper as he leaned towards the hole.

"Mess-mend!" was immediately heard from inside and through the opening appeared the head of the plumber, Van Hope.

"Is that you, Willings? I'm fixing the pipes here. And what are you doing?"

"I'm working on the locks. Tell me, please, Van Hope, do you have Mike-the-Magician's trademark on all the things down there?"

"On almost everything, Willings. Only the wallpaper factory in

Beandorf has let us down. The fellows over there still haven't signed up in our union and their things don't fit with ours. It's a real nuisance that right here behind the wallpaper there's a door with the trademark that goes right into the upper room of our good old Russian prince, but the wallpaper isn't under our control."

"We've got to put pressure on Beandorf. Warn Mike Thingsmaster. And make sure, Van Hope, that you stay in the pipe until tomorrow. There's bound to be some interesting communications going on."

After this Willings closed the parquet, and cheerfully whistling, set about examining the lock. This he did in the strangest possible manner. For example, he took a magnifying glass and carefully peered through it at the tumblers in the locks, at the keyholes, at the hinges on the doors, dressers and wardrobes and each time he nodded his head approvingly. Taking a peek together with him, I saw through the magnifying glass only two microscopic letters, one of which stood within the other, tiny like protozoa: And that was all.

His examination finished, Willings firmly locked one of the doors with a key and then he went up to the same door and without taking out the key he ran his nail along some kind of invisible strip. The door immediately opened quietly although the key was still stuck in the lock as before.

"Mend-mess!" someone called loudly from inside the wall.

"Mess-mend!" Willings replied promptly. The wall opened up and with a piece of material fabric in his hands the wallpaper hanger emerged into the room. His face was anxious.

"Willings, let everyone know immediately all down the line. Something is going on here. The ex-president No Hom has just arrived by express from San Francisco. They just rang up from the docks to say that Lord Hardstone is expected. It's no coincidence. I think it's time for us to finish our repairs, everything down to the last detail is ready."

"Van Hope told me about the wallpaper..."

"Yes, it's going to prevent us from hearing what's going on in the Russian'ss room and the room adjoining his. But it's not a catastrophe. Set up the sentries, brother, and get yourself out of here as fast as you can."

Both immediately stepped behind the wall and without making a sound found themselves in the room of the telephone operator, Miss Totter. They exchanged the same mysterious greeting with her and then they exited by a side door and emerged directly on the noisy street.

Meanwhile General Gibgeld and Viscount de Montmorency had happily concluded their protracted dinner, washed it down properly, had a smoke and were chatting quietly as they made their way to their adjacent apartments, No. 2 A-B.

CHAPTER 6
A CONFERENCE IN THE ABSENCE OF THE CHAIRMAN

General Gibgeld entered the room first. Impatiently he paced back and forth twice from one corner to the other, waiting until the Viscount would laboriously lower himself into an armchair. Then he went up to the door, glanced out into the corridor, locked the door and returned to the Viscount:

"Without beating around the bush do you know the state of our affairs?"

"Just as much as you do, General," Montmorency replied languidly. "As you know, I despise every kind of ideology. The arguments of our patron Kressling get on my nerves. If it weren't for the dollars, pounds and francs whereby he accompanies them..."

"You're mistaken, Viscount!"

"Don't shake the floor like that, it goes right through the chair and vibrates in my spine," the Frenchman declared reproachfully.

"You're mistaken, Viscount, not to pay any attention to Jack Kressling's theory. It is the most suitable theory in a world of chaos and anarchy such as our unpleasant planet is in the midst of becoming."

"It's sufficient that he is paying us and is about to reinstall us as the leaders of our countries. I am utterly in agreement that leaders are enthroned from above, that power, as the church says, comes from God. And if he succeeds in establishing governments everywhere which correspond to the divine scheme, and if they will be able to maintain themselves..."

"With an iron hand!" interrupted the General, his gold braid tinkling.

"...Then Kressling will have a powerful basis of support against these vulgar people who call themselves communists."

"Sh-sh!" whispered the General.

Someone was knocking at the door. A servant delivered the visiting card of the Russian nobleman, Prince Feofan Ivanovich Obolonkin, on a tray. This was the third year that the Prince had been living in New York, occupying room No. 40 on the second floor, and all bills which he received were sent to the head of the Russian Provisional Government in Paris who continued to support its members of court and diplomatic representatives. Malicious tongues, incidently, insisted that in Berlin, Rome, Madrid and London as well there were ruling members from the dynasty of the Russian throne and that the diplomatic corps displayed a tendency for the continuous growth of its population, but this really concerns the realm of statistics and not belletristics.

The General glanced at the visiting card and nodded affirmatively to the servant. The door opened once more and this time a puny old fellow with a monocle in one eye, a red nose, trembling legs with joints severely afflicted with gout, slid sideways into the room.

"My regards, Gibgeld. Good evening, Viscount. I bid you welcome on your arrival. I am very, very pleased. The papers, you know, have become somewhat indecipherable. They've confused the royal birthday of his Highness the Autocrat of All The Tula Province, Mavrikii Ioannovich, with General Wrangel's rescue on land and sea, and because of this I had to arrive late. I have been receiving deputations from early morning onwards."

"What?" the General repeated distractedly. "Mavrikii? Ah, yes, yes, Tula Province. He's the pretender for the national separatists who are known under the name of *Russia and Samovar.** I know, I know, do sit down, Prince, you are not in the least late. We are expecting still another person!"

"Incidently," the Viscount drawled, "My dearest Obolonkin, did your neighbor give you any instructions before his departure?"

"You are speaking of Signor Gregorio Cice? No, he simply informed me that he would appear without fail at the required moment." With these words Feofan Ivanovich reached out towards the small table where the General's Havana cigars lay.

"A strange person, this Cice," the Viscount said, lowering his voice, "he comes and goes like a wizard, never once missing an important moment. He gives no account of himself except to Kressling, he twists and turns the League and each of us any way he pleases."

"He's a great mystifier" noted the General, "and that impresses Kressling."

"Indeed, a vigorous person. As far as the female sex is concerned, you can rest assured—I do keep an eye out—an extraordinary vigor and an utterly complete neutrality," interposed Prince Feofan. "Not at all like the banker Westinghouse. The latter, during your absence... you couldn't begin to imagine!"

"How has Westinghouse distinguished himself?" the Viscount inquired lazily.

But Feofan Ivanovich was not fated to explain himself. The door opened wide once more, this time admitting Doctor Lepsius into the room.

In order to avoid the burdensome ceremonies, the reader himself may at this point insert "greetings," "how are you doing" and other such phrases which serve as the customary vocabulary among civilized people. I am omitting all of this and shall commence at the point where Doctor Lepsius, in keeping with his profession, set about outfitting himself with his instruments.

Every doctor must possess the following: a stethoscope, a small hammer, a prescription booklet, a watch, tongue depressors and—preferably—an electric lamp with a head band. All of these were in Lepsius' possession. All of these he dragged out and then set about his business.

"I haven't examined your heart and lungs for so long, Your Excellency," muttered Lepsius, "your pulse is fine, alright. I don't care for the coloring of your face, and your neck as well. But tell me, please, what about those symptoms which afflicted you during the past year?"

"You mean my spine? In fact, they have not gone away, Doctor. I would like to have you do something about them."

"The spine, damn it all," interrupted Montmorency. "It's been a month now that I've been vexed by this unaccountable limp which for some reason or other causes a pain in my spine. Take a look at me as well, Lepsius."

The doctor's little eyes started to dance like phosphorescent lights beneath his spectacles. All three steps leading up to his nose were compressed into an excited little ball. He sprang up, almost scattering his instruments in his haste.

"I must examine you. It's essential for you to disrobe. We shall go into the neighboring room."

"That's the way he always is," said Gibgeld with a sigh after the Viscount and Lepsius disappeared behind the door. "You hardly mention the spine, or more precisely the sciatic nerve, and our Doctor changes completely: he becomes excited, dashes about, undresses the patient and examines him with the utmost curiosity. When there's no reason for an examination, he manufactures one in his head. I have seen three Turkish boys, pretenders to the renaissance of the Ottoman Empire, whom he contrived to examine for no good reason at all, under the pretext of some ailment or other..."

Meanwhile in the neighboring room, Viscount de Montmorency was languidly permitting Doctor Lepsius to study his naked spine. The fat man was completely beside himself. He puffed, scampered like a rabbit around the patient, muttering all the while something in Latin and, finally, fell completely silent in contemplation.

What was he looking at? He was looking at the spine of the young Frenchman which so gracefully intersected his white body interlaced with pale blue veins. Everything seemed to be in order, but the treacherous magnifying lens in Lepsius' trembling hand pointed to a small spot the size of a pinhead which felt like a small swelling.

"There it is, there it is," whispered Lepsius, forgetting himself, with an expression of ecstasy and horror on his face. And suddenly he put an incongruous question to the Viscount which did not amaze the Frenchman simply because his languor was no stronger than all his other faculties.

"Have you at any time experienced a severe fright, Viscount?"

"During the Russian Revolution, when I was deprived of my franchise," the Frenchman replied with a shudder. "I do not like revolutions. At that time I had to flee from the Bolsheviks and the territory of my franchise into Persia."

"Excellent, excellent, get dressed, we shall prescribe some marvellous drops for you."

Meanwhile there came another knock at the General's door. Two new guests entered: a tall, red-haired Englishman all saturated with the strongest smell of tobacco, and a strange creature who had just lost a hundred million subjects who had banished him from his own land.

"Your humblest servant and ally, No Hom," this creature presented his name with Asiatic politeness as he widened his mouth into a smile.

"Lord Hardstone," the Englishman presented himself curtly.

"Hearty handshakes," again "greetings," "how are you doing," etc., etc.. But Lord Hardstone was not disposed to waste time. He glanced around, looked at his watch and spoke abruptly:

"I have just seen Kressling. He orders us to begin the meeting without delay."

"Excuse me, but Cice is still not here."

"He will be. Dear Gibgeld. Dismiss, if you please, this fat man, he is a doctor, so it seems?"

"Doctor Lepsius."

"Ah, so this is the famous Lepsius! Pleased to make your acquaintance. However, time is precious. I declare the meeting open in the name of the chairman. I request all outsiders to leave!"

Lepsius never managed to receive his honorarium from the guests of the *Patrician*. Nonetheless, he always took his leave in a state that resembled ecstasy. Just as he was doing at this moment, pressing his cane to himself, he sprang out of No. 2 A-B with a look of rapture on his face and without ceasing to mutter to himself: "so that's how it is!" and went down to the car that was waiting for him.

Setto from Diarbekir watched him leave with reproach.

"A vain man," he said to his wife, "just go and give him any of those pretenders and presidents there. Any old Turkish pasha making his living by begging in American antechambers is more interesting to him than a proper Armenian laborer. All of these illustrious sham moguls of both sexes, and all their lackeys to boot, I'd happily exchange them all for a good tomato salad..."

"With onion," echoed his spouse, sighing.

CHAPTER 7
A WORLD BEHIND WALLS

As soon as Lepsius departed, a lackey led the limping Viscount to an armchair beside Gibgeld, helped him to sit down and then left. Prince Feofan Obolonkin, with a delicate prancing step, went up to the table together with No Hom, still attempting to relate what had happened to Baron Westinghouse. But at the moment Baron Westinghouse himself appeared at the door, a youthful-looking old man with a powdered nose, dyed moustache and a wallflower in his lapel—and that put an end to all of Obolonkin's attempts. At the very last moment when Lord Hardstone, raising his eyebrows, pulled his watch for the fifth time from his pocket, Rockefeller Junior appeared, a smallish, pimply-faced dandy who excused himself before all those present for the absence of Rockefeller Senior.

"Is your daddy still sick?" inquired Feofan Ivanovich with curiosity.

"He is still finding it difficult to recover after the usurpation of power in the Russian Empire," Rockefeller Junior replied readily.

The illness of the number two American millionaire after Kressling had occurred immediately after the Russian Revolution and the collapse of the Interventionist Division which had been mustered, equipped and trained at his expense. This was one of the beloved themes of the illustrious clientele which had gathered in the Hotel *Patrician*. However, today that particular theme fared no better than the adventures of Baron Westinghouse.

"Do be seated, gentlemen claimants!" announced Lord Hardstone in a thunderous voice.

Those present seated themselves around the table. Overhead, in a chimney flue, a young man with a vividly black nose, black cheeks and forehead, also settled down more comfortably, that is, he pushed his legs above his head into an extension of the flue and let his head hang downwards, pressing his ear to an indiscernible crack.

"We shall exchange basic news about our efforts to create harmonious governments in both hemispheres of the earth without waiting for Signor Cice, gentlemen!" Hardstone began once more. "Time is precious..."

"How do you like that for courtesy!" whispered Tom the chimneysweep to himself, spitting down below. "How does he know that every moment counts for me as well?"

"...time is precious," repeated Hardstone, "inasmuch as the shares on today's stock market have begun to fall and even..." at this point he shrugged with the appearance of a certain skeptical disbelief in his own words, "...even the pound sterling has stumbled."

Exclamations of genuine sympathy resounded about the table.

"In order to conceal the conspiracy of what will now be said, let us move without delay, gentlemen, on the express wish of Signor Cice, to his room, the key to which," Lord Hardstone pulled from his pocket a key of an unusually bizarre shape, "Cice himself has passed on to me..."

But Tom the chimneysweep was not about to listen any further. Quicker than a monkey he scrambled through the flue, crawled into a kind of damper, wriggled through it, hung suspended over an empty bathroom, dropped down, leapt through it into the lavatory and there he bumped right into the maid Jenny who was cleaning up the fixtures.

"Eek!" shrieked Jenny, "Eek! Who are you?"

"I'm the devil, honey. By God, I'm the devil."

"Since when have devils started to swear by God," declared an uncertain Jenny as she thought to herself: "Just wait, Mrs. Thindick will burst with envy if she finds out that I saw a real devil."

But the time she spent on her reflections were a godsend for Tom. He slowly inched backwards towards the door, opened it and disappeared.

Jenny's mouth was wide open.

"After this you'd better believe that minister Russell," she mumbled to herself, in a state of spiritual shock, not taking her eyes from the door. "How come he tells us that miracles are the work of God. It looks like devils too can work their own miracles. Just look at that, my friends, he passed right through a locked door and here it is locked again from my side."

Meanwhile, Tom, flying like an arrow along the corridor, stepped into a wardrobe, made two or three turns in the wall and found himself in front of Signor Cice's door. But he was late. The meeting had already begun—right under his nose. And thanks to the irresponsibility of the fellows at the wallpaper factory in Beandorf, he could not get inside. Tom almost wept from fury, something which, naturally, would have very much damaged the professional coloring of his face. A fireplace was nearby. He sadly entered it and dropped into the flue. Down below, beneath the terrible heat of the kitchen range, in a network of every conceivable flue and pipe, Tom pressed a button and whispered:

"Mend-mess."

"Mess-mend," came the immediate response.

The boiler opened up, revealing Van Hope sitting peacefully there with rubber earphones on.

"Why have you left your watch-post, Tom?"

"Because, damn them, they've moved into that Italian's room!"

"The room without a number?"

"That's the one, Van Hope. I made a real fool out of myself. I scampered behind the walls, landed right on the head of some honey, and I even managed to more or less get clear of that mess, but then I couldn't think of anything else to do."

"True, Tom, you've never been especially good at that. I'm amazed that the fellows even gave you that job. Well, O.K. Shut up and listen. Hello, Miss Totter!"

Through one of the rubber phones could be heard:

"It's me, is that you, Van Hope?"

"Yes, it is. Connect me with Mike."

"I can't right now, the office needs me. Hang on."

Van Hope and Tom began to wait in silence. In two minutes Miss Totter'ss voice came through:

"Van Hope, go ahead. I've connected you with Mike."

From somewhere terribly far off came a hollow sound:

"What's the matter?"

"Thingsmaster, help us," Van Hope began into the phone, "the conference has been transferred to the room without a number. Tom and I can't do anything there. And they must be whispering about something really important."

"Do you know how to rig up the mirror equipment?" The sounds vibrated through the earpieces. Thingsmaster was trying to talk clearly.

Van Hope looked at Tom, Tom looked at Van Hope.

"Seems like we don't know how, Mike," Van Hope answered with embarrassment.

"I'm coming myself," resounded through the telephone.

No sooner had the plumber hung up his rubberized telephone than the chimneysweep poked him gently in the side—not without a certain spitefulness:

"It's obvious, Van Hope, that you too are not particularly remarkable for that same thing..."

"What do you mean?"

"For brains."

And before Van Hope could give him a cuff, Tom had flown up to the very top of the boiler and began to dangle cheerfully by his heels from there.

Meanwhile a broad-shouldered, red-bearded athletic type in a worker's shirt that was belted in, laid down his wood plane by the bench in the brightly lit workshop of a woodworking factory, cleaned the wood shavings off himself, glanced all around and suddenly disappeared into the wall. He rushed as fast as his legs would carry him along the dark passageways that were only a few feet wide, moving sideways, now and then shaking himself off from the dirt and drops of water. After ten minutes the passageways widened, his feet felt for the steps and then ran up them, and suddenly the blond head of Thingsmaster, with his cheerful pale blue eyes looking out from under the even bushy eyebrows, emerged through a crack into the light. He glanced around: it was a telegraph tower, the highest point in the factory town of Middletown. From here, from a height of several hundred feet, a network of steel wires, carrying more than just communications, disappeared towards New York. A portion of the network served as a gigantic elevators, another portion was used to transport square bundles of Middletown's hay to Rolley's horse stables which were located not far from the *Patrician*. Precisely at that moment, two strapping workers hung a chain from a compressed bale of hay to a steel loop on a wire.

"Mend-mess," the worker in the work shirt said to them.

"Mess-mend," both replied, "Want to go for a ride, Mike? Get on, get on."

In a second, lying on the bale of hay, pressing his arms tightly around the sides, Thingsmaster was flying with the speed of an arrow towards New York. Down below him along the telephone wires the secrets of invisible people were being carried. The melancholy Tony White, a telegraph operator, was writing them down on paper. Even lower down, along the ground, travelled a famous express from a North American trunkline; but it was supposed to cover the distance between Middletown and New York in half an hour, whereas Mike Thingsmaster did it in seven and three-quarter minutes. Tony White had not even managed to take the first telegram down when our traveller jumped onto the roof of the stables without anyone noticing him and disappeared into one of the openings between the metal panels. In three minutes he had reached the boiler pipe where Van Hope, in helpless rage with Tom, was bombarding his heels with spitballs made from newspaper.

Mike Thingsmaster gave both of them a reproachful look.

"I see that you're enjoying yourselves here, fellows. Whereas the people upstairs, you can rest assured, are not wasting time. Quick march upstairs!"

He turned on his pocket flashlight and all three rushed through the flues. But Thingsmaster suddenly stopped, pressed his ear to the metallic skin of the flue, listened closely, produced an inaudible exclamation, then retraced several steps. Here he stopped once again, took out a measuring tape, paper and a pencil and began to measure something out. Apparently the results of his measurements did not console him very much, because Van Hope and Tom heard the humorous whistling which served Mike as a sign of extreme annoyance. To their amazement he took out a hammer which he used to tap at various places in the corridor. Thereupon, without saying a single word, he continued in the earlier direction but without his earlier haste. Entering a glass-fronted closet, from where it was possible to view the door of the unnumbered room, he turned around to his companions:

"Fellows, listen and remember: besides our passageways, there is yet another one that leads into this room. It wasn't made by our union. It must have been here from the first day of the hotel's existence. And someone has just gone through this passageway—ahead of you and me.

Tom and Van Hope exchanged uncertain glances. They were not inclined to believe just any old paper calculations. But before they could respond, the door to the room opened slowly and into the corridor emerged the entire company that we are familiar with. The Russian Prince immediately took leave of his companions and went off to his own room. Gibgeld and Hardstone, supporting the severely limping Viscount, went downstairs to their apartments, while the smiling No Hom got on the lift: for economic reasons he lived on the very top floor.

"Now we can enter," whispered Thingsmaster. "The person who came by way of the secret passage has already made his way back, I hear the scraping on the other side of the partition."

They carefully emerged from the closet, partially opened the door and noiselessly, one after the other, entered the room without a number.

CHAPTER 8
MIRROR-ASSISTANTS

It was the most ordinary "room" in the hotel although it had been left without a number for some reason. It was furnished in an incomparably less lavish fashion than Gibgeld's apartment. But even here, as had been the case there, mirrors stretched the length of the wall along the base of which were tropical plants. There were three mirrors, one on each wall.

Thingsmaster went up to one of them, pulled out his magnifying glass and pointed out to his companions two microscopic letters "mm" in the corner:

"These mirrors are the handiwork of our fellows from the photo-chemical works and the technician Sorrow from the "Secret Works." Take a look with both eyes and learn how to operate them.

One: Mike turned the mirror around on its own axis, stopping it at right angles. Two: Mike removed from beneath the glass, directly from a zinc plate, a very thin packet of film. Three: from somewhere on the side he pulled out a new packet— and swung the mirror back into place. Then they went out of the room, locked it and Thingsmaster passed through the wall to Miss Totter.

The packet of film was dropped into a tin with a pink liquid. Then it was pulled out. Then placed into a small machine with a little lamp at the front resembling a cannon. The lights were extinguished, the front of the machine lit up and a round spot was formed on the wall.

"Learn, my friends," said Thingsmaster, "not everything is in our hands yet. There are occasions when we are powerless to penetrate the enemy. Today we didn't succeed in hearing what they were discussing among themselves but nevertheless we can still see them. Sorrow's mirror apparatus is constructed in such a fashion that when the switch is turned, all three mirrors will project everything that is taking place within the field of the photographic camera. The noiseless shooting is about to begin this very moment—be good enough to take a look."

He turned the handle of the machine and on the illuminated screen appeared a depiction of the room they had just left. It was not empty. Inside it the very same people whom they had just watched leaving, were now moving around and seating themselves around a table.

Tom and Van Hope gave a cheerful cry. True, not a single sound reached them but at the same time they could now watch them unhindered.

"Learn to lip-read!" said Mike. He sat down in front of the screen, cranking through each scene several times, slowing down the movement so that the people on the screen seemed to be swimming in water. Every one of them was known to the "Mess-mend" Union from photographs in newspapers and from the hiding-places of the *Patrician*. Just as though he were reading a book out loud Mike reproduced word by word the following for Tom and Van Hope: "They're waiting for instructions... the German is strongly rebuking our handsome little Viscount for something, and he is barely moving his lips in response. The Englishman with the pipe is silent. The Russian Prince is flitting from one to the other with questions—look there, his eyes are inquiring, his ears are sharpened, he still doesn't know anything. The Englishman is telling him 'quiet!' Learn, fellows, in all languages you can tell from the lips when the word "quiet!' is being spoken. It's like this, the lower lip is pushed forward and it looks as though the upper lip is being pushed up by the proboscis..."

But what's this? Van Hope and Tom let out a cry. Mike whispered to himself: "Cice!"

A curious confusion was underway on the screen. A trapdoor opened directly from below into the midst of the argument, and climbing slowly out of it, as though in some fairytale ballet, was a smallish black figure. Although the figure remained on the screen, for some reason or other it was difficult for our viewers to see it very clearly, just as though it were all enveloped in mist.

"Darn, it's sort of dark, I can't make it out," complained Tom straining his eyes as hard as he could.

Only Thingsmaster gazed relentlessly at the screen. The black figure pulled a piece of paper out of his briefcase and quickly read it aloud. Indignation, amazement, triumph were clearly expressed on the faces of the others. Then the black figure raised its hand, said something and everyone nodded their head in response... Now the figure opened wide the briefcase, replaced the page which had just been read. Black-gloved hands moved quickly—what's that? Bundles, straight from the bank— one, two—with American dollar bills of the highest denominations. The eyes of everyone in the room fastened on the bundles and the number of bundles kept increasing. Palms were stretched out for them. The black figure passed them out left and right with an abrupt motion. A moment later—and he had jumped back through the trapdoor. The remainder then made their way to the door... Darkness... Light once again. And this time Tom shouted in rapture:

"Look, look, there we are!"

The film came to an end. Thingsmaster took it out and placed it in a fireproof wall-safe. Then he turned thoughtfully to Tom and Van Hope:

"We must find out precisely what is being cooked up here. Go on, fellows, through the flues and find your replacements. It's important for us to establish in the first place whether they will be staying in the building or whether they'll be dispersing after the payment, and if they are going to disperse—then where to. This is your main business now!"

"What about you, Mike?"

"I have to go back to the factory. We have some pressing business this evening, brothers. The boss is decorating his villa and we'll have to do our utmost, you understand. After all, he does have some pretty important gatherings!"

With these words Thingsmaster took his leave, entered the wall—and was gone. Miss Totter gazed dreamily after him. Tom and Van Hope dispersed to their sentry posts with a sigh. But all their efforts were in vain, that entire long night was wasted—neither Gibgeld, nor Montmorency, nor even the English lord had any subsequent conversations, and the secret of their meeting remained unrevealed for the time being. Furthermore, they were apparently not about to depart from the *Patrician* either.

Meanwhile, Thingsmaster emerged onto the street, calmly walked around the building and then once again entered the *Patricia* from the main entry as though nothing were amiss. Sticking his hands in his pockets and whistling, he went up to the desk. Here he stopped and calmly removed his cap.

Setto from Diarbekir, finishing the calculation of his weekly deficit, raised his head.

"Greetings, boss."

"Hello, Michael, what can I do for you?"

"Maybe you need some renovations?"

"God bless you, Michael, for those words," interjected Setto's wife who shared her husband's indomitable passion for renovation. "You fixed everything up for us last year so properly and cheaply!"

"But now I could fix it even better."

"Impossible, Michael," Setto replied sadly. "I've got enough pretenders here to sink a ship—just let them pay their bill first, then they can go ahead and drown! How can I do any kind of renovations?"

"A pity, a real pity, I was hoping to redo everything like new upstairs, particularly in the room without a number."

"Michael, I've made an agreement not to touch that room and I don't dare. You yourself know that a former president built this hotel for me so that he wouldn't meet another Armenian fool like me a second time either on land or sea. So then he went and made a condition: that this room would never be touched, summer or winter. And I did such a sinful thing, I decorated it, on your advice, with mirrors."

"But who actually built the hotel for you, boss, if it wasn't the ex-president himself?"

"A foreign architect was hired, Michael. And they recruited the workers from the same place as the architect."

"So, that's the way it is. A pity, boss. All the best!"

And this time Thingsmaster hurried off to Middletown.

CHAPTER 9
THE BIZARRE HABITS OF BANKER WESTINGHOUSE'S CONCUBINE

If Feofan Ivanovich had not been prevented from speaking out about the banker Westinghouse, he would have said the following:

"Westinghouse, hee-hee-hee, has acquired a concubine... And not just any old one, but can you imagine—one in a mask. Yes, it's true, in a mask. An ephemeral woman, elegant, with a sylphlike walk, and she only makes an appearance in a mask. I am convinced that she is speculating on male curiosity. If I were about five or six years younger..."

Prince Feofan was not lying. The events, as noted by the New York press, were as follows:

A week before, in the *Concordia* theater at the opera *Suleiman*, the public had suddenly seen a beautifully built woman wearing a mask in one of the fashionable boxes. As though nothing were amiss, this woman was watching the stage with a pair of eyes that glittered through the almond-shaped slits of a silk mask and was not at all embarrassed over the lorgnettes and opera glasses directed her way from all sides. She wrapped her bare shoulders in a luxurious fur, read her program and, in short, behaved quite naturally. New Yorkers were struck. No one could recognize the unknown woman. Rumors circulated to the effect that it was an illustrious foreigner whose face had been disfigured by smallpox. Then the curiosity was replaced by sympathy and for a while the incident was forgotten.

Two days later the woman in the mask reappeared for a drive along Washington Avenue, but this time she was not alone. In the carriage with her sat the banker, Westinghouse, an old roué who was known to all of America for his equipages and mistresses. Westinghouse was a bachelor. He had no female kin. There was not a single woman who would agree to take a ride in his carriage. The conclusion was clear: the mysterious mask was a child of that same world whence had emerged Violetta and Manon Lescault.

In New York there was not the same cult of courtesans which had been characteristic of Paris during the times of Balzac. But a woman who knew how to attract attention to herself with her bizarre behavior, merited a certain amount of respect. Attempts were made to photograph the woman in the mask, to catch her unawares. Love letters were written to her, flowers and gifts sent—all in vain. She proved to be beyond the reach of anyone, no matter who they were. Banker Westinghouse, who accepted the congratulations of friends with a smile, would shrug his shoulders in response to all their inquiries.

"My children, she is a pearl of creation! I assure you, I would marry her if only she would agree. But show her to you?—No! Not to anyone, at any time, not until the day I die!"

You may imagine how consumed with curiosity was the *jeune monde* of New York! The representatives of the business empires pulled faces from envy. One of them, who had only just finished Harvard, the overstuffed sybarite, Pommberbock, took it into his head to outdo Westinghouse: he took the little Flora from the *corps de ballet*, outfitted her in a mask and walked along Fifth Avenue with her, but the partisans of the lady in the mask shamed him with their catcalls and Flora could no longer dare to appear on the street. Ultimately, the masked lady was made into something akin to a parimutual betting machine and people made bets according to her, swore by her, guessed at the weather, good fortune, wins, etc., according to the color of her costumes.

The girls, too, were no less intrigued. In the depths of their hearts all of them wanted to look like the lady in the mask. Seamstresses constantly received the following commission: make it in the style of the lady in the mask.

But not a single one experienced such amorous rapute, such worship for the masked lady as did the daughter of Senator Notabit, the mischievous Grace. Grace is sitting at this very moment in her music study with her teacher, Miss Orton, and is making vain attempts to pound out Beethoven's Fourteenth Sonata. She is twenty years old, curly-headed like a young lad, freckle-faced, with a somewhat large but cute mouth, and agile like a lizard. She could not be called attractive. But with her one immediately felt like a person who, without rhyme or reason has been challenged to a bout of Chinese boxing. Grace hit a false chord, Miss Orton made a nervous cry, Grace turned to her, embraced her impetuously and exclaimed:

"Miss Orton, dearest, it's simply beyond me! I saw the mask today in front of a flower shop. If only you knew what handsome legs she has! I did something silly, I seized her by the dress and confessed my love for her."

"What happened then?" smiled and asked the teacher who was, one might have said, a sleek, hunchbacked, lopsided young lady with hair combed straight back, and wearing an extremely ill-fitting dress. Her voice, incidentally, was very musical and resembled the murmuring of a lute.

"Oh, Miss Orton! The trouble was that that vile old fogey, banker Westinghouse, came like a bolt out of the blue and announced venomously: 'Miss Notabit, I have the honor of accompanying you into the store'. And before I managed to gather my wits, he had stuck me into the store and the mask had flitted off into a carriage and disappeared."

"Well, Grace, that was very imprudent on your part. Do not forget that you are the daughter of a senator."

"As though I needed reminding about that, Miss Orton. I categorically declare: I am in love with the lady in the mask. I sense that that accursed Westinghouse is tormenting her. I am determined to save her..." One-two, one-two... The immortal trio from the Fourteenth Sonata disintegrated into pieces under her energetic fingers.

"My God," sighed Miss Orton, "you really do not understand Beethoven."

We don't know what Grace would have replied to her if at that very moment the door had not been flung wide open and someone's strange, bass-like, manly voice had not declared:

"Dear Grace, at last!"

Miss Orton gave a severe start, no doubt from surprise. Into the music study came a very dark, elegantly dressed girl with large crimson lips, red hair, and wearing furs despite the fact that it was May. It was Miss Claire Wesson, the niece of Morlender's second spouse and Grace's bosom-friend from school days.

"Claire! You're here at last!" Grace scattered the music hither and yon, leapt up and hung on her neck. "One small moment, Miss Orton, forgive me, please. I'll finish the lesson, just let us say hello to each other."

Miss Orton did not even consider making a protest. With a poor person's patience, she rested her hands on her knees, sat down in a darkened corner and remained there silently for more than half an hour while the girls forgot about her in the midst of their chattering. They chattered in a way befitting to a pair of young idlers of the privileged class, about one thing and another: about the Warsaw Opera, Rachmaninoff's concerts, the young Arthur Morlender, and again about the lady in the mask. The following became clear: by preference Claire talked about Arthur, and by preference Grace talked about the mask.

"This Arthur of yours, he's a proper milksop," the senator's daughter let fly towards the end of their conversation, "tell me at least whether he's seen my masked lady even one little old time?"

"Mister Morlender is not interested in courtesans," Claire replied drily, "all his thoughts are devoured by revenge. You do know that his father was killed by the Bolsheviks, that has now been proven without a doubt. He is preparing to stir up all of Europe against them."

"Fie, how silly. Claire, you know what? I very much want you to take a look at the masked lady; I'd be interested to learn what your opinion is. She is all chic, elegance, fascination, well, I can't even tell you what she's like. But the main thing is that she seems frightfully unhappy to me."

"Grace, I'm telling you again that neither I nor Arthur are interested in women like that."

"You're talking as though you were engaged."

Claire flared up, Grace pouted. The conversation was broken off. Miss Orton glanced at her watch, quietly stood up from her place, inconspicuously put her hat on, dropped the veil over her face, took leave of the two girls and, limping heavily, went out of the music study.

Claire watched her departure with amazement.

"Grace, I cannot comprehend why you are taking lessons from this hideous hunchbacked, limping old maid who resembles more a laundress than a musician. After all, you might have found yourself an excellent teacher!"

Grace jumped up from her place and firmly shut the door. She flared up from anger:

"Shame on you!" she whispered to her friend. "Miss Orton hasn't yet managed to go down the stairs, she probably heard everything. And she is not at all a monster, but..."

At this point Grace stopped and realized that never once, *never once* had she given any thought to Miss Orton's exterior appearance. Giving her curls a shake, the girl began to recollect her teacher, her face, the eyes, the smile, the hands. True, she kept her eyes lowered and disfigured them with her spectacles, she wore gloves on her hands because of rheumatism, her hair was slicked down into a net, she smiled once in a blue moon, but all the same, all the same, if she recollected... Grace's face suddenly became illuminated in positive triumph. She gave her friend a triumphant look and concluded quite unexpectedly for herself:

"But all the same I tell you—Miss Orton is a beautiful woman."

CHAPTER 10
THE MUSIC TEACHER AND THE LAWYER

Poor Miss Orton had heard everything that Claire had said. Apparently it did not unduly distress her. She simply buttoned up her knitted jacket over her breast and began to limp even more severely. Reaching Seventh Avenue, she climbed into a bus, rode for half an hour and got out directly in front of a dark old house in the style of the preceding century, one of the few remnants of antiquity which had been preserved in New York.

A few minutes elapsed before the door was opened for her. A youth in a jacket with epaulettes asked her in a hoarse voice (his face was red from tears):

"Who are you looking for?"

"I must see the lawyer Kraft. Here is my card."

The boy looked at the girl in amazement, at the same time as his hand automatically took the card.

"Is the lawyer at home?" she repeated once more.

An old negro came up to the boy and his face was also swollen from crying. With a trembling hand he pushed him aside and uttered:

"The Miss will forgive us. The Miss can't see the lawyer. Massah Kraft died more than a week ago, he had an automobile accident."

"He died? My Lord, my Lord!"

Miss Orton seemed utterly shaken. She turned so pale that the negro supported her out of sympathy and leading her up to a wicker chair, suggested that she sit down:

"But what about his papers now? Is someone taking the lawyer's place?"

"There, upstairs, in the deceased's office they'll give you all the information," the negro replied darkly and his round eyes flashed like those of a wild beast. "The Massah was hardly dead before they came to lord it over everyone: confiscated all his papers, broke open the files and then sealed everything with red seals. They've certainly replaced him already, without any sign of conscience, the Miss can rest assured. As for us, his loyal old servants, we're being dismissed."

The girl listened until the negro had finished and then silently she made her way up the staircase. But halfway up she stopped and turned her head in his direction.

"Tell me," she whispered as quietly as possible, "what is the name of the person who is replacing Mr. Kraft?"

The negro looked up at her from down below, his eyes still flashing darkly and replied quietly:

"He's a real devil, Miss. A plague for one and all to have any business with him. But there's no way I can tell you his name. All I know is that his assistants address him as Signor Gregorio."

Miss Orton climbed the staircase, this time without turning around, and entered the general office.

Kraft's former assistants were sitting here, all those who were being "dismissed," including his young male secretary, Druck. He was turning over affairs to the new secretary and four small, swarthy persons were peering fixedly over his shoulder. Apparently they were all concerned with the analysis of the papers left behind after Kraft.

Miss Orton took them in at a glance. Then, submitting to that faithful instinct possessed by very sensitive people who have been overtaken by misfortune, she moved directly towards Druck.

He was a young man with a wide, clever face, puffy cheeks and a dimple on his chin. Those who knew Druck more closely would have said that he merely pretended to be more obtuse and flighty than he actually was. At that particular moment Druck portrayed such simplemindedness, such doltishness, that the four swarthy-faced young gents exchanged looks with one another, shrugged their shoulders and one after the other retreated from him to the more intelligent, and apparently for that very reason, more interesting assistants of the lawyer.

But it was precisely to this imbecile that Miss Orton now made her way. Approaching him, she lifted her veil, removed her spectacles from her eyes and stared directly into his eyes. Druck froze on the spot as though he had been hypnotized. Then Miss Orton replaced her glasses, lowered the veil and quietly declared:

"I have come here with a large request. Morlender has died, and his will is supposed to be in the possession of Lawyer Kraft. I have come to find out about the contents of this will."

"What is your name?" asked Druck submissively, winking unmistakably for her benefit in the direction of the swarthy-faced gentlemen.

"Miss Orton."

"Miss... what is it? Burton, Morton... Ah, Orton." He wrote something down on a paper and handed it to the girl. "There, be good enough to ask the courier in front of that door to let you in directly to Signor Gregorio, the executor assigned to the take-over of Lawyer Kraft's archives." Having said that, he once more winked unmistakably at her, but indicating the paper this time.

Miss Orton read the slip of paper. At that very moment one of the swarthy-faced gentlemen came right up to her, trying to look into her hands. But he did not succeed and he muttered angrily:

"Hey, Druck, what did you write for the Miss?"

"My own name," Miss Orton interjected in a calm and quiet voice, as she folded and hid the slip of paper in her purse, "no doubt to give to the courier. Thank you, Mr. Druck, if that is your name," she turned to the secretary who had once more assumed a very doltish look, "but there's no need for such a note, because I do have my own card."

She produced a card from her purse and handed it to the swarthy-faced gentleman.

Grumbling angrily, his small coffee-colored eyes flashing, he took the card and personally went through the dark oak door.

He reemerged from there in a few minutes. The expression on his face had changed radically. Glowing with courtesy and making two or three bows, he invited Miss Orton into Signor Gregorio's office, retreating all the while backwards before her towards the door, like some lackey out of an operetta. No sooner had she entered and the oak door had closed tightly behind her than he made a sign to his colleagues. Immediately one of them, the one who was sitting nearest the telephone, picked up the receiver and on an internal line notified someone in a whisper that "Netty will have to buy herself a new hat."

We cannot say whether all these machinations pleased the tow-headed Druck, inasmuch as there was an expression of submissive tranquillity on his face, and judging by the sheeplike expression of his eyes, he hardly seemed to be sorting the manuscripts before him in any sensible fashion.

Meanwhile, Miss Orton had crossed the threshold into a large room with heavy leather furniture and stained Gothic windows where formerly the lawyer Kraft had received his visitors. She entered, limping severely and painfully hunched over. And at that precise moment, despite the fact that there was nothing extraordinary either in the room or in the person inside it, a sixth sense sent a shiver down her spine and made the hair rise in terror on her head.

Sitting at the desk was a man in black who had just replaced the telephone receiver. With a hand encased in a black glove, he raised her card to his eyes.

"You are Miss Orton? Do take a seat, please." It was the most ordinary voice in the world.

She sat down and took several moments to set herself right. During that time, the stranger closely examined her from head to toe and asked her once more:

"So, Miss Orton, you are one of the clients of the deceased Kraft. In what way can I be of service to you?"

"I am not a client of Lawyer Kraft. I came to ask for one solitary favor. I have learned that Jeremy Morlender left a will before he departed for Europe. Now he is dead. Would it be possible for you to acquaint me with his will?"

"Nothing could be easier, Miss Orton. Unfortunately, I must inform you that the will of which you speak, has not been located among Kraft's papers, and, moreover, it is rendered null and void by the final will of the deceased which was drawn up in Russia. Here is an exact copy of the last will for you."

He handed Miss Orton a paper and the girl read the document which is already known to the reader. Having read it through twice, she stood up and returned the paper to the stranger.

"I thank you. You do not recall whether the name of Orton has been mentioned in any of Kraft's papers?"

"There are quite a few of his papers. But insofar as I can recall, I have not encountered your name."

Having spoken thus, he once more carefully studied the girl. Through her spectacles and veil, Miss Orton studied him as well and then, suddenly shuddering, she lowered her eyes. Sitting before her all the while was nothing more than an impeccably dressed man with a swarthy face, black moustache and bloodless yellow lips.

Miss Orton returned to the general office, limping more severely than usual, and nodding good-bye to the lawyer's clerk, she went down the stairs. There she loitered about for a while, keeping an eye out for the kind old negro who had admitted her into the house. Then she wandered over to the bus stop and taking shelter in the shade of a large metal umbrella, behind the back of a dozing fat man, she read once more the note which Druck had handed to her. This is what was written there:

"Brooklyn Street, No. 8, Druck, 4:00 p.m."

"Apparently this Druck knows something. But who is playing the lord in Kraft's archives, and by what right?" She firmly resolved to go to the indicated address, and in order to fill in the remaining time, she made her way to the embankment. Passing two or three blocks, she came out to the shining ribbon of the Hudson which was almost deserted at that particular place. No steamers or motorboats were to be seen. Down below, beneath the granite slabs of the embankment, a special May cleaning of the sewer pipes was in progress. Two blue-collar workers, one young, the other old, were resting on the excavated roadway, and were hungrily eating their sausage.

Miss Orton walked along the shore, without taking notice of the fact that a relentless companion was tailing her. He was a puny, dark-skinned man, with shoulder blades that worked under his shirt, with slightly swollen joints in his hands. His eyes were sunken, mournful, desolate, like those of a confirmed alcoholic who had been forced into sobriety for the time being. Under his nose, above the bloodless yellow lips, were black cat-like whiskers. He walked along, looking this way and that and then suddenly, without a single sound, at a deserted turning, he pulled something out from under his shirt, leapt noiselessly up to Miss Orton and swung his arm. A fleeting instant—and the wretched girl, with a knife between her shoulders, without uttering a cry, without a moan, tumbled from the embankment into the Hudson. The man waited for almost a minute. Everything was just as deserted as before. Then he turned around and disappeared into a sidestreet.

The blue-collar workers, their sausage finished, had returned to work.

"Willings," said one of them, "I don't like it. A lame girl was passing along here and suddenly there's no trace of her, just like she had plunged into the water."

"I heard the splash of water too. Let's go down, Ned, down below and give Laurie a knock,—he's laying pipe right under the embankment."

"Alright!" the other replied and jumped into the opening.

CHAPTER 11
THE TIMBER BARGE

A strike was in progress not only at the metallurgical factory in Sweaton. In addition to the telegraph operators and postal workers at Roven Square, almost all the factories and plants in Middletown had followed suit. Only the woodworking factory—the pride of Mr. Kressling—remained loyal to its owner and did not go on strike.

But in order not to starve, the workers heeded the advice of Mike and went their individual ways to find piecemeal work wherever possible—and, incidentally to check for the microscopic "mm" on installations whose secret, except for the members of the "Mess-Mend" Union, was unknown either in the Old World, or the New, either in this world or the one beyond.

Young Laurence Laine from the "Secret Works," which had also gone on strike a few days before, found a job laying drainage sewers deep below the embankment, alongside the Hudson itself. The waves were even lapping at Laurie's very feet after he had made a place for himself on two metal pillars and was now working with a benzine torch in his hand. Laurie had been mending pipes from early morning in that uncomfortable pose, neither whistling nor humming lest he might lose his balance and plop into the water. Finally, extremely tired, he stuck his belongings deep inside a hole between two girders, stretched his limbs as much as possible and pulled out a hunk of bread from inside his shirt. But it was not to be. He had barely managed to raise it to his mouth when something came flying past him from above, somersaulting in the air and thudding heavily into the Hudson.

"Strange," Laurie thought, "I wonder if it was a suicide? Besides, anyone else would have cried out or started to flounder about, but there was nothing but ripples in the water from this one."

He trained his eyes on the water, noticed nothing suspicious and again was about to eat. He was, however, interrupted once more. To the left, out of the dark tunnel from where he had made his way to this spot, a knocking sound rang out and the familiar word reached him:

"Mend-mess."

"Mess-mend," Laurie replied hurriedly, grabbing his safety hooks and jumping acrobatically into the tunnel. "Who's there? What's wrong?"

Surfacing out of the tunnel came the mud-covered heads of Willings and his friend, Ned.

"Listen, Laurie, didn't a person just fall past you into the water?"

"A heavy object fell, but I couldn't see what kind. I didn't hear any cry."

"Laurie, it might have been a lame girl. We watched her walking along and then suddenly she disappeared no one knows where."

"Strange," replied Laurie. "Wait for me, fellows, I'll dive down myself. Attach yourselves to my hooks and keep an eye out to see if I drag anything out. If I don't appear for a long time, come and give me a hand."

"Okay," replied the workers, "but what are you going to do with her if you pull her out?"

Laurie looked the Hudson over thoughtfully. It was deserted at this spot with the exception of a small inlet where an old barge stood loaded up with timber. At that hour there was not a single living soul on it.

"Over there, on that barge," he replied carelessly, tossed off the iron clamps and chain by means of which he had clung to his risky perch, swung his arms out, described an arc and flew headlong into the Hudson.

Willings and Ned had meanwhile fastened themselves to the iron hooks with much kicking and grunting and clung to the pillars with their knees as they began to look in the direction where wide ripples were spreading out.

"Clever fellow," said Willings, "he's only been in our Union for no more than a week. And he's as good as Thingsmaster."

"What's so clever?" replied Ned. "There's never been one smarter than our Mike, and there sure won't be either."

"Why doesn't he come up? I'll count to a hundred and you keep an eye out... Well, any sign of him?"

"No."

Willings counted to a hundred once more. But there was still no sign of Laurie. Then they decided to dive down after him, swung out by the hooks and plunged awkwardly to where Laurie had disappeared. In a few seconds they both surfaced, snorting water, and at that very moment they caught sight of Laurie. He was swimming about half a dozen yards away from them, dragging a heavy object behind him and calling to them at the top of his voice. The wind, however, carried his words away and they could not make anything out. Talking it over, they both decided to swim after Laurie. A short time later, breathing heavily and spitting, both workers swam as far as the barge where Laurie was waiting for them, too weak to use his own strength to lift his heavy catch out of the water.

It was a woman in a dark dress and a knitted jacket who had apparently lost consciousness. Her face was completely wrapped up in a veil which had stuck together in an impenetrable clump. One leg appeared to be longer than the other.

"So it is the lame girl after all," cried Willings, "but who could have pushed that poor wretch into the water? Is she alive, Laurie?"

"Let's take a look," the latter replied.

All three of them pulled her up onto the barge and following the rules for life-saving they turned her face down. At that very moment they all gave a loud cry: a knife was sticking out from between the wretched girl's shoulder blades.

"Murder," Willings muttered in a hollow voice, "Damn it all, Laurie, this is a nasty piece of work! Leave the girl like she is and Ned you run for the police and a doctor."

"Wait a minute," replied Laurie, "there's something funny here. Did you ever see, brothers, a knife stuck into someone without a single drop of blood? There's not even a trace of it here, her dress is pretty clean and there was no blood in the water."

He went up to the girl, touched her foot and then, kneeling down, began to feel along her back. A smile stretched practically from ear to ear. With an abrupt motion he tore the jacket off the girl together with a portion of her back and the knife sticking in it. The other workers gasped.

"She must have been a professional beggar," said Laurie, "a beggar wearing an artificial hump for greater effect. Let's carry her under the cabin awning and bring her back to consciousness."

They carried the girl inside the boat where a miserable sleeping-place had been set up beneath a piece of tarpaulin, laid her down on the straw and began to pull the sticky veil off her. This turned out to be more difficult than imagined, but when Laurie resorted to his penknife and tore the sticky blue netting from the girl's face, it turned out that the dye from the veil had stained her face a proper blue. Smiling despite himself, Willings brought a handful of water. Laurie took the girl's round, dark spectacles off and began to wash the face of the drowned girl before him. Imagine the amazement of all three when once the blue color had been washed away they suddenly saw before them the face of a marvellous, flawless beauty.

"Ho-ho!" said Laurie as he pulled the ugly hairnet away and wet, chestnut curls spilled over the girl's shoulders. "There was no need for someone like her to go begging. Instead of begging for half-a-cent with an artificial hump, she could have raked in hundreds of dollars with her pretty little face."

"But after all the poor girl was lame!" Ned declared with compassion.

"Lame?" Laurie drawled. "Let's just take a look and see how lame she is."

He leaned over her and examined the enormous fat legs of the girl with amazement. He had to admit that they were ugly in the extreme and one leg was practically several inches longer than the other.

"Hm-m, Laurie, looks like you're a little disappointed in your pretty girl?" Willings asked.

But Laurie quickly set about pulling off the girl's high, coarse shoes. They were soaked through and the undertaking was all that easy. But when success came, Laurie triumphantly stuck a large boot with a false sole cast from iron under the nose of his mocker and happily announced:

"Now I understand why she didn't come to the surface but went straight down to the bottom. With weights like that she never could have surfaced in her life if I hadn't grabbed her by the dress on the very bottom."

Willings and Ned fell silent after that. Curiosity aroused, they pulled an entire wad of cotton batten and rags from the girl, together with her stockings, revealing two miniature legs as white as marble. Now lying before them, barely covered with the remainder of her wet clothing, was the most perfectly beautiful woman imaginable.

"Well, now," said Willings thoughtfully, "there's mystery here, brothers. Wee should let Mike know."

"But let's give her some whiskey first," replied Laurie, as he opened the girl's mouth and poured some of the bracing moisture through her clenched teeth.

A few moments passed during which all three admired the beautiful girl in spite of themselves. At last she sighed and opened eyes that were blue like violets.

At precisely that moment a deathly pallor spread through her face and neck. A wild terror flashed in her eyes. She shrieked, leapt up and rushed inside the boat.

"Calm down, Miss!" Laurie cried out after her. "Really, calm down. We're honest fellows, local workers. We dragged you up from the bottom of the Hudson. And even if we did take your hump and false shoe off, there's no harm done. You can rest assured that we won't interfere in your secrets."

The wretched girl turned around and came back to them again, examining each one of them with an attentive gaze.

"I want to believe your words," she said slowly, "you saved my life and that's good. But you could subject me to a fate a thousand times worse than rotting at the bottom of the Hudson if you hand me over to whoever it may have been."

Laurie exchanged looks with his comrades.

"I'm calling Mike to witness that we won't hand you over, Miss. Not me, not them" he declared solemnly. "We have no stronger word to give you than that. And if you require help, then we can provide you with the kind of help that you have never dreamt about in your wildest dreams."

"Fine," replied the girl. "Now one of you give me your clothing, destroy the remainder of my own clothing and the rest of you can take me somewhere to a safe place and hide me because now there is no safe refuge for me in all of New York."

Before she could even finish her request, Laurie had disappeared behind the tarpaulin and threw out his own boots, trousers and jacket. Meanwhile, Willings and Ned had gathered her clothing into a ball, tied it to the heavy shoes and thrown it into the water.

"Fellows," Laurie shouted to them, "take the Miss to Middletown, straight to Mike's place and make sure that not a single hair on her head..."

"Okay, just shut up now. Sit there in your birthday suit until we send someone."

"And one more request," interjected the girl who had now been transformed into a handsome young boy with chestnut colored curls scattered over her shoulders. "When you get your clothing and get off the barge, you must go to a Mr. Druck at No. 8 Brooklyn Street. Inform him that you have come from Miss Orton who was the victim of a murder attempt but who was saved by you. And have him pass on to you everything that he intended to pass on to me. Understand?"

"Point for point," replied Laurie from behind the tarpaulin. "It'll be done, Miss!"

For a long while he watched through a hole as his comrades led the exquisite boy from the barge along the dizzying gangway to the shore.

CHAPTER 12
MIKE THINGSMASTER AT DAY'S END

It had grown dark. The long working day in Middletown was drawing to a close. The exhausted workers spilled forth in a throng from those few factories and mines which had not joined in the strike. The workers, both men and women, came running out of the wide-open doors of the woodworking factory. Only in a single department at the "Secret Works" were lights still burning, and would burn all night, even though no one could see that from behind the shielding fence, nor could a pilot even see from up above. Jack Kressling's "Secret Works" were working around the clock.

And there was Jack himself. He was riding on top of a grey English mare up into the hills where his extraordinary villa *Ephemerides*, constructed with fantastic lavishness, was glittering with a thousand lights. While the soft silver horseshoes of the mare lightly touched the special bridle path which had been built for the master of the city alongside the ordinary roadway, Kressling's workers, exhausted by their hard day, dispersed in the direction of their quarters. Jack's workers lived worse than dogs. Not because they were badly paid. No, on the contrary, they were paid a great deal. Jack Kressling had devised his own system of wages. He kept the workers only until the age of thirty. No sooner was your thirtieth year celebrated, then off you went, the devil cared where, you had to move over for the next. But as long as you were still only seventeen, twenty, twenty-five—Jack Kressling would give. And he gave generously: fistfuls of dollars every Saturday from the pay wicket. But he did not give for nothing—work! work! work! another hour, another hour, another hour... And choking over the thought that after thirty—the prescribed time—they could expect poverty and unemployment right up until the grave, Kressling's workers, in the hope of saving at least something for that rainy day, and rushing like madmen, they would work, work, work—ten, twelve, fourteen, and after fourteen even sixteen, twenty, twenty-four hours a day, sleeping only once in three days, eating their food right beside the machinery, chewing coffee beans in order to whip up their energy and the clarity of their minds. But if you think that they were able to save up in this fashion at least something for the day when they would celebrate (or bemoan) their thirtieth birthday, then go and pay them a visit, only not in the workers' settlement of Middletown, but farther down, at the Middletown cemetery: there they all are lying in a row. And Jack Kressling did not scrimp when he put up their headstones.

Incidentally, that was the way it had been five years before. But now it was not like that. From the time when the giant Michael Thingsmaster had raised his blond head at the woodworking factory, people worked and worked, but no more than the prescribed time and they no longer were dying by their thirtieth year; and between their lips, like a rabbit in a burrow, sat a smile like a little ball. Mike Thingsmaster knew what he was doing. It was not in vain that those two tiny, microscopic letters "mm" were spreading rapidly from there to all corners of America and beyond, to mighty steamers, to airplanes, to dirigibles, to trains and buses, to hotels and offices, and it was not in vain that more and more workers both on this side as well as the other side of the ocean knew what these letters signified and how to use them.

Mike Thingsmaster did not live in the workers' settlement. He had built a shack for himself out of cast-off wood on the outskirts of Middletown, right beside the telegraph tower. In this shack he would spend those two or three hours a day that were left over after the greatest and most highly diversified activity. He knew how to sleep both sitting and on his feet. But he always ate without fail at home, taking from the hands of the old cook an enormous soup dish with the aromatic, "long-life stew" that was known to all of Middletown and which the old woman knew how to prepare to perfection. Here there were pieces of meat gristle, potatoes, onion, parsnips, carrot, pepper, and in addition, a kind of medicinal herb which was sent to Mike by oil-field workers in Mexico. Mike had neither wife nor children. When he ate his stew, Beauty, an enormous dog and Thingsmaster's loyal friend and comrade, would lie stretched out at his feet under the table, following lovingly every movement of his hand.

Mike's wooden spoon had just barely touched the half-cleaned bottom of his cherished soup dish, and Beauty, licking her chops had just swallowed the gristle which had been tossed to her, when the door to the shack opened without a knock and an elderly little man with a small goatee peeked in. Before continuing our story, we shall introduce this elderly man to the reader.

Who of you does not know about Edison? His fame is spread throughout the entire globe!

But does anyone know the technician Sorrow? No one!

The technician Sorrow, despite his age, was always in motion. He loved to stroll about with his hands behind his back. He was almost never sitting; he walked while he worked, he walked while talking with you, he walked while he ate and even walked while he was sitting—the latter was only possible because the technician Sorrow had devised a moving seat for himself, a kind of walking chair. He loved to chat, mixing now and then some Latin rhetoric into his speech:

"Life is mobility, death is immobility; just you stand there gaping or take a seat, and it's got you by the tail, brothers, one-two-three. That's your *pax vobiscum* for you, just like the catholic priests sing about."

The rumor circulated that as a young lad the technician Sorrow had been a close friend of Edison's. Once they had had a chat at the work bench.

"Hm-m" Edison is supposed to have said, "I'm going to invent the kind of thing that will make people gasp. Kings will greet me with a handshake, the most esteemed professors will come to learn from me."

"But then what?" asked Sorrow.

"And then I'm going to live and invent. I'll live in my own palace and I'll invent one miracle after another."

Sorrow said nothing during these speeches. But to tell the truth, he didn't care for them.

"What's the meaning of it?" he thought to himself. "Edison isn't thinking like a fellow-worker. He's a worker himself, but he's thinking about kings. Let's see where he ends up."

Edison ended up precisely where he intended. Telephones, gramophones, phonographs, trams, an innumerable multitude of miracles ended up in the hands of kings and rich men, increasing their comforts and adorning their lives.

"Now that's what a simple worker can do!" said Edison during a reception where a king greeted him with a handshake.

Edison's former fellow-workers were proud of him. The workers frequently drank to his health, squandering their weekly wages. The technician Sorrow looked on all of this in silence and shook his head.

"You're envious," they said to him at the factory.

But the technician Sorrow continued to be silent and shake his head. At that time he was an assistant to the engineer Jeremy Morlender at Kressling's steel foundry. He repaired machines, fixed screws, lubricated, oiled, stripped down and reassembled machine parts that did not function—in short, he was a small fry at the factory. But Jeremy

Morlender's keen gaze immediately discerned the unusual inventive capabilities of the technician Sorrow. He took him under his wing, taught him drafting, design and high mathematics. As precipitously as Jeremy Morlender climbed up the career ladder, he dragged behind himself his own right-hand man, the technician Sorrow. But neither Morlender, or even Jack Kressling had any hold over him. They could offer him a million for an extra hour's work, but the technician Sorrow would not even bat an eye. He would take off his blue coveralls, wash his hands under the faucet, place them behind his back and leave for home, whistling some tune or other. And what he did at home no one knew, not even his landlady.

On that day when Michael Thingsmaster delivered his first speech which initiated a new Middletown era, the technician Sorrow knocked at his door after work, came in, closed the door and began:

"Thingsmaster, you're precisely the man that I've been waiting almost thirty years for. Put your hand in my pocket!"

Mike Thingsmaster put his hand into his pocket, pulled out a sheaf of papers and glanced questioningly at the technician Sorrow.

"Walk beside me and listen," Sorrow said in a whisper. And so they walked all evening, all night and all morning, right up until the whistle gave the signal for work. And a short while later, from all the factories, from the mines, pits, docks, wharfs, from the mills, the elevators, from depots, from garages, from repair shops, the cheerful symbol of "mm" poured forth on cheerful things that had been trained to all of the technician Sorrow's secrets.

It was this same small, unremarkable man with a face that was crisscrossed with an entire network of fine, thoughtful wrinkles who had just looked into Thingsmaster's shack with a very serious expression in his eyes.

"Mike," Sorrow said after they had exchanged a firm handshake and the cook had placed before him a wooden soup dish of her "long-life stew" steaming with all the aromas of her kitchen, "Mike, my comrade, something has happened. I received a letter from Engineer Morlender."

"Senior or junior?"

"From Jeremy Morlender himself. His handwriting, a Soviet postmark, mailed in Russia. Written in a fury—he's pressing me to hurry up with the conclusion of the work in our department, he assures me that until we've put an end to this plague of Russian communism there'll never be a single day of peace for us, that the Russians have made up their minds to destroy America and the Americans, that he himself, with his own eyes and ears, had reason to be convinced of this, and that from this day forward the fate of the world was in our hands, in the hands of Jack Kressling's "Secret Works."

"These don't sound like Jeremy's words!"

"And immediately after receiving the letter I learn about his death, Mike. You yourself read in the newspaper that Morlender's body was supposed to have been found in the middle of the night in Petrograd, then delivered to us with every possible precaution by the representatives of a neutral state which has accreditation in Russia and that supposedly we already have conclusive evidence in our hands about the violent death of Morlender at the hands of the Bolsheviks."

"But the Russians did print a statement of denial!"

"But it wasn't reprinted here. But listen further. Today, at the end of the work shift, I was summoned to Jack Kressling's own office. And there I was told that I would be named the chief engineer at the "Secret Works" and beginning the very first day I'm to speed up a certain piece of work which we know by the code "AO.""

"An exploding clock with a range of half-a-kilometer?"

"Exactly!"

"At the woodworking factory we're making an ebony case for it."

"What should I do, Mike? From the very moment when I'm named to the job, and that won't be any later than three days from now, I won't dare to take a step without being checked and searched, I won't be able to step out of line... I couldn't even think of getting in touch with you and the fellows, so maybe I should refuse the work. But you yourself understand that our success depends on me getting my hands into this business and not refusing to do so under any circumstances!"

"Yes," Mike answered slowly, pushing aside the empty soup dish, "it's a complicated situation. Even now, before you've even begun to work, he's got a hundred eyes watching you. We must not, absolutely must not draw suspicion on our Union. And the most important thing is that we still haven't got hold of all the threads, we don't know everything that is being plotted. And for us to wait is particularly..."

Beauty leapt out from under the table and hurtled towards the door, barking threateningly.

Knock-knock-knock—came the sound, not very loudly, but quite insistently.

Knock-knock-knock!

CHAPTER 13
THE ADVENTURES OF DRUCK

As soon as business came to a close in Kraft's office, Mr. Druck gave a wide yawn, produced an expression of blissful fatigue on his face, peeked in a small mirror, smoothed his hair down and then, good-naturedly bidding his colleagues good-bye, he made his way homeward, swinging his walking-stick.

Mr. Druck was not your usual kind of fellow. He knew full well that people did not have eyes in their backs. But on the other hand, he was aware of the fact that watch and jewelry stores did have two-way mirrors which could replace any eye of yours regardless of where it was placed. Apparently at precisely that moment Mr. Druck was about to acquire some new cuff-links, in consequence of which there was absolutely no limits to his rapture as he stood before the display windows of Leon's the Jewelers. With mouth broadly agape and devouring a pair of diamond cuff-links with his eyes, Mr. Druck remained standing there until he espied the man who was relentlessly trailing him. Then he entered the store, purchased the cuff-links, chatted with the jeweller about one thing and another, exited by way of the back-door onto another street and made his way to Brooklyn Street on a streetcar. The fact of the matter was that Mr. Druck had read all of Gaborieau and Arthur Conan Doyle. For a long while now Mr. Druck had felt the urge to become involved in some monstrous crime in the capacity of a detective. And finally it looked as though his hopes were about to be realized.

Arriving home and dining quickly, he locked himself up in his room, raised a small rug near the bed and then a piece of the parquet flooring. He pulled out an envelope on which was written in Mr. Druck's minute handwriting:

THE MYSTERY OF JEREMY MORLENDER

He drew several sheets of paper out of it, added yet another page of writing to them and then hid everything back in the old place. That done, Druck took up one more sheet of paper and wrote to the Attorney General of the State of Illinois the following amusing letter:

> Mister Attorney General, Fearing for my life, I am requesting you to be on the alert. In my hands I hold the threads to an intriguing incident. If I am killed or if I should disappear, I am requesting you to remove immediately an envelope from a secret hiding place in my

room at No. 8 Brooklyn Street, the twelfth piece of parquet from the left-hand window, to read that letter and initiate a judicial investigation. I am writing specifically to you and to no one else inasmuch as you have distinguished yourself by your fascination for criminal mysteries. Robert Druck, Clerk.

The letter written and sealed, he glanced at his watch and went up to the window. It was a warm day, and Mrs. Druck had left the windows open in his room. From here a portion of the street was visible and Mr. Druck espied the black automobile which had stopped at the entrance. His heart experienced a pleasurable contraction when he caught sight of the four swarthy-faced men jumping one after the other out of the automobile.

"It's beginning," he whispered ecstatically to himself, "four against one!"

He placed the sealed envelope, which had been addressed to the Attorney General of Illinois, on the window-sill, covered it with the blind and then laid down on the couch, pretending to be asleep. "It'll be interesting to see," he thought, "how they'll begin? Maybe they'll offer me a million dollars for my part in the affair?"

But the encounter with his colleagues proved to be much more prosaic than Mr. Druck's musings. They come into his room, closed the doors firmly and one of them said to Druck in a whisper:

"Listen here. Signor Gregorio does not intend to deprive you of your good name, he wished to put an end to the business quietly. You've cleaned out Kraft'ss cashbox. Return the money immediately or we'll go to the police."

Druck leapt up from the couch, his mouth agape. His round face assumed a stupid, insulted expression, his ears turned red like a small boy's—and this time Mr. Druck was not pretending one little bit.

"How dare you," he roared fiercely. "You are mad!"

"Don't shout, Druck, you don't want to get your mom excited. Prove it if it wasn't you; you had the key to the cashbox. It's been unlocked and cleaned out right down to the last cent."

"But I had already left!" Druck exclaimed in bewilderment.

"Then be good enough to go and take a look to see who might have done it in your absence."

Feverishly Druck grabbed his hat and ran downstairs without even saying good-bye to his mother. He was beside himself. He forgot about Arthur Conan Doyle and the Attorney General. He was shaking from the insult as only those honest young people of twenty-two years of age with round faces and pale blue eyes, such as Druck had, could shake.

The swarthy-faced men climbed into the automobile and Druck joined them. The chauffeur took the steering wheel, the automobile flew like an arrow. The clerks were telling one another about various instances of theft which had been perpetrated by secretaries. They expressed their indignation and disapproval. They referred to the lack of trust displayed by someone or other. Druck reddened and puffed, he was ready to thrash all four. Then suddenly, glancing out the window, he saw something strange: this was not at all the road to Kraft's office! They were hurtling along a deserted waterfront roadway, they were driving out of New York, they were flying along to no one knew where, only it certainly was not to Kraft's...

"Hey!" he exclaimed, and at that precise moment, a blow knocked him over. In a second Druck was sitting calmly with a gag in his mouth and his hands tightly tied. A half-hour later the automobile drove up to an impenetrable black fence on a deserted road. Behind this impenetrable fence stretched a park where quiet people in white gowns roamed about, invisible from the road. Several muscular men in white overalls with a red cross on the sleeve dragged the floundering Mr. Druck out of the automobile, picked him up like a kitten and carried him into an enormous gloomy building with numerous corridors and numbered doors.

"A dangerously violent case," said someone in metallic voice, "put him in number one hundred and thirty-two."

And Mr. Druck was put into number one hundred and thirty-two where he was supposed to disappear, in all probability, forever. The swarthy-faced clerks said good-bye to the orderlies, the gates banged shut once more, the automobile drove back.

I might now have concluded this unpleasant chapter if, in fact, a most ordinary crow had not become involved. This crow lived in the square of the Catholic church on Brooklyn Street. According to the custom of its forebears, it was supposed to make itself a nest. This serious matter was fraught with great difficulties in New York, because there were far more crows in the city than trees, and the crows had already long before raised the question among themselves of the lack of building space.

And so, our crow was thoughtfully flying about the roofs, keeping an eye out for twigs, sticks, small branches and the like, when suddenly its eyes fell on a beautiful white envelope on one of the window sills. It cawed, looked around on all sides, quickly seized the envelope and carried it off to the highest tree in the square where it was transformed into the solid bottom of a very comfortable nest. The Attorney General of the State of Illinois, for this reason, did not receive the opportunity to uncover a new mystery crime, but at the same time many other people, right down to the police who found absolutely nothing in the room of the "fugitive Druck" were likewise deprived of the same opportunity.

CHAPTER 14
THE ADVENTURES OF LAURIE

"Yes," Laurie said to himself, "her name is Miss Orton. Orton... Almost a familiar name... And so beautiful. But be good enough to tell me what I'm supposed to do here all naked until the fellows send a pair of trousers. And Orton, Orton— where have I heard that name?"

He came out from under the tarpaulin and, depressed, began to pace about the boat only in his shirt, like the first man from the most distant age of our planet. But suddenly his foot stumbled against something and he fell.

"Looks like the hump. So it is, they forgot to toss it off the boat."

Dreamily he picked up Miss Orton's false hump and even sniffed it, surrendering to the pleasant recollection when suddenly his eyes fell on the protruding knife.

Laurie pulled it out of the hump instantly and began to examine it from all sides. However young he might have been, he still knew two things: first of all, that he was looking at "material evidence," and secondly, that every mystery can be solved if you can get hold of one of its links.

The knife was not American. It was not English. The strange trademark bewildered him: something in the shape of the swastika. The knife was sharp as a razor and appeared to be colored along the edges. Laurie raised it to the light, looked it over carefully, and then, obeying some hidden voice, stuck it back into the same piece of hump and wrapped everything up into a bundle after tearing off the edge of his shirt.

Then he took up his pacing once more in order to keep warm. Dusk was approaching, it was getting cold. The barge was a most desolate spot. Beside the straw bedding underneath the tarpaulin, there was nothing else, and all around this shelter towered the lumber in unbroken walls.

Laurie was chilled through. Despair had already overtaken him as he thought that he had been forgotten and he began furiously to restack the logs in order to construct a warmer shelter for himself for the night. Unpiling two rows of logs, he began on the third when suddenly a completely empty, dark space opened up before him. Crying out involuntarily, Laurie looked all around him. Everything was just as deserted as before. Then he bravely entered the passage. For a while it was dark and damp, but about ten steps later his fumbling hands found a small door. He opened it and gasped. Before him was a small round room with a skylight up above, illuminated by the sunset. Along the walls were couches, in the middle of the room stood a woman's dressing table covered with a multitude of tins of makeup. Piled all around in disorder were every imaginable piece of clothing, beginning with a worker's shirt and ending with a marvellous suit-coat. The clothing belonged to a man, of medium size.

"Now here's a chance to cover up my nakedness" Laurie grinned, but before setting about to do so, he went back out on the barge and took a look around. Laurie had sharp eyes. In the fading light of dust he distinguished a lonely figure far away on the shore. Quicker than a squirrel he immediately arranged the wood as before, destroyed all traces of his presence on the barge, took the bundle with the knife in his teeth and jumped into the water. Circling the boat, he lay right in its shadow, carefully keeping his eyes on the moving figure. It could be one of his fellows with clothing for Laurie, but it could also be the owner of the barge and Laurie now understood full well that it would have been more than just an idle matter to meet him.

The figure gradually approached; it kept stopping right at the shore and would look for a long while all around the Hudson. Then it walked up and down the embankment twice, looking hither and yon, and finally, climbed stealthily down to the gangway. It was a stranger. Laurie could not comprehend why he felt a sudden, childish terror, and without considering it for long, he dove underwater.

Swimming underwater was a piece of cake for Laurie. But this time he also had to press the bundle to himself with his elbow and work without that hand free, which made the swimming doubly difficult for him. Nonetheless, compressing his lungs, holding his breath and without surfacing Laurie moved forward along the murky green waterway until he had exhausted the entire supply of oxygen. Then he surfaced and regained his breath. The barge was far away and no one was visible on it. In front of Laurie granite blocks loomed darkly and he turned out to be close to his work-place.

A few moments later he reached the iron rings, leapt up like a fish, latched on to them and dove into the tunnel. Here he was totally safe. It now remained to save whoever had been given the task of bringing clothing to the barge.

Hanging on to his bundle, Laurie rushed along the tunnel as fast as his legs would carry him. It was damp, wet, almost dark here. Invisible cracks barely admitted the light. About a thousand paces along Laurie reached an overpass from where a racket and whistling noise came—the subway passed by there. He was now faced with the prospect of appearing naked in front of people.

What to do? Laurie sat down and started to ponder. Aha! Clever people are never at a loss. He pulled off the shirt, stuck his legs into the sleeves and tied the shirt tightly around his waist. His trousers were ready. Then he climbed up the overpass, used his hand to pick up the tar which had dripped onto the steps and smeared himself from head to toe. Now he was a genuine black man with a bundle in his hands. With little effort he made his way to the underground railway station, found the wall with the hidden symbol "mm," opened it up and then moving through another steel passageway found himself in a compartment that no one knew about and that was not subject to travel fare. It was located between the firebox and the bathroom, and had been constructed by the fellows from the Chicago railway car works. He got off at Brooklyn Street, passed through the wall again, avoiding the turnstile, and paused out on the street, deep in thought.

What to do now? He had to let Willings in Middletown know about the barge. But they must already have sent someone there. Laurie hoped that it wasn't some fool. He would see a stranger on the barge, turn around and leave. But what if he didn't? At the recollection of the figure of the stranger climbing stealthily up the gangway, a shudder stole over him once more.

Raising his eyes mechanically, he saw that he was standing before a large old building with No. 8 on it. He immediately remembered Miss Orton's instructions and going up to the massive doorway, began to read the metallic little plates which covered most of the doors. There were the queerest names here. It was exclusively clerks that lived here. An anthill of clerks. With great difficulty Laurie sought out the modest title:

ROBERT DRUCK
clerk

and a moment later he was already climbing up the long, official-looking staircase which smelled of dampness, cats and rubbish bins.

A neat old woman with bulging eyes that were still teary at that given moment, opened he door. Immediately, without saying a single word, she took a good crust of bread from the table and handed it to Laurie, taking him for a beggar.

"I'll gladly eat it, ma'am, and wish you good health," said Laurie, "only it's not bread that I need, but Mister Druck himself."

"Bob isn't here," Mrs. Druck said in a trembling voice and the tears trickled down her cheeks.

"What do you mean he isn't? But when will he be?"

"I don't know a thing," the old woman continued to weep, "eat the bread and if you want, I'll give you some pudding, but you won't see my dearest, no, you won't see him."

"But what happened to him? Don't be afraid, ma'am, get it off your chest. I'm a good friend of your Bob's even though for various reasons I have to go around looking like this."

"Oh, my Lord, Mister, I don't know what your name is, the whole business doesn't make any sense. Exactly at four o'clock, just as always, Bob came home from work so kind and cheerful. Mama, he said, I'm expecting a certain lady, so if she comes, bring her right in to me. He ate and then went to lie down in his room. I was washing dishes in the kitchen and suddenly four of the strangest people covered with buttons all over came and they asked for Bob. I said: are you from the lady? They said yes. I took them to Bob and a minute later they all came out together, and Bob with them, rushing, rushing down the stairs; Bob didn't even say good-bye to me. I looked out the window and I saw a black automobile driving away from us and he was gone. I waited an hour, I waited two hours—no Bob. And then just a while ago, o-oh,.. my dearest... The police came, they sealed up Bob's room, turned everything upside down in my room and said that my Bob was supposed to have robbed Lawyer Kraft and run off with the money... Only that could never be, it could never be!"

Once again the old woman burst into tears.

Laurie stood for a while in utter bewilderment, then he politely bowed and left. He knew neither Druck nor the lawyer Kraft. Not without grief he was thinking:

"Is Miss Orton really mixed up in that kind of business?"

And he didn't even manage to think it through before he hit himself on the head. "Orton, Orton,—that was the name of an unassuming typist at their "Secret Works" before he left the plant and joined the "Mess-Mend" Union. Only she was actually much older in age. Laurie had seen her fleetingly a few times. But could this really be the same one?"

CHAPTER 15
MISS ORTON'S CONFESSION

Meanwhile it was not without an obvious pleasure that Ned and Willings had been taking the taciturn, good-looking girl through various backstreets and thus reaching the station by a roundabout way. They had decided not to take her into the secret compartment between the firebox and the bathroom—it would have meant giving away the secrets of their Union to a stranger. Therefore, digging around in their pockets and under their shirts, they gathered all the money they had on them and grudgingly furnished themselves with tickets.

But no sooner did the rescued girl hear the name of "Middletown" than she gave a start and halted. The earlier pallor which had disappeared now spread once more through her face and terror flashed in her eyes.

"My God, you've betrayed me!" she cried, fleeing from them into the first handy sidestreet. "You've betrayed me so basely, so shamelessly!"

The staid Willings was insulted and stopped. Ned, glancing at him, did the same. And perhaps it was precisely this that had a greater effect on the wretched girl than anything else the two of them might have done or said. She halted as well.

"Let me go..." Her voice started to tremble.

"My God, but where will I go now? Wouldn't it have been better to be lying on the bottom of the Hudson?"

"Miss, you're all wrong. And you're insulting honest working people for nothing. We all live and work in Middletown. Michael Thingsmaster lives and works in Middletown. We wanted to take you there to him. But if you don't want to, then you don't have to, but you're insulting us for nothing!"

With her head hanging the girl quietly went up to them.

"Forgive me. Take me and lead me wherever you intended. Only we'll have to wait until the day is over and do it in the dark. Otherwise... otherwise I could be recognized there."

Willings and Ned exchanged looks of distress. Taking the tickets out of his pocket, Ned returned to the wicket and cashed them in, then the three of them, while they waited for darkness, walked and walked along some backstreets until it had finally turned dark enough for the girl to agree to go to Middletown.

And now the three of them were in Middletown. By a roundabout route, along the fences of the working town, they had picked their way to Michael Thingsmaster's shack. The silence distressed both Willings and Ned, particularly the talkative Ned. All during that long journey he had tormented himself searching in vain for some kind of decent topic of conversation. But, other than the story about how Tom's wife had poured dishwater over her husband, he could not think of a single thing. And he decided not to tell even this story, realizing that the miss was probably sufficiently fed up with her own sojourn in a wet place.

"Knock-knock-knock" Willings banged on the door.

"Knock-knock-knock," Ned insistently added himself.

The door of the shack opened and a curly blond giant with a pipe in his mouth appeared in the doorway. Beauty stopped barking. She sniffed at Willings, then the rest, and immediately held out a fuzzy paw to each of the arrivals. It was warm and cozy in Mike's little room. Willings seated the young lad who was trembling from cold in a chair beside the fireplace and briefly told Thingsmaster about what had happened. During the story Mike looked attentively at his strange guest a few times and when Willings finally fell silent, Mike got up from his place, took his pipe out of his mouth, went up to Miss Orton and offered her his broad hand. Mike Thingsmaster did not offer his hand to just anyone. Miss Orton put her icy little fingers in his.

"Go and send someone to Laurie's rescue," Mike said to Willings and Ned.

While all this was taking place between him and the arrivals, the technician Sorrow, who had gone off into the farthest corner, was also gazing with great curiosity at the girl who was dressed like a boy but who responded to the name of "Miss Orton."

Willings and Ned left. Thingsmaster moved his chair up to the armchair, added some coal to the fire and declared in his soft voice:

"The world isn't a big place, my dear Miss. It's even quite a small one. I recognized you immediately because I often saw you walking along our streets with a music folder on your way to study at your school. Aren't you the daughter of the typist Mrs. Orton, who works in Morlender's office?"

The girl turned her face to the back of the chair, buried herself in it and began to weep desperately. The technician Sorrow went up to Mike on his tiptoes from the corner and said in a whisper:

"Used to work, Mike, used to work. Didn't you know? It's been some days since she passed away."

With an abrupt movement Miss Orton turned towards them once more. Her tears had dried. It was strange to see the cold expression of hatred which disfigured this very youthful and beautiful face:

"Who are you, what kind of people are you?" she asked, also in a whisper.

"Miss, you're with honest people. I am not going to question you about anything, but if you require help, then give us the whole truth."

"I will tell you the whole truth and you will be the first ones to hear it from me. Only beware, you will have to pay a cruel price for your kindness. I am a wretched creature, I have terrible enemies and my cruelest enemy is myself."

"Enough, my child," Thingsmaster spoke softly, "let's have it all out in the open, just the way it is."

For several moments Miss Orton gazed at the fire. Her eyes had assumed a bitter and wild expression. Then she slowly began to speak, without ever taking her eyes off the fire:

"My name is Vivian Orton. I am the daughter of Captain Orton. He died ten years ago, leaving my mother and me without any means whatsoever. I was studying at the time and still a young girl. In order to allow me to finish school, my mother took a position as a typist in Morlender's office... At that time my mother's beauty was in full bloom. I finished school and learned that she was in love with Morelender."

"Senior or junior?" Thingsmaster interrupted.

"Jeremy Morlender. You know him, he seemed to be an honorable man. At that time we were living very modestly, in a very small house, with a single servant. Mother was very happy, she was expecting a child. They were supposed to be married a month ago, and, as I recall, he was terribly embarrassed to say anything to his son about it... But both of us did believe him. Mama got ready for the wedding. I helped her. Then unexpectedly Morlender was sent on a business trip to Russia. Before his departure he quickly dropped by to tell us about it and promised that immediately upon his return he would be with us. There was no news for about a month. Then a letter and parcel arrived from him."

At this point Miss Orton paused once again in order to choke back with a shudder the sob which was rising in her throat.

"I can't even tell you how overjoyed we were. The letter was from Russia, with an unfamiliar stamp. And in the parcel were some unusual candies and cookies."

"What did he write about?" Sorrow asked.

"About the fact that he would soon be returning and that the wedding would take place immediately. Mama and I organized a celebration. She cleared off the table, decorated it with flowers, laid it out with the sweets that had been sent and then sat down in an armchair. I sat down beside her, but for some reason or other my heart was heavy and I didn't feel like eating a thing. Mama took one of the attractive sweets from the bowl and sighed:

"How painful it is for me, Vivian, that with the exception of our Kate there's no one we can invite and show our hospitality to."

"She put the sweet in her mouth and suddenly leapt up from her place. I managed to catch sight of the terrible shudder that ran across her face. She did not even cry out. I rushed to her. She was dead. I dashed into the kitchen—Kate had disappeared. Then I seized another sweet and without really being aware of what I was doing, I stuck it into my pocket and then, wracked by the most horrible shaking fit, bent down beside mama. It wasn't grief, nor was it terror. At that moment I felt only one thing: hatred! Hatred overwhelmed me and made my heart pound so painfully, I almost lost consciousness. I swore to myself by every fiber in my body that I would kill Morlender, that I would have revenge on him for mama and for her unborn child. At that moment a strange man in glasses entered the room without knocking or asking permission. He announced that he was the coroner and that our Kate had run to get him. I understood at once that I was surrounded by enemies and had to remain silent in order to save my own life. He asked what mama had died from. I replied that it had probably been because of her heart. He asked whether she had suffered from a heart condition earlier. I replied that she had. He immediately filled out a death certificate and mama was buried the following day. While I was at the funeral someone came and took away from us everything that Morlender had sent. Kate didn't return. A few days later I managed to find a doctor who conducted an analysis of the sweet that I had concealed. He said that it was full of the most terrible poison and it would kill immediately upon touching the tongue. At my request he gave me a written analysis of that sweet. A short time later I noticed that I was being followed. Then I pretended to be completely harmless, my behavior was quiet, ingenuous and unassuming. I was left in peace. In order to wipe away all traces I moved to New York..."

Miss Orton faltered here. Thingsmaster laid his hand on her head and said soothingly:

"Go ahead, my child."

"The entire meaning of my life became concentrated on a single thought: to have revenge. My life was consumed by a single emotion: hatred. I began to give music lessons, disfiguring myself beyond recognition. But it was impossible to have revenge from my position as a semi-impoverished music teacher. The banker Westinghouse was a frequent visitor to the house where I was a music teacher. It seemed to me that he was the suitable person. And I let him believe that... that..."

Miss Orton dropped her head. Sorrow and compassion passed over Thingsmaster's broad face. The girl continued:

"I had to get to know all of them and yet remain unknown to anyone, and so I made up the game with the mask. I'm that famous 'masked lady' with whom all of New York is intrigued. And then, suddenly having achieved my purpose after paying for it with my honor, with my conscience, with myself, I suddenly learned that Morlender was already dead. He had escaped my vengeance. I rushed off to his lawyer, Kraft, who had known my deceased mother, but he had died, and instead of him in the office... instead of him in the office... It's strange," she interrupted herself, clutching her forehead with her hand, "I have a marvellous memory, I always remember everything, but right now I cannot recollect who was in the office instead of Kraft... I don't even recall what I talked about with him. But I do remember Morlender's will: it turns out that he was married—married to Kressling's secretary, Elizabeth Wesson. He married her right before his departure, on that very day when he dropped in on my mother... He left all his belongings to her despite the fact that he had told my mother before he left that he would take care of her. And he bequeathed his invention and his plans to the struggle against the Russian communists."

"Miss Orton!" Thingsmaster cried. "What you're saying is a very important matter. You're not confused, you haven't made a mistake, have you?"

"No, there's no mistake. I read it with my own eyes. But before I left the office, a young man, Druck, gave me his address so that I could drop in on him at four o'clock. It seemed to me that he knew some secret or other, but that he was afraid of something or somebody... Druck, No. 8 Brooklyn Street. I walked down to the Hudson in order to kill time until four o'clock, and I can't remember anything else..."

A terrible pallor covered her cheeks. She dropped her head on her chest and whispered:

"I feel so terrible, so strange that I seem to have become so forgetful."

Thingsmaster looked at her attentively and brought her some water and whiskey. After she had drunk it and regained her composure, he asked her:

"My dear Miss, tell me what your intentions are now?"

"To have revenge on Morlender," the girl replied slowly. "That's impossible with him now, he's dead,—it means it will have to be on Arthur Morlender, his son."

Silence set in. Thingsmaster stirred the coals in the fireplace, paced several times around the room, then stopped and peered at the pale girl.

"Listen to me, Miss Orton. You've fallen among people whose purpose in life is the struggle not only with all the Morlenders, but with those who manipulate these Morlenders like puppets. But, my dear Miss, we are engaged in this struggle not because we hate individual people, and we desire no personal reprisal. We are engaged in this struggle because the children of the poor are perishing in cellars where they are deprived of the sun and the air, because in times of war our lads are being sent to kill others who are just as unfortunate as they are themselves, or because they are driven into the mines and factories during times of peace. We are engaged in a struggle not in order to have revenge. We want to establish justice on earth and a bright life for every person, from the first to the last. Do you understand me?"

"Thingsmaster!" the girl cried, leaping up from her place. "I would like to feel what you are saying. But right now I can't, I can't do it! The image of my poor mother, so basely, so treacherously murdered, is before my eyes. There is no such thing as life for me until I can appease this horrible hatred which has transfixed me like some mortal disease. And if you won't let me have my revenge, it doesn't matter, I'll work alone, I'll return to New York and continue my horrible comedy..."

She dashed for the door, forgetting that she was wearing Laurie Lane's working outfit. Mike took her by the shoulder and sat her down once again in the armchair:

"You'll stay here with us until you've sorted yourself out," he said simply. "Willings, Ned!"

The two friends came running into the room—so quickly that there was no need to ask them whether they had been far away or whether their ears had picked up what had been said in the room. Mike Thingsmaster was just preparing to give them their instructions when the door swung wide open once more and this time, all smeared in tar, Laurie came running into the room. Without stopping to catch his breath, still running, he cried:

"Thingsmaster! Here's the knife she was stabbed with. I was at the druggist: he said that the blade was smeared with a terrible African poison. And you, Miss Orton, you'd better not worry about Druck. He's taken off. They say that he robbed Kraft and took off with his money!"

"Quiet, Laurie," Thingsmaster stopped him. "Put the knife on the table and don't frighten the poor miss. Let me ask one of you fellows to have a talk with my cook and get Miss Orton some women's clothes."

"By the way, Mike," Laurie continued to produce his news, "the timber barge on the Hudson turned out to have a secret room. And its owner, its owner... Damn it, I can't remember what it was about him... I hope the fellows didn't bump into him when they brought the clothing there?"

"What do you mean, Laurie," Willings replied, "Otto, the baker, went down there for you and, search as he might, he couldn't find a trace of the barge. It's vanished, as though we only dreamt it!"

"Vanished!" Laurie repeated, and the shiver of incomprehensible terror ran up and down his spine.

CHAPTER 16
LEPSIUS SEES THE HAND

"Toby!" Doctor Lepsius shouted as he entered his room after an innumerable and exhausting series of appointments. "Where has he gotten to, the sneaky fish, the penguin, that gangrenous tumor! Toby! Toby!"

The taciturn mulatto with puffy eyelids emerged from the side and halted in front of the doctor with an expression of utter indifference.

"Toby. Warn the duty nurse and wait for me. We are going to see his Highnesss Bugas XXXI. And if you're going to fall asleep with your mouth wide open like a dead fish, I'll pour gunpowder down there and blow you up together with all your giblets!"

Doctor Lepsius had been in a bad mood all day. His housekeeper, Miss Small, had announced that she had ordered a new hearing aid from Germany and now, thanks be to heaven, she would be able to hear like everyone else. Miss Small even hinted to Doctor Lepsius that now she would not be wanting for suitors.

If a thousand horse powered engine had been added to the belltower of the Church of the Forty Martyrs, the Doctor's nervous shock could not have been more terrifying than at the thought of his housekeeper speaking, hearing and married all at once. And it was precisely at that very moment when Doctor Lepsius' discovery had been transformed from a brilliant guess into a bizarre fact and when all that was lacking was to synthesize the findings and multiply the examples. He sat down at his desk and opened a secret drawer. At the bottom of it lay a manuscript. Lepsius put his spectacles on, took it out and opened it at a page which had been carefully noted with a bookmark.

It was a very curious notebook. To look at, it was in no way different from the ordinary case histories maintained by doctors who have extensive practices. But in place of the designations of illnesses which may even have been encoded in a learned Latin, in place of all manner of cases of diabetes, brucellosis, meningitis and endocarditis, there were notes which were more reminiscent of a politician's or a sociologist's diary than that of a doctor's. Taking a very old, chewed up, ordinary quilll pen (Lepsius could not stand the so-called fountain pens, believing that it was better for a pen to work well for a short while than badly forever), he removed an invisible hair from it, pulled the inkwell closer, dipped the quill into it and entered under the name of "Montmorency" in the fine tracery of a doctor's hand: "Complains of the terror experienced from the Russian Revolution."

The symptoms of Lepsius' patients, if one were to take a peek into his notebook, were on the whole remarkably uniform: an oppressive fear over their fortunes which had been invested in real estate; a depressed mood at the thought of a strike in their factories; a horror before the future; the terror experienced when they crossed borders in order to save themselves from the pursuit of an enraged people; a gloomy mood at the thought of the advent of an economic crisis; despair connected with the relentless decline of shares on the stock market; a terrifying dream that repeated itself every night: numerous footsteps on the staircase, coming closer and closer, pounding at the door, the heavy breathing of a mob—then a mass of people, of the lower classes, breaking down the door into the bedroom...

"Hm-hm," Lepsius repeated to himself with complete and heart-felt satisfaction, "there are already sufficiently numerous examples for me to draw up classifications!"

And he took a ruler, turned the notebook to a fresh page and divided it in half with a neat line. On the top left-hand side of the page he wrote:

Depression on economic grounds

On the top-right hand side of the page he entered:

Depression due to banishment from native country by fellow-countrymen.

Entering approximately a dozen names under the first heading (on the left) and a similar number of names under the second heading (on the right), Lepsius began to ponder. The three steps of his chin, lower lip and upper lip fell into a certain undulating motion: Doctor Lepsius was smiling, smiling to himself—with a mixture of inquisitiveness and irony.

"The amazing fact in this entire chain of ailments," he muttered to himself, "is not that they all lead to one and the same physiological syndrome. The amazing thing is that the patients from the left-hand column become linked to the patients from the right-hand column in the hope of salvation, whereas the patients from the right-hand column become linked to the patients of the left-hand column in the hope of getting the dollars which will enable them to regain their former position in the world. Yes, this is truly amazing!"

Sighing deeply, Lepsius closed the notebook just as though he were parting with a packet of love letters that were dear to his heart. Then they were back in their old place in the secret drawer, and the drawer was slammed shut and locked by means known only to him. Stretching and sighing deeply again, Lepsius did several light gymnastic exercises and went out through an inner door onto the asphalt-covered courtyard with a cheerful step.

At the bottom of the courtyard, in front of the door to the concrete building that resembled a garage, the taciturn duty nurse in a white cloak was waiting for him, holding the same kind of cloak, white as snow, in her hands. The immutable Toby was there as well. Going quickly up to the duty nurse, Lepsius had himself dressed in the cloak, but personally tied up the strings at the collar and wrists and then marched forward through the half-opened door, accompanied by the taciturn duty nurse and Toby.

If from the exterior the clinic building resembled a garage, then from within this impression was instantly converted into amazement and rapture. The ideal clinic for the most precious clients could not have been better outfitted. Luxury and comfort right down to the greenhouse flowers and beautiful works of art. For the time being all of this was being utilized only by a single patient of Doctor Lepsius' who had already reached that particular stage when a prone position was preferable to a sitting or standing position.

In a luxurious chamber, on a couch truly decorated with regal lavishness, lounged the sole patient of the clinic, invisible behind a thick cloud of bluish cigar smoke. On the small table beside him were all the accessories for that insane drink whose composition according to the connoisseurs was just as irrepeatable and unique as a chess game. In other words—for the cocktail. The gentle aroma of a fine dinner which had not yet been dispelled by the Swedish *magnetoventilator,* showed that the cocktail had already been drunk and the patient had finished dining.

"Get rid of the nurse and the mulatto," a senile fickle voice was heard, accompanied by a dry coughing.

"As you wish, your Highness," the doctor replied and motioned Toby and the duty nurse away with a nod of his head. Then he went up to the regal couch and sat down on a chair beside the patient. Through the blue smoke the doctor saw a blotchy-faced little old man with a straggly growth of hair at his temples and on his chin. The naked scalp displayed depressions and lumps which mercilessly disfigured that precious vessel where the human brain was customarily accommodated. Prickly little eyes gazed piercingly and irritably out from under shaggy grey brows.

"How are my offspring and better half doing?" Are they still trying to legally prove my irresponsibility and sink their teeth into my capital?" he squeaked, wanting to lower his voice. And then immediately, without waiting for a reply: "What about my disguise? No one suspects?"

"No one suspects anything, Mr. Rockefeller," Lepsius replied. As far as everyone is concerned, you are travelling on your yacht in keeping with your doctor's advice,—whereas my personnel are convinced that it is an Indian emperor, Bugas XXXI, who is under my treatment. So, allow me to examine the condition of your spine."

A marvellous spectacle for Doctor Lepsius! It seemed that no matter how long he looked at the barely noticeable protuberance with a small swelling at the middle of the spine—the *vertebra media*, according to his terminology—the doctor could not tire of his contemplation. Hardly surprising if one considered that the entire interest of his life, all the observations of his mature years, were being confirmed by that strange deformity which he was encountering more and more frequently—and only in a specific category of people.

"You must, you really must, go to the gymnastic room, your Highness! Without exercising you are risking... hm-hm... the chance of assuming a certain horizontal position in your movements which would be embarrassing in view of our European dress.

The old man produced a whistling sound—he could not bear the gymnastic room. But the doctor was implacable. The faithful Toby was summoned to the scene.

"Help his Highness to put on his trunks," Lepsius ordered in a stern voice, "and go through the cycle of vertical exercises with him. And beware if you run across the street afterwards to the confectioner's and take up various conversations with him, because then I'll sell you to the War Ministry as cannon fodder. Take my cloak, I must go."

Giving the necessary instructions to the duty nurse, Lepsius went out, climbed into the automobile that was waiting for him and ordered the chauffeur to drive to Doctor Bentrovato who had a model clinic and an X-ray room.

He was not doing this entirely by choice. He was afraid that his discovery would be stolen right out from under his nose. Muttering through his teeth, Lepsius climbed the stairs and fell into the hands of two young girls with pencils and notepads.

"Forty dollars," one girl spoke out.

"Put it here," the other confirmed, holding a box overflowing with money out to him.

"My dears," Lepsius replied softly, "I ask for more than that."

And waving them aside with his hands, he entered directly into his colleague's reception room.

Bentrovato was in the midst of receiving patients. A multitude of people were waiting for him, amusing themselves with all manner of distractions which had been placed at the disposition of the patients in waiting rooms. Here there were books in all the languages, dominoes, chess, sewing and knitting for the women, toys for the children, refreshing drinks. Passing through into the neighboring room, and from there into the X-ray room, Lepsius came to a halt. It was semi-dark in the room. A red lamp illuminated the room with a dim light. Behind a shield and in front of a screen stood a man who was undergoing an X-ray examination. Lepsius could not make out his innards and merely saw the shadow from a smallish, oblong head and a hand which had been carelessly flung behind the back of a chair and protruded from behind the shield.

Lepsius sat down indifferently in an armchair, waiting for the end of the consultation. He looked about distractedly here and there and experienced an irresistible attack of yawning. Then suddenly, completely by chance, his eyes fastened on the above-mentioned hand.

"What's that... Where the devil was it?" Where had Doctor Lepsius seen that hand, thin, weak, with swollen joints?

But no matter how hard he concentrated his memory, no answer came. The fingers continued to lie there so lifelessly, then suddenly they convulsed, as though they had grasped at something, slid off and disappeared.

Bentrovato let his patient out through the side door of the X-ray room.

"Greetings, greetings, Lepsius. What can I do for you?"

"Greetings, Bentrovato. Who was it you had here?"

"You wish to check and see if I am withholding professional secrets?"

Lepsius looked askance at his colleague in annoyance.

"I dropped in on you, my revered friend, with a request to conduct an X-ray examination of a certain degenerated subject. The sooner the better."

"Fine, at the very first opening. Wait a moment, we'll write it down: "The twenty-eighth of August of next year at four-thirty in the afternoon."

Bentrovato entered it onto his pad with a smile and handed a copy of the notation to his colleague.

Lepsius' broad face did not express anything other than gratitude. But on the staircase he clenched his fists, crimsoned and leapt at the doorman with a fierce expression on his face:

"Who passed by here just now, eh?"

The doorman raised his shoulders phlegmatically:

"Lots of people have been going by... The fruit-vendor Bear, Professor Hiserton, the navigation officer Kovalkovsky."

Lepsius climbed into the automobile, carefully committing to memory the three names he had heard.

CHAPTER 17
THE CONFERENCE AT
THE VILLA *EPHEMIRIDES*

"Mrs. Thindick," said Jenny the maid, a lean individual in spectacles and with compressed lips, "Mrs. Thindick, why do you boast day and night about those Siamese twins as though you yourself had given birth to them?"

Jenny's impudence provoked a giggle of approval in the kitchen of the hotel *Patrician*.

"Miss Jenny," replied Mrs. Thindick in an icy voice, "do express yourself more carefully. I have no intention of boasting. I am simply stating the fact that I have Siamese twins for cousins and that no one else but me has Siamese twins as cousins. There are as many separate male and female cousins as you like, but no one, ever, has had a "pair."

"And what kind of sense are you trying to make out of that?"

"*Miss* Jenny, I am not talking about 'sense'. I am simply stating a fact. I am not to blame if people are envious of their fellows."

"Not likely!" Jenny flared up. "Who cares about your pair when I've seen the devil himself!"

A tomb-like silence held sway in the kitchen of the hotel *Patrician*. Jenny was well known as the most truthful girl in New York. But to have seen the devil. That was a bit much.

"Believe it or not, but I did see the devil himself," Jenny repeated with a catch in her voice, "I was cleaning up in the bathroom, and he landed right on my head from the ceiling, then he backed off and disappeared through the wall."

Mrs. Thindick triumphantly looked around at the entire kitchen staff: it was obvious that Jenny was lying.

The wretched girl flared up red as a beet. Tears began to well up in her eyes.

"Strike me down if it isn't so. And the devil was all black, naked, with no tail, a black nose and white teeth."

"Ah, Jenny," sighed the messenger, an elderly man who had dreams of legal marriage, "and you know I was just about to propose..."

But at this point, with the speed of lightning, right through the ceiling, a naked, black devil without a tail tumbled onto Mrs. Thindick's back, leapt up like a cat and disappeared into the chimney. Mrs. Thindick emitted a piercing shriek and fell unconscious. Meanwhile, the incautious Tom, cursing his clumsiness, flew as fast as his legs would carry him through the flue pipe onto the neighboring roof and from there he climbed down onto Broadway Street and made directly for the telegraph building.

The passers-by jumped aside from the flying chimneysweep who was clearing, or, more precisely, dirtying a pathway with his elbows. Finally he was upstairs in the compartment of the chief telegraph operator and came to a halt in order to catch his breath.

The melancholic Tony White, with a blond curl on his forehead and a black lady's bow instead of a tie, glanced through the wicket, recognized Tom, took a blank form and immediately placed the two letters "mm" in the corner.

"Go ahead," he prompted Tom.

"The telephone is broken, Tony, and we need Mike desperately," Tom explained, breathing deeply, "send it urgently right away."

"Alright, dictate it." And Tony wrote the following according to the chimneysweep's dictation:

> "Middletown. To Mike. The public is meeting today at 9:00 p.m. Kressling's villa *Ephemirides*. Important conference. Everyone there."

Tom dictated it in a whisper and then took off like a flash of lightning. Tony White made inquiries as to whether the Middletown telephone which had been broken by a storm in the night, would soon be fixed and when he learned that it would still be an hour, he himself sat down at the telegraph transmitter. He tapped out "mm" at the head. The letters ran along the line and all the telegraph operators immediately began to hop as they abandoned their work and transmitted the message urgently. His business done, Tony rolled the telegram form up into a tube and burned it, then he appeared at the wicket where a very long line of cursing New Yorkers were waiting for him.

In a quarter of an hour a quick-witted telegraph operator from the city of Middletown, on his way to delivering telegrams, dropped into the woodworking factory for some reason. Seeing that there were only workers and none of the bosses around, he slipped a white piece of paper into Thingsmaster's hand, lit up a cigarette and hurried on his way. Mike read it through and burned the paper. Then he gave a few instructions into a rubberized tube without leaving his work bench and continued to work as hard as he could, whistling a tune.

Meanwhile, a warm May evening was descending. After the thunderstorm in the night, Middletown was refreshed and had bloom. Escort motorcycles were travelling up and down the main thoroughfare into the hills—it meant that Jack Kressling was expecting guests. High up in the hills where it had just turned to dusk, a fantastic sea of light began to glitter, resembling a horde of giant fireflies or a fistful of diamonds as big as cannon balls. It was the glitter from the famous villa *Ephemerides* which had been constructed according to Morlender's special plans and seemed to be all made of iron lacework, extremely delicate wood-carving and crystal suffused with electrical light.

Jack Kressling had created a "kingdom of light" for himself, as was reported in the rather diffident newspapers that were published with the aid of his finances. He had found the means to dispense with people. Everything in his glittering villa was controlled and set in motion by innumerable electrical motors, and the radiant rooms were enlivened only with Kressling's beloved friends: the monkey Frou-Frou, the English mare, Esmeralda, two young crocodiles which he had shipped from Egypt and kept in a gold swimming pool, and the former secretary Elizabeth Wesson, who was now the inconsolable widow of Morlender. This company was entirely sufficient for Kressling. In his opinion, people were too unscrupulous and he found absolutely nothing that was amusing in two-legged creatures. Jack Kressling despised humanity.

No sooner had the powerful sounds of Beethoven's Ninth Symphony pealed on the electric clock of *Ephemerides* then Kressling arose from his chair and pressed a button. It should be said that his clock struck the first nine hours with Beethoven's Nine Symphonies; however, the performance of the tenth, eleventh and twelfth hours, much to the surprise of his guests, were dedicated to the miaoing of a cat, the sound of the cuckoo and the cry of the owl. When he was queried, he would reply unsmilingly: music should not intrude on the hour of love, the hour of death and the hour of knowledge.

"Nine o'clock," Kressling said to himself, "It's time." With these very words he sat down in an armchair and crossed his legs. At that very moment the armchair was elevated together with him through the crystal ceilings and floor-coverings to the topmost story where there was a luxurious room with a richly decorated table in its midst. Kressling strolled lazily over the carpets pushing buttons here and there—and fragrances began to stream into the room, flowers were scattered about, crystal casks with cool liquids floated in. From below and from above, on platinum shelves, plates converged and distributed themselves about the table.

No doubt the reader is expecting, by way of a completion to the aforementioned marvels, a supplementary, detailed description of all the possible viands and beverages that would have graced the table of a billionaire. But for reasons of which the reader will become aware further on, I am forced to forego this for the moment.

Kressling had not managed to press the final button when the two-way window mirror showed him several automobiles approaching along the main driveway. He quickly activated the wall switches and the suspension elevator brought his distinguished visitors one after the other up to the room.

Assembled here were General Gibgeld, Viscount Montmorency, Lord Hardstone, Prince Obolonkin, ex-Regent Don Carlos de Los Patrias, ex-Presidents No Hom, Uno Si Nogi and Sidi Yama and yet another couple of claimants to presidential posts.

Here there were Italians, Austrians, Rumanians, Poles, all of whom had been banished from their homelands. Big businessmen were also with them. The famous German, Stinnes, his friend Krupp, the banker Westinghouse, the English merchant Rothschild and the young Junius Rockefeller. Also among the guests, but keeping off to the side, was Arthur, the young and morose son of the engineer Morlender, who was visiting Kressling for the first time and wearing a mourning band around his sleeve in memory of his deceased father. As usual, only Signor Cice was not present.

"Be seated, gentlemen." Kressling said in his customary and not particularly polite voice, "I beg you to excuse my crocodiles who couldn't wait for you and have already finished dining earlier."

At the mention of the word "dining," those who had already been guests of Kressling's could not restrain themselves from a somewhat crooked expression. The platinum shelves fell into operation once more. Dishes of pure gold distributed themselves smoothly over the table. On one of them was toasted barley bread from the State of Wisconsin; another one contained finely sliced onion; a third had tiny slices of an excellent Chicago cheese. In cups of rare porcelain which floated up to and placed themselves around the table was that white substance which Russians call sour clotted cream, the Caucasians "matsoni," and learned dieticians "lacto bacillae." A cooled mixture of hydrogen and oxygen called water was poured into crystal goblets.

"Let us dine, gentlemen," Jack Kressling declared politely, being the first to set an example by taking a bite of the barley bread with onion. "We, the masters of the world's greatest capital, know the vulgar dream of the lower classes and the laboring masses of mankind to stuff their bellies with food. This alone shows their inability to rule the world. Give them power—and in a year you won't recognize them because their bodies would have become so rounded and their eyes would be swimming in fat; and a year after that no doctors would be able to save them from their obesity and gout. The knowledge of how to live, to dress, to spend money, to preserve longevity, the knowledge of how to understand and know the measure of things—this is the privilege of those who hold in their hands all the possibilities of being excessive! After six, gentlemen, in general I eat nothing, I only drink Vichy. But for the sake of hospitality..."

Prince Obolonkin, dispiritedly soaking his mustache in the clotted cream and eating it together with four pieces of cheese which he had grabbed as a single slice, strove to support the conversation:

"The French say: if you want a thrifty wife, don't marry a poor girl. From lack of habit she'll go and spend money like one possessed. Whereas a rich girl has an immunity and she'll be penny-wise!"

But the rest of the guests, probably from an acute awareness of measure, did not take up the dinner conversation and finished dining as quickly as possible. Passing into Kressling's study, the gathering seated itself around a circular ebony table.

"My friends," Jack Kressling began in a somewhat softened voice, "you know the mighty purpose which inspires our union. The threat of communism hangs over the world. This threat is both material and spiritual. Above all it is essential to destroy it in a material fashion. Communists have the habit of always referring to the masses and the people—and therein lies their weak point. We are realists. You and I can see from experience that history is determined by governments, by people who have been given power over the masses. They are the ones who declare wars. They conclude pacts. They produce loans. They issue laws. They have the army and the police. If you establish the kind of power everywhere that understands the mighty genius of capitalism and that despises the inert jumble of communism, by the time you count to three you'll be finished with the bearers of this plague, the communists, by using restriction, arrest, jail and the gallows. And where the communists have seized power—I have in mind Russia—there you must secretly establish power over their power, you must destroy the very authorities themselves by dispatching murderers and saboteurs, those heroic warriors for the sacred freedom of capital on earth! In other words—let us declare communism illegal. Terrorism! Terrorism! That is what I consider to be the correct American policy, gentlemen!"

"All of that is very fine, although rather disturbing," Viscount Montmorency muttered lazily. "But how are you going to bring it about in practical terms?"

"We will not interrupt the chief," Lord Hardstone said decisively, slightly raising his hand.

"Our forces, or more precisely, our personnel, have various functions although their purpose is but one," Kressling continued, nodding slightly in the direction of Lord Hardstone. "A portion of us, those, for example, like your esteemed father, Junius," he turned to Rockefeller Junior, "are giving money, a great deal of money, insofar as this business requires billions. Millions and billions are being given by Stinnes, Krupp, Rothschild and myself who am in charge of our alliance. Others, like those worthy future rulers of their countries who have gathered here, will give their experience, their positions, and their future politics when we will have re-established their power in their countries. Yet others, finally, will give their irreproachable service to us, according to their conviction, just like the final heir of that mighty lineage of mesmerists and rulers of the human soul, of the counts Caliostro,—Signor Gregorio Cice..."

At this point Kressling's speech was interrupted by the stormy applause of those present.

"Signor Gregorio Cice," Kressling repeated with emphasis. "You know how his talented forebears served the Bourbons and various other dynasties and restrained the vain revolutionary attempts of the rabble. A mesmerist and hypnotist in the service of a legal king or president is a mighty support for power; it counts no less than the support of the church..."

Again the orator was interrupted, this time by Prince Obolonkin:

"I can affirm that! While Grishka Rasputin was alive, the greatest hypnotist and mesmerist ever, autocracy held sway in Russia. Grishka was killed—and the revolution began. That's a fact!"

"And there is yet another category of supporters required for our undertaking. I mean youth, the personal avengers. My brilliant engineer and assistant, the best engineer-inventor in America, Jeremy Morlender, was treacherously and underhandedly killed by the Bolsheviks in Russia. I have suffered a terrible loss. But the son of my dear deceased friend, the young engineer Arthur Morlender, wishes to risk his life in order to avenge his father. Introduce yourselves, gentlemen."

Arthur and those present exchanged handshakes. Jack Kressling began once again:

"At this point we are shifting to concrete measures. As you know, the so-called 'toilers' (as though you and I, gentlemen, did not toil!) love to send delegations and gifts to Russia. We are preparing a nice little gift like that from our toilers to the Russians. It will be presented in the fall, on the anniversary of their Revolution, in Petersburg, at the spot where all the communist authorities will be gathered simultaneously. And it will be presented by an American communist, the engineer Vasilov, or to be more precise, by Mr. Arthur Morlender—disguised as Vasilov.. The local Russians, my dear Prince Obolonkin, have unfortunately slipped away from under your tutelage. A portion of the youth are enthused with the propaganda from Soviet Russia. Vasilov, as you can see, is even a member of the communist party and people say that he is loyal. He's getting ready to leave for Russia and in the fall he'll be given the responsibility of presenting a nice little 'gift'—one of Morlender's beautiful inventions. To our enormous satisfaction, Arthur, you resemble this Vasilov a great deal—for example, the same size, color of hair, and features; the rest will be taken care of with make-up. You will be given the most detailed instructions in due time. And you, Prince Feofan, you will recruit a small but powerful governmental group of Russians for a seizure of power when our little 'gift' annihilates the Soviet commissars. I hope, gentlemen, that everything is clear to you at this present stage of our struggle?"

"Excellent! Marvellous! We congratulate you, Mr. Morlender! Allow us to shake your hand!"—flowed from all sides.

The mood of those present became particularly elated at the moment when the host proposed, in place of the patriotic liquid from American plumbing, to condescend to have some champagne of foreign vintage for the conclusion of the conference. Kressling himself, contrary to habit, drank and toasted with his guests and upon their departure showed them the two crocodiles slumbering peacefully at the bottom of the swimming pool.

With the conference terminated and the champagne drunk, Kressling's clock screeched like an owl. One after the other the guests departed into the gloom of the warm May night. Suffering from interminable insomnia, Kressling alone was destined to pace back and forth for long hours through the gleaming halls of *Ephemigrides*.

Meanwhile, in the dark storeroom of a small cottage where Mike Thingsmaster lived, everything that had taken place in *Ephemerides* was being projected onto a screen and recorded on a phonograph. The fellows watched and listened, their fists clenched: and in their midst, in the modest dress of a working woman, was Vivian Orton.

CHAPTER 18
VASILOV AND HIS WIFE

Every honorable communist puts duty first and his wife second. Every wife strives to put herself first and everything else second.

Comrade Vasilov, a member of the New York communist party, found himselff precisely in this family state of affairs. Returning from a late night meeting of the party he woke his wife up and said:

"Katya Ivanovna, we are going to Russia."

"I'm happy to hear that," she replied, half-awake. "The *Amelia* is sailing the day after tomorrow. We'll go together with Mrs. Deboshir."

"You and I are going on the *Torpedo*," comrade Vasilov objected, "those are the instructions I've received."

"Did you really think that you wouldn't have to take your own wife into consideration regardless of whatever instructions you may have received?!"

"Instructions, my dear," Vasilov repeated patiently. He had committed but one folly in his life: marriage. And now he had to suffer all of its consequences.

"Instructions," his wife repeated.

"Instructions!"

"Instructions!"

"Instructions!"

"Ha! If you're going to be worse than any alarm clock and not let me get my sleep, then I'm telling you: I am going on the *Amelia*—and that's final!"

"As you wish," Vasilov answered tiredly, sighing bitterly and starting to undress.

The following morning Katya Ivanovna arose when it was barely light, gave her sleeping husband a scornful look and in her most fashionable hat scurried out onto the street. At the gate stood a messenger. He was stroking his beard. The beard had a respectable look.

"Messenger," Katya Ivanovna called, "do you know where the steamers and information offices are and where one has to board in order to go to Russia?"

"Nothing to it, ma'am," he replied, coughing thickly, "you go on home and do whatever you like. And with your permission I'll take care of a ticket for you and bring it to the house. Just remember, messenger No. 7."

"Would you really do that? But you see, the problem is that my husband and I are at odds. I want to go on the steamer *Amelia* together with

Mrs. Deboshir. Can you get me a ticket for the *Amelia*?"

"Easy as pie, ma'am."

"Well here you are. Take the money. And here are the documents. And you know what? Don't bring the ticket for me to my house, but straight to Mrs. Deboshir, Roven Square, No. 10."

"First thing tomorrow morning, ma'am, and everything'll be arranged perfectly."

Ecstatic over her plan, Katya Ivanovna pulled out a notebook, pencil and envelope and energetically turned the messenger's back towards herself.

"No. 7, I'll just lean on you for a moment... There we are. I want to write my husband a letter."

In crooked letters she scrawled on the messenger's back:

"Vasilov! You need to be taught a lesson and so here are my own instructions to you: I am going on the *Amelia* with Mrs. Deboshir. I'm not coming back home. Pack all my things, the lilac dress and my music for singing. I hope that you too will go on the *Amelia*, otherwise we'll meet on the quay in Kronstadt. Your wife, Katya Ivanovna."

"Here," she said, "take this letter upstairs, straight to this address. Toss him the letter on the bed and run back. If he asks you any questions—give him the silence of the grave. Understand?"

"Impossible not to, ma'am," the messenger smirked. He watched while the cheerful lady, opening an umbrella over her head, rushed off in the direction of Roven Square. Then he quickly ran his eyes over the letter he had been given. Then he glanced at the address, shook his head and went upstairs with the letter. Managing to rouse Vasilov, he shoved the letter into his hand and without answering any of his questions ran back downstairs.

Up until this point, Jones, a longtime messenger in this area, acted as he had been ordered. But once on the street he displayed an unexpected independence; namely, he went up to a sewer pipe, took a quick look around and then disappeared in the sewer with the speed of a rat. The dark, damp passageway brought him out first of all onto stone steps, then to the subway station. Jones chose his moment and leapt into the narrow crack between the steel panelling of the car: he was in a compartment between the toilet and the firebox where he was not subject to the fare.

The honest Jones made several transfers, plunged once more into an underground passage, got soaked, dirty, and messed up his beard, but still managed to reach that hot spot right under the kitchen of the *Patrician* where the plumber Van Hope was sitting in a flue with rubberized earpieces on.

"Mend-mess," the messenger uttered, puffing.

"Mess-mend," replied Van Hope. "Is that you, Jones? Well, what's up?"

"Vasilov's wife has instructed me to buy her a ticket for the *Amelia*. You see, she wants to travel on her own. Tomorrow morning I have to take her ticket and documents to her girl friend's address."

"Okay, Jones, do your business. I'll pass everything on to Mike. But watch out, Jones, that nothing happens to Vasilov. Put your boys on every corner, keep a close eye on him until he gets on the ship's boarding ladder. Put the papers here."

Wetting a pencil in his mouth, Jones the messenger sketched out a detailed report of everything that had happened to him that morning, added from memory a copy of Katya Ivanovna's letter, stacked all this beside Van Hope and quickly popped out of the flue, through the wall, and ended up directly around the corner from the *Patrician* where the steamship, railway and airline offices were located.

Meanwhile, comrade Vasilov had finished reading, with some annoyance, his wife's note. He knew that it would have been easier to find some way of squaring a circle then to come to any accord with his wife's intentions, and for that reason he waved his hand and busied himself with the packing. Vasilov was a well-built, agile, clean-shaven fellow who had managed to become significantly Americanized during the long years of his stay in America. Beside his activity in the party, he was an excellent engineer and was now travelling to his native land with a mandate in his pocket and a passionate desire to work in Russian factories and plants. Managing somehow to fit Katya Ivanovna's innumerable items of frippery, the lilac dress and song music into the suitcase, he distributed his own personal papers among his pockets, also stuck the missive there that he had just received, took his hat and made his way to buy himself a second-class ticket on the steamer *Torpedo* which was sailing for Europe in three days' time.

CHAPTER 19
A PLEASANT ACQUAINTANCE

The entrance where Jones and Katya Ivanovna had conversed only seemed at first glance to be deserted. Both of them had barely managed to go their own ways when a short, dark-skinned man in an unusual suit with shiny buttons emerged from behind a coat rack. He stepped into a telephone booth, dialed an indecipherable number and when he was connected he passed on the information in a whisper that "Netty will have to buy herself a new hat." That was all that was said and not a single thing more. It would have been impossible to say what connection this had with the subsequent events, yet without reaching the home of Mrs. Deboshir, Katya Ivanovna felt a sudden desire to have a rest.

She glanced around and saw a lone bench standing not far away in a small and empty square. Going up to it, Katya Ivanovna cracked her knuckles, tossed her head back and yawned several times from some inexplicable fatigue. There was no sun in the sky, her eyes never bothered her but all the same it seemed to her that something in the shape of a red sun spot was dancing before her eyes.

"Strange," this stubborn lady said to herself. "Exceedingly strange. I want to sleep although I have no intention of sleeping. I don't care for this."

Meanwhile a man of medium height, stylishly dressed, thoughtful, one might even say, sad, walked through the square. His hands, with slightly swollen joints, hung limply, his eyes were sunken, doleful, mournful, like those of an inveterate alcoholic who had been forced into temporary sobriety. Under his nose were sparse, cat-like whiskers.

He lowered himself onto the bench beside her, sighed deeply and covered his swarthy face with his hands.

Katya Ivanovna felt a strange pounding of her heart.

The stranger sighed once more and whispered:

"I won't get over this. I haven't the strength to live. Let me die!"

"Everyone has some grief," Mrs. Vasilov noted tenderly, moving closer to the stranger. "Today is one thing, but tomorrow is different. Sometimes both are filled with grief at the same time. One has to temper one's character like steel."

"I haven't the strength," came a hoarse sound from the direction of the stranger.

"Pull yourself together, sir, and you'll get over it."

"Give me your hand, Miss, the tender hand of a woman. Fill me with your balsam."

Katya Ivanovna unhesitatingly removed her fine cotton glove and held out her energetic hand to the stranger. Immediately an electrical current passed through her entire body, making her head spin, but in a pleasant way. Accustomed to self-analysis, she thought with amazement:

"It seems as though I'm falling in love. This is strange. I am falling in love although I have no intention of falling in love."

Meanwhile the stranger imbibed her balsam by the barrelful through her outstretched hand. He pressed his nose, his lips and his cheeks to her hand, caressed it, ran it over his eyes, tucked it under his shirt and stung it with his coarse little whiskers.

"Woman!" he exclaimed in a sudden piercing voice. "Be an angel! Be a sister of mercy. Sacrifice an hour or two for me, rid me of this demon of suicide."

The way things happened, Katya Ivanovna simply could not have refused him anything. She thought that it would be fine to arrive at Mrs. Deboshir's at four p.m., stood up from the bench, took the proffered hand and with the other hand raised her umbrella over the suffering stranger.

"In a moment of sorrow," she instructed with a firm yet tender voice, "the most important thing, my dear sir, is decorum for society's sake. When you behave with decorum for society's sake, sir, you will become convinced that in addition to you there are other people, a great number of other people, with their own sorrows and joys. This will console you and broaden your horizons."

"You are right," the stranger whispered hoarsely. "Let's go straight to where we can meet society. Let's get on a steamer and go to the Bourneville Forest."

Mrs. Vasilov had never been in the Bourneville Forest and did not know whether society might be found there or not. Nonetheless she had been very flattered by the fact that her words had had such a decisive effect on the wretched man.

They got on a steamer and travelled peacefully for two stops, leaving New York behind and sailing rather far in the direction of Sweaton. During the trip Katya Ivanovna began a conversation on generally instructive topics such as: what lives in water and what lives on land; do fish have wings and birds fins; who had invented steam heating and why houses with steam heating do not move but steamers do. Two or three times she had to seize and stop the stranger from his intention of jumping overboard and committing suicide.

Finally, at the third stop, they got off the steamer onto land. The spot was rather deserted. The Rockefeller mines began here and were overgrown with thick scrub, rocks and a small forest, gloomy and unpleasant in appearance since it consisted of aspen and juniper.

Mrs. Vasilov shuddered:

"Where are you taking me?" she whispered anxiously when the stranger started to drag her directly into this very forest which bore the proud designation of *Bourneville*. "What do you want from me, dear sir? There's no society here, there aren't even any people!"

But Katya Ivanovna's companion was transformed. His dull eyes came to life, his thin body grew taut, his muscles became steel. He stared fixedly at her and dragged her after him into the forest without answering her questions. A strange weakness came over Mrs. Vasilov. Her arms and legs grew leaden, there was a bitter taste in her mouth, an inexplicable mist filled her head. She could no longer remember anything other than the need to reach the forest, and somehow dragging herself up to the first aspen, she collapsed heavily onto a mound.

"I feel queer," she whispered softly. "I don't intend to, but I feel nauseous." The stranger pulled out a small box with round, pale blue capsules and handed it to Katya Ivanovna. Practically automatically she took a small capsule and and placed it in her mouth. At that very second, a terrible shudder passed through her body from head to heels and the wretched woman tumbled headfirst into a ravine. The man leapt down there after her, made certain that she was dead, dragged some brushwood, fallen branches and bows of aspen and covered up the body of his victim.

Then he glanced around, stepped behind a tree and disappeared. Everything all around was just as deserted as before. The aspens were rustling. A lonely timber barge floated motionless on the Hudson.

CHAPTER 20
THE DEPARTURE OF THE AMELIA

Jack Kressling never allowed himself to grow loud in his anger, all the more so in the case of Signor Gregorio Cice. In this regard he had taken lessons in restraint from his crocodiles. And right at that very moment, sitting a little apprehensively in front of a small, swarthy man of an indeterminate appearance who had draped a thin, weak arm that was lightly swollen at the joints over the back of a chair, he did not become angry, but spoke in a dry, deadly cool voice as he looked past his partner:

"And so, with Jeremy Morlender you've met with failure. That is the first failure for Signor Gregorio Cice. It's all the more annoying because this technician Sorrow has proven to be a striking fool and nonentity... I can't understand why, or with what purpose, Morlender kept him and praised him."

"In everything else—a complete success," replied Signor Cice, raising slightly his upper lip which made the small brush of his cat-like whiskers bristle.

"I know, I know, and nonetheless..."

Jack Kressling sighed deeply. He had wasted the entire morning on clarifying Sorrow's inventive capacities. The technician had dragged along a whole folder of illiterate diagrams; stumbling over his words, he had spoken such unbearable, high-falutin nonsense about the fact that he had invented a perpetual mobile out of a pair of boots and an old drainpipe; he had developed some theories about growing lentils on asphalt and when Jack Kressling had finally become convinced of his utter worthlessness, he had dismissed him. And for a long while afterwards he had gone on shouting something at the office door and had not wanted to leave. There was at least one consolation: the hatred of this man Sorrow for the communists.

Jack Kressling called himself the most clever industrialist in the States. It was not by chance that at hundreds of his plants in Middletown there was definitely not a single worker who was suspected of having communist sympathies. Expensively paid agents, such as the elderly and solid carpenter Willings, for example, would talk with a sigh about the fact that he was paying them for nothing... Incidentally, Willings was to be sent without fail on the *Amelia* to Russia with a shipment from the Hoover Works and a few other things...

"And so, you'll inform Willings about his secret departure on the *Amelia*, whereas you yourself will depart on the *Torpedo* according to the instructions that were worked out," Kressling concluded his conversation with the taciturn Signor Cice.

Meanwhile, Willings and Sorrow were also concluding their conversation— with Mike Thingsmaster.

"Ugh, it's not easy to play the fool," said the old-timer, Sorrow. "You should have seen the way they laid out Morlender's most secret plans in front of me, and I, like a jackass, could only flap my ears—trying on the sly to imprint them in my memory."

"It's no easier playing the spy," Willings objected morosely. "That's why you'ree free of my unslumbering eye, Sorrow, and free to go where you have to now!"

At this point, both friends, and Mike included, burst cheerfully into laughter.

These were the circumstances under which the old-timer, Sorrow, who had been dismissed by Jack Kressling, was able to get a job as a fitter in the engine room of the steamer *Amelia* which had been hired to carry freight for the Hoover Company. Two hours before departure, he was on the quay observing the loading of the steamer.

An Irishman, MacKinley, the captain of the steamer, was sucking on his pipe as he strolled about on board. The cranes were transferring one thing after another onto the ship: barrels of fat, compressed bales of corn and sugar, crates of canned milk, sacks with corn meal: all of this was earmarked for the intestines of the starving Russian people as a substitute for raising them to the heights of American civilization. The workers who were loading the ship, winked cheerfully at Sorrow and he winked back in turn.

Then suddenly Jones, the messenger, red-faced, puffing, dishevelled, flew headlong onto the quay, looked around here and there, ran up to the technician Sorrow and trying to catch his breath whispered to him:

"Vasilov's wife can't be found anywhere. Maybe you've seen her among the passengers?"

Sorrow shook his head negatively.

"What should I do now?" whined Jones. "This cantankerous dame, no doubt, is sleeping in. But where am I suppose to look for her? She wasn't at her friend's, she didn't go back home, and look, I don't dare ask her husband whether he knows where his own wife has run off to. What am I supposed to do with the ticket, with her documents, what am I going to do with her change? Who's going to pay me my commission?"

"Talk to Mike about it," Sorrow answered phlegmatically, continuing to pace up and down the quay. "And hurry, altogether there's one hour and fifty-eight-and-a-half-minutes left until sailing."

Jones leapt up as though he had been stung, dashed between the lamp standards hither and yon, plunged through the ground and within ten minutes he was speeding on a wooden chair along a wire from the roof of Rolley's Stables higher and higher towards the Middletown tower. The journey was a risky one: the wires were whistling around him; bales of hay could come flying down on top of him from above if the fellows did not manage to hold them back; the electrical current could be cut off. But the honest messenger, Jones, had no other means of getting to Middletown in time, and he had to take a chance.

"You say that no one has seen her anywhere?" Thingsmaster asked, after hearing Jones's confused account.

"You've got it, Mike."

"That means that the poor woman has been waylaid. That means that a trap is also waiting for Vasilov. They'll waylay Vasilov as well and send the conspirator Morlender instead."

"Vasilov is going on the *Torpedo*, Mike, you have lots of time, but what am I supposed to do with the ticket, the documents, the change? Who's going to pay my commission?" whined the honest Jones. "The *Amelia* already has her steam up, I'm telling you!"

Thingsmaster did not need long to consider.

"Just hang on a second!" he shouted decisively. "Miss Orton, my child, come here as quickly as you can!"

Miss Orton appeared in the doorway.

"Listen. Here are documents and a ticket for you. You are leaving in an hour on the steamer *Amelia* as the wife of the communist Vasilov bound for Kronstadt. Your husband is also going there, but on the *Torpedo*. By whim you are taking the *Amelia*. You will meet him on the Kronstadt quay. You will whisper to him that you have been sent by the workers in place of his wife in order to protect his life from any attempts on it and you will reveal to him the plot of the fascist organisation... You understand?"

"Yes," replied Miss Orton. "Thank you, Michael Thingsmaster. You'll be happy that you have given me this mission."

"Wait a minute. It could happen that Vasilov will be waylaid and instead of him Arthur Morlender will be sent..."

"A-ah!" the sound came through the girl's clenched teeth.

"Then you must take revenge, Miss Orton. But do it properly. You'll be the wife of a conspirator, you'll pretend that you don't suspect the substitution. This will be all the easier inasmuch as he himself doesn't know who his wife is. You'll be guarding him day and night and uncovering, step by step, thread by thread, this treacherous plot until all the threads will be in your hands. Then you will reveal everything to the Soviet government. Do you understand?"

"Yes," exclaimed the girl. "And I thank you once more."

"You must get her to the *Amelia* immediately," Thingsmaster turned to Jones the messenger. "Hand her over to Sorrow and have Sorrow provide her with everything she needs. While underway have Sorrow get a radio report from the *Torpedo* every hour. We'll send the fitter Bisk to guard Vasilov's life. Understand? Go ahead."

"Mike," the poor Jones moaned, scratching at his beard. "But who's going to pay my commission? Who am I supposed to give the change to?"

"Take the change for yourself in place of the commission," shouted Thingsmaster, grabbing both Jones and the girl by the hand and dragging them off towards the telegraph tower.

In half-an-hour an attractive young lady wearing a dark veil occupied a first-class cabin on the steamer *Amelia*, and Sorrow received Thingsmaster's highly detailed directions from Jones.

The gangway was raised. Smoke surged out of the smokestack. The deck, the promenades, the innumerable portholes of cabins were filled with protruding heads, hats and handkerchiefs. There was nothing but waving, whistling, screeching and nodding—and in reply came waving, whistling, screeching and nodding from a quay that was overflowing with people. The steamer *Amelia* made a beautiful turn and with a puff set sail on its long voyage.

CHAPTER 21
THE DANGEROUS JOURNEY
OF THE DOG BEAUTY

Having sent Sorrow and Willings off to do their business, and having said good-bye to Miss Orton, Mike Thingsmaster finally gave vent to his feelings.

Rarely could it be said that he had been seen in such anger as he now was. Mike struck the table with his fist:

"Killing women, the scoundrels! If only I could get on the tracks of that man!"

"Mend-mess," came the sound of the wall.

"Mess-mend," he replied quickly and with the agility of a monkey the chimneysweep Tom sprang into the room.

"Mike," he began, stammering.

"Well?"

"Mike, even though people are saying that I seem like a devil, I hope you won't take offence, Mike, but I myself am beginning to fear the devil. Look here, Mike, Van Hope and I are keeping an eye on the *Patrician* day and night, just as you ordered. Only there we are, sitting in the wall, while underneath us, in the wall, too, someone, would you believe it, is keeping an eye on us. And by gum, Mike, if I'm a devil only because of some false slander, the real devil for sure is walking around underneath us in the wall, I'd wager my own head on that!"

"You mean that you're still hearing steps in the underground passage?"

"Call it the underground passage if you like, but Van Hope and I call it the devil's passage!"

Thingsmaster gazed at the broad black mug of Tom, was about to say a few words to him, but waved his hand and went up to the door with a determined step. Opening it he shouted ut into the darkness:

"Beauty, Beauty!"

Immediately an enormous white dog with golden spots tore into the room. It leapt around Thingsmaster, wagged its tail, crouched down on its forepaws, whined in a friendly way, then jumped up onto its hind legs and embraced its master with the most passionate tenderness. Finally, settling down, it licked his nose, curled up on the floor and laid its snout on his dusty boot.

"Beauty," Mike said tenderly, bending over to his friend. The white tail began to drum energetically in response. "Beauty, I need you to do something important for me. Something dangerous, do you understand?"

The tail's rhythmic motion showed that Beauty was ready for anything.

"I can't send a person there, Beauty, because it smells strongly of murder. But you would know how to get yourself out of a jam. But keep a sharp lookout, Beauty, keep a sharp lookout, my buddy, for the person that you and I are hunting for—your master's greatest enemy."

"Gr-r-r-r!" came the sound from below.

"And the greatest enemy of mankind. Be careful, old girl."

"Gr-r-r-r! Ruff-ruff!" Beauty barked fiercely and laid a paw on Thingsmaster's knees.

"Mike," Tom said entreatingly, "what have you got on your mind? What can a dog do against the devil!"

But Thingsmaster did not care for superfluous words. He examined Beauty's teeth, ears and paws, attached a metallic shield fine as cambric to the dog's chest and tied a string to her collar with pieces of meat strung on it.

"Look, Beauty, one piece a day and no more," he said to the clever dog who followed his every movement.

Glancing around, he stuck a flashlight into his pocket and a few other odds and ends, nodded to Tom and set out on his way.

Meanwhile, in the kitchen of the hotel *Patrician*, a solemn conference between the service personnel and the administration was in progress. Mrs. Thindick was representing the former, while the latter was headed by Setto from Diarbekir.

"Briefly, I am saying," Mrs. Thindick began, compressing her lips, "from the day Mr. Thindick, my husband, died, not a single male hand, to say nothing of the male foot, has touched my shoulders. I have suffered damages. I positively insist on compensation for those damages which I have suffered from the touch of male feet on my shoulders within the property of your hotel, Mr. Setto."

"That's right!" the entire kitchen supported her in a chorus. "On account of the damages—she's hit it right on the head. We too have suffered damages boss. And if it goes on, and on, then at any old time every god-loving day devils can come showering down on us from the ceiling and you could lose your work force before you know it."

Mrs. Thindick turned with displeasure to her audience:

"Let's not get our legal claims mixed up," she said firmly. "As every justice-of-the-peace knows, I can count on special support from society because society does take into account acts of God. I must stand by the honor of my name. I have the positive intention of protecting my name from the advances of gentlemen of unknown origin within the bounds of your hotel, Mr. Setto."

Setto from Diarbekir took his pipe out of his mouth, looked around at all those present, and calmly declared:

"That's right. You are suffering damages and I am suffering damages. As this clever woman, Mrs. Thindick, affirms, a non-paying element has taken up residence all over my hotel. Let's sort the situation out. Wife, come here, sort the situation out. I employ a doorman, I employ a messenger, I employ a guard, I employ a valet, I employ a waiter, I employ a maid. Is what I'm saying correct, wife?"

"The absolute truth, Setto."

"And I employ, now you listen to me carefully, Mrs. Thindick, I employ a woman to look after the doorman, the messenger, the guard, the valet, the waiter and the maid. And what comes of it? You cannot even find out who the occupant is who has taken up residence in the walls of my hotel and is illegally violating my territory. And so the question arises, Mrs. Thindick, just what are you receiving your salary for, eh?"

This kind uf turnabout was not at all to the liking of the service personnel.

"But my shoulders, Mr. Setto!" Mrs. Thindick exclaimed in confusion.

"Well, my dear Mrs. Thindick," the implacable Setto continued, "even if you were a young girl, Mrs. Thindick, really, if you'll forgive me saying so, it would have been more to the point to start not at the shoulders but at an entirely different place."

Mrs. Thindick shrieked as though she had been stung and covered her face with both her hands. A roar of laughter resounded in the kitchen. And Setto from Diarbekir, taking his wife by the arm, went off to his own quarters as though nothing were amiss.

While this remarkable conversation was taking place in the kitchen, upstairs, in front of the room without a number, Mike with his dog, Tom the chimneysweep and the plumber Van Hope suddenly appeared and jumped noiselessly out of the glass-doored closet.

Mike pressed an invisible button and the door together with the lock and bolt quietly separated from the wall. There was no one in the room. In general, Signor Cice's dwelling created the strange impression of being uninhabited. The bed appeared to be untouched, the chairs unmoved, the window curtains never raised. Mike shook his head and made directly for the spot where the trap door was supposed to be situated.

"Not a single square of this floor has been equipped with our trademark," he whispered to his companions. "It seems to me, lads, that we are in the lair of some monstrous beast. All the rest of them are just loudmouths compared to him."

He got down on his knees, pulled out a magnifying glass and studied the surface of the floor for a long while. Then he jumped up and ran to the wall. Here a small nail had been hammered in and a wall calendar hung crookedly from it. Thingsmaster pushed the calendar aside and showed Tom and Van Hope a barely noticeable bulge underneath the wallpaper. He pressed it, returned to the floor and once again studied it closely through his magnifying glass. Between two pieces of parquet a barely noticeable crack now appeared. Thingsmaster pulled out a fine strip of steel and went to work with it. The crack widened, the parquet shifted, moved hesitatingly and then slowly rose upright. A black hole gaped down below.

"Beauty!" Thingsmaster called the dog.

"Fellows, look at what's happening to her!" Tom exclaimed.

The dog's limbs were shaking all over, and she was yawning so hard that it seemed as though her jaws were being stretched with boot-irons and the fur on her back was bristling.

"I told you, Mike, I told you," Tom muttered in terror. "Don't get mixed up with the devil! What's the point of destroying the dog!"

But Thingsmaster also seemed surprised, all the more so since he felt overcome by the same irresistible need to yawn. However, he began to look not at the dog, but at the windows, the shutters and the drapes. He pushed a chair forward, jumped up on it and began to rummage around the muslin curtains which hung down in folds. Finding something, he tore it loose and jumped down onto the floor. Only the tearing sound of a string being broken could be heard in the room, and at that very moment the dog stopped trembling. She raised her intelligent face to her master and started to wag her tail.

Thingsmaster went up to Tom and Van Hope and opened his hand. In it lay a round piece of glass of a strange color, a clouded milky color with a mixture of warm crimson such as one sees in the eyes of a newborn calf.

"Fabionite," Mike said, immediately squeezing the stone tight once again. "The technician Sorrow can tell you some interesting things about it, fellows. It's an artificial stone which was manufactured by the chemist Fabio-Duzzi a year-and-a-half ago in one of the factories in France. I can't imagine how and why it turned up here. This thing could put an entire army to sleep if you direct the light rays on it."

He hid the piece of glass in his pocket and again went up to the hole.

"Beauty, my girl, come on over here!"

Beauty went up to her master without displaying any terror this time. But the scent which came out of the subterranean passage apparently had an arousing effect on her. The fur on Beauty's back bristled and her nostrils sniffed the air unceasingly. Thingsmaster took her face in both of his hands and gazed fixedly into the dog's clever eyes.

"Beauty," he said slowly. "Go on into the hole. Don't fall into anyone's hands. Follow where the hole goes and where the other exit is. Come back to Middletown and show us all where you managed to come out. Understand?"

Beauty whined, poking at her master with her nose.

"Go on. One—two—three!"

Beauty took one more look at the three people standing over the trap door, wagged her tail and in a wink disappeared through the hole without a sound. The three of them waited for her for about ten minutes, listening for every little sound. But all was quiet. The dog did not return.

Then Thingsmaster closed the trap door. He replaced the calendar the way it had been hanging earlier. He put everything back the way it had been and left the room together with his companions.

CHAPTER 22
THE HAREWAY DOCKS

Three miles from New York, on the way to Sweaton, towered the famous Hareway Docks. The steamship *Torpedo* which had been sent here for repairs, was not ready for sailing. It had been cleaned inside and out, refitted, redecorated, repainted and was now casting cheerful sidelong glances at us with a thousand bulging, round cabin portholes which resembled frogs' eyes.

The sailors, who were by now fed up with running around town and had nothing left to drink, were gathered like a friendly family in the engine compartment. Tobacco smoke enveloped everything like a steam bath. The sailors were exchanging strange tales and whiling away the leisure time left to them before the sailing of the *Torpedo*.

"Well, boys," said the new mechanic who had been recommended to the *Torpedo* by the docker's union, a cheerful Scotsman by the name of Bisk, "the *Torpedo* could go ahead and weigh anchor this very moment. We've done such a good job refitting her. Douglas and Burley Brothers can be satisfied."

"The captain would have been satisfied," said the old sailor Xavier, who had been silent up until now. "But Douglas and Burley Brothers won't have a single word to say."

"Shut up!" shouted a sailor who was as pale as death and had eyes that were ringed with black circles. This was Dan who until recently had been a cheerful daredevil, and friend and drinking companion of the unfortunate Dip, but now Dan was drained, sickly, a mere shadow of himself, a man who was afraid to look back over his shoulder.

"What's happened to you, you old woman!" Xavier growled back angrily. "If I want to talk out loud then it means that I can talk out loud. I'm no fool. I can look after myself. You, my friend, have been here for three days," he turned to Bisk once more. "And if you spend another three, then you'll be cursing the day and hour that brought you aboard our *Torpedo*."

"Well, I'm not chicken!" Bisk laughed. "The laddie you're looking at has also had to go through just about everything there is. But who is the captain of the *Torpedo*, if it isn't Jackson from Hammerfordt?"

"Jackson's been gone for a year already. He was a captain that was one of a kind. A fellow would never say a bad word about Jackson even if he were drunk. But now we have..."

"Shut up!" Dan interrupted him again, shaking all over as though in a fever.

This time the old Xavier seemed to obey Dan. In any event he shut his mouth and had no wish to continue the conversation.

"What's the name of the new captain?" asked Bisk, looking around at the sailors. Their faces were gloomy. Someone answered unwillingly:

"Captain Gregoire,"

"What is he, a Frenchman or something?"

"Could be a Frenchman, could be the devil," Xavier butted in again. "The one thing is that he's a redhead. People with that color of hair have no reason to go poking their noses into the life of the sea. If you've got red hair, then go and work in a bank, you've got no business at sea if you don't want to call down misfortune on the whole ship's company. There's never been a situation yet where the ocean calmly put up with a redheaded person."

The conversation broke off. The sailors hid in each of their nooks and it was difficult to tell whether it was from the dim light or from the tobacco smoke, but their faces had turned grey. Bisk emerged out of the engine compartment onto the companionway, went about a hundred steps, looked all around himself, quickly ran his finger along a steel panel and disappeared into the crack which appeared. The panel immediately closed up and Bisk found himself in a tiny but very comfortable little room with a ventilator in the ceiling and an electric light on the side—all of which had been made by the fellows from the shipworks and which was not subject to fares. On the table in front of Bisk lay a notebook, and in the table an inkwell had been fixed and a pen hung on a long chain. Bisk opened to the first page of the notebook—*The Report of Bisk Concerning the Journey of the Torpedo*—and wrote on the first page:

> The person of Captain Gregoire, judging from the stories of the sailors, seems to be very suspicious. All in all, about 980 passengers have registered. Several people, in addition to Vasilov, are travelling to Russia. He is registered for a second class cabin, No. ll7, which is situated between the boarding ramp and the quarters of the crew personnel. I examined it and found nothing suspicious. Just in case, I also examined the adjoining quarters. Apparently the steel for the panelling throughout all of the crew's quarters has not come from our metalurigical works. Not one of the panels bears our trademark. I did not manage to get through to the captain's quarters. Among the passengers bound for Russia, the following are suspicious: the banker Westinghouse and Senator Notabit with his daughter. According to rumors, Westinghouse is travelling to distract himself after the disappearance of his mistress, whereas Senator Notabit is indulging the whim of his daughter who has been, for some time, fol-

lowing the banker Westinghouse without any apparent reason. Still a complete mystery is the absence on the steamship of Arthur Morlender who, according to the plans of the fascists, is supposed to be travelling incognito to Soviet Russia. Among the passengers there isn't a single person who could prove to be Morlender in disguise.

Having written down all of this, Bisk tore out the sheet, sealed it in an envelope, emerged quietly from the compartment and within a minute was already in the post office compartment where our old friend, Miss Totter, was in charge. She had been placed there directly from the *Patrician* on the recommendation of Setto's distinguished guests.

"Miss Totter," said Bisk, "here's the first letter for Mike. I hope that there'll be a good dozen of them to follow and I also hope that you and I will arrive safely in Kronstadt."

Miss Totter said nothing in reply, took the letter and went up to one of the numerous dark cages hanging in the room. The microscopic letters "mm" were marked on the doors.

"These are Mike's pigeons," Miss Totter whispered and sighed with melancholy. Then she took one of the messenger pigeons, placed the letter in a little sack on its breast, opened the upper window and released the bird.

Bisk started to whistle like a man who had fulfilled his duty, shoved his hands into his pockets and took the shortest route back to his cabin, that is, he opened the panelling and plunged into the narrow passage running between the walls. He had been walking along in the darkness for not more than two minutes when suddenly he froze as though rivetted to the spot. A whistling sound came through the wall very close to him. A moment later the sound turned into a scatching and someone passed by in the wall so close to Bisk, so audibly, that the mechanic involuntarily moved away although the person passing by was separated from him by a steel sheet. At the very same time something clanged overhead with a soft grating sound, just as though someone had closed an invisible hatch.

But it was with good reason that the Scotsman Bisk did not consider himself a chicken. He waited for several minutes, opened the panelling and emerged onto the companionway without entering his own compartment.

"An addition will have to be made to the letter. And rather quickly at that!" he said to himself philosophically.

Meanwhile, sailors were running past him with the cry:

"Weigh anchor, weigh anchor. Orders from the captain to weigh anchor on the *Torpedo* and make for New York harbor. Sailing time tomorrow morning."

Bisk stopped a young man running past him and asked him:
"When was the order given? Is the captain really on the *Torpedo*?"
"None of us have seen the captain," the young sailor whispered in his ear. "But the order came from the navigation officer."
And the blue-eyed young sailor dashed headlong on his way.

CHAPTER 23
THE SAILING OF THE TORPEDO

There was no reason to call it a fine day for the sailing of the steamship. The rain had been pouring down since morning. The water in the Hudson had risen half a foot. All the privately owned boats standing by the quay had been smashed to smithereens by a hurricane in the night.

And, finally, the morning newspapers had reported the current prices of American wheat, mentioning at the same time three other events: in a ravine near the Bourneville Forest, the completely disfigured corpse of an unknown woman had been found; the secretary of the deceased lawyer, Kraft, had run off without a trace after robbing the cashbox; the coffin with Jeremy Morlender's body, which had been scheduled for opening due to the petition of the deceased's wet-nurse and his distant relatives who had arrived from Europe, had suddenly been stolen from Kressling's family chapel by unknown malefactors and despite all manner of searching had not yet been uncovered...

Doctor Lepsius, after reading all of this, let the paper fall weakly onto his knees and leaned back against the chair in utter exhaustion. He felt a flood of hatred towards humanity. He was at a loss to understand what powers forced him to live and work for the good of that same humanity...

But a moment later Doctor Lepsius' innate optimism regained the upper hand and he turned the page of the newspaper in the hope of finding respite for his soul in the theatrical, marriage, sports, stock and other similarly entertaining columns.

Then suddenly his eyes fell on several lines printed in italics. Beside himself with wrath Lepsius read the following:

Yesterday, at seven o'clock in the evening, in the Church of the Forty Martyrs, there took place the marriage ceremony of the spinster Miss Small and Mr. Nathaniel Epidermis, the major-domo of our famous X-ray specialist, Bentrovato. Present on the bride's side were Mr. and Mrs. Small from

Middletown; on the groom's side was Dr. Bentrovato himself who at the same time was reading a lecture to a thick crowd of youths assembled around him about X-raying infants in the mother's womb in order to determine their sex.

Lepsius jumped to his feet, crumpling the newspaper convulsively. He was seeing red. He waved his hand, tore his hat off the hook and fell headlong down the stairs.

Doctor Lepsius was positively sputtering. If he had not been a doctor he would have run off immediately to a doctor in order to have his blood let or, at the very least, to get some kind of prescription written in Latin which, as is well known, does have its positive side, since it provides visual proof of the intelligence behind the expense to you.

But even this consolation was denied to him. And for that reason, Lepsius ran as fast as his legs would carry him along the street. He was fleeing from the accursed perfidy of his housekeeper, he was fleeing blindly ahead until he came running right up to the Hudson.

The rain seemed to be coming down in buckets. Newspaper vendors and shoeshine boys were in hiding. The infrequent pedestrians belonged to that order of people who were tramps. The mist thickened along the streets of New York, hovered over the Hudson, enveloped the entire quay to such an extent that the Hareway lighthouse was casting bands of light from its lamp over the entire stretch of the bay, while the quay was lit up with electric lights at twelve noon.

Lepsius was soaked through to the skin and it was not without surprise that he noted that he had come out in the direction of the landing where the *Torpedo*, flooded with a thousand lights, was standing ready to board passengers. However, the gangway had not yet been lowered. The crowd standing in the rain kept expressing signs of a frightening impatience.

"They're afraid of demonstrations," said someone beside Lepsius in a peevish voice. "As though there were demonstrations these days!"

"Just wait and see," replied someone else. "After all, the communists are sending their representative to the Soviet Committee of Deputies. Take a look, they've come to see him off, by God, no worse than a president would get."

At this moment only Lepsius noticed the extraordinary mixture of people and took a more attentive look around.

The entire enormous square around him was overflowing with people in caps and workers' jackets. They had come here straight from the factories without having time to change their clothing. Their faces were aflame with inspiration, their hands were reaching out from all sides towards comrade Vasilov who was standing in their midst wearing his travelling suit.

"Tell them, Vasilov, that we're not dozing!" someone shouted, waving his cap. "We won't miss our hour by sleeping in!"

"Greetings to Lenin!" another one shouted.

The crowd pressed in from all sides, definitely not letting anyone get through to Vasilov from that half of the quay where a more distinguished public had gathered. Lepsius caught sight of Westinghouse over there, with an elegant travelling bag in his hand and a monocle in his eye. Not far from him was the curly-headed Grace, plucking at her father, looking around in all directions, her eyes searching for someone. They were accompanied by young girls, ladies and their beaux in dress jackets from Fifth Avenue, vainly trying to hide from the rain beneath a canvas awning. But the clutch of fashionable New Yorkers who were departing for Europe to refresh themselves, was completely lost amid the thousand-strong crowd of workers who were rumbling deeply like the sea. A policeman who was gingerly picking his way towards them, pretended that he was in control of the situation when the workers began to shift him around from one place to the other like a ball.

Lepsius extricated himself from the crowd and reached the side of the *Torpedo* itself where the heads of the warrant officers and sailors stuck out from the bridge.

"Kovalkovsky!" someone shouted. "It's time to lower the boarding ramp. Give the orders!"

An extremely fat warrant officer, pink-faced like a cherub and with lips like bedroom slippers, ran off to give the order. Lepsius glanced at his hands and feet with a critical eye, pulled out the notebook where three surnames were written— 1. The fruit-vendor Bear 2. Professor Hiserton 3. Navigation Officer Kovalkovsky— and crossed out the last one in the list.

Meanwhile, two men who had climbed onto the anchor chain of the *Torpedo* were exchanging whispers. One of them was the chimneysweep, Tom; the other was the mechanic Bisk.

"Mike wants you to know that he got the letter. Morlender's absence is much more suspicious than his presence. Mike fears for Vasilov's life. Watch out, Bisk, protect him with your own hide and don't spare yourself."

"I know," replied Bisk. "But what about the dog, has it come back?"

"No, Mike is really suffering. The dog has disappeared. It must have been stabbed with a knife. Well, good-bye, Bisk, send us the news."

"Good-bye, Tom, don't worry."

Tom jumped down, onto the mooring cable, sprang clear, made a pirouette and disappeared in the water.

The boarding ramp was lowered. Greetings, best wishes, farewells. A few pairs of sharp eyes belonging to people of the same profession, but, apparently, working for different masters, and obviously unaware of one another, were turning each passenger inside out with their eyes as he or she walked up the ramp to where the tickets and documents were being examined.

"One."

"Two."

"Three."

"Four."

"Five."

There was no Morlender. There was not even anyone resembling Morlender.

The distinguished public passed by and the communist Vasilov walked up the ramp. He was pale from excitement. The distinguished public awarded him a jeering whistle.

But the whistling was immediately drowned in the roar of the thousand-voiced crowd who tossed their hats, handkerchiefs and caps skyward.

"Hurrah! Vasilov! Hurrah! Soviet Russia! Off you go, comrade, give our regards to the boys, tell them to keep a firm grip! And hail to Lenin!"

The roar became thunderous, and joining in with it, as though supporting the workers' voices, was the mighty whistle of the steam siren, the groan of the ramp being raised, the clanking of the chains, the whistle of the wind, the straining of the blocks and tackles. The *Torpedo* slowly got underway.

The steamship had already made off into the outer reaches of the bay, the fog had now covered up the thousands of lights which flooded its decks and cabins, but the thunderous cries and greetings to Lenin still continued to shake the quay, causing a few people both in New York and on the steamship to experience a justifiable pounding of their hearts.

CHAPTER 24
THE DIARY OF BISK

We weighed anchor at noon on the 19th of May. I was busy in the engine room and for about three hours I couldn't get out on deck. It was a calm day, nothing happening, if the strange story of a certain sailor by the name of Dan, a proper coward and epileptic, is not taken into account. He told the story of how several times he was supposed to have heard a drawn-out, inhuman howling coming from below where the sailors sleep. We all went there in order to calm him down but we didn't hear anything. Dan is acting strange. Today he had an attack, he howled, collapsed headlong onto the ground and foam came out of his mouth. I thought that his own howling hardly bore any resemblance to that of a human.

When I got an hour-and-a-half break, I hurried up onto the deck on the pretext of checking the electrical wiring. Everything was in order. The deck reminds one of the president's reception room in the White House: tropical plants in pots, carpets and statues everywhere. At five o'clock the passengers listened to a small concert and drank tea on the deck. Vasilov didn't come up out of his cabin. I went down to his quarters through our passageway, opened a peephole and took a look in at him. I was surprised by what he was doing: he was squatting in the middle of the cabin, holding a revolver in his hands and watching the door. His face seemed distracted and frightened to me. I tossed a note to him inside the room:

"You have someone to protect you here. Let me know what you are afraid of and leave a note on your table. Keep calm on the outside. Spend all your time with the other passengers."

He picked up the note, read it and instead of a reply he said in a whisper:

"I'm asking whoever it was who gave me that note to come into the cabin."

Then I emerged from behind the panelling into the corridor and knocked on his door. He half-opened the door, holding the revolver in his hand, looked me over and then let me in. I identified myself and said that I was travelling with him right to Kronstadt in order to guard his life. He smiled and showed me a ball of paper on which the following was written in crude letters and completely ungrammatical speech:

You will die as soon as you cross the threshold of your cabin.

Vasilov looked at me fixedly while I read the piece of paper and then declared:

"You see, I've got plenty of people concerned about me already. One advised me to be with the passengers, the other tells me not to leave the cabin. Whose advice am I supposed to listen to? How do I know who's my enemy and who's my friend?"

Before replying, I read the piece of paper once more. It was a filthy sheet of paper torn out of the ship's galley book. Whoever had written it had left traces of a greasy thumb on it. It was difficult to imagine that the note had come from the enemy's camp.

"Listen!" I cried putting together a plan of action. "Take this note and go with it to the navigation officer and say that you're upset and want to be placed either in a second-class cabin or in the open ward of the ship's sick bay. This is the wisest thing we can come up with."

Vasilov shook his head: "I still don't feel good about crossing the threshold of this cabin."

"You should be afraid to stay in it!" I continued, influenced by my thoughts. "And so you won't be worried about your life, watch this."

With these words I opened the door wide open, went out into the passageway and calmly announced as I turned to him, at the very same time as I clearly caught out of the corner of my eye the tail of someone's black frock coat disappearing behind the handrail:

"Everything's in order here, sir... It must have been a fuse that has blown down below."

Vasilov followed me out and together we went up on deck. I tried to keep myself close beside him in order to shield him with my own skin in the event of danger. But nothing of the sort happened and he safely reached the glass booth where the fat navigation officer Kovalkovsky was sitting. I busied myself with my electrical wires which I had contrived to ruin as a precaution and watched as Kovalkovsky read the note handed to him. His fat face flushed with displeasure and he shrugged his shoulders several times. Then he got up and Vasilov followed him in the direction of the sick bay.

I couldn't go there as well. But, as soon as I fixed the wiring I went back up towards the companionway from where the second-class cabins and the crew's quarters were visible. To my amazement, I caught sight of a short, completely unfamiliar man in a long black frock coat standing directly in front of Vasilov's cabin. He was red-headed. I could not restrain myself from giving a start. At that very moment he turned around and glanced at me. He was an unattractive man with vague eyes.

They sized me up without any expression, exactly like those of a fish lying on the beach or like those of an inveterate alcoholic if you kept him on straight water for about three days. I don't know why, but I felt goose bumps all over my body. I remembered the words of old Xavier.

"It must be Captain Gregoire," I thought and hurried to conceal myself from the deck. Down below, in front of the engine room, rumors were circulating about Dan's sickness. The Portuguese, Picherga, my immediate superior, turned on me.

"You should go off for strolls less often, Bisk! We've had to carry that miserable Dan to the sick bay, he's no good to me now and you've been ordered on duty for the whole night without relief, so get on with it, if you please."

"Who gave the order?"

"The order's been given and that's that!" Picherga replied sullenly. "Don't you worry, if the bosses feel like dumping overtime on you for any old reason, then they can go ahead and suck the blood out of you!"

Grumbling and swearing, he gradually let it slip out to me that Captain Gregoire has personally designated me for night duty on the engines and that the *Torpedo* had been ordered to increase its speed to maximum because of information received on the radio about an approaching storm.

"We'll have to cut right through its path, that's all there is to it." Picherga puffed behind his reeking pipe.

I didn't care much for this but there was nothing I could do. I decided to play along, stay on duty for two or three hours, but then to slip away to the toilet under the pretext of being sick and try to get through the wall to Miss Totter. The report to Mike about everything that had happened was in my pocket. And so, I stayed, put on my overalls and glasses, extinguished my pipe and went into the engine room.

The iron beasts were doing their work without complaint. Opening and closing their jaws, chewing up one minute after another with their cog-like teeth, devouring time with an insatiable gluttony. One hour, two, three—I suddenly clutched at my stomach, gave a groan and ran out past a handful of workers into the dark corridor from where it took a little effort for me to slip behind the panelling, make two or three turns inside the wall and then knock at Miss Totter's.

"Mend-mess!"

Not a sound.

"Mend-mess!"

Miss Totter was not answering.

What was going on? I peeked through a crack: Miss Totter was lying on the floor in the pose of someone sleeping, her papers were scattered about, the fresh sea air was streaming in through the porthole, Miss Totter's drawers were all pulled out, and the pigeons, Mike's famous pigeons—there wasn't a trace of them.

CHAPTER 25
BISK'S DIARY CONTINUED

"—Bisk! Where the hell did you disappear to?" I heard the voice of the Portuguese.

I had to return to the engine room without being able to make any sense of the reason for Miss Totter's sleepfulness and the disappearance of Mike Thingsmaster's'ss pigeons.

All night long the *Torpedo* churned out its full revolutions. While the passengers were soundly asleep, the boiler was threatening to burst from the pressure, the stokers danced around the fireboxes like devils, and on the other side of the walls a diabolical storm raged and tossed before the *Torpedo*.

By the time morning came, when I was already stumbling about from fatigue, the Portuguese arrived to relieve me and I ran off to my quarters, crawled into the first bunk I came upon, beside a loudly snoring sailor, and without undressing, was about to fall asleep.

Then suddenly, from beneath the floor, a partially muffled howling reached our ears—a creepy and inhuman howling that made my hair stand on end. I leapt up, wide awake. Several other sailors awoke and sat up, their naked legs dangling from their bunks. We listened carefully. The howling sound repeated itself once more and this time it was so piercing, so forlorn, that many of the sailors rushed together into a terror-stricken herd.

"Boys, that's the captain's dead dog howling!" Xavier said in a hoarse voice, and the sailors began to shake in terror. My neighbor dashed to his bed and buried his head under his pillow.

"Shut up, Xavier. It's enough to make one stck without you saying anything," someone rebuked the old man.

"I won't shut up," Xavier whispered stubbornly. "It's clear as day, the dead dog has started to howl again. It can only mean that we're going to have another corpse, boys, you just mark my words."

"What do you mean, a dead dog," I butted in.

"You see, lad, on the ship we used to have a dog, from Jackson, the former captain. He went away but left the dog, only it didn't take a liking to the redhead, I mean Captain Gregoire. And the dog took on a strange habit: it would howl just before someone died. Believe it or not, every time we sailed, it would no sooner begin to howl then we would find out that we had someone dead. The redhead sure didn't care much for that and so once when he was walking past the dog, he raised his foot and the dog ups and starts to growl. But he raised his foot and then he brought it right down on the dog's head and cracked its skull with his heel. That redhead had the strength not of a human, but of the devil himself!"

"But the dog still goes on howling before someone dies," a young sailor added in a whisper, his teeth chattering in terror.

And as though in direct affirmation, a protracted, inhuman howling reached us from right under the bunks, as though the howling creature has moved over to us while we were talking.

The sailors dashed to their bunks in terror, and I too leapt under my blanket, not so much from terror as from exhaustion, and I immediately fell into a death-like sleep.

I awoke at the second shift change. The morning bell was jangling as loud as possible in our ears, giving the first call to breakfast. The sailors jumped up, turning over the warm bunks to their bone-weary fellow workers.

When I went into the bathroom and put my head under a stream of cold water, old Xavier waited for the right moment and whispered to me:

"A corpse really had been found. The telegraph operator died at the very same time as the dog was howling

I leapt up from under the tap and without drying myself, I hurtled into the engine room.

"Picherga!" I shouted. "Is it true that Miss Totter has died? What did she die of?"

"Don't holler," the Portuguese answered phlegmatically. "Must have been the storm frightened the poor girl too much or she overate and her heart couldn't take it. After all, she was over forty even if she did wear brightly colored scarves."

I started to work. From that moment it was clear to me that the smallest indiscretion would hasten my own death. I used my first free moment to put down these pages and to get a bottle ready in my hideout. Then I slipped into the sick bay where I was admitted with difficulty. I went to visit Dan.

The wretched epileptic was lying motionless; his lips had turned blue and were tightly drawn. I had to make a special effort to get him to open his mouth.

What did they want from him, he said. He was determined to die and the sooner the better. It's impossible for a man who has seen Satan to go on living, he claimed. And he watched Satan kill his friend, Dip... No, no one had been brought into the sick bay except for himself, he said. The passengers' ward was next door; but there was a common office for both wards in the sick bay; he would have known immediately it there had been another patient except for himself...

With these words Dan fell silent and turned his back to me. I had squeezed everything I needed out of the poor wretch and with trepidation I slipped out onto the deck. It meant that Vasilov had not spent the night in the sick bay. I was angry at him for his lack of caution. Why had he not listened to my considered advice?

Up above, in a small salon, it was noisy. Passengers from the first and second class were milling around Kovalkovsky and talk was about the death of the telegraph operator.

"I demand that a disinfection be carried out!" An elderly woman from cabin No. 7 was shouting hysterically.

"But for pity's sake, after all she did die from a heart attack."

The man who had said this in such a cheerful voice, was standing with his back to me. I looked and then sighed in relief. It was Vasilov in person—alive, cheerful, talkative, in no way reminiscent of the frightened passenger from the day before. He was alive—a weight fell from my shoulders, thank God! I wanted to go up to him, but I was afraid of being seen by the navigation officer.

Meanwhile, Vasilov was chatting in a lively fashion with the passengers. He calmed the muttering, elderly woman down, picked up the delicate little handkerchief which had been dropped by Senator Notabit's daughter—in short, he was acting like a regular man of the world.

"How do you like those manners," I thought to myself, not without some malice, and choosing my moment, I touched him on the shoulder when he went to a chair with a newspaper in his hands.

"Why didn't you spend the night in the sick bay?"

Vasilov quickly turned around and looked at me with a sharp gaze.

Boys! It was Vasilov, it was his face, his nose, lips, hair, jacket, trousers, vest, shoes, it was Vasilov, I'm telling you, and yet it wasn't him! It was someone else completely, or I'm not Bisk, the Scotsman! I couldn't hold back and I gave a start.

"What's the matter?" he asked, smilingly, this same Vasilov, this specter off Vasilov, I don't know what to call him—but I did not answer. My teeth were chattering, I dashed headlong down below, to his cabin.

I managed to get behind the panelling without being noticed by anyone. I looked through the peephole: everything was as before in Vasilov's cabin, even the revolver was lying on the table and in the corner stood his untouched suitcase. Was I dreaming, or something? Wasn't I having a nightmare? But unless a double had assumed my identity as well, that man up above was not Vasilov, no, no, no!

I went out into the passageway once more in order to make my way to my hideout. Running down the companionway, I caught sight of a red-headed man in a black frock coat not more than two steps behind me. He was hurrying after me, lightly touching the handrail with an emaciated and lifeless hand whose joints were badly swollen. I tore foreward as fast as my legs would carry me, outstripped him by about twenty paces, turned a corner and flew through the narrow opening like an arrow.

Ah-ah-ah! Saved, if only for an hour, but saved! I looked around, carefully locked all the exits in my hideout, got my paper and ink ready, and brought my diary up to date. Now I'm working it all up inside the bottle and going to throw it into the sea after writing with a piece of diamond on the glass:

Whoever might fish this bottle out of the ocean, as long as he turns out to be a working man, he'll get it to Michael Thingsmaster. There are so many more of our boys scattered all over the wide world then we even know about ourselves.

And I was just about to stick the paper into the bottle when I heard the sound of water pouring in. It turned out that a crack the width of two fingers had opened up overhead and water was gushing in. I tasted it on my tongue—salty. I hurtled to the exit—it wouldn't open. I had been caught as though in a mousetrap. The water will fill up in about two hours and I'll drown. I'm hiding the paper in the bottle, corking it up, trying to widen the crack so that I can throw the bottle out of the cabin. Boys, remember the Scotsman, Bisk! Warn the ones on the *Amelia* that they've made the substitution. Beware of Captain Gregoire! Mend-mess!

CHAPTER 26
THE SENATOR'S DAUGHTER

"My dear, you are behaving indecently." Senator Notabit said to his daughter, Grace, who was lying on the couch with her two feet higher than her head and resting on the back of her father's chair.

"That may well be so, papa," Grace replied. "Your remarks don't offend me. If it pleases you, then say as much as you like."

"It's not a question of whether it pleases *me*, my daughter," the

Senator objected reproachfully, "but whether you are going to pay attention to what I am saying."

"Don't count on me, daddy dear. It's never yet succeeded that my father could count on such a silly girl like me. I implore you, just do whatever you please."

The Senator was silent for a few moments, completely at a loss. Incidentally, it was not by chance that he was a senator and it was not by chance that he attended the official and personal receptions of the president. It was no effort for him simply to blow his nose and then get back down to business again.

"You are behaving indecently," he began once more. "You're literally neverr more than a step away from Westinghouse. I might understand it if it were due to tender feelings. Many marriages in New York have arisen from tender feelings that were spawned by a steamship's rolling, pitching and other manifestations of a galvanic order that are possible at sea. But in the present circumstances it apparently has nothing to do with tender feelings."

"Papa. How can you say such things to me!" Grace cried with displeasure, leaping up from the couch. "How can you abuse the fact that I am an orphan, that I have no mother. Boo-hoo!" She immediately burst into tears, stamped her feet on the floor and shook her head with such force as to make one think that it was not a head but rather a ripe apple tree.

"But what have I gone and said now?" the confused senator muttered.

"You-ou said,.. you sa-said..." wept the wretched Grace. "You said that thing about galvanic... no, I can't repeat it."

"Well, now, enough, enough," the senator declared in a conciliatory voice, patting his daughter on the back. "I really do know that I've got a wonderful little girl in you, Grace, that you're a fine girl, an educated girl. Don't weep in such a terrible fashion, it'll be bad for your lungs!"

"I-I won't, papa, dear," Grace wept. "Oh, you don't know how heavy it makes my heart whenever I remember that I have no mommy... My wardrobe, you know... and the hats... and there's no one, no one, ever!"

Grace's feet were again showing some intention of beginning to drum on the floor. The senator was utterly destroyed. He went limp and wiped away a tear. He crawled into his side pocket for his billfold.

"Enough, enough, Grace. We can straighten all that out on the continent. You'll see, honey, that your father also attaches importance to such things as a wardrobe."

"And hats!" Grace exclaimed.

"And hats, kitten. Give your papa a kiss. Hide these bills in your purse."

Grace brushed her father's cheek, hid the bills in her purse and once more curled up on the couch.

Meanwhile, the senator, who had gone off into his own cabin, surrendered to sweet and proud thoughts.

"Just like her deceased mother!" he whispered to himself with emotion. "Just as meek, tender and forgiving. Give her a caress, console her with some trifle and she'll immediately forget everything. A baby, a perfect baby."

He stretched peacefully on the bed, closed his eyes and fell asleep.

Meanwhile, the baby, after lying there for a short while, leapt up, listened for her father's snore, brushed her curls and sticking something behind her wide silk sash, softly made her way out of the cabin.

Banker Westinghouse, who had grown old and emaciated, was sitting in his own cabin at a table that had been fastened to the floor, drinking whiskey and soda and feverishly looking through the New York newspapers. This old roué had been knocked off course. He was suffering from something akin to melancholy. He was languishing for his mysterious Mask who had left him one fine May day and had never returned. Someone knocked at the cabin.

"Come in," he muttered distractedly. The door opened, someone quickly entered the cabin, stopped right beside him and Westinghouse did not have the time to raise his eyes before he found the muzzle of a pretty little lady's revolver poking at him and heard a woman's voice declaring in a threatening tone:

"Hands up!"

During his entire banking experience, Westinghouse had never felt such alarm. He wanted to raise his hands, but they were shaking and positively refused to tear themselves loose from the protective surface of the table.

"Hands up, you old rat! One, two, three!"

"Miss Notabit," Westinghouse implored, making out at last who the curly-headed bandit was. "I'm willing to raise my hands as soon as they'll do so. I have a weak heart. Put that dangerous toy down."

"I have no intention of doing so," Grace replied calmly. "I'll keep it there until I find out from you what I need to know. You good-for-nothing tyrant, despot, Dardenelle Turk, what've you done with the Mask? Answer right this minute, where is she, where've you hidden her?"

"Honestly, Miss Notabit, you are desperately mistaken. I have been crushed, thrown over, abandoned, she ran away from me. I'm suffering, and you are asking me questions which I myself am prepared to ask with a gun in my hands."

"Just as I thought," drawled Miss Grace. "Let's have the proof, you old fogey!"

Westinghouse bit his tongue in fury. He grabbed the newspapers off the table, a whole pile of newspapers and waved them in Miss Notabit's face.

"Read them!" he moaned in despair.

Grace gathered up the newspapers in one hand, holding her other hand level with the banker's nose. She immediately saw several announcements underlined in red pencil.

"The banker Westinghouse is imploring Vivi to come back, promising to give her all his wealth."

"The banker Westinghouse is offering Vivi, in the event of her return to him, legal marriage."

"The banker Westinghouse begs Vivi to drop in on him if only for a moment in order to get a diamond necklace..."

"Hm!" Grace murmured uncertainly, after she had read all the announcements. "But then why ever did you leave for Europe?"

"I'm about to take Steinach's treatment," muttered Westinghouse, starting to cough.

Grace tossed him a disdainful look and puffed out her lips.

"And to this man," she declared in a decimating voice, "to this man belongs the most beautiful woman in the world. And I considered him a despot! Pfui!"

She wanted to back away towards the door without lowering her revolver when suddenly her eyes fell on another announcement in the latest edition of a New York newspaper which had just been dropped onto the *Torpedo* by airmail. Notice was given there about a modest celebration that had taken place in the private residence of the Morlenders' on Riverside Drive: a close circle of intimates celebrated the marriage of Mr. Arthur Morlander and Miss Claire Wesson in circumstances that were very modest due to the period of mourning.

Grace waved her revolver in irritation as though it were a whip, gave a whistle like a boy and ran out of the cabin, leaving a shaken Mr. Westinghouse with both hands raised to the sky precisely at a moment when there was not the slightest need.

CHAPTER 27
PARTLY ON LAND AND PARTLY ON WATER

"Claire married that calf, Arthur!" Miss Notabit said to herself angrily, tossing her revolver on the table. "She really has gone and married him, the silly girl!"

"Arthur married that redhead, Claire!" Doctor Lepsius said to himself in amazement, both pairs of eyes, including both his spectacles and his own eyes, goggling at the morning edition of the newspaper lying in front of him. "Simply unbelievable! Arthur, a misogynist, a confirmed bachelor who was prepared to destroy all the women in the world, who hated Mrs. Wesson and that moustached niece of hers—he's married Claire. Toby! Toby!"

With a gaping mouth the mulatto silent appeared out of nowhere beside the doctor's chair.

"Toby. Pinch me. Ai! I'm not dreaming! Toby, is it daytime or nighttime? Is this me or not me?"

The mulatto gave a blank look, silently slobbering.

"Oh, you fool!" the doctor cursed and struck him across the legs with his cane. "Now I can see at least that you are really you. Go away!"

Toby disappeared just as wordlessly as he had suddenly appeared. Doctor Lepsius again read the announcement and at the same moment a threatening crease appeared on his forehead.

"Aha," he said to himself. "Aha! 'A close circle of intimates...' Since when, dear friends, are you excluding Doctor Lepsius from among your intimates! A wedding—and I'm a superfluous person. A wedding—and Doctor Lepsius is forgotten as though he could only be remembered when someone has the flu', catarrh or constipation. Just you wait!"

The three steps that led up to his nose went off in various directions: a sign of extreme anxiety in Doctor Lepsius. He leapt up with uncustomary agility, tossed on his jacket, took his hat and cane and immediately left the house. Along the way he bought flowers. And with a malicious smile on his lips, a bouquet of flowers in his hand, Doctor Lepsius gave an energetic ring at the front door of the Morlender's private residence.

"Not at home," said a servant.

"I know perfectly well, Peter, now let's have a look to see whether your ear is still running," And Doctor Lepsius peeked into Peter's ear where there had not been any discharge for a long while, tossed Peter his hat and cane and firmly opened the door into the salon.

On a soft divan, her legs comfortably curled up, sat Mrs. Elizabeth Morlender, doing silk embroidery on a piece of velvet. Directly opposite her on a couch, Miss Claire Wessen was half-reclining and doing nothing. Seeing Doctor Lepsius, both of them leapt up and cried out.

"Allow me to insist on the rights of an old, albeit forgotten friend!" the doctor declared gallantly, holding out the flowers. "I am pleased that people who are dear to my heart have become united into an even more tightly knit family. But where is Arthur then? Allow me to press him to my heart."

Mrs. Morlender exchanged a fleeting look with her niece.

"Thank you, Doctor," she uttered, somewhat confused. "Unfortunately, you won't be able to see Arthur. He's ill, very ill, and we are receiving absolutely no one."

"Arthur is ill!" Lepsius cried. "Take me to him." With these words he pulled his stethoscope and various other professional instruments out of his pocket.

"Er, that is, he... he's ill in a completely different way," Mrs. Morlender became utterly confused.

"He's not ill in the area of your specialty, Doctor," Clair interrupted in her masculine bass voice. "Doctor Bentrovato is taking care of him."

Lepsius halted without being able to believe his ears. He chewed on his lips, making an effort to utter at least one word, looked at Mrs. Elizabeth Morlender, looked at Miss Claire Wessen and turning around, headed out of this house with a firm step.

Peter handed him his hat and cane and whispered in his ear with a mysterious look on his face:

"Mister Lepsius, go down to the servants' quarters. Polly wants to have a chat with you. It's an ugly business, this, sir!"

It was as though an electric current had passed through the doctor's body. He gave a jump and smacked himself on the forehead. He twisted his lips sardonically. And without questioning Peter any further he ran down to the servants' quarters.

The negress Polly had been on the verge of dying for some time. But it was clear from the gloomy expression on her face that earthly matters were stubbornly preventing her from doing so. And thus, taking heart from day to day, she kept postponing her death.

Seeing Doctor Lepsius she sent everyone else out of the servants' quarters, seized him by the shoulder with her black wizened hand and began to whisper, her eyes flashing darkly:

"Massah Lepsius didn't listen to me. Old Polly knows a great deal! Polly has the Gonewalkin' Stone. She knew right away that it wasn't Massah Jeremy lying in Massah Jeremy's coffin. She told you, Massah

Lepsius, get them to open up the coffin. And then they went and stole the coffin. They hid it from everyone's eyes and from the eyes of the Gonewalkin' Stone. Now, you listen to me, Massah Lepsius, you listen good. Master Arthur gets married to that yellow-faced witch, fine. But who saw Master Arthur? And who was at the wedding? No one, no one, no one! There was one German and one Russian, and there was one Frenchman, and there was a priest who nobody knew and there wasn't a single servant, not a single good negro. There was no Polly. There was no Massah Lepsius. And now it's been three days since anyone has seen Master Arthur, three days, you hear!"

Having said all of this, old Polly rolled her eyes, gave a choking sound, shuddered and died. Doctor Lepsius had heard all of Polly's pre-death monolog without batting an eye. He called the servants, who entered the servants' quarters shaking in terror, ordered them to be silent about everything they had heard from Polly and quickly went off home.

Here he paced back and forth for some time, neither summoning Toby nor showing any signs of anger as would have been his custom. Then he sat down at his desk, took a piece of paper and wrote:

> To the Attorney General of the State of Illinois.
> From Doctor Lepsius. a Knight of the Order of the White Banner, and an esteemed member of Boston University.
>
> My Highly Esteemed Mr. Attorney General!
>
> Not long ago it was printed in the newspapers that you are the national pride of America in the realm of solving mysterious crimes. In the article it was said that compared with you, Nat Pinkerton, Nick Carter and Sherlock Holmes were no better than common chimneysweeps. I am appealing to you for help in an extremely bizarre affair. You have heard that Jeremy Morlender was killed in Russia. There is reason to believe that he was definitely not killed by the persons who have been officially accused. At the present time his son, Arthur Morlender, has disappeared although his relatives are concealing his disappearance. In the name of justice and for the salvation of the young man's life, give this mysterious affair your attention.
>
> Your respectful servant, etc., etc.

After writing the letter, Doctor Lepsius sealed it, pasted a stamp on it and summoned Toby.

"Toby," he commanded, "give this letter to Miss Small and tell her to drop it in the mailbox immediately."

Toby grabbed the letter and rushed headlong to the upper floor where the former Miss Small, her sleeves rolled up, was ironing the linen of her husband, Nathaniel, who had dropped in on her for a wee half-hour. While the iron was heating up on the stove, the newlyweds busied themselves with kisses.

"Miss Small!" Toby yelled. "Take this letter and drop it in the mailbox."

"I'm not Miss Small to you, you yellow loudmouth! Twenty times a day I tell you: Mrs. Epidermis, Mrs. Nathaniel Epidermis."

"But how am I to blame, if Massah Lepsius himself!..." whimpered Toby.

Mrs. Epidermis grandly took the letter and waved it in the air.

"No you just listen to this, Toby, you mulatto. If your master in his old age is jealous of me or wants to play up to me or has got some funny business up his sleeve, just remember, you monkey, I'm not that kind of woman! I can hear everything that's said to my face and behind my back, thanks to this Berlin hearing aid. So there! And here's what I think of your master!"

The next thing you know, the letter flew out the open window, right onto the street. Nathaniel started to giggle ecstatically. Toby shrieked and rushed downstairs to fetch the abused letter. But, alas, no matter how much he searched for it on the sidewalk and the road, it did not turn up anywhere. One could put one's firm faith in Toby: he was not about to tell his master, waking or sleeping, what had happened.

As for the reader, he is entitled to know that the letter fell directly onto a vehicle with prize-winning rabbits which were being sent home from a New York livestock breeding exhibition.

CHAPTER 28
ENTIRELY ON DRY LAND

The sun was roasting over Middletown, the birds singing, the trees bursting into leaf; in short, mother nature was keeping up to the dot with the calendar although it had to be confessed that it was becoming more and more difficult for the old woman every year.

The workshop in the woodworking factory was flooded with daylight. The cheerful giant, Michael Thingsmaster, wearing a work-apron and with a pipe in his mouth, was working away full steam with a wood plane, brushing the beads of sweat from his face. His curly blond hair was sticking to his forehead, his apron was fluttering like a sail, the wood shavings were flying with a whistling sound in all directions. A fine, smooth piece of work was emerging out of Michael Thingsmaster's hands and it winked at him with its two eyes:

Mike held it up to the light, admired it, pulled out his pipe and began to sing under his breath as he looked at his piece of work:

> With wooden lathe and plane and glue,
> We promise husbands fine for you.
> From workers' hands and craftsmen's too,
> Are born our daughters—such pretty things.
>
> Go forth on guard where foes do dwell,
> In banks and belle-etages as well,
> Return from there to tattle-tell
> About their regal lords and kings.

Everyone knows Thingsmaster's little melody. One after the other, the workers gathered around Mike, smiling and joining in the melody.

"Well, how're things, Mike? How's the Kressling intrigue proceeding?"

Thingsmaster held up a marvellous square box made from a rare Brazilian red tree.

"There it is, fellows," he said with a smile. "All that has to be done is to decorate it with carving and hand it over to the optical works where the technician Sorrow has already taken care of everything. They'll put it in and set it up and the thing'll be all ready!"

"Clever!" the workers burst into laughter. "And do the chemists know?"

"The chemists can be relied on. The daughter will never go against the father, never, just remember that, fellows."

"Do you know the secret, Mike?"

"Don't pester me, I won't tell you. Besides, brothers, it's not for our brains. The technician Sorrow is just making something more complicated in Latin."

The workers grabbed at their stomachs as they burst with laughter. But as though he had not noticed, Mike swept the wood shavings from his apron, put his cap on and went home to while away the half-hour assigned by Jack Kressling for the lunch break.

It had become melancholy in Thingsmaster's little house without the faithful Beauty. The cook placed a bowl of Thingsmaster's beloved "long-life stew" on the table, strained some watery beer into a mug and sat down to eat with him. Silently and quickly she ladled out spoonfuls into the bowl, but suddenly the attic window started to rattle.

"A pigeon!" Mike exclaimed and throwing down his spoon, he rushed up into the attic. In fact, one of Mike's messenger pigeons was flapping against the window. Opening the window wide, he caught the pigeon, stroked it and stuck his fingers into the little sack around its neck.

"Strange!" he muttered, letting the pigeon slip from his fingers. "No note either from Bisk or from Miss Totter."

He had barely managed to say that when another eight messenger pigeons flew one after the other through the attic window and settled down with affectionate cooing sounds on his shoulders and head. The pigeons were alive and well, the little sacks around their necks were perfectly in order but not one of them had brought Mike a letter.

"A disaster!" Mike exclaimed. He set the pigeons on their perches, watered and fed them, then ran off to the nearest radio station.

"Mend-mess!"

"Mess-mend! What's up, Mike?" The duty operator asked curtly as he busied himself with receiving the despatches.

"Send a radio message to the *Amelia*, old buddy."

"Sure. Who to?"

"The technician Sorrow. Tell him this: "Nine pigeons have returned without letters. I suspect a disaster. Beware of a substitution in Kronstadt."'

"It'll be taken care of, Mike. A big gamble, eh?"

"Life or death," Mike replied, putting two fingers to his cap and rushing headlong back to the factory.

The cook carefully ate her portion of the stew and glanced out the window to see whether Mike was coming. Then she sighed, scratched her ear and honestly divided the remainder of the stew into two portions, eating her portion and licking the spoon.

"We're poor people, but honest ones," she whispered under her breath, going outside and waiting for Mike. "He'll come back any moment now and eat his portion, exactly one-half."

However, Mike did not come even then. Sighing more loudly, the cook again divided the remainder into two equal halves and ate her portion without touching a single drop of her neighbor's. In this fashion she kept dividing and eating right up until dusk and not a single wooden spoonful remained of Mike's portion. Sighing, the cook cleared away the dishes and lay down to have a tiny nap.

Meanwhile Thingsmaster had pulled a hot crust of bread out from under his shirt and chewing it up on the go was carrying the coffer he had made back to his own little house to finish the unusual overtime work for Kressling: namely, to cover the rare wood with the finest carving, to bring to life a hundred-odd web-footed birds, hunting dogs, vixens, rabbits, fine steeds and hunters on horseback, in tall hats with feathers, in swirling capes, wearing hawking gloves. And to chisel out around the beasts and people a path, to plant it with the leaves of ferns, ashes, populars and oak, to place a hut off to the side. In short, to introduce such wonders, such fine bits of work that everyone would admire it and praise it. And to put in one corner two tiny letters that would be invisible to the human eye so that his fellow worker would look through a magnifying glass and say:

"How can you miss that clever devil of a Thingsmaster? Who besides him could think up a piece of work like that?!"

In order to dampen the powerful feeling of inner anxiety, Mike lit the lamp, started to work with a very fine chisel and purred his melody:

> On kulak's carts so richly laden,
> Upon the general's mighty gun,
> On all the rich man's source of fun,
> Our trademark travels through the land.
>
> For all our fathers' calloused pains,
> For all our want and bitter chains,
> Avenge yourselves in labor plain
> Creating marvels with your worker's hand.

CHAPTER 29
THE AMELIA UNDER FULL STEAM

The beautiful young woman wearing a veil and registered in the log under the name of Katya Ivanovna Vasilova, created a deep impression on the male population of the *Amelia*.

Captain MacKinley, the Irishman, took to stuffing his pipe with the best grade of tobacco. The navigation officer who usually walked around with baggy trousers, put on foot-straps. And Mr. Pell, the very same Mr. Pell who supplied gunpowder and spirits to the Indo-Chinese; spirits and the Bible to the Caliphs; spirits, the Bible, and beads to the New Zealanders; sal ammoniac, beads and the Bible to the Zulus; dried maize, milled maize, ground maize, maize in the form of rice and maize in the form of saccharine to the Russians (which led one of his colleagues to remark with refined wit: "There's your Ara-Massacre"*—this very same Mr. Pell, thin, sophisticated and red-haired, suddenly became talkative like a Russian emigrant.

Dressed in a sandy-colored linen suit, cleanly shaven with the exception of his cheeks where sufficient red hair had been allowed to grow in order to sport the so-called "Yankee style", Mr. Pell spent a great deal of time on the deck, gnawing at the golden knob of his walking stick. Mrs. Vasilova had only to appear anywhere and Mr. Pell would take the knob of his walking stick out of his mouth, use the point of the stick to touch the surrounding barrels, crates and sacks, name their contents, the number of kilos, the cost price per kilo, the retail price per kilo, the percentage of falsely designated weight, the percentage of falsely designated measure, the percentage of moisture acquired during the complete journey and, finally, the percentage of his own profit, calculating according to the general sum of heads or, to be precise, the number of customers' mouths. Mr. Pell called his speech a public lecture. With purely American self-restraint, he repeated it several times until he noticed that Mrs. Vasilova, stopping nearby, was listening carefully to what he was saying. Mr. Pell immediately removed his hat and bowed.

The young woman raised eyes the color of violets to him:

"Excuse me, sir, but you appear to be a specialist in the Russian people?" she asked with enchanting diffidence.

"Ah-ha!" Mr. Pell replied in a promising voice.

"Might it be possible (a timid glance and smile)... Might it be possible (the violet-colored eyes were fixed downward, on the tiny point of a delicate little shoe) for you to acquaint me with commonly used Russian expressions?"

"With the utmost willingness " Mr. Pell exclaimed, leaning on a crate of corn and pulling out a notebook. "Now, for your first orientation in a Russian city... you'll enter a restaurant and ask for the national dishes... Allow me, I'll read them to you," and Mr. Pell read through the list: "Cabbage soup, poorridge, fancakes, aigues..."

"No, no," Mrs. Vasilova interrupted him with a gentle sigh, "I would like to know words that are completely different and if possible, to ask you to write them down for me in English letters. For example, the word 'husband', then the words 'be careful'..."

"Ah-ha!" the American smiled sourly. "A very dangerous choice of words. In Russian the word for 'husband' is 'hashbean' or more familiarly, 'hashy', whereas your warning must be pronounced in the following fashion: 'Take careacute."'

"Thank you," the young woman declared sweetly, writing these words down in her little book. "Sir, I am Russian in origin but I have completely forgotten my native language. Especially after suffering from seasickness... Such a strange sickness, it has deprived me of the memory of events, people, time sequence..."

"Are you really suffering from seasickness?"

"At night in my cabin," Mrs. Vasilova said in embarrassment and went off after caressing Mr. Pell with an enchanting curtsy."

She had not gone ten steps when a strange groaning sound issued out of a crate of maize on the left. Shuddering, she retreated to the right, but from a box of maize standing there she now heard a clearly audible puffing sound. The frightened good-looking young woman ran directly into a pile of sacks and suddenly a heavy and suppressed sigh reached her ears and one of the sacks began to move unmistakably. By now it was far too much for her sensitive nerves. She covered her face with her hands and rushed down the companionway to her own cabin.

Mrs. Vasilova had a very elegant first-class cabin. Considering that the steamship *Amelia* was such an old and small wreck of a ship and relied more on cargo than on passengers, it was a very pretty cabin. Padded furniture was fastened to the floor; the mirror and coat-rack were screwed into the walls; there were carpets, rugs and curtains everywhere. The phoney Katya Ivanovna hurried to the couch, pulled off her stockings and threw both hands behind her head. Her chestnut brown locks which had come loose from her coiffure stretched in soft strands alongside her fresh, pale cheeks; her violet-colored eyes grew dark; her lips worked painfully.

Katya Ivanovna, or rather Vivian Orton, was thinking about what awaited her in Kronstadt. She was travelling to an insane country that Thingsmaster called mighty. She was travelling to a people whom Thingsmaster called brilliant. She had been thinking about this country and passionately wanted to see it. She was also thinking about the man whom she was supposed to meet in Kronstadt. This was Vasilov and she would go up to him and say: "Take careacute", but if it was Arthur Morlender, she would have to say to him in a tender voice.: "Hashy" and begin the horrible comedy—God willing, the final comedy of her life...

Vivian let her eyelashes droop tiredly. She was sick with a hatred that was destroying her more effectively than any poison could. But she had her own poison, a real poison, which would work like lightning and it was hidden in the mechanism of her tiny gold watch. Vivian was not about to kill Morlender with it, she was keeping this poison for herself. Vivian would uncover all the secrets of her enemy, she would read his thoughts entirely, she would get to know his plans and then turn him over to the people so that the Soviet people themselves could settle accounts with him, just as he deserved...

Her eyelashes fluttered and cruel wrinkles formed at the corners of her exquisite mouth.

A knock at the door. Vivian leapt up and her face immediately assumed its former naive expression.

"Who's there?"

The head of a short man poked itself into the cabin. It was the technician Sorrow. He entered at once, folded his hands behind his back and whispered in an upset voice:

"My dear Miss Orton, We received a radio message from New York, from Michael Thingsmaster..."

"And so?"

"Prepare yourself for the worst, Miss Orton, Mike suspects a disaster. He thinks that Vasilov has been killed and replaced by someone... By whom—I don't know.. In all probability, by Morlender, according to the plan of the plotters."

Vivian said nothing in response. Her hands were convulsively clenched into fists.

"And one thing more, my dear Miss, the *Amelia* is way behind schedule. We won't arrive in Kronstadt until tomorrow. And the *Torpedo* will arrive at the same time as us, or even earlier. We picked it up on the radio and learned that it has been running at top speed. It's gained two days."

"Fine," Vivian replied slowly. "Don't worry, Sorrow, my friend, I remember alll your instructions, I know my duty and I shall fulfill it."

CHAPTER 30
ARTHUR FACE-TO-FACE WITH THE READER

We left the *Torpedo* at that ill-fated moment when Bisk, the sailors, the wretched Dan, Picherga the Portuguese, the phoney Vasilov, the daughter of the senator and even the banker Westinghouse were seized with terror. Incidentally, not all of them for the same reason by any means. Leaving aside any psychological analysis, I must briefly name these reasons:

Westinghouse was terror-stricken because he was frightened by the senator's daughter.

The senator's daughter was terror-stricken because her final hope for finding the mask had disappeared.

Bisk was terror-stricken because he was perishing.

The sailors were terror-stricken because of a new, piercing shriek underneath the deck which augured of yet another corpse.

The Portuguese Picherga was in terror not so much because of the disappearance of Bisk as of the quantity of work which henceforth had fallen to his lot.

The wretched Dan's terror had established itself once and for all in his confrontation with Satan.

As far as the terror of the phoney Vasilov is concerned, it is impossible to discuss it in just a few words, and the careful development of this chapter, I trust, will gradually prepare the reader's understanding of it.

Mr. Arthur Morlender, since in fact this is who he was, had completely and unconditionally acquiesced to the will of the people who had despatched him. Life had ceased to interest him. He had decided to become the instrument of revenge and nothing more. He did not ask questions about anything and no one had volunteered anything other than cut and dried instructions: do this, that and the other.

For the first day he had sat patiently hidden in the narrow, black cabin from which apparently there was no way out. The wall would slide open and a mechanical conveyor would pass food and drink in to him. But when the *Torpedo* was one day's sail from New York, the very same conveyor had subsequently disgorged the shoes, trousers, waistcoat, jacket, collar, tie, cuff links, cuffs and other objects taken from the unfortunate Vasilov and still warm from his body.

Arthur Morlender had obediently put everything on. A short time later, an opening in the wall the size of a man had noiselessly slid open and a short man had entered the room wearing a mask and a monk's hooded cloak. With a sign he showed Morlender that he was supposed to sit down in front of a mirror and then he pulled out a variety of jars and small bottles, and with a black-gloved hand began to skillfully make him up to resemble Vasilov. It should be said, incidently, that the latter was not at all difficult, since the young Morlender and the communist Vasilov were amazingly similar to each other—a circumstance which had been taken into consideration by the plotters earlier. And so, the unfamiliar hand applied a thin layer of make-up, showed Arthur how to do this without his help and then the man in the hooded cloak disappeard without a word from where he had appeared.

At that very same moment, a dry voice that seemed familiar to Morlender, issued from the opening:

"The time has come for your performance, Mr. Morlender. From now on you are the communist Vasilov. You are Russian, but you have lived since childhood in the States and you do not know Russian. You will have to act quickly, cautiously, without vascillation. You will now receive money, poisons, and a weapon. Your basic task is to consolidate yourself at the principal Russian metallurgical factory in order to blow it up, while having simultaneously prepared explosions in other Russian centers of production, and to gain the confidence of the communist leaders in order to prepare for their mass destruction at a day to be determined by us. Conduct yourself tactfully. Perform your role with talent. The League of Imperialists has invested its complete trust in you."

With these words the voice fell silent and through the opening he was handed an imposing wad of Soviet money, a small bottle of poison, several tablets which were unfamiliar to Arthur, a small box with pale blue capsules and a noiseless American automatic pistol of the newest construction.

He had barely time to gather his wits from everything he had heard when the floor beneath him began to rock slowly and descend. In a moment the movement ceased, a dry grating sound was heard overhead. Arthur looked around and discovered himself in Vasilov's cabin where everything was located in the very same order as when the unfortunate American communist had been alive. The door to the cabin was half-open.

Morlender locked it with a key, went up to the mirror and examined himself from head to toe. Then he stuck his hands into his pockets pulled out all of Vasilov's documents and set about studying them attentively. There were quiet a few of them—a party booklet, a police certificate, letters and recommendations from New York communists. And there were the envelopes addressed to Russian officials. And a letter from Petrograd where he, Anton Vasilov, had been invited by the chief engineer at the Putilov Works. And there was—what the devil was that?!

Morlender held a crushed ball of paper in his hands, with letters scratched illiterately in pencil on it. When he finally was able to decipher its contents, an angry shriek almost burst forth from the breast of the phoney Vasilov.

He wanted, like one possessed, to pound on the walls with his fists, but no one would have responded and not a single crack would have opened up! Nothing but silence around him. The storm was seething outside the window. Morlender fell with terror into a chair.

He was prepared to do anything, only not this. He was ready to sacrifice his own life twenty times over in order to wipe from the face of the earth those treacherous people who had killed his father. But to have a wife... To have a stubborn and illiterate wife by the name of Katya Ivanovna, who out of pure stubbornness was travelling on a different steamship and would be waiting for him in Kronstadt!... It was impossible for, Arthur Morlender, this mighty misogynist, to cope with the terror in whose grip he now found himself.

For a long while he sat as if crucified. But little by little his thoughts gained clarity.

Ultimately, the plotters knew what they were doing and, perhaps, he would need this same Katya Ivanovna as a helper... Moreover—Morlender glanced out the porthole—the storm showed no sign of abating and the *Torpedo* was being tossed about like a chip. Was there not some hope that the leaky old *Amelia* would disintegrate into smithereens from the force of the storm before it ever arrived in Kronstadt? And, finally, Arthur Morlender had the right to defend his freedom. He... aha! Now there was a brilliant idea. He had experienced a serious bout of seasickness that had totally upset his spiritual equanimity. He had to rest, he did not have the strength to fulfill his conjugal obligations, he had lost his memory for many things, for names, for events in the past. He would have to act distracted and irritable. He would not let her open her mouth, damn it!.. All the same, better a fictitious wife than a real one, if fate had seen fit to make him a married man...

Despite this entire flood of prudent ideas, Arthur Morlender felt himself to be anything but calm.

For the remainder of the entire journey, he attempted on many occasions to contact the mysterious people who were directing his fate.

Several times a day he would ask for Captain Gregoire, but neither the Captain, nor the plotters, gave any further signs of life from themselves. He was left to his own devices.

The storm abated, the *Torpedo* slowly entered the Finnish Gulf.

The phoney Vasilov stood on the deck of the steamship, nervously examining the outlines of Kronstadt floating closer through his binoculars. The weather was cold, a biting northeasterly wind was blowing.

The navigation officer Kovalkovsky was running about the deck with an angry face. Damn this country! They actually had to put into a port where you would not find a single decent person and where workers headed the government.

Meanwhile, in the boiler room, in the engine room, in the kitchen, in the wheelhouse, excitement was also reigning, and the closer the steamship approached land, the more and more powerful that excitement became.

"And I'm telling you, brothers," Xavier was holding forth, pale with excitement. "Here we are sitting, you and I, sweating blood, and that pig of a navigation officer, to say nothing about the redhead, can go ahead and punch you in the teeth any old time, whereas there, my boys, ho, ho, ho! There our brother worker is number one. There the admiral himself comes from the ordinary sailors and walks arm-in-arm with the stoker, that's the way it is!"

"And in the factories the workers are the directors!" the Portuguese Picherga shouted through his clenched teeth.

"Get to work, you bastards! I'll give it to you!" Kovalkovsky's voice screeched from up above. "And I don't want any of you showing your mugs to the shore, understand?"

Grumbling, the sailors dispersed to their places.

Kronstadt. The deserted embankment passed before Arthur's binoculars (from now on we will call him Vasilov). The *Torpedo* moved closer and closer. In the misty northern sky, like specters, ranged the distant towers, peaks and cupolas of Petrograd.

Then they came to a stop.

The ramp was lowered.

Kovalkovsky, the navigation officer, with a malicious look on his face, showed Vasilov the way off. The steamship seemed dead, there was not a living soul anywhere.

But when Vasilov, with suitcase in hand, climbed down in the company of a handsome Russian Red Army soldier and two customs officials, the sailors from the *Torpedo* could bear it no longer: they streamed out in a crowd onto the deck, with Xavier at their head, and began to holler, all of them, regardless of who they were—American, Germans, Italians, Portuguese, Frenchmen, Abyssinians, Englishmen, Swiss, Jamaicans:

"Hurrah! All right, Russian comrades!"

"Well done, boys!" shouted the Red Army soldier, turning around.

"Greetings to the American workers."

Both sides felt a surge of enthusiasm although the words they were uttering were incomprehensible to both one and the other. Navigation officer Kovalkovsky, like a lion lying in ambush, jumped into the thick of his sailors.

Meanwhile, several young people in military outfits approached Vasilov, exchanged greetings with him in perfect English and introduced themselves as his future party comrades. One of them politely brought forth someone from behind barrels piled in a heap and said:

"Your wife has been waiting for you since morning, comrade Vasilov."

The wretched Vasilov gave a shudder, turned cold, raised his eyes and...

CHAPTER 31
YANKEES IN PETROGRAD

Instead of a cantankerous and stubborn woman who was full to overflowing with vices, a beautiful woman stood before Vasilov. She glanced at him, stammered and gave him her icy little fingers.

The people in military caps led them to an automobile, seated them, one jumped in beside the driver, the others raised their hands to say good-bye and the automobile dashed towards Petrograd.

Vasilov watched his wife distractedly. He would have gladly fastened his mind on any flaw of hers in order to stir up his hatred. But Katya Ivanovna was distressingly appealing, distressingly perfect. Every movement of hers was full of grace, her voice resembled the warbling of a flute; she did not say or do anything out of place, nothing of the sort that would have justified his contempt.

Meanwhile, the magnificent streets of Petrograd whizzed past them. They did not resemble in the slightest the tumble-down hovels depicted in the New York street newspapers. Palatial houses stood in rows, mirrored in the green water of the canals. The automobiles and motorcycles darted back and forth, motorboats ran up and down the canals, and the pedestrians scurried along the street with amazing speed. Vasilov and his wife barely had time to take their eyes off each other before they were rivetted on their surroundings.

"How different it is!" Vasilov muttered. "Dear Sir, that is, comrade, how different all this is to the photographs in our American newspapers!"

The man in the military jacket smiled cheerfully.

"My name is Evgeny Barfuss. You'll find a great deal that's different from what the capitalists write about us. We would have perished long ago, my dear comrades, if we hadn't put several inventions into operation... Do you see those towers there?"

They were now dashing along the embankment of the tumultuous Moika which was sending its waves rolling through the entire city.

To the left and right of the Moika ranged strange pyramids decorated on top with enormous porcelain cups that made them resemble candle-holders. A network of endless wires stretched from the pyramids over the entire city.

"What is it?" Vasilov blurted out.

"These are electrical transformers of colossal powers," replied comrade Barfuss. "This is our pride and joy that you're looking at. Thanks to these transmitters we are able to electrify in a split-second the entire space above a city to a height of more than a thousand meters which makes us inaccessible to any enemy air force. When information reached us about the Americans inventing a kind of explosive material, we, in our turn, also busied ourselves with technical matters. But our purpose is not to attack, but to defend. We have electrified enormous air spaces over all of our cities and production sites. Explosive materials will be discharged above us without inflicting the least amount of damage to our country. We have fortified our borders with thousands of electrical batteries, thanks to which we can repel any army with the help of but a single electrician from our Petrograd Central Aero-Electrical station. And we are making newer discoveries in this direction all the time!"

At that moment Vasilov felt truly like the son of Jeremy Morlender.

"Yes!" He blurted out with no lack of enthusiasm. "Here in Russia, you're certainly not dozing away. But tell me then, how can such a simple, average engineer like myself be of use to you?"

A grin slid across the face of comrade Barfuss.

"Dear comrade Vasilov, we need people like you more than anyone else, you see..."

He leaned over to Vasilov's ear and continued with a smile:

"Because we have almost no average people here. No one wants to be an average person. The times have made superhuman demands on us— to keep giving more and more, to raise the average human norm. But this norm is necessary to maintain an equilibrium. Now you understand why you are such a welcome guest for us!"

Vasilov bit his lip from a certain amount of injured pride. At that moment the automobile braked in front of a palatial building on Moika

Street. Comrade Barfuss gave him his hand and said:

"A room has been set aside for you in this building. Have a rest. In two hours a motorcycle will be given to you for your first trip to the factory."

The driver placed both suitcases on the ground and Vasilov distractedly picked up one and the other. They walked through the entrance, climbed the stairs, and guided by the directions of everyone they met, they finally reached their room. It was a very comfortable bedroom with two beds, a stove in one corner, two writing desks, two book shelves, two windows and two inscriptions on two walls:

Be mindful of time!
Join the League of Time!

"An amazing country!" Katya Ivanovna whispered. They glanced at each other and suddenly remembered that during that entire hour they had not thought about themselves or about the revenge that had brought them this far.

CHAPTER 32
HUSBAND, WIFE AND DOG

Katya Ivanovna blushed as she caught herself in mid-thought. Vasilov blushed for the very same reason. With irritation he flung his hat on one of the beds, sat down and announced:

"After your behaviour in New York, Kate, I imagine that you don't have any expectations of affection from me!"

Katya Ivanovna remained silent and turned her back to him.

"I should forewarn you," Vasilov continued in despair, "seasickness has had a severe effect on me. I got on the ship as one person, but left it as a completely different one..."

"Of course!" the young woman snapped caustically.

"What are you muttering?" Vasilov grew confused. "You must understand me once and for all. I cannot refuse you any comradely attention, but I am dead as far as anything else is concerned. I came here in order to work and... I am positively begging you, Kate, to leave me in peace!"

He sighed with relief, looked around and noticing a fine Chinese screen in a corner, dragged it into the middle of the room.

"You and I will divide the territory in a friendly fashion. That part of the room over there is yours. Take that bed for yourself, and that wall, that desk, and that placard, in short, everything which is on that side of the boundary, and organize yourself there as you please. And I likewise will be completely free over here!"

He set up the screen, fencing off his corner from Katya Ivanovna's eyes, tossed off his jacket and stretched out on the bed with pleasure.

"I've cut her short right at the outset!" he thought with a certain amount of self-satisfaction. "Now just let her try to start anything. It would be interesting to know whether all these novelists who sing the praises of love and beautiful women, whether they do so with genuine sincerity? I am almost certain that they are simply getting themselves worked up over the thought of their honorarium."

With this purely American conclusion, he closed his eyes and pretended to doze off.

Abandoned in her territory, Katya Ivanovna remained motionless for a few moments. Her two tiny, delicate ears, peeking out from beneath her chestnut-colored locks of hair, had turned crimson. Morlender's words and behavior had been precisely the kind to arouse all the fury of hatred in her heart. Her teeth clenched, hands balled into fist , she mentally reviewed the entire plan of strategy which she had thought out while she had still been on the steamship, then she tossed her curls, ran her hand over her face and—stepped across the enemy's border.

Vasilov heard the light steps, opened his eyes and at that very moment slender fingers appeared right beside his very cheeks. The unbearable Katya Ivanovna was sitting on the edge of his bed, her feet dangling over the edge as though nothing were amiss, she was gazing serenely at him with her violet-colored eyes.

"What do you wish?" he muttered impatiently. "I thought I had been completely frank with you."

"Of course!" she replied and laughed, purling just like a flute on its tendermost note. "But, dearest Tony, after all you didn't wait for my response. You must hearr the other side out..."

"The devil with her, that's quite logical," Vasilov thought to himself and pulled the blanket right up under his chin.

"Yes, you must hear me out," she continued, running her hand absent-mindedly over his face and diligently smoothing out every wrinkle on his forehead with her finger. "The thing is that seasickness... oh, that damned seasickness! It has made a completely new person of me as well. I don't even recognize myself. I'm guilty before you, dearest, I know that... But never, never again..."

Katya Ivanovna wiped a tiny pearl from her eyelashes and laid her head right on the chest of the dumbfounded Vasilov.

"I feel so wretched, Tony! You mustn't scold me any more. And then..." She stammered.

Vasilov lay there, involuntarily inhaling the fragrance of her hair and looking at the pink little tip of her ear.

"I must admit," he thought to himself, "that among the zoological individuals bearing the designation of women, she is rather an inoffensive example."

"I can only whisper this in your ear," Katya Ivanovna continued to purl. "Turn your head."

She brushed his ear with her lips, waited for a few moments during which he experienced a state which he mentally described as "fairly tolerable" and then she whispered:

"Tony, it looks as though I'm about to present you with a baby."

Damn it! If a galvanic stream had been poured into his ear, Vasilov would not have leapt up higher than he did at that moment. He flew off the bed, flung the pillow into one corner, the blanket into another, and began to stamp his bare feet in a fury.

"The devil! The devil alone knows what's going on!" he started to shout with a completely distorted face. "I'm sending you back to New York! I'll hand you over to the law! Leave me alone!"

Katya Ivanovna turned pale and raised her hands as though she were protecting herself from a blow. Her lips squeezed tightly like flower petals. She stood before him—the incarnation of purity, innocence and despair—and gazed at him with such wide, such helpless eyes, that Vasilov suddenly fell silent, waved his hand and sought refuge in the other half of the room.

"What am I going to do?" he thought in a frenzy. "It's as clear as day that she's the real wife of Vasilov... She suspects nothing... and just the way she contrived, despite all the quarrels... A vile, scatterbrained, criminal woman! To make love to this vulgar communist!.."

The stream of his thoughts were making such capricious zigzags that as the author I would have been completely out of my mind if it had gone on for a long while yet. Fortunately, he stepped smartly up to Katya Ivanovna and without looking her in the eye, declared in an official voice:

"I deny, categorically deny, that this is my child! You can do as you wish. I wash my hands."

With these words he put on his shoes, jacket, hat, glanced at his watch and went out in order to have a stroll in front of the house on Moika Street in the hope of finding anyone who could save him from a hateful *tête-à-tête* with Katya Ivanovna.

Katya Ivanovna watched him go with a cruel smirk on her lips. She was satisfied with herself. And as for him, that pitiful little boy with an eccentric nature, he was weak, distracted, hot-tempered, impatient, witless, stubborn and nervous, just like Jeremy Morlender. And it was just as easy to wind him around her little finger as the old man Westinghouse...

But this beautiful young woman who was so satisfied with herself, then behaved with purely feminine illogicality. After the cruel smirk, her eyes began to glitter with despair, she went up to her bed and suddenly fell on the pillow and burst into tears.

"Knock-knock, scratch-scratch..."

What were those strange sounds at the door? Someone was poking at it with their blunt muzzle, scratching with claws, gnawing on a hinge... Katya Ivanovna raised her head and listened.

"Ruff! Arf! Ruff!" The sound now came quite clearly from behind the door. Then a few more dull thuds, scratching, whining, and the door blew wide open in front of some kind of shapeless, enormous clump of fur and dirt which burst into the room like a whirlwind.

A second later, the filthy clump, like a ball, flew directly onto Katya Ivanovna's bed, started to wag it tail furiously, embraced her and licked her on the mouth, nose and chin.

"Beauty!" the young woman cried. "Beauty! Beauty!"

Yes, it was in fact her, Michael Thingsmaster's faithful Beauty, but what a sight!! Scruffy, wild-looking, dishevelled and so filthy that her fur was matted in clumps. She whined and kept poking her nose at Katya Ivanovna, circled around the room, sniffing every corner.

Finally, calming down, Beauty sat down at her feet, laid her paw on her knees and fixed her expressive eyes on Katya Ivanovna.

"How did you get here, Beauty?" Mrs. Vasilova asked.

Beauty whined and waggled her paw. Only then did the young woman notice the filthy striped scrap of material covered with dark spots on her paw. She carefully undid it, went up to the window and examined the spots covering it. They resembled blood. She was intrigued by the symmetry of their positioning. Having spread the scrap out on the window-sill, she read one letter after the other:

"Bisk. *Torpedo*."

The dog watched her with intelligent eyes. As soon as Katya Ivannvna turned once more to her, she started to wag her tail and began to tear her collar from her neck with her forepaws, making curious motions.

"Is there something else, Beauty?"

But of course, there was sure to be something else there. Push her head back, reach your hand behind the collar and tear loose the envelope which had been tied there with great ingenuity so that a dog's paw would find it difficult to rip it free, nor would not be able to reach it with its nose or teeth! That's it. Now open it. Read it!"

Katya Ivanovna tore the letter free in silence, unsealed it and read:

To the Attorney General of the State of Illinois

Most Esteemed Sir,

If you have already received my preceding letter and have retrieved the package from my secret hiding-place, you will not be uninterested to learn of the sequel to the Morlender affair. In my hands I hold all of its threads. I have been placed in a lunatic asylum and there is no better place from which to investigate the principal criminal. You will understand what I mean if you demand the release from cell No. 132 of the lunatic *Robert Druck*.

CHAPTER 33
AID FOR THE STARVING AND THE ATTENDANT CIRCUMSTANCES

Whereas the *Torpedo* disembarked Vasilov, sealed itself up like a medieval knight in armor and made off into the heart of the gulf, the silent and sullen *Amelia* spent all day and much of the night unloading its goods.

Mister Pell, with his walking stick in hand, was running hither and yon, periodically letting fly with his entire vocabulary of Russian words. Sacks, barrels, crates swung from the deck to the shore, and from there they were transferred to enormous trucks. The technician Sorrow, who was under orders from Mr. Pell, was observing the work with his hands folded behind his back.

At that very moment, from a barrel which stood alongside him, there came a drawn-out sigh. Sorrow listened more closely and tapped the barrel with his foot.

"Hey!" came the sound from the barrel. "Hey, Sorrow, old buddy! Mend-mess!"

It had been spoken in the clearest language for the technician Sorrow. With lightning-like quickness he glanced around and whispered in response: "Mess-mend"... and knocked out the bottom of the barrel. A familiar head immediately popped out to greet Sorrow, followed by a neck, and shoulders, and then the body with various other appendages, and out of the barrel leapt an agile Laurie Lane, thin, cheerful and dishevelled.

"Sorrow! Some bread and shot of whiskey!" he whispered to him in a pleading voice. "I tell you it was just like the life of that there Greek, what's his name, Diogenes, who was devilishly deprived of all comforts, especially the way I was sealed in."

Sorrow gave him some bread, hid him behind a barricade of sacks and crates, put his hands behind his back and declared sternly:

"You'd better explain to me now, Laurie Lane, why the goodness you stuck yourself in one of Hoover's barrels and cast off on the *Amelia* without asking Mike?"

"And what about you?" Laurie asked, chewing his bread with the force of millstones.

"You know quite well that I left on Mike's orders in order to investigate those fascist dogs."

"Well, I came to work for Soviet Russia!" Laurie replied unperturbed and stuck the final crust of bread into his mouth. And if you want to give me a hand in that, Sorrow, old friend, then don't wait a single moment. By the way..." Laurie stammered and turned red as a beet. "By the way, I'd like to know, Sorrow, what you've done with Miss Orton, that is, Mrs. Vasilova?"

"So that's it!" drawled Sorrow significantly. "You're a fine one, I'll say, Lauriee Lane, metalworker!" There's no way of knowing what Laurie, turning an even deeper crimson, would have replied to him, because a strange cracking sound suddenly came from a neighboring crate.

"Cre-eak, cre-eak!" Came the strange sounds from the crate. Sorrow frowned, walked up to the crate and pounded on it with all his might.

"Sorrow, mend-mess!" came the pitiful sound from there.

Laurie and the technician Sorrow, exchanged glances, tore the lid off the crate and before their eyes appeared the esteemed carpenter Willings, all scrunched up in the shape of an English lock and looking at them with pitiful, starving eyes.

"Willings!" Laurie exclaimed.

"Willings! It's you!" the technician Sorrow let escape in despair.

"It's me, fellows, really me! It can now be said that I've experienced the worst possible thing we can expect in this world: being hermetically sealed in, no more no less! After that I'm not even afraid of death, no, not a single bit afraid of death, any kind of death at all, even the plague."

"Stop philosophizing," Sorrow replied sullenly, "better you tell me how you, a pillar of our Union, the staid fellow, Willings, how you could copy a young lad like Lane and jump in a crate for the sake of a skirt?"

"No, Sorrow, no, not for a skirt! You're wrong!" Willings replied angrily. "Brother, I may have come in a crate, but I've got all my documents, just as official as any of your old dopelimats. Kressling himself sent me, brothers, to watch and report... As far as the skirt is concerned, well, brother, I've seen Miss Orton in our Laurie's trousers and whether she's got Laurie's trousers on or a drum case or the esteemed banner of Boston University, well I'd follow her whereever she wanted, may I be struck down on the spot if it ain't so!"

"That's right!" someone declared beside him.

All three gave a start and turned around in every direction. But there was not a soul around, and the stevedores were bustling about way off in the distance, in the company of Mr. Pell.

"That's right," someone repeated once more, and a sack that was lying at the technician Sorrow's feet, abruptly altered its shape.

"The devil with you, whoever you are," the technician said, giving the sack a whack with his open hand. "I'll pack you off to the bakeshop and we'll let them figure out over there what to bake out of you, you no-good loafer, coward, deserter!"

"Don't do that, Sorrow," the bag declared, ripped itself in half and out of it emerged no other than Ned.

"Just as I thought," Laurie burst into laughter, "Well, boys, now our whole team's here in person. We saved her from the Hudson, so that means it's preordained for us to stay right on her heels."

"We'll see about that," grumbled Sorrow. "First of all I'll take you to get yourselves registered, boys, and then I'll fix you up with some work. You can breathe the same air as Miss Orton if you like, but I am firmly forbidding you to see her."

"You can't do that!" Laurie exclaimed.

"You can't do that!" Willings lowed.

"You can't do that!" Ned hissed.

And as though to bear their words out, suddenly there appeared on the embankment a tall, thin figure in a white outfit, in a halo of chestnut curls. And following on her heels, a big, shaggy, filthy dog, wagging its tail. The figure was looking all around from under a little white hand until suddenly she noticed the technician Sorrow and our three friends. The she gave a joyful cry, clapped her hands and rushed towards them as fast as her legs could carry her. In two leaps the dog overtook her and hurled itself at the technician Sorrow's feet, started to whine and pounded its tail in a frenzy.

"I'll be damned if it isn't Beauty!" the stunned techician blurted out and with all his might squeezed the stained and scruffed-up dog in his embrace, leaving his comrades to address similar emotions to Miss Orton.

CHAPTER 34
MISTER VASILOV IN
THE LAND OF MIRACLES

Vasilov leapt out of the entryway, trying not to think about anything. But, after lighting up a cigarette and making two or three turns in front of the house, he calmed down and busied himself with an investigation of the surrounding area. The house in which they had been billetted was of an ancient construction, probably dating from the times of Peter the Great. The original core had been rebuilt several times and because of the multitude of architectural styles seemed unattractive although grandiose. It had been turned into a dormitory for artists and writers. Newly arrived communists were also placed here. Almost at every entryway stood an automobile and with a purring sound motorcycles were constantly arriving on the fly. He had not managed to go more than a few steps when his attention was attracted to a woman beggar.

It was an old woman in a dress full of holes, wearing men's boots and with a piece of window curtain over her head. Her face was so creased, drawn and flabby that it looked more like a piece of leather than a human face. Her eyes were white from age and seemed vacant. She was standing motionless and the passers-by were throwing money of their own accord into her outstretched palm. He hardly had time to look her over when a tall greyheaded man emerged through a gateway, his face disfigured by dark spots and with two walleyes that were barely visible beneath his thick grey brows. He came out limping, looked around in all directions, and without noticing Vasilov, quickly went up to the old woman. Imagine the surprise of Vasilov when the old man respectfully kissed her hand, gave her the most courtly bow and pronounced in exquisite English:

"And how is your rheumatism, Princess?"

"Oh, I'm not complaining," the beggar woman replied coquettishly. "I trust you have read the last speech of our beloved monarch?"

"Indeed, I have, and I carry it in my heart!"

"Still on guard?"

"Still on guard!"

After the exchange of formal salutations, the old man ran limping back through the gateway, and the old woman froze in her former pose.

"A fine place where the beggars resemble courtiers," Vasilov muttered and moved further on, looking and listening. At that moment an automobile sporting a red flag came flying out onto the street. Two ordinary workers in patched jackets were sitting in it, carrying on a lively conversation about something with an imposing looking man in a military uniform. No sooner was the automobile noticed on the street than the pedestrians raised their hats and many shouted something by way of greeting.

"Must be an important person in the city," thought Vasilov, "it's funny that he travels about with ordinary workers."

At that moment the automobile which had been flying along with all its might, came to a halt as though rooted to the spot.

"What's happened? Who could interfere with the passage of such an important person in the city?" Vasilov continued to muse as he looked all around the practically deserted street. Well, how do you like that! Crossing the street were several pairs of tiny children dressed in identical poor clothing and wearing identical caps on their shaven heads. They were being led by a plain woman in glasses who resembled a quaker. She was waving her arms energetically and as she led the last pair of her charges right under the nose of the automobile, she gave the chauffeur a majestic wave of her hand after which he started the car. In truth, it was an extraordinary spectacle! Poor, homeless children were walking like the offspring of an English peer or American billionaire, blocking the way of an important person in the city...

Vasilov shrugged and hastened his step, passing the tumultuous Moika. He found himself in a gloomy square built up with old, dark buildings with grey walls that were mouldy and peeling.

"This must be a hangout for crime and poverty, just like in all big cities!" he thought to himself fingering his wallet in his pocket and cautiously moving on farther. As though to confirm his words, curious people began to converge on the gloomy square from all directions. Dressed in old, discolored clothing, in chintz kerchiefs and vizor caps, they walked in a throng, carrying some strange objects in their hands. And what was the most amazing thing of all was that these people were almost entirely elderly folk. Grey-headed and wrinkled, with dark calloused hands, some of them hunched over, others limping, some leaning on a cane, some stomping along on a wooden stump instead of a leg.

"Invalids? Criminals? Beggars?!" Vasilov did not know what to think. Meanwhile the passers-by began to enter one of the houses. There was no doorman at the door, nor even a watchman. Vasilov mixed in with the mob, slipped through the door and began to walk up the staircase.

"Now I'll find out what kind of hangout this is," he thought with the curiosity of a tourist. Meanwhile they entered a large, bright room which was equipped with tables and benches. An enormous blackhoard hung on the wall. On a low platform stood a man in a blue shirt. The people who entered, slid along the benches and sat down beside one another and ley before themselves objects they had brought with them and which resembled prayerbooks. The man in the blue shirt raised his hand.

"Aha!" thought Vasilov. "This is some kind of religious sect. It must mean that here too they have something resembling our own unbearable New York pharisees. The preacher is going to begin his sermon... How boring! I'm leaving!"

He did not manage to do so before the men and women had opened their booklets which resembled prayerbooks and the man in the blue shirt had written on the board in chalk... the large letter "A".

Vasilov looked around on all sides. The faces of the people around him were gleaming with the most genuine attentiveness, their foreheads were furrowed, their mouths half-opened, repeating the letter which had been written on the board, while the prayerbooks lying open before these candidates for another world proved to be nothing other than ABC books!

This Vasilov could not bear. He leapt up and ran out onto the street; he was choking from amazement. Turning around towards the door, he was able to decipher with the greatest difficulty the mysterious title on the sign: "School for the Liquidation of Illiteracy".

"A mad people!" he exclaimed in English. Teaching the alphabet to old people! And they're learning, damn it, and it seems they're even learning with pleasure!"

"Excuse me, sir, are you English?" Someone asked him in English as they bent right over his ear.

Vasilov shot a quick glance and saw a big man, tall like an athlete, with military bearing, the grey moustache of a general and the smart uniform of a commanding officer. He was standing beside Vasilov on the pavement, watching the columns of cavalry soldiers riding through the square in orderly formation.

"Yes," Vasilov answered automatically, "I'm a tourist... This is my first time in the country."

"Do you mind telling me why you were so soundly amazed?"

"I was amazed at the mad behavior of the old people who are learning the alphabet in this building over here on the right."

"Oh, sir, that is one of the methods of rejuvenation which we are practicing," the commander replied with a smile. "I myself took an examinatian in political literacy not long ago. And I can go as far as to assure you that I would not trade either my cavalry or my Red Guardsmen for any other army in the world,—that's how pleasant it's been for me to begin my life anew."

He placed two fingers to his cap, bowed politely to Vasilov and climbed onto his motorcycle.

Hatred and amazement mingled in Vasilov. He watched the cavalry pass by, prancing on their way through the square, and then he turned back towards Moika Street. By the entryway where their quarters were located, two men in military jackets were standing, gazing about in every direction. One of them was Evgeny Barfuss. The other, tall, gray-eyed, with a pipe in his mouth, was a stranger to Vasilov. Both immediately came up to him, Barfuss took him by the arm, the tall man introduced himself:

"Rebrov," and signaled to an automobile to drive up.

"Comrade Rebrov will drive you to the Putilov Works, we've been waiting ten minutes for you," Barfuss said hurriedly. "You'll receive all necessary explanations from him, he is your immediate superior."

With these words, Barfuss raised his fingers to his cap, climbed onto a motorcycle and disappeared like a bolt of lightning.

The phoney Vasilov climbed into the automobile, Rebrov jumped in after him, the driver took the wheel and they drove off from the living quarters.

Arthur gave his neighbor a sideways glance. He was a well-built muscular man with a face that looked young for his age, with stern, thin lips and a refined line to his chin. His ears were small, almost without lobes.

"The aristocrats haven't died out yet in this land of the workers and peasants," Vasilov thought ironically. "I'll lay odds that my supervisors are the offspring of those ancient generations that used to flog their serfs."

"Comrade," he turned to him. "You must have worked at the Putilov Works earlier?"

Rebrov removed his pipe from his mouth and replied in good English:

"You guessed it."

"Where did you study to be an engineer? It must have been in England?"

"You guessed right again," Rebrov smiled. "If what I did in England can be called 'studying to be an engineer', then I studied in England."

Vasilov thought for a few moments how to renew his questioning. But before he could open his mouth, Rebrov tapped out his pipe, stuck it into his pocket with a quick motion, turned to Vasilov a face that was so striking in its refinement and subtlety, and began in a friendly voice:

"You see, I'm a greaser at the Putilov Works, but my father was a carpenter at the same Works. When I was seventeen I was sent off to Siberia, I escaped to England and managed to learn a few things there working as a stoker for Parkins in Birmingham. The fellows elected me as the director after the Revolution. Well, my skills were of some use."

"What the devil!" thought Vasilov, bringing up the devil at least for the hundredth time that day. "I can't understand this country even if thirty of the German Baedeker guides described it in thirty different languages. I refuse to try and understand it."

They were now flying along a broad avenue fringed with marvellous linden trees. The fleet-footed pedestrians were scurrying back and forth. The palatial buildings gave way to shady gardens with canals and ponds dug out in them, and finally, off in the distance, in a blue and completely cloudless sky, the gigantic outlines of thousands of factory chimneys of varying length, breadth and shape began to loom up. It was an entire forest of protuberances towering up to the sky, resembling puffed-out lips, but emitting an unusually fine amount of smoke and leaving no trace of their breath in the sky.

"Our factory district," Rebrov began, pointing in that direction with his finger. "We have concentrated all of our production in one place. Previously, Petrograd was encircled on all four sides by factories under operation, but now we have transferred them to this hilly area and converted them into an experimental research division. In essence, you are entering an industrial museum, an industrial school, an industrial academy, that's what the old Putilov Works have become here. Take a look over here: you see these three rings that resemble three stories in a building?"

Vasilov looked where Rebrov was pointing and saw a strange spectacle: down below, enclosed by a stone wall, ran the ring of the first tier. Spiral staircases proceeded upward from it to the circle of the second tier which was also enclosed by a wall. At the very top of the extremely light, refined, compact architecture, which reminded one of a wooden structure, arose the third ring which was crowned by the wings of wind turbines, landing platforms for aircraft, an aerial network for communications and an entire sea of red flags fluttering within this network of chimneys and wires like crimson poppies in the midst of ears of wheat. This spectacle, with all of its dizzying profusion of colors and symmetry, cast a powerful spell over Vasilov.

"Do you really call this a factory district?" he exclaimed in amazement. "It looks more like an international exhibition!"

"You didn't let me finish," Rebrov smiled. "Here before you is the triumph of the method of economic indivisibility, still in its experimental-scientific state. You will have to study it in order to work together with us. Take a look down there, to the first circle: it encompasses the river bank of the Neva, tracts of Finnish granite, peat moss bogs on the west, a portion of forest on the east. Located down there for us are the raw resources. These Toksovsky Highlands which come down to us all the way from the Finnish border, contain the richest minerals, valuable timber, pitch, all the imaginable mineral resources which we require. The gigantic wall around the first tier serves as an electrical transmitter for the colossal electrical energy from the Volkhov Power Station which helps in blasting out the mineral wealth and transporting it higher up to the second tier. Take a look a little higher," continued Rebrov, moving from his spot and pointing straight ahead for Vasilov while putting his other arm around Vasilov's shoulders. "Take a look over there: that's the second ring. There we have the processing industry. Do you see the smoke and glare from the enormous blast furnaces, do you hear the clanging of the iron cogs, the whine of the saws, the grinding of the wheels, the din of the engines? There the raw materials become processed materials, nature's gifts are transformed into the products of work. And still higher—raise your eyes—the crown of this entire industrial settlement is the manufacturing industry which makes the manufactured goods out of all this material and churns them out onto thousands of our elevated transport conveyors leading into the city, the port, the surrounding areas and to the trunkline railway stations..."

"Marvellous!" Vasilov exclaimed, again feeling himself the son of the engineer Morlender. "I am proud that I've come to work with you. But, comrade, I don't see what the sense of your method of economic indivisibility is, other than a territorial integration of all areas of production?"

"What the sense of our indivisible method is? You haven't seen that yet, although you already have a premonition of it. Comrade Enno, the supervisor for the method will tell you about that. Here he is, by the entrance to the settlement. He's already seen us and is waving to us."

The driver braked, Vasilov and Rebrov jumped out onto the granite slabs of the road and walked forward to meet the blond-haired, almost albino man with pink cheeks and shining blue eyes who looked simultaneously like an old man and a child.

"Welcome, dear comrade," he said in the most pleasant voice, holding out his hand to Vasilov. "We'll go to the factory by a roundabout way and I'll give you a little guided tour."

Meanwhile, comrade Rebrov, nodding to them, had already leapt onto some kind of platform, fastened a metal ring around his wrist and before Vasilov could say anything to him, was already flying off on the mobile platform into he depths of a stone corridor.

"Let's go, my friend, let's go," the red-cheeked man said tenderly as he took Vasilov by the arm. "You and I will make the long way on our own two feet because it's always been more useful for a person to find out something new through a certain amount of effort rather than by entertaining ease."

He also spoke English, but with a slight accent. Leading Vasilov out onto a granite balcony, he directed his attention down below, to a vast area of fields planted with the most varied of crops. From the wet quadrangles of the rice plantation to the arid bamboo fields, from the Icelandic moss to the coconut tree groves— there was everything here. Various people were working in each field, representatives were here from all nations and all peoples.

"Don't be amazed at all of this, there's no sorcery here," said Enno to the stunned Vasilov. "You see the tower in each of the fields. This is the famous Savali regulator which has been adapted to our own invention of an electro-climate. We can determine the moisture and temperature with complete uniformity for a predetermined area, preventing its escape into the atmosphere by means of the fact that we create transmissive magnetic currents of great force all around it just as though we were sealing it in from above. This invention is worthy of even greater possibilities and for that reason we are applying it here simply by way of an initial experiment. Our fields are serving as an agricultural experimental station, and nothing more; the raw products coming from there are still very insignificant. Now turn around."

"The entire length of this ground area is taken up by mines and small raw mineral extraction centers, still experimental as well. You and I will make the rounds of them and along the way I'll reveal the secret of our method to you."

They walked along the asphalt and granite pathways. Each step revealed more and more new vistas to them. Thousands of mechanisms were in operation extracting coal, salt, peat, clay. The blades of windmills were turning, the wood saws whined incessantly, the axes chopped. And all the workers they met would nod in a friendly fashion at them, turning their cheerful, happy faces towards Vasilov. There was not a single one who did not smile. Happiness shone in every look.

"Look at them," Enno began. "They are happy. We have produced the mightiest revolution in the world, but we would have been fools if we had not gone further, my friend. Once we seized the means of production, we wanted to make man happy."

"Utopia!" Vasilov sighed.

"Exactly," Enno affirmed with enthusiasm. "We set ourselves the task of realizing a utopia. The best of our brains sat over this problem for many days. Only two things can give complete happiness: creation and knowledge. But up until now, those who created, knew nothing, whereas those who knew, created nothing. That monstrous mongrel of the past—the absent-minded professor and the worker-automaton—had to disappear once and for all! We firmly resolved to make production knowledgeable and knowledge productive. How was it possible to achieve that? That, my friend, is precisely where we were helped by the method of economic indivisibility. Yes, impoverished, exhausted, hungry, deprived of products and a market, we began by trying out the method of economic indivisibility on our own skin. That was a cruel time of hunger and collapse. We planted potatoes in drawers from desks, we tanned our own leather for boots, sewed those boots, dyed old cloth, got hold of raw materials, processed them and manufactured things out of them in order to stay alive—and in fact through necessity itself we arrived at a cyclical process in the mechanics of the economy through the dependence on the productivity of one another. Our 'method of economic indivisibility' consists of the fact that not a single one of our workers from this day forth will take up his work without a complete understanding of all the links of production. He will fashion the head of a nail knowing not only about the extraction of that mineral, but about its chemical composition and its makeup on the one hand, while at the same time he'll know about the role of his nail in the most complicated of manufactured items, beginning with furniture and finishing with a tiny screw in a microscope. In other words, my friend, we have replanted our production according to the system of an *orchestra*. From the drummer to the violinist—everyone will fulfill his part in the general symphony; but everyone will be able to hear that same *general symphony*, and not just his own part. Do you understand?"

With amazement Vasilov listened to Enno's ecstatic words.

While he was musing, a group of workers with the numerals II and III on their sleeves walked past them.

"Look at that, those are the visitors from the second and third production tiers. Each of them is going to his neighboring territory in order to study the economic link. Our workers, engineers, apprentices, inventors are no longer separated into groups. In practical terms we don't have an apprentice who doesn't work and a worker who doesn't apprentice. But now I must take leave of you. Stand on that square and hang on to the metal rings, it will take you up to the Putilov Works!"

Enno gave him a friendly wave of good-bye and joined one of the workers' groups. Stunned by everything he had seen, Vasilov stepped almost unconsciously onto the indicated square and barely had time to grab the rings before he took off from one floor to the next along a stone shaft and came to a halt on his square in the midst of a small granite courtyard.

Rebrov came out to meet him, took him by the arm and led him to the factory.

CHAPTER 35
THE FIRST CONJUGAL NIGHT OF THE VASILOVS

It was already dark when Vasilov finally tore himself away from his workbench. Amazing things had happened to him. He had stood obediently at his workbench all the while, turning out metal encasements for the porcelain cups of the electrical transmitters. He had experienced an extraordinary pleasure throughout the working process. The workers around him were of all nationalities. Everyone understood a few words in the language of the other and a number of them made up groups to practice their new language. He had been treated not as a superior but as an equal. In the midst of the jokes and songs he had managed to learn what for him were new phrases in Russian. And when he joined up with the excursion going to the first and third tiers, his rapture turned to exultation.

"I've fallen in love with the settlement and my workbench," he said to Rebrov when the latter had come to force him away from his work. "This is a marvellous thing, this is better than any gymnastics, boxing or football! I've become positively cheerful here!"

With great regret he removed his foot from the operating pedal, rolled down the tucked-up sleeves of his shirt, removed his overalls and jumped into his jacket.

"I'm ready to spend a whole twenty-four hours here!"

"You can come here at nine o'clock in the morning and stay until eleven at night, in other words, your entire waking day," Rebrov replied with a smile. "But it's not allowed to do more than that. In the Soviet Republic every laborer must faithfully observe the rest period at night, from eleven at night until eight in the morning. Otherwise he wouldn't have the strength to work."

With these words, Rebrov took Vasilov to the showers and showed him the moving platform that carried our hero down below in a few moments. It had become fresh, the sky was strewn with enormous stars, from the experimental fields wafted the extraordinary fragrance of the tropics and the polar summer. Vasilov ran down the stairs to the automobile awaiting him, relishing the soft night air, the starry sky and the elasticity of his pulsating and refreshed body. But when the automobile had carried him to the fateful house on Moika Street, Vasilov gave a shudder and struck his forehead. He had forgotten about the secret instructions of the fascists as well as his phoney wife and his role of conspirator!

His heart contracted and a cold shiver ran down his spine. It was this very same extraordinary, amazing, thrice-dear county that he was supposed to help destroy, cover with blood, make barren and allow to be overrun with enemies. It was these brilliant and likeable people who had come from all corners of the world, with their noble faces, with their blazing eyes with their cheerful eyes, that he was supposed to betray and murder so treacherously!

He knew that not a single drop of his former hatred remained in him. He knew that the spirit of old Morlender, like his own, was rejoicing inside him, at this miraculous spectacle of labor which he had just seen in the settlement.

"Father would have fallen in love with them, just as I have," he whispered with certainty. "What the devil made him begin to spy on them... Well, enough! Maybe he wasn't killed by them, but by *someone else?*"

At that instant he sensed the hairs on the back of his neck bristling in terror.

Stop! The driver braked in front of the dark door of the quarters where he caught a fleeting glimpse of that same old beggar woman.

Vasilov climbed out slowly and then walked slowly up the stairs of his building. He had experienced so much during that day that even the woman who was waiting for him upstairs seemed to be a good comrade to him now. How good it would have been to tell her the whole truth! He did not know what they had done with her husband. He did not know what they would even do to him.

Knocking at the door and receiving no reply, he turned the handle and entered the room. It was completely dark, the curtains had been lowered over the windows, and Mrs. Vasilova, judging from her even breathing, was already asleep.

Vasilov jumped for his desk and lit the lamp. On the table supper had been prepared and there was a glass of cold tea. His bed has been turned back, a clean nightshirt lay on the pillow and soft slippers were on the bedside rug. He took all these comforts in with a glance and involuntarily smiled. There they were, all the virtues of family life!

Vasilov tossed off his jacket and dusty shoes. He would have liked to have a smoke and was already reaching out for the lighter when suddenly he stopped. This woman... whoever she was, maybe tobacco smoke might be unpleasant to her. He would have liked to read for a while but it might have awakened her... Shocking! The only thing left to do was to get undressed and go to sleep. There they were, all the inconveniences of family life!

Vasilov carefully sat down on the bed and began to muse. His nerves did not want to settle down. He was wound up, aroused, on fire. He went from exultation to gloomy despair. He was confused. He did not know what to do. He cracked his knuckles with anguish and at that very moment heard the soft whisper of Mrs. Vasilova:

"Tony..."

There was so much enchantment in her sleepy purling voice that Vasilov involuntarily arose from his spot. He made an allusion to the devil under his breath—for the thousandth and final time that day—and crossed on tiptoe to the borderline he had laid down, stopping beside the bed of his wife.

She was asleep. In the feeble brightness of the electric light he saw an enchanting creature who had thrown the blanket off her legs and was barely covered by batiste and lace. She had placed one hand on her breast and the other was flung out behind her head. Her mouth was half-open, the chestnut curls fell over her eyes, a dark shadow from her eyelashes lay on her cheek, deepening the sleepy blush even more, like that of a child.

He spied the dimples on her elbows and the round, smooth shoulder. He saw the measured movement of her nightgown over her breasts, a form which would have fascinated an artist for ages. It had to be confessed that Arthur Morlender did not hasten to part with this spectacle which is so troublesome for every honorable misogynist.

Mrs. Vasilova gave a deep sigh in her sleep and smiled, revealing the gleaming row of pearls that were her teeth. Her lower lip was pouting with childlike capriciousness. She muttered once more:

"Tony-y," and turned over on her other side.

It would have been safer for Vasilov to make a strategic retreat while the opportunity existed. But he had fortified himself with the thought that he ought to study his enemy properly.

"Upon closer examination things often prove to turn out quite differently!" He thought hypocritically. "After all, I do have the right to do so inasmuch as no provisions were made for her in the instructions delivered to me."

The happy thought about his instructions inspired him with a new idea. Was it not possible, bearing in mind this fact that was so unforseen, shocking, upsetting and embarrassing to him—namely, this wife who claimed to be his own wife— was it not possible now to refuse to carry out his instructions? Let Kressling blame himself! He leaned with one hand against the wall, right above the head of his wife, and to keep his balance he stuck the other one carefully under her pillow. He felt the warmth and languor of her body, he felt the beating of her heart. Instead of studying his adversary, Mr. Vasilov froze in this utterly awkward pose and closed his eyes.

Meanwhile, a kind of magic change took place in the face of this sleeping beauty. Her eyelashes and nostrils began to flutter, her lips pressed together, her brows frowned. She sighed once more, opened her arms wide and suddenly—wound them around Vasilov's neck. Her skin was silky and cool. Perhaps it was precisely for this reason that Mr. Arthur Morlender turned pale and cold like a corpse.

"Kate, are you awake?" he said hoarsely. "I'm sorry. Let me go."

But Kate did not let him go. Closing her eyes as before and without brushing the curls from her face, she kept bending Morlender's blond head closer and closer until his lips were touching her breast. If my novel were a Greek tragedy, at this point there would have appeared the shaken chorus of misogynists with threatening and wailing verses suitable to the situation and the scattering of ashes in their hair (or bald heads). However, nothing of the sort will happen in my novel, and if the heart of Mr. Morlender was pounding furiously at this moment, scorning all the normal pulse prescribed by medicine, then his watch, operated by a cold-blooded mechanism, was ticking precisely the same as before.

"Kate, forgive me, forgive me!" Morlender whispered, covering her eyes with kisses. "I... O-oh, forgive me!"

He was unable to speak. Never before in his life had he felt such a penetrating, invincible, almost unbearable, ecstasy. He was utterly overwhelmed by it, like a whirlwind. Freeing his hand from under the pillow, he brushed away the curls from the forehead of his phoney wife, ran his trembling fingers over her forehead and cheeks, tilted her face back by the chin, still stunned by the discovery of this unprecedented marvel.

Arthur Morlender had never loved a single woman before that evening. Arthur Morlender, for the first time, had encountered that unique and most mighty of wonders of the earthly sphere which was called woman. And suddenly he felt his unbearable excitement dissolve into a whirlwind of tears which streamed down his cheeks.

At this very instant, Vivian raised her eyelids. Their eyes met. Morlender staggered back and shrieked. He stood up, covered his face and like a lunatic strode off to his own section. He sat down on his bed without taking his hands away from his face—and was to sit like that right up until morning.

I do not have the slightest intention of watching over him, and, what would be even worse, to anaesthetize the reader together with myself. And for that reason I'll say quite directly what had happened within his heart. At certain moments, a person is able to perceive things with an almost savage instinct. With all the nerves of his shaken being Morlender had espied the look of hatred flashing at him out of the violet eyes of Mrs. Vasilova. At that very second it had become perfectly clear to him that she was the same kind of Kate as he was Tony.

Vivian was lying quietly in her bed like a mouse. Her breast and neck were spattered with Morlander's tears. Biting her lower lip, Vivian gazed into the darkness with fixed eyes. She had given herself away to Morlender. She had given her body to the vile old man, she had been ready to do anything in order to have her revenge—and yet she had not been brave enough to lie to Morlender! There was nothing in the world, there was no revenge that could have made her continue this contrived comedy...

Thus, two hearts in the grip of a mania for revenge had on one and the same day declared their capitulation.

"But how is all of this connected to your laboratory?" Morlender asked with interest. They had already driven up to a high and narrow tower which was surrounded by several rows of wire and were now climbing up its gently sloping steps.

"I'll tell you why," replied Rebrov, entering his small, comfortable office and hanging his hat on the rack. "Sit down, I'll explain everything."

Without a word, he placed before the phoney Vasilov a strange contraption that consisted of metal connections, plates with openings and a tiny magnet.

"Before showing you a single experiment, I'll tell you about the thoughts that led us to it. It's now been a year since our best scholars set themselves the task of joining science with practice. But not only in the usual sense in which that is generally said. We want to unite in the minds of people the principal and most important theoretic accomplishments of science, the laws which it has discovered, with common everyday affairs. Take the law of gravity, it has thousands of ramifications in science, but the volleyball player hardly stops to consider them when he throws the ball; the mountain climber, picking his way with grapnels along a terrifying icy path, does not bother to recollect them; the cook who is preparing porridge or coffee, suspects nothing about them. Or the familiar proposition in physics: 'For every action there is an equal and opposite reaction'—who thinks about it at every step of his practical activity? We have entered the age of explosives. The principal instrument of destruction has become the explosive. And what do people do? They invent counter-explosives. And what do they do after a war? They liquidate the remaining sources of explosives, the various mines and bombs, by way of finding them and exploding them. They are exploded after measures have been taken—and the danger of a chance explosion involving victims is eliminated. We, the Soviet people, are surrounded by enemies and if we were to waste our time on arming ourselves against encroachment with weapons and methods of encroachment, then we wouldn't have the strength or the means left for the mighty tasks of creation."

Rebrov fell silent, turned on the strange apparatus and placed a small ampoule into one of its openings.

"Take a look, this litttte toy is a genuine bomb of a specific explosive force. I am placing it in a cradle in our apparatus which is called an 'automatic discharger', and it appears as though nothing is happening to it, no noise, no crash, no ignition of flames. But—during these few seconds it has actually been discharged. Why? Because loading and discharging are two episodes in one and the same process which are subject to the passage of time plus the influence of specific eternal forces. We do not let the enemy's bomb go so far as to explode; we do not want to deactivate mines with the aid of an explosion. On the contrary, we place the bomb in those conditions under which the elements leading to the explosion are stably returned of their own accord to their former, neutral state by means of a third agent. This third agent—is our secret. If an explosion is caused by a bump, friction, fire, contact between chemical elements and their compounds, we can eliminate, with the aid of this third agent, the specific effects of all these actions. If an explosion is caused by a breakdown in the elements, our 'Third Agent' will simply not allow that breakdown to take place, it will stabilize the elements. We are being aided in this business by science's most general laws and principles which until now mankind has not yet learned to utilize in a conscious fashion, and which we are now taking advantage of at every step of the way."

"You mean, your apparatus is a model..."

"Yes, this is a model for gigantic installations which are being brought into operation right now, when our motherland is being threatened by invasion. You already know about one of them—that's our Aero-Electric Station."

"You are merely disarming the blow which is about to be delivered to you? Nothing more?"

"Yes, for the time being we are simply disarming any possible blows, and preserving our enormous reserves of energy which would otherwise be doomed to dispersal... But our scholars are thinking ahead as well. In the neighboring room of this tower," Rebrov straightened up and lightly touched the stone wall, "my comrade is seriously engaged in work on a small practical deduction based on the principle that "for every action there is an equal and opposite reaction'. But for the time being we're not telling anyone about this."

Morlender sat for a few moments in silence.

"My father," he blurted involuntarily...

"Your father?"

"Yes, my father, the inventor, Morlender..."

And as soon as he said that, he turned pale, leapt up from his place and Rebrov likewise turned pale and arose from his place.

Absentmindedly, Arthur had let the cat out of the bag. He was not sorry that he had. He stood there with his head hanging, pale, like death, not denying what he had said and explaining nothing. Rebrov waited a short while, then he pressed a button. Two Red Army soldiers loomed in the doorway. They went up to Morlender and took firm hold of him, one at his right elbow, the other at his left.

CHAPTER 37
THE SECRET OF THE CHEKA

In America Arthur Morlender had heard quite a bit about the terrifying Cheka of the Bolsheviks. The newspapers had printed sensational confessions by White Russian émigrés about how they had been tortured by incredible instruments that had not even been known in the Middle Ages. Some refugee landowner had serialized an entire novel by the title of *The Secret of the Cheka* in one issue after the other of the *Chicago Sunday* and then had admitted to his friends whenever they got drunk that "if it hadn't been for that dear old Cheka—God bless it—I'd have absolutely nothing for grub." And so now Arthur was sitting in that same Cheka, in a comfortable chair, in front of a table on which stood a glass of tea and two ham sandwiches which had been pushed towards him by a handsome, dark-skinned investigator in a military uniform and with a dozen medals on his chest.

"And so you're the son of the famous inventor, Morlender," he said thoughtfully, tapping the tip of his pencil on the table in front of himself. "But why didn't you come here under your own name? You would have been afforded the most generous hospitality. What purpose did this masquerade serve? And where is the real Vasilov? Answer these questions in order, please."

"I am the son of the famous inventor, Arthur Morlender," the arrested man said with a heavy sigh. "My father was killed in Russia by the Bolsheviks, or so I was told by the head of the organization that my father worked for, Jack Kressling the billionaire. I swore to have revenge on my father's murderers. Jack Kressling and his friends arranged this masquerade, equipped me with money, weapons, poison, bombs and sent me here under the name of Vasilov. Where the real Vasilov is, I don't know. A woman came with me who pretends to be the wife of Vasilov. Who she is, I also don't know. That's everything. No, that's not everything, incidentally. When I saw your country and your people, from the first day I began to doubt the fact that my father was killed by your people. And the desire to avenge him was extinguished in me."

"You are right, Morlender left here alive and well." The investigator rang, a youngish Red Army man entered. "Sidorov, a copy from the ship's log of the *Torpedo*!"

When the copy was delivered, the investigator leafed through it until he had hunted down the page.

"Read it, there's the entry: "A cabin reserved to New York on the sixth of July...' But what's this?" The investigator suddenly turned red and read the following line: '...remained unoccupied'." Once more, more forcefully than before, he pressed the button. "Sidorov, find out immediately, where, when, and by what means, the engineer Jeremy Morlender, who was a guest in the Soviet Union for about a month, left our country!"

While Sidorov disappeared soundlessly to fulfill the order, the investigator gazed sympathetically at Arthur.

"To tell the truth, we did not attribute any significance to the newspaper furor surrounding this phoney murder. After all, the things they do write about over there! And where do they get it from? But didn't this whole affair seem strange to you? Tell me, what about your father's estate, his famous invention that has provoked rumors in both hemispheres, a new form of some kind of energy? Are you yourself working on it?"

Arthur had already begun to get accustomed to the investigater's manner of asking not one, but an entire series of questions. He understood that with a group of several questions posed all at once, the investigator was helping him to see the connection between various things that had eluded him earlier. And, bearing this connection in mind, he replied:

"My father's invention was not bequeathed to me. Father wrote a new will in Russia. According to this new will, the invention was supposed to be used for the struggle against the communists. But now, it all seems strange to me. I was his only son. For some reason or other, father deprived me of all of his fortune. Everything was awarded to his new wife, whose existence I had not even suspected."

"And who is this new wife?"

"The former secretary of Jack Kressling."

As he answered, Arthur Morlender himself saw how his answers became linked into a circle and how all of them pointed to a single person. Listening to him, the investigator nodded his head in understanding. He had managed, in the course of those moments, to contact someone on the telephone, he listened to them, gave brief replies into the mouthpiece and continued to watch Morlender. And when he put the telephone down, he turned to face Morlender full on.

"There's no need to wait for Sidorov. I was just speaking with the person who had the responsibility of guiding your father around our country and who was present when he departed. This person has informed me of some curious things. They'll be here in a moment."

All this time, Rebrov had been sitting by the window and smoking his pipe. He had not intruded with a single word into the conversation. But when the investigator fell silent, and Morlender, his chin on his chest, was mentally resurrecting in his mind everything that had happened to him in New York, Rebrov said quietly:

"The engineer Jeremy Morlender was at our place as well, at the experimental division. He acted very friendly. It doesn't seem likely that he would have bequeathed his new discovery you were telling us about to the struggle against communism."

He did not manage to finish before the door was softly opened, and on the threshold appeared the "person" about whom the investigator had been talking. This person—an attractive and stern young lady with curly hair and a gold pince-nez on her acquiline nose, wearing Swedish suede shoes, a Finnish jumper, and a Parisian blouse—took them all in with a questioning look in her eyes.

"Here, let me introduce you," the investigator smiled broadly, "the well-known interpreter, a worker in the commissariat of foreign affairs, a trusted person, you can rely on her every word. Sit down, comrade Serezhkina. Repeat for those present what you just informed me."

Comrade Serezhkina pulled a fine Estonian notebook out of her Italian purse with a view of Mount Vesuvius, opened it up and, peering into it, rapped out:

"Mister Jeremy Morlender visited four of our Republics, eight regional centers, Moscow, Petrograd, twelve factories, had conversations and meetings with academicians, professors, workers, planners, spent three days at the Central Aero-Electric Station, was received by the leaders of our government, stepped before the microphone with words of gratitude and great satisfaction, spoke in favor of closer contact between the sciences here and abroad. According to his wish, a ticket was reserved for him on the steamship *Torpedo* departing for New York on the sixth of July. But Mister Jeremy did not depart on this steamship."

"Did not depart!" Arthur whispered. "Why not?"

"For the reason that on the morning of the fourth a private American airplane for the exclusive use of the capitalist Jack Kressling, landed at the Petrograd airport. Information was given by the pilot to the effect that he had to find Mister Jeremy that same day and offer to fly him back immediately for some unavoidable reason. I personally accompanied Mister Morlender at six o'clock in the morning and was a witness to his departure by air. Mister Morlender did not have time to request the money back for the cabin on the *Torpedo*."

"But his coffin arrived on the *Torpedo*," Arthur let drop in a hoarse voice. "What nasty business is lurking behind all of this?"

"You figure it out!" the investigator said curtly and amiably. "Comrade Serezhkina, you may go. And now I am going to ask you to inform us what specifically the organizers of your disguise wanted from you, the same organizers who in all probability murdered the unfortunate Vasilov. Be very precise in your answers. This time I'm going to record them!"

Arthur Morlender stuck his hand in his pockets and subsequently pulled out and distributed in front of the investigator everything that he had received from Kressling's gang. One after the other, the investigator picked up the "material evidence." He held the ampoule up to the light and carefully looked at its contents, counted the little blue capsules in the box, weighed in the palm of his hand the loaded automatic pistol of the latest design. He thumbed the thick packet of new Soviet bills as though it were a deck of cards. Then he pushed everything off to the side, pronounced "...good" and again selected the ampoule out of the pile.

"Rebrov, take that for your laboratory. Well, now, I'm listening to you, Morlender!"

"In addition to all the sabotage which I was to carry out at my discretion, I am supposed to present a gift—an explosive contrivance—which will be sent to me from America. For the time being I don't know the specific time, the operation or the nature of this gift."

The investigator recorded the last word, stuck the pen back into the inkwell, handed to Arthur what he had written and gave him the pen to sign.

Morlender read it through and signed. He felt immeasurably exhausted. He sat and waited for them to send him off to jail. But Rebrov suddenly stood up, went up to him as though nothing were amiss, took him by the arm and pulled him after himself towards the door. The investigator shouted after them:

"Don't forget to go on playing your part! And don't be afraid of anything— we'll take measures. Under no circumstances should you have anything further to do with us, otherwise they might get suspicious and kill you before we can get to the bottom of this business. Good-bye and good luck!"

To Morlender's great amazement, he now understood that they believed him, that he was free, and, the main thing, that from now on he was not alone in the world.

CHAPTER 38
THE PERSONNEL OF PRINCE OBOLONKIN

Several days that were saturated with labor, perception and friendship passed for Arthur Morlender. From Rebrov he learned the details of his father's visit to the laboratory. He heard, at his request, the precisely reproduced words and speeches of the senior Morlender. He comprehended what it was that must have taken place in his father, the kind of enormous breakthrough in his views. And the criminal role of Kressling and his gang became more obvious to him. Somewhere in New York they had killed his father in order to gain control over his invention. Somewhere in the ocean they had loaded the coffin onto the *Torpedo*. He had paid a visit to the port, had learned about the day and hour of the next arrival of the *Torpedo* and had decided to have a talk with the captain. All these thoughts and actions had devoured the time left over to Arthur after work. And still, whenever he returned to his room, its emptiness would make his heart contract. How different it was to return now than it had been the first time! The room was dark, uncomfortable, the bundle with Katya Ivanovna's bedding had been cleared away, her bed had been laid out with clean, cold linen, the fragrance of her delicate perfume had dissipated; no one was there to wait for him, to hate him... Hatred! Regardless of whoever had sent Kate to him, the hatred—that had been so piercing, passionate and flashing in the depths of her eyes—that had been occasioned by something personal. Where was she from? Who and what were behind this woman?

Despite himself he thought about her more and more. It was not that first and final night that would arise in his imagination, but rather the involuntary friendly exchange of glances when they both had arrived at their quarters from the steamship and they had both been in the grip of their first Russian impressions. It had been a look of mutual understanding, of sympathy, of like minds, a look out of which some explanation might have followed. Not a single person out of Kressling's pack could have produced a look like that. Why, oh why had he not explained himself to her? And where was she now, what had happened to her? Arthur had changed so deeply during those days that he was certain that a change had occurred in her as well.

But time passed and Kate still did not return. In the corner behind the screen stood her suitcase which had been delivered together with his own. He had not so much as touched it. He was waiting for someone to come for it or send for it. Meanwhile, the morning arrived when the *Torpedo* was once again supposed to enter the port of Kronstadt. Having forewarned Rebrov the evening before, Arthur Morlender left to meet it as soon as it was barely light.

But where was Vivian Orton all during those days? On that horrible morning when she had run out onto Moika Street, she had but one thing on her mind: to find Sorrow somehow. His address and the map which had been carefully sketched in his own hand were safe in her pocket. But it had not been all that easy to figure out the map of a large city! Smoothing out the crumpled bit of paper, Vivian had walked uncertainly along the streets, counting off each corner and then turning down the street where it was seemingly required. But the streets went on and on, the turnings multiplied and multiplied; however, the street whose name was written on the paper, kept eluding her. She was afraid to ask. The people were hurrying along the streets and they did not have the time to stop. Thirst was tormenting her. Her eyes began to search for a water fountain, a faucet, a kiosk with drinks. First she searched down one, then another street opening and suddenly she understood in horror that she was lost. The part of the city that she had ended up in was gloomy and squalid. Dark, tatty little dwellings of the barrack type of construction, with filthy gateways that exhaled a deathly cold and the odor of cats. Pipes everywhere, pipes on the roofs, pipes sticking through window vents wafting black soot and smoke directly unto the streets, broken windowpanes pasted over with paper... With something akin to despair, Vivian entered one black maw of a gateway and halted without knowing what to do next. And suddenly she heard English being spoken. Someone had greeted someone in her native language!

Seized with joy, without leaving much to thought, Vivian rushed at the person who was speaking.

"I beg of you, help me, I'm lost," she blurted out hurriedly, addressing the dark figures in the entrance. "I need the harbour, the Fifth Red Fleet..."

And only then did she look more closely at whom she had addressed. Two beggars in unlikely rags were standing before her, huddled against the wall: an old woman with a crutch and an old man with two walleyes.

"The harbor, the Fifth Red Fleet dock," the old man repeated in a squeaky voice, fastening his horrible walleyes on her. "Yes, it's not far away, my dear. Come, come, come, we'll show you!" With these words he seized her tightly by the right arm, while the old woman, changing her crutch to her other arm, quickly took hold of Vivian's left arm. Vivian reacted with a quick movement to free herself from these grasping, filthy hands, but she was hemmed in from both sides.

She attempted to cry out. A bony hand covered her mouth. Slowly, step by step, the beggars dragged her deeper and deeper into the entryway until they found themselves in a filthy, stone courtyard in the midst of tall, gloomy blocks of houses illuminated by a miserly square of sky above.

"Just mention the devil's name..." the old man began playfully, but speaking in French this time.

"... And he'll show up before you know it," the old woman completed the proverb. She gave Vivian a sideways glance. But the girl, who was seized by terror, seemed to comprehend nothing. They were now heading somewhere down the damp steps, into a filthy basement room. Raising her crutch, the old woman knocked at the door. A bolt squeaked immediately, a door chain rattled, a key was turned in the lock... An emaciated, deeply etched face peered out into the semi-gloom.

"Is that you, princess?"

"Quick, quick, let us in! Make sure you close the door tightly behind us," the old man muttered hoarsely, shoving Vivian in front of him. "We've been lucky.. The birdie has flown into the cage herself!"

He unclenched the claw-like fingers that were holding the girl's arm. She was about to dash back, towards the door, but a terrible blow knocked her back into the room. It was a strange room: small, cramped, hung with washed out grey-blue rugs, furnished with some kind of gilded and threadbare furniture, vases, clocks, and piled up with bags and sacks of flour and barley, reeking of musty onions, dust and mouse dirt.

"Where am I, where have I ended up?" Vivian asked in terror, gazing all around uncomprehendingly.

But the old man continued in French out of spite, this time addressing the person who had let them in, a creature of indeterminate sex and enveloped in some kind of robe:

"Obolonkin will be pleased... In his last instructions he advised us to isolate this good-looker. It looks as though all bets are lost on Morlender—it didn't take him long to get together with the reds..."

"It was incautious to drag her here, Kammerherr! To the hideout where all our personnel get together!" muttered the master of the room grumpily.

Personnel, hideout, princess, Kammerherr... Vivian's brain was working feverishly. The name of "Obolonkin" which the old man had mentioned to the other beggars, was familiar to her: in New York, at Westinghouse's receptions, she had met the devious, pushy old codger, Prince Feofan Obolonkin. The banker had told her that he was a famous émigré from Russia who was high up in the service of the next heir to the Russian throne. It meant that right here, in Petrograd, there was a hornets' nest of these people—"personnel", a "hideout"... And Morlender, the "Tony" of her horrible comedy, had refused to serve the capitalists and had gone to the side of the Bolsheviks...

Meanwhile, the old man got a bundle of thick rope and a ball of rags out of a drawer: Vivian had no time to gather her wits before she was seized once more and she felt iron fingers boring into both of her cheeks, forcing her jaws open, and a filthy gag smelling of mouse dirt was stuffed deeply into her mouth. While the old man tied the struggling girl with the rope, the old woman was pronouncing sentence in a malicious voice.

"May there be a swift, swift end to this age of darkness! An end to the barbarism! Our beloved monarch will return!"

"And, princess, our patriotism will not be forgotten," the old man with the walleyes replied in similar spirit.

CHAPTER 39
MRS. DRUCK'S CAT

It's one and the same thing: either you go on mourning, or you fulfill your obligations. But when you are mourning while fulfilling your obligations, or you are fulfilling your obligations while mourning, then at best you are like the salt industry that consumes the very product of its labor without any profit left over.

Mrs. Druck's cat had come to this conclusion precisely at that moment when its fur had begun to resemble alum crystals and the milk which it was lapping up, had begun to resemble pickle brine.

Mrs. Druck was bedewing with tears her household furnishings by night and by day.

"Molly," she affirmed, pressing the cat to herself, "it really is true that he was a remarkable child, my Bob, even before he was born. I used to sit by the window and he would give a poke with his fist, like a woodpecker. 'Septimius,' I would say, 'our little boy has started to stir once more.' 'How do you know that it's a boy,' he would reply... And I... o-o-oh, Molly, o-o-oh, how wretched my life is! I would reply, 'Septimius, you'll see,' I used to say, 'that for sure it'll be a boy... a boy-oy-oy!..'"

At this point, Mrs. Druck's agitation would reach such a point that tears the size of peas would begin to drum right on Molly's back, driving the cat into a torment of tail twitching.

"Molly, come here," Mrs. Druck would call her a few minutes later as she poured her some milk. "Go ahead and eat, for yourself and for our little darling... how he used to love milk. 'Drink,' I used to say to him, and he, o-o-oh, I haven't the strength, o-o-oh, if only I were dead. He used to an-answer, 'Goo-goo... more, mummy!'"

Mrs. Druck's sobbings would last until the dish in her trembling hands would be filled far beyond the point of overflowing. Molly would give a shudder with her entire body, as she dipped her tongue, curled like a tube, into it. But after two or three gulps she would snort furiously, get her fur up and fly like an arrow to the kitchen, straight to the washtub, in the hope of refreshing herself with some fresh water. Alas! In the world that surrounded Mrs. Druck, there was no fresh water. The moisture that had been entrusted to her care, had stagnated in her stomach like stalagmites and stalactites. If Molly had been acquainted with the Bible, she might have compared her mistress to Lot's wife who was turned into a pillar of salt when she looked back into her past.

But Molly was not acquainted with the Bible and one fine morning she leapt out the window and from there to the drain pipe, from the pipe into someone's flowerpot, from the flowerpot head over heels down, down, down over the stone projections until she fastened with all her strength onto a woman's blonde-curled coiffure that was set with combs, pins and forget-me-nots.

"Ai!" shrieked the owner of the coiffure. "I'm done for! Save me! A flying mouse!"*

"Nathaniel, save me, I'm dying!" whined the former Miss Small, for, in fact, it was her. "Whether it's a mouse or a cat, it's chewing its way into my innards! It'lll suck me dry!"

Even by now it was apparent that there was no longer any harmony of spirit between the Epidermises. In any event, her husband regarded the threat of Miss Small's innards being sucked dry with a complete passiveness to fate.

"Monster!" shrieked the former Miss Small, wielding her umbrella at her husband. "I'll die without making a new will, I'll die, yes I will, I will! As before, everything will go to the aunt of my deceased brother's wife!"

This time Nathaniel Epidermis gave a shudder. Before his eyes arose the aunt of Miss Small's brother's wife in the role of heiress to his own wife's inheritance.. He seized the clinging cat by the scruff of its neck, and tore it loose. Something tore apart like an automobile tire, and flew onto the road like a wheel.

A deafening roar of laughter issued from the passers-by, a shopkeeper, a newspaper boy and a shoeshine boy. Mister Epidermis looked and froze. His wife stood before him, balder than Bismarck, bald as a skating rink, bald as a billiard ball.

"You've tricked me!" he roared. "You despicable intriguer, you'll pay for this!. Where's my lawyer! A lawsuit!"

Meanwhile, the attention of the passersby was drawn away from the couple by another extraordinary spectacle: the unfortunate Molly, all twisted up in the curls and forget-me-nots of Miss Small, went completely crazy and was rolling ahead like a wheel, with papers, rags, straw, horse dung and cigarette butts clinging to her all along the way.

"Ha-ha-ha!" roared the street urchins as they dashed along after her.

"What's going on!" the baker asked, sticking his head out the window and fastening his gaze with terror on the wheel flying past. But at that very second, the wheel gave a hop, bit him on the nose and turning a sommersault in mid-air, flew on.

"Grab it, catch it! A salamander!" And the baker, with a rolling-pin in his hand, leapt through the window, dashed after the wheel, furiously scattering flour through the air and over the sidewalk.

A policeman vainly tried to stop the insane procession by holding up both of his traffic flags. But it dashed on and on from one sidestreet to the next, until the policeman had summoned an entire detachment of the police with his whistle and was dashing after it. Crowds of people jammed all the sidewalks. The deacon from the Church of the Forty Martyrs, for a small offering, allowed those wishing to do so to find a seat for themselves on the Church's ballustrades. The windows and roofs were scattered with the curious. Establishments were forced to declare a recess.

"I'll tell you what that is," said a clerk to three young ladies. "It's a rush on stocks, word of honor."

"Where did you get that from?" said a neighbor, growing enraged. "Nothing of the sort! Ask the baker, he says that it's an advertisement for the *Salamander Insurance Company*."

"No, it isn't! No, it isn't!" cried the urchins. "It's a toy dirigible!"

But the wheel kept rolling and rolling. Foam was dripping from Molly's snout, her yellow eyes were flashing in utter madness, the fur on her back was standing upright. Dashing hither and yon, but crashing everywhere into barriers of hooting urchins, Molly hurtled into the one and only free sidestreet which led to a square, and spinning like a top, she flew up into a tree precisely to the spot where a crow's nest loomed blackly among the branches.

"Caw-w-w!" the crow cawed as she squatted over her eggs. But there was nowhere for Molly to retreat to. Hissing and trembling, caught up in the curls, forget-me-nots, paper and dung, she advanced on the crow, emitting a piercing war cry. The crow ruffled its feathers in turn, raised its wings, opened its beak and hurtled straight for Molly. While this bloody duel was taking place high up in the tree, down below, in the square, other events were transpiring.

Two parties had taken shape in the salamander chase: one was dashing towards the square from the direction of the church and was led by representative Pirouette who had been involuntarily caught up in the rush together with his secretary, briefcase, and bulldog. The other party, which came flying from the opposite direction, consisting of newspaper vendors, shoeshine boys and street urchins, had produced as their leader a fat, ruddy-faced fellow wearing an army shirt and a straw hat on his head.

The two speeding parties bumped into each other, got mixed up into a knot, and the church deacon, together with representative Pirouette, were the recipients of a large bump on the forehead from the ruddy-faced man.

"Sir!" the representative exclaimed with displeasure. "I am untouchable! How dare you!"

"Tough luck! Don't butt in!" roared the ruddy-faced man.

"Give it to him!. Slug him!" shouted the aroused Yankees in support from all sides. "Let him have-it good!"

"Police!" shouted the representative. "Riot! Propaganda! The government and the church are being insulted here!"

"That's right," the baker interjected sullenly. "It's the Bolsheviks, fellows! You wouldn't believe how sneaky they are, the dogs! They let a salamander loose in order to agitate for a trade agreement. But it'll be the kiss of death for our grain, strike me down if it isn't true!"

"True, true!" the church deacon supported him as he pressed a copper coin to the bump on his forehead. "Vote against them until that salamander rots!"

"Big deal!" roared the ruddy-faced man. "A trade agreement! What's bad about trading with Soviet Russia? I'm a trading man myself. Step forward whoever's against the agreement! Quick march!"

Representative Pirouette glanced around on all sides. His party watched him with burning eyes. He understood that he could lose his popularity, shoved his bulldog and secretary aside, tossed his briefcase down, threw off his jacket, rolled up his sleeves and with a cry of "Down with the agreement!" he plunged into hand-to-hand combat. A half-hour later, a detachment of police separated the combatants that were for and against the agreement, and an ambulance was loaded up with gentlemen who had received injuries for their principles. The fat man had come out the victor, whereas the representative had lost his bulldog, briefcase and popularity.

The duel between the unfortunate Molly and the crow had ended no less tragically. Giving a final squawk over her shredded nest and crushed eggs, the practical-minded crow seized the envelope containing Druck's letter, and like the Easterner who carried the roof of his home on his shoulders, she set out on a distant emigration with her precious object. As far as Molly was concerned, she was lying on the ground with pecked-out eyes and broken back. May she rest in peace! She had sacrificed her life for the development of our novel.

CHAPTER 40
LEPSIUS MEETS BEAR THE FRUIT VENDOR

Toby had just finished cleaning the first boot and was on the verge of dozing off for a bit before getting to work on the second, when suddenly someone knocked softly on the kitchen door. He armed himself with a broom in order to chase away any beggars and opened the door just far enough to stick his weapon through it, but at that very moment the broom dropped out of his hands and his mouth opened like a bird's beak. The fact was that it was not a beggar on the other side of the door, but someone else.

From the front, this other person resembled Miss Small to a terrible degree. Those were Miss Small's eyes, Miss Small's nose, Miss Small's mouth and Miss Small's lace shawl. But from above, this person reminded one of a round apothecary globe filled with crimson acids. And this person was acting not at all like Miss Small: there was no swearing, no spitting, no standing with hands on hips, no pushing with elbow or stomach, but instead Toby heard a gentle voice saying:

"Dear, sweet Toby, please let me in!"

The mulatto stepped backwards, frightened to death. The person entered, removed a shawl, hung it on a hook and bleated in an even more touching voice:

"Please get me some ashes from the stove, Toby my dearest!"

Toby fetched a whole spoonful of ashes, shaking all the while from terror.

"And now lift it up, dearest, and pour it over my head!"

But at this point, the scoop dropped out of Toby's trembling hands and Toby, breaking into convulsive sobs, dashed up the stairs, climbed into a closet and hid his head between his knees.

Meanwhile, this specter of Miss Small manifested neither irritation nor annoyance. It patiently bent over the stove, gathered together a fistful of ashes and smeared its round head, not to excess, but rather more to indicate the symbolic nature of this operation.

Then Miss Small timidly proceeded to the doctor's study, halting timidly on the threshold and folding her hands over her stomach.

Lepsius raised his eyes from the medical book about spinal columns and frowned threateningly.

"Miss Small, what is the meaning of this? If I am not mistaken, I am seeing you without your wig and with your scalp smeared with soot. What the devil is the meaning of such a demonstration?"

"It's not a demonstration, sir, oh no! You shouldn't even think such a thing, forr the sake of my immortal soul! Repentance, sir, the most profound, pure-hearted and fatal kind of repentance!"

"Stop talking nonsense. What's the matter?"

"Sir, I am repenting the fact that I did not heed your fatherly advice. Madness led me to make fun of it! Fate has chastised me most cruelly, sir. You were right, right three times over. My innocence has been defamed, my feelings trampled, my ideals cast down. Sir, the ruins are smouldering in the midst of the flowering vale!"

"What kind of recitation is this?" Lepsius grew furious and threw his book on the floor. "If you and that Nathaniel Epidermis of yours are about to blackmail me..."

"Nathaniel Epidermis is finished, sir!" Miss Small replied curtly. "Forget about him. From this day forth, sir, I am devoted to your household, body and soul."

We have no idea of what further touching scene Miss Small still had in store because, fortunately for Doctor Lepsius, a piercing bell resounded and Toby flew into the room, still pale all over from terror.

"Some ruddy-faced gentleman is asking for you, sir," he stammered, trying to catch his breath. "And blood is dripping from him!"

Doctor Lepsius gave his housekeeper and his servant a silent glance, mentally arrived at an unsettling conclusion and set out for his reception room.

The mulatto proved to be correct. In the doctor's reception room stood a fat, ruddy-faced man in an army shirt and blood was flowing from his face.

"Pleased to meet you," he said, shaking the doctor's hand energetically. "I'm the fruit vendor, Bear, from Lincoln Place, there was a bit of a free-for-all on political grounds... I was driving past and suddenly noticed your shingle, and here I am before you, with all the earmarks of a patient, if it could be put that way!"

A minute later he was already sitting in an armchair, washed and bandaged by Doctor Lepsius' skillful hands. The doctor was studying him closely from all sides, examining his enormous fingers with steely nails and healthy ribs, and he asked a question that was quite unexpected for the fat man:

"Were you receiving X-ray treatments at Bentrovato's, Mister Bear?"

"That's right. How did you know?"

"Why shouldn't I? It was on the day when someone else was being X-rayed with you... what's his name?! What the devil, a small man, looked like a drunkard and had gouty hands... What is it?"

"Professor Hiserton!" the fruit vendor interrupted him in a satisfied voice. "Sure, sure! A big-shot! Because of him they wouldn't even let me into the reception room, as though they could keep Bear the fruit vendor from Lincoln Place out! Naturally, I went right in and that character didn't like it one bit. And to tell you the truth, he was right to try and hide from his neighbors. If I were him, I'd have found myself a cave and sat in it like a toad the whole live-long day."

"How strangely you speak of Professor Hiserton!" Lepsius objected. Outwardly he was calm, but the three steps leading up to his nose were trembling like a bloodhound. "Why should he hide?"

"Well, get someone else who wants to tell you about that. I'm keeping my mouth shut. Ask at Lincoln Place about Bear the fruit vendor and everyone will tell you that he knows how to keep a secret. I'm not one of those to go around ringing bells!"

"A praiseworthy quality," Lepsius noted sourly as he arranged his surgical instruments in a crystal glass with alcohol. "A valuable quality in every profession. It seems that you deal in fruit, Mister Bear?"

"Seems!" the fat man exclaimed. "It would have been better if you had said about Shakespeare that it *seems* as though he wrote plays! All of New York knows about Bear's fruit! All of Fifth Avenue eats Bear's fruit. The fattest pear carries my name, and all you can say is 'It seems...' If your mouth has ever watered, then it is because of my pears, sir!"

"I don't dispute it, Mister Bear, I don't dispute it. I'm a man of science and I avoid modishness. But you must admit that still you do exaggerate the quality of your goods."

These words, which were uttered in the most inoffensive voice, infuriated the fat man beyond any jesting. He clenched his fists and arose from his place.

"I'll tell you what, sir, just you come to me. I'll force you to take your words back. You taste all my varieties one after the other, or else."

"Or else what?"

"You'll choke on them!"

With these words, Bear puffed up and assumed the most challenging pose. Doctor Lepsius slapped him affably on the shoulder.

"I'm not refusing, my kindest Mister Bear. But in order that the treat shouldn't be, so to speak, one-sided, allow me to take a wicker basket with me in the automobile..."

He winked at the fruit vendor, and the fruit vendor winked back at him. Toby was summoned and was also winked at, whereas Toby, in turn, winked at the chauffeur as he placed a basket of bottles in the automobile. The chauffeur winked at himself as he took the wheel, and Doctor Lepsius sped off with Bear the fruit vendor to Lincoln Place, to Bear's magnificent greenhouse for fruit.

Here there was everything that grew on the face of the earth, beginning with Icelandic moss and ending with coconuts. Bear gave orders for every example from his fruit kingdom to be brought to the doctor on crystal plates, while the doctor, in turn, ordered the bottles he had brought to be uncorked.

Two hours later, Doctor Lepsius and Bear were addressing each other in familiar terms.

"I'm going to marry you," Bear said, as he embraced Lepsius by the waist and kissed him on his metallic buttons, "you wonderful fellow. I'm going to marry you to a pomegranate pear."

"No, don't," replied Lepsius, wiping away the tears, "you love Professor Hiserton! Better you marry Hiserton off!"

"Who told you that? To hell with Hiserton! Don't spoil my good mood, drink! I'm going to marry you to a pineapple melon!"

The friends embraced once more and exchanged kisses. But Lepsius could not hide the tears that were streaming down his face in rivulets. His new friend tried in vain to wipe them away with his own hand, using cigarette paper, he tried in vain to persuade him not to weep, but Doctor Lepsius was inconsolable. Faced with such despair, Bear the fruit vendor tore the bandages off himself and swore to commit suicide.

"I-I'll st-stop!" the doctor burbled, restraining his tears. "I'll stop! Dear, old buddy of mine, give me a hug. Tell me that you'll put the bandages back on. Telll me that that accursed Hiserton... will go off to a cave!"

"The best place for him!" snarled the fruit vendor darkly as he pressed Lepsius to himself. "Judge for yourself, where else could a man hide himself who-o..." He burped, lowered his head to the table and closed his eyes.

"Bear, baby!" Lepsius was shaking him. "Go on! I beg of you! Who... what?"

"Whose... whose... body..." babbled the fruit vendor and this time began to snore like a steam kettle.

Intoxication disappeared from Doctor Lepsius as though it had never been there. In a fury he poked at the fat man, broke an empty bottle and ran out of the greenhouse into the open air, clenching his fists.

"Just you wait, just you wait!" he muttered fiercely. "I'll find out why you disguised yourself! Why you came waltzing up to me all concerned about the fate of that crushed sailor! Why you were being X-rayed! Why you put the fear of the devil into this blockhead! Why you call yourself Professor Hiserton! Why you have those joints in your hands, those joints... those nice little joints—I'll be damned if they don't correspond to all the symptoms I've gathered together!"

CHAPTER 41
THE TRADE AGREEMENT

"Did you hear what happened at the stuck exchange?"

"No, what?"

"Better run and buy gold! Jack Kressling is in favor of a trade agreement with Russia!"

"Kressling? You're off your rocker, it can't be!"

But the helpful acquaintance waved his hand and dashed off to spread panic at every intersection on Broadway.

In the leather-upholstered room of the stock exchange where only the money tsars of America were admitted, Jack Kressling sat with his grey eyes fixed on the tip of his cigar and was talking to the Secretary of Congress:

"You'll send a telegram about this all down the line. Harvard University ought to put together a resolution. The society for the dissemination of innocent knowledge should do likewise. It's essential to organize a demonstration on the part of the negroes. Decorate a few houses, shall we say every tenth house, with mourning flags."

"Excuse me, sir," the Secretary interrupted respectfully, "I have not quite understood you. Are you speaking about a joyful or a sad demonstration?"

Kressling raised his brows and gave him a contemptuous look:

"I have taken the lead at the stock exchange on an agreement with Soviet Russia. America should put on its mourning clothes."

"Aha," the secretary pronounced profoundly, turning as red as a lobster. But in the depths of his heart he comprehended nothing.

"But a portion of the intelligentsia, you should be aware, only a portion will express its satisfaction. It will announce a fund-raising drive for the presentation of a valuable gift to the leaders of the Soviet Republic. You will be the first to contribute a thousand dollars..."

The Secretary of Congress shrank back in his chair.

"Nonsense," Kressling said sternly, pulling a check book out of his pocket and tossing it on the table. "Fill in the necessary figures here, I've already signed each check. The gift is already prepared. It's a timepiece in a case of redwood—a symbol of labor and economy. Take care of putting the letter together with the usual appropriate sentiments, put in a few quotations from our Emerson and the Bolshevik Professor Kogan... The gift is to be sent in the name of those who are supporters of the Soviets and is to be delivered through a member of the communist party who has been sent to Russia. Enough, I'm tired."

The secretary dashed out of the room all in a sweat. He had to get in touch with Washington. In utter despair he rushed down the stairs, buzzing like a beehive. The main hall of the stock exchange was filled to overflowing. The blackboard was being rubbed off continuously with an eraser. The figures grew. A small man with chalk in his hand kept adding fresh circles to the board. The White Russian émigrés from the far right of the Socialist Revolutionaries had kept their word by forewarning Jack Kressling that a terrorist attempt had been planned against him at three minutes past five at the left entrance in the stock exchange.

The perpetrator of all this panic finished smoking his cigar, stood up and slowly went down the stairs. Down below, in the vestibule, two borzoi dogs and a crate of crocodiles were waiting for him. He petted his favorites, glanced at the clock— five o'clock—and nodded to his servant. The latter raised his eyebrows and nodded to the doorman. The doorman dashed out onto the street and cried in a loud voice:

"A car for Mister Kressling's dogs!"

A glossy Italian automobile upholstered with lilac-colored silk inside, rolled effortlessly up to the entrance. The servant lifted the dogs by the collar and they seated themselves on the seat while the chauffeur took the wheel.

"A car for Mister Kressling's crocodiles!"

Immediately on the heels of the first automobile a second one in the form of a stylish sedan with central heating and pineapples in tubs rolled up to the entrance. The servant and the doorman carried the crate of crocodiles into it and the automobile departed in the direction of the first.

"Mister Kressling's mare!"

America's best horse, the famous Esmeralda, with a white patch on her chest, chomping on her mouthpiece and rolling her brown eyes, pranced up to the entrance, trying to break free of the jockey's grasp. A murmur of rapture escaped from the public. Even the stock exchange brokers forgot about their business deals for a moment. A policeman, a shoeshine boy, a newspaper vendor and a cigarette vendor stood around the entrance, their mouths agape with fascination. The whirring sound of a movie camera could be heard. The clock over the stock exchange pointed precisely to three minutes past five.

In the indentation between two niches stood a sullen-faced man in a Mexican sombrero with a long black cloak tossed over one shoulder, twisting his lips sardonically.

"Window dressing!" he muttered with hatred. "I can't waste our last bomb on that kind of charlatan."

And enveloping himself in the folds of his cloak, he tossed the long strands of his hair, stuck the bomb back into his pocket and gloomily made off for the bus stop where he was forced to put up with a multitude of curious looks before the next vehicle arrived.

Meanwhile Jack Kressling lazily swung his foot into the stirrup, looked around in expectation of the bomb-hurler, shrugged his shoulders and in a moment his imposing figure was resting in the saddle as though it were made of bronze and the tamed Esmeralda was prancing down Broadway, lightly touching the asphalt with her silver horseshoes.

Meanwhile, workers had carried a magnificently packed box into the New York Customs. A round wax seal was affixed to it there. It was addressed to Petrograd, to comrade Vasilov, from an entire series of sympathetic organizations. The policeman on duty kept shrugging his shoulders and muttering into his moustache:

"Just look at all the fuss! And no custom duties or examination either! I'll bet the voters put some real pressure on more than one elected representative for this kind of fantasy. Bah, Washington, Washington!" Then suddenly a strange cold shiver ran down his spine and the policeman interrupted his thoughts as he felt someone's hand on himself.

"Who's that? What the devil are you doing in customs, sir?"

Before him stood a short man in a black two-piece suit. His eyes were vacant, mournful, like those of an inveterate drunk and who's gone a week without any vodka. He had put his left hand on the policeman's shoulder. The cold shiver travelled down the custom official's spine once more. He looked at the stranger with inexplicable terror.

"Is the packing alright my friend?" the stranger asked softly, barely moving his bloodless lips.

"I'm not responsible for that, sir," the policeman blurted feverishly and began to shake like a leaf. "The workers delivered the box all sewn up and sealed."

"Get out of here!"

The stranger's voice, as he pronounced these words, was quiet and unemotional. His gaze, which rested on the policeman, seemed to be completely expressionless. Nonetheless, the policeman's terror mounted with each moment, and his teeth began to clatter against one another.

"I-I-I do-don't have the right, s-s-sir!"

"Get out of here at once."

The policeman pulled out a handkerchief, wiped away the sweat which was streaming in cold drops from his forehead and slowly, slowly, retreated into the corridor, and from there into the dark square.

"What's happened to you?" asked a custom's official who was passing by. "You didn't get hold of some gasoline instead of whiskey, did you?"

"You knows," the policeman replied, articulating his tongue with difficulty and looking around with an expression of terror, "a man came in here... just an ordinary kind of person... and he asked, he asked... wait, let me think... that's strange!" he interrupted himself and gave his companion a wild look. "I'm not drunk and I'm not dreaming, but strike me dead if I can remember what he even asked about!"

CHAPTER 42
READ THE NEWSPAPER!

"Tom Tops!" shouted the editor of the *New York Illustrated Gazette*. "Tom Tops!"

"That's me, sir."

"I know it's you! I'm positive it's you! But right now I need some Soviet illustrations, and not you, sir! Do you understand?"

"I understand quite well, sir."

"What the devil do I need your understanding for, you impudent fellow!" The editor ground his teeth. "I keep you employed and pay your salary not for your understanding! The whole issue is dedicated to Soviet Russia, three articles about the trade agreement, eight about the psychiatrists' convention, and there's not a single illustration!"

"There are illustrations, sir! Lord Cecil's dog in the president's cabriolet, the latest attire of the princess of Monaco, the tea service which has been purchased by Mr. Kressling for forty thousand dollars and the collection of pine cones in Wisconsin."

"You're making fun of me! I'm telling you that there's not a single illustration on the essential thing. I'm ruined, I'll be made a laughing stock! The socialists will sell out their entire supply of papers and we'll be left high and dry! And all because of you! Damn you, can't you get hold of at least some kind of picture of a factory, even three-quarters of one, half-turned around, even back to front at least! But with some ideology in it, fellow!"

"Not a word more, sir!" Tom Tops exclaimed, getting up and grabbing his photographic equipment. "You've given me an idea which will bring in brilliant results! Just wait, sir... Wait for me at the workshop."

With these words, Tops ran out onto the street and flew to the automobile garage like a madman.

Late that evening, the editor and Tops were sitting feverishly at the printer's, looking over the numerous prints and trying to decide, with the help of the typesetters, the important question about what caption to place under each photograph.

The following morning, the New York business people unfolded with pleasure the biggest issue of the *Illustrated Gazette* yet. In it was everything that human curiosity could long for.

The Inhabitants of the City of Tula Write a Letter to Jack Kressling!

A photograph from our own correspondent! With their backs turned to the viewers, a group of people, their heads bowed, were doing something above a table that sported red flags on the left and right. The group of people, to be sure, reminded one, from its composition, of the painting by the Russian artist Repin—something about a letter to some sultan—but it would have been impossible to call it a plagiarism inasmuch as the crowd of people writing the letter had been photographed from the back.

The Bolsheviks Greet the Arrival of an American Steamship!

Directly under the very bow of a real American steamship which blotted out the harbor and horizon with its bulk, people were crowding together, smacking strongly of jobless American workers as far as could be judged from their hunched backs.

On and on went the numerous shots of various city backyards and chimneys smoking against the horizon with the depiction of aroused mobs of people with their backs turned to the viewers. And only one face, which the readers could recognize without difficulty is that of the youthful Tom Tops, the *Illustrated Gazette's* own correspondent from New York, was turned to face them, in its full frontal view. Tom Tops' hand was being shaken by some important Bolshevik whose back was turned to the viewer, holding scissors in his left hand in order to cut the ribbon opening a factory ready for operation...

That day, the circulation of the *Illustrated Gazette* surpassed all expectations. On the streets, the squares, the crossroads, the trams, shoving one another, women, men, youths, lads and even pickpockets were enthusiastically buying the newspaper, some of them with their very own money, others with money that they had earned by the sweat of their brow from other people's pockets.

Towards evening the crush became all the more terrible because a rumor was circulating that the issue had been seized. The editor was ringing his hands. Tom Tops turned sick from worry. The Boston clerics had made an open inquiry to the government, asking whether they really did not understand the insulting allusion cast by the Bolsheviks at the United States of America?

"Why..." the clerics inquired, "why have they all turned their posteriors towards us?"

At the woodworking plant in Middletown, no less of an uproar held sway. The workers who had just read the newspaper were milling around the blond-haired giant who was wielding his wood plane.

"Thingsmaster," said one of them, striking him on the shoulder, "looks like that thingamabob was sent to Petrograd ahead of schedule!"

"It'll get a few things done," winked another worker, collapsing from laughter. "Just read the front page, boys!"

The newspaper made the rounds by hand until it arrived at the best scholar who raised his voice for the whole shop to hear.

"Two events," so ran the headline, "highlight the celebration of science and trade: these are the trade agreement with Russia and the convention of psychiatrists in Petrograd to which we are sending the best representatives of medicine. It is to be hoped that there is some purpose behind our food products gaining inroads into the Soviet Republic at the same time as our medicine. It is a well-known fact and no secret to anyone that medical aid in America has risen to unseen heights, and a statistical calculation has recently revealed that for every restaurant we have three hospitals and 1758 doctors in private practice. Readers, buy 'Antigastritis' pills by Doctor Pommer which will instantaneously remove the aftereffects of overindulgence in eating!"

"Hang on, what are you reading there?" Michael Thingsmaster interrupted. "Forget that part and dig a little deeper."

The local scholar omitted a column and to the approving cries of "aha", he read the following:

"On the morning of the designated day there will take place a ceremonial sitting of the Petrograd Soviet during which a gift of a luxurious timepiece in a redwood case will be presented to the Russian commissars in the name of the group of Americans who have introduced the trade agreement. On the evening of the same day the opening of the convention of psychiatrists will take place not only in the presence of learned delegates from all around the world, but also in the presence of our own authorities and citizens who will be in Petrograd on the occasion of the trade agreement."

"Damn it!" the workers from the woodworking plant exclaimed after they had laughed to their heart's content. "And we have to sit here at our work benches and wait for the news."

Unwillingly they dispersed to their places, and that particular day there was no doubt the Jack Kressling suffered a loss inasmuch as work did not seem to go well even in the hands of Thingsmaster himself.

During the lunch break, everyone scattered off to their homes. Mike had not yet managed to reach the threshold of his little wooden cottage when his sharp eyes picked out an unusual picture.

His cook, her kerchief tied up right under her nose, was energetically fighting off the embraces of an enormous white dog while the fat captain, MacKinley, was darting all around her in the vain hope of shaking her hand.

"Beauty, MacKinley!" Thingsmaster roared at the top of his lungs and dashed towards the cottage.

Ten minutes later, when the white ball had leapt about four times over her master's head, licking his nose and cheeks along the way, and then had frozen in bliss with its snout stuck in his palm, MacKinley finally managed to receive from the cook a handshake in return and letting his breath out, said to Thingsmaster:

"Sorrow sends his greetings, Mike. Things are going smooth as silk. Laurie, Ned and Willings are there too. Beauty arrived on the *Torpedo* with this here scrap from Bisk and also with a letter addressed to the Attorney General of Illinois which I sent on to the address. Here's a copy of it."

MacKinley had never uttered that kind of speech before in his life inasmuch as he was an honest Irishman. Up until now, his words had been restricted to a purely evangelical "yes, yes" and "no, no", with the addition of the tiny little word "vodka!"

For that reason it was completely understandable that he was utterly weakened and would have dropped into the arms of the cook if the latter had not brought him a proper tumblerful which she tried out twice along the way in order to test its contents.

"We're poor, but honest people, sir," she declared firmly, taking a third swallow from the tumbler. "We never bring a guest anything, be it alcohol or ordinary water, without checking to see—gulp, gulp—whether or not—gulp—it smells right, sir!"

MacKinley would obviously have preferred to dispense with this courtesy. While he was finishing off the tumbler, the Middletown telegraph operator came running up to Thingsmaster, and looking around on all sides, whispered:

"Mend-mess!"

"Mess-mend," replied Mike. "What's happened?"

"A despatch, Mike," the telegraph operator answered anxiously and handed him a piece of paper. It was from the fellows at Customs. The fellows informed him that an unknown man had gained access to the parcel addressed to Vasilov and had spent about an hour alone with it.

Thingsmaster read the note through twice and fell into thought as he bit his lips. His wide blue eyes glanced down, at Beauty, and, suddenly making up his mind, he took the dog by the collar.

"Things have taken a turn for the worse, MacKinley, it looks as though they've uncovered our work," he said to the Irishman who was wiping his lips. "Go tell them at the plant that I've come down with a fever. Meanwhile Beauty and I (the dog started to wag its tail furiously), Beauty and I will follow the parcel, and my name isn't Thingsmaster if I won't mix up the cards of that Gregorio Cice!"

CHAPTER 43
MORLENDER IN ACTION

A light, grey rain was spitting, settling on faces and clothing like microscopic rainy dust particles. Arthur Morlender, pacing back and forth along the moorage, gave a shiver and felt a slight chill. To tell the truth, the fine Petrograd rain was not the reason for it. All during these past days, Morlender had been suffering from the revolting sensation of an animal that was being hunted. He kept sensing a pair of implacable eyes on his back; he would see a fine shadow along the street that would appear and disappear behind his own shadow; everytime when he had to enter his building or come out onto the street, he would encounter first that old beggar woman, and then the tall man with a crutch and two walleyes whom he had seen the very first day of his arrival. And in the morning when he had barely gone down the stairs, a strange eastern man, swarthy like a Moor, turned up at the door. Actually, it was the shoeshine boy. He was constantly sitting there, by the entryway of No. 81 Moika Street, with his numerous wares spread out on his wooden footstool: laces for shoes, brushes, rubber heels, soles, insoles. And down below, under the stool, he spread out a whole series of tins with shoe polish. Barely catching sight of a passerby, the shoeshine boy would strike up some kind of folk song which would go something like this:

Azer-Azer-Azer-bai-djan!
Romashvili—Yerevan!

Arthur Morlender had already allowed him to clean his shoes a couple of times.

But something amazing happened today. Today the shoeshine boy, who contrary to custom had appeared at daybreak, was the first to speak, asking to clean his shoes and he even seized hold of him by the foot, although Morlender was afraid of being late for the arrival of the *Torpedo* and was not about to stop. But he did not even manage to make a move to refuse before both sides of his shoe were smeared with a thick paste, and the shoeshine boy, without raising his head from his work, suddenly declared softly in the purest English with an American accent:

"Mister Morlender, do you know what's happened to your honey of a wife?"

"Who are you?" the stunned Morlender was barely able to utter.

"Don't look as though you're talking to me... I've been ordered to follow you by Jack Kressling. But I'm not a member of their gang. My name is Willings, Willings the locksmith. I'm keeping an eye on you so as to avoid falling under suspicion, and I report the obvious truth: that you've been to the Cheka, that you've given them all the poison and bombs, that it looks as though you've crossed over from Kressling's camp to the other side. I make these reports, but actually I'm keeping an eye on you and guarding you, according to the decision of the opposite side, so that in case of any machinations I can save your life. Understand?"

"I do," replied Morlender, although he understood little more than nothing. "But Kate, Katya Ivanovna, who is she? On whose side?"

"Assigned to you from the opposite side, that is, from ours, from the workers' side. Don't worry, it must have become completely clear to her which side you went over to."

Arthur turned a deep red.

"But where is she?"

Willings dropped his brush and immedeately retrieved it. His face showed grief.

"First a polish, then a shine. Move the tip of your shoe closer, that's it... We were hoping to find out from you... Gone, the girl, I mean. It's a big loss to us..."

But at this point, a motorcycle drove up and Willings fell sternly silent, gathering up his brushes and shoeshine rags. Arthur Morlender arrived at the quay with an anxiety that was gnawing away at his heart. Kate had disappeared! The girl's friends did not know where she was—and he had been the one who had chased her out from under the roof she had shared with him in a foreign country. But now the *Torpedo* was drawing near. Ten minutes conversation with the captain and he would know about the secret of his father's demise...

"You were completely correct in coming yourself to receive the box which you'll present to the local people from a group of American laborers!" Captain Gregoire began politely, as soon as Morlender stepped onto the deck. "Demonstrations are not allowed on the quay. But it seems as though one is about to be arranged right now..." He pointed with his finger down below, and turning around, Morlender saw that a crowd was gathering by the boarding ramp, someone tossed a hat in the air and someone was shouting: "Hail to the trade agreement!"

"Come along with me," the captain continued, going on ahead and showing the way. "Here's my private quarters. Boy!"

Without giving him time to finish, a boy came running with a tray.

Glasses were filled, cigars lit, and Morlender found himself sitting in a comfortable chair. But the captain, as though struck by some sort of amazement, would not lower his piercing gaze from Morlender's face. Struggling with the invincible passivity that was overwhelming him, a passivity that was akin to sleeping with both eyes open, Arthur Morlender finally found the words that had been hovering at the tip of his tongue for many days:

"Captain, I have a question for you. Precisely where and how did the coffin with my father, Jeremy Morlender, end up on your ship? My mother-in-law as far as I recall, spoke with you, but I did not..." He wanted to continue but stopped short. The strange, dilating gaze of the captain had nailed his tongue to the roof of his mouth, had bound up all his limbs, had caused the hair to bristle on his head. His mouth had become unbearably dry. He finally opened his mouth, gulped in some air and—let his head fall onto his chest. He was asleep.

Captain Gregoire rang twice. Warrant officer Kovalkovsky entered together with a tall, grey-headed man with two walleyes who is familiar to our reader as the disguised count.

"You were correct," the captain announced dryly. "It is essential to get him out of the way, but not to do away with him for the time being. Take him where the box will be kept and where his accomplice is being held. I departed with a strict directive from Jack Kressling to send Vasilov as a visitor, before the presentation of the gift, to the Central Aero-Electrical Station, merely to have to a look around, to become familiar with it, to talk, and nothing more. On his departure he was supposed to leave this slow-working pellet there without being noticed. But this man has betrayed us. He is useless. However, if you can disguise one person, then you can disguise another. You, Count, are of the same size for example... The make-up artist who created Vasilov out of

Morlender, is here. He'll make you look like him and you'll assume the assignment for the Aero-Electrical Station. As for this one," Captain Gregoire touched Arthur's legs with the tip of his shoe, "we'll keep this one under hypnosis and send him to deliver the gift."

"Excellent!" the counterfeit beggar responded acidly. "They'll trust him. Only remove his documents for me..."

Bt it was in vain that the captain rummaged around in the pockets of the sleeping Morlender. Morlender had left his documents on his table. The shoeshine boy, after finishing his job, had taken but a moment to peek into the room Morlender had left in order to convince himself one more futile time that Miss Orton was not hiding somewhere in the vicinity. But once he had gained entry into the room and seeing Vasilov's documents on the table, the staid Willings had put them into his chest pocket just in case, or for any future unforeseen circumstances. For this reason, Captain Gregoire did not find anything on Morlender.

"You'll go down to the factory, Count, and ask them to give you a pass to the chief electrician at the station, that's all there is to it. But now—as quickly as possible, regain your youth, take off your wig, walleyes, eyebrows, wrinkles and turn yourself over to the hands of our magician. And one thing more: the phonograph will reproduce Vasilov's speech a few times for you and you'll practice in your room in order to assimilate his intonation and pitch."

CHAPTER 44
IN THE LAIR OF THE BEAST

One hour, then two, passed. Miraculous transformations were taking place all this while beneath the hands of the unknown make-up artist in the very same cabin where not long before the young Arthur Morlender had sat before him in the role of a newly arisen Vasilov. The dry and wiry Russian count did not resemble Morlender in very much other than, perhaps, his build and bearing. But after removing and cleaning away the coarse layers which had transformed the count into an old beggar, the make-up artist set to work with his tweezers and brushes. Slowly, slowly, in this lean count of indeterminate age, the features of that same Vasilov began to appear more and more: the skin was smoothed out, the wrinkles disappeared, the corners of the lips were lifted, the puffy jowls disappeared, eyebrows grew up anew under the fingers of the make-up artist. The work was delicate but durable. In the very same place, in the very same cabin, that very same person emerged, practically in the very same spot where he had been murdered not long before. And all this while, Arthur Morlender was lying in a deep sleep in the cabin of Captain Gregoire.

When at last the work of the unknown make-up artist had been concluded, the captain and warrant officer Kovalkovsky bent over Morlender. They took his clothing and shoes off, picked him up from the chair, and with considerable difficulty, stuffed the motionless body into a large box standing in a corner of the cabin. A lid with inconspicuous openings for air was lowered and nails were hammered in. Sailors who had been summoned were sewing up the box with canvas, when suddenly the captain was anxiously called by the make-up artist. The shoes which had been taken from Morlender's feet—there was no way they would fit the narrow but unusually long foot of the count! Another half-hour elapsed before they came up with a suitable pair of shoes from the wardrobe of warrant officer Kovalkovsky. But the warrant officer, meanwhile, was out on deck, cursing vilely. The fact was that the mixed crowd which had gathered before the *Torpedo*, kept growing and growing. When the overhead crane was letting the first crate unloaded from the *Torpedo* swing down to the ground, loud cries resounded: "This is a gift of friendship!"... "An American parcel from the workers!"... "Hail to friendship with American laborers!" The box was quickly seized down below by the sailors from the *Torpedo*, but a second one to replace it came swinging through the air. The public had not expected that and they began to discuss and figure out who and what was being sent to whom in this second box. While the sailors were grabbing the second box as well, and putting both of them on a cart, dragging it along the cement roadway away from the quay, up above, on the deck, the engineer Vasilov had appeared. He descended the landing ramp in silence: the phonograph had not yet taught him all the peculiarities of Morlender's speech. On his way down, he turned once more to the *Torpedo* and waved at Captain Gregoire.

At that moment, he was noticed by the carpenter Willings who had rushed to the moorage in the same swarthy-faced disguise of the shoeshine boy with which he had established himself on Moika Street.

"Seems like my boy is alive and well and is even parting with the captain on friendly terms!" he thought to himself with relief. "But what's this?"

Rubbing his eyes, he worked his way closer to the ramp. Vasilov, who was descending the steps let his eyes meet with those of Willings—but the eyes were those of a stranger, and their expression bore nothing, no recognition whatsoever. However, Willings was not looking at his face now. He was looking at his shoes. In the morning he himself had cleaned Morlender's black American shoes and had shined them to a brilliant gloss. But these were brown, Swedish boots, three or four sizes larger.

"Aha!" Willings thought, turned to the crowd, sought out Ned, found him and called him over with a nod of his neck.

"Ned," he whispered to him in a barely audible voice, "it's my job to follow this guy. I don't think it's Morlender. But you watch where they take those boxess over there, not just the one, but both of them. Do it anyway you can even if you have to split yourself in two, but don't lose one or the other."

Ned nodded and immediately faded into the background. The staid Willings, in his swarthy-faced disguise, was about to try and shout something like "Hurray for Vasilov" together with the crowd and even to block Vasilov's way, clumsily kicking him with the toe of his boot. But there was not a flicker of anything familiar in the eyes of the man passing by. Raising his hat, bowing left and right, not at all with the quick and light walk of Morlender, but even with a certain predilection for an artificial limp, the counterfeit Vasilov passed by on his way to the car that was waiting for him.

Meanwhile, the real Morlender, tightly packed up in the box, was quickly transported to a spot where he was rudely tossed on the floor. But he did not feel the bumps, just as he did not hear the banging and creaking of tools that were tearing the lid off above him, nor was he aware of the musty stream of air when the lid was removed. Morlender was still asleep, although not so deeply. He was picked up and lowered onto a rug and tied up to the legs of a massive oak table. Then his hands and feet were tightly bound up and the canvas that the box had been sewn up in was tossed over him. Having done all of that, the people left without paying the slightest attention to the other bound person who was lying in the opposite corner.

When the steps had died away and silence had reigned for about two minutes, the bound figure in the corner manifested several signs of life. It made a few convulsive movements resembling the twitching of a fish that was trying to swim on land—and rolling over from side to side, it began gradually to crawl, or rather, to roll, towards the sleeping Morlender. At the same time a gradual transition was taking place. Sleep was beginning to leave him, and the vital signs of life—currents of air, clenched hands, renewed circulation, a sunbeam falling on his face from the window, and, finally, the breathing of some other person beside him—began to attract him more and more strongly to consciousness. The sunbeam, which had tickled his nostrils, caused an unexpected sneeze, and together with the sneeze, Morlender opened his eyes and felt himself vilely sick. Nausea rose in his throat, his hands and feet ached. He let his eyes wonder hither and yon, and suddenly he saw Katya Ivanovna beside him on the floor.

It was an utterly new Kate. Her face had grown thin, yellow and blue shadows of hunger and suffering lay on it. Her curls were dishevelled and matted in a ball. The nails of her bound hands were filthy and torn—from her vain attempts to break the rope. A gag stuck out of her mouth. But even like that she seemed closer, more understandable and human to him.

"Crawl closer to my fingers so that I can pull the gag out," he whispered in a barely audible voice. It was not easy. The taut ropes had made his hands swell up. But his fingers were dexterous and long. Making the tips off his fingers meet with difficulty, he used them to seize the torn edge of the gag. The girl helped him, pulling her head back carefully. Inch by inch the revolting rag was finally pulled out, but Kate could not immediately move her lips which had turned blue.

"Where are we?" he asked quietly.

"With the enemies of the Soviet people, the White Guards," she replied with difficulty. "You should keep silent for a while, otherwise you'll be sick and there's no water here. Five days, maybe ten, I don't know how many days it's been since the day I left you. I haven't seen any bread or water. I'm living on what they inject under my skin. How did you fall into their hands?"

"What about you?"

"I got lost, trying to find my way to friends, and I crawled right into the beast's lair... My name isn't Katya Ivanovna. I'm Vivian Orton, the daughter of a typist from Kressling's office. Your father was in love with my mother. She was poisoned... she was poisoned to make it look as though your father had done it... I wanted to take revenge on his son because of her..."

Morlender turned to her, ignoring both his nausea and the pain in his hands from the ropes that were cutting into his fingers. He looked at her with the serious, honest look of youth that has stumbled into wrong, and she returned his look with the same kind of serious, honest look.

"Kate... Vivian! Father never would have done that, he couldn't have... Never, do you understand?"

"I'm beginning to think that way."

"And I was deceived as well. Even now we're comrades in misfortune. Forget and forgive the past. We'll untangle ourselves from this together. Move closer, I'll chew through your ropes with my teeth."

She rolled over flat against him and with his strong teeth he began to split one thread after another in order to bite through her ropes. Then with one hand free she loosened his knots. And they untied the ropes without saying anything, but by simply infusing every movement with a secret, inner tranquility that was born of their presence together, of the slaking of their thirst for each other, a thirst which they themselves did not even suspect as yet. Vivian and Morlender freed themselves from their bonds, at the same time unconsciously strengthening other ties that bound their youthful hearts.

CHAPTER 45
THE ELECTRICIAN
AT THE AERO-ELECTRIC STATION

All during these days the technician Sorrow lay in inactivity: an attack of his old swamp fever which had been contracted in his youth in the damp shafts of the Kresslings', suddenly knocked him off his feet. Cursing his illness, he vented his spleen on his three faithful friends who uncomplainingly took turns looking after him and carrying out important work around the city. Sorrow knew all of the unsettling news: Mike had telegraphed him that at the last moment Kressling had apparently changed the mechanism in the watch which had been so cleverly disarmed by the technician Sorrow. And Laurie Lane, on his orders, had already gotten in touch with the Soviet authorities and had related all the details to them. Sorrow knew as well about the events which were coming up in Petrograd: the ceremonial sitting of the Petrograd Soviet and the convention of psychiatrists. Feeling much better today, he had already arisen, dressed and exchanged his prone position for an ambulatory one. When his three faithful friends—the blond-haired Laurie, the taciturn Ned and the staid Willings in the disguise of a shoeshine boy—had taken a peek into his room, they had seen the old-timer Sorrow, with hands folded behind his back, pacing back and forth, back and forth, from wall to wall, in the confined space of his room.

"Sit down. Let's have your report, fellows!" he nodded to them, impatiently continuing his pacing which the fever had kept him from for so long. "What's new? Where's Mike? Has the *Torpedo* arrived? Has Miss Orton been found? Why don't you begin, Laurie."

The wretched Laurie turned red and looked with downcast eyes. All that time, day and night, he had searched without success for the vanished, attractive Miss Orton. He had not been successful in finding a trace or a clue to preserve even a crumb of hope for the possibility of seeing her alive. His face was sullen and distrought.

"I'm ashamed, Sorrow, I've found nothing. Miss Vivian Orton disappeared so suddenly, so completely that not even Morlender could help. Willings says that he hasn't seen her from the moment she went out through the door of her room. And no one has come to ask for the trunk."

Sorrow shook his head. Laurie's wretched look prevented him from using the word that was hovering at the tip of his tongue.

"You, Ned?" he asked after an indeterminate, painful silence for all concerned.

"My news will be better. Two boxes—note, not one, but two—have been unloaded from the *Torpedo*. I followed them to where they were delivered. Both were taken to the same place. One of them—I know this for sure because I picked it out with my magnifying glass—is our trademark, so it must be the clock itself, Sorrow. What's in the other, I have no idea."

The staid Willings assiduously cleared his throat:

"My news is important. I am reporting, first of all, that I've looked over all the passengers. Mike wasn't to be seen among them. Secondly, Morlender went to Captain Gregoire, sat for about two hours in his cabin, then came out of there... Well, Sorrow, get ready for a surprise, old boy! Someone in disguise came out again. Done up like Vasilov, you can't deny that, only it wasn't Morlender. But where Morlender himself is, whether he's dead or alive, I don't know. And that's not all. The new Vasilov went from the *Torpedo* directly to the factory. And what do you think he did there? He made a lot of effort to get himself a pass to the Central Aero-Electrical Station."

"The Aero-Electrical Station!" Sorrow cried with extreme anxiety as he interrupted his pacing. "We didn't foresee that! Measures will have to be taken. But why a pass from the factory? After all his pockets are full of documents and everyone believes him, Willings."

The swarthy-faced shoeshine boy guffawed, pulled a wallet out of his wide trousers, and from the wallet several pieces of paper that were lightly smeared with shoe polish, and spread them out before the technician Sorrow.

"Here are those same documents from Morlender's room."

"Good work," Sorrow praised him. "Here's what we'll do, boys. There's little time to forewarn the Soviet authorities and we can't go pestering them with every little trifle. Where's your new boy, Willings?"

"At the factory. He can't do anything until tomorrow. Entry to the Station has already been terminated for today!"

"Good! Laurie, the tins with the make-up!"

Not without some surprise Laurie brought him a box with colored creams.

"Well, now, all three of you sit down here in a row so that I won't have to do you up separately!"

Laurie, Willings and Ned seated themselves on a bench, looking at Sorrow in confusion.

Sorrow soaked a rag in water, and, one-two-three, tore the blond moustache and brows from Laurie, the entire eastern get-up from Willings and then wiped them all down with the wet rag. That finished, he took up a brush, three blond wigs, nose pincers and various other secrets of the make-up trade and quickly began to go to work on all three of the boys, smearing them in equal measure and with impartiality. A half-hour later, three young fellows were sitting before him, made up with no small artistry to resemble to unfortunate Vasilov or Arthur Morlender.

"One might say that it's not particularly fine work, a bit coarse," Sorrow declared, admiring his handiwork, "but it'll do for our purposes. Laurie, do we have any formal attire?"

"For one gentleman, Sorrow, over there in the closet."

Sorrow pulled out a new black, two-piece suit, high shoes, a top hat, tie, gloves and walking stick, and gave it all a critical glance.

"Not bad, fellows," he declared, his mind made up, "we'll split up one gentlemen's outfit among three, it'll do like that."

A minute had hardly passed before Willings was flaunting a marvellous suit jacket; Ned was in a pair of stylish trousers; and Laurie was dressed in top hat, patent leather high shoes, gloves and walking stick, or more properly expressed: *arrayed* in top hat, patent leather high shoes, gloves and walking stick.

"Honest to goodness," Sorrow said, "you'll more than do under any circumstances! And now take these here documents!"

He gave Laurie the letter of recommendation made out in Vasilov's name, to Ned he gave an identity card in Vasilov's name, and to Willings, the party card made out in Vasilov's name. In a serious voice he declared:

"Listen to me carefully, fellows. I'm not afraid of an explosion. Whether they've changed the mechanism or not, in any event the Soviet authorities have been forewarned. The one thing that we have to fear is an accident to the electrician at the Aero-Electric Station. Do you understand? It's not likely that the new Morlender will try to get to him first thing tomorrow morning. And so, fellows, here's a little bit of work for you to do. First thing tomorrow morning, go to the Aero-Electric station and have a little chat with the electrician, giving your name as Vasilov..."

"Talk about what?" Laurie asked in surprise.

"I'll tell you about what," Sorrow winked, "about a bribe, naturally. You'll say to him, for example, won't he sell out the Soviet authorities for decent currency and loosen a few screws here and there for you."

"Sorrow, you're off your rocker!" Willings blurted.

"I don't think so," Sorrow replied tranquilly. "Of course, the first one isn't going to escape going to jail, and then the second one comes along and does the same. Using a bit of clever diplomacy, one can count on the fact that the second one will end up in the slammer too, and at the same time along comes the third Vasilov."

"But what the devil's the point?" moaned Ned.

"The point is, you son-of-a-blockhead, is that they won't even give the fourth Vasilov a chance to speak—do you understand?"

The fellows exchanged looks and burst into laughter, tried to fall on Sorrow to give him a kiss, but Sorrow turned away just in time in order to save the valuable make-up job on the faces of his comrades.

The Aero-Electrical Station was the most closely guarded point in the city. The chief electrician who was in charge of the electrification of the atmosphere, remained inside it day and night, deprived, like the Roman Pope, of the right to enter any other territory. Meanwhile, aircraft constantly patrolled the sky, guarding the gigantic electrical transmitters. At the first warning of danger, a colossal lever, that controlled transmission power over a twenty kilometer chain of steel grid-work, was supposed to send up a fiery shield of electricity to a height of a thousand meters above Petrograd. At the same time, the entire city would be switched off from the electrical network and be plunged into absolute darkness.

Down below, at the gates to the station, stood a platoon of guards that were relieved every half-hour.

Early in the morning, before the detachment of guards that had just come off duty had a chance to march off for a rest, saluting their relief on the way, a frivolous-looking young man in a top hat and with a walking stick appered on the parade square. He advanced, waving all his limbs in front of him, sucking his stomach in as far as possible, so that his miserable excuse for a jacket and his patched trousers completely faded into the background before the eye of the observer.

"I'm the communist Vasilov," he blurted out abruptly and stuck a document in the face of the guard on duty. "I have to see the head electrician at once!"

The document was read and accepted, and Vasilov was accompanied to the first inner yard into which he ran, waving his gloves.

All the gates were passed, but not without some difficulty.

The experimental Aero-Electrical Station. The chief electrician, a grey-headed man with a set and stern face, came to meet the visitor.

"Comrade... eh... do you speak English?"

"Yes," replied the chief electrician.

"I've come... eh... at the request of a certain government. Mr. Electrician, do you know what the exchange value of the dollar is? What's your opinion on the exchange value of the almighty Dollar?"

The chief electrician stared at the strange man in amazement.

"Enough of playing the fool!" the man in the top hat said in a conciliatory voice and grabbed the electrician by the shoulder. "Spoil all this song-and-dance here! My government won't be miserly! A thousand billion... In a wink of an eye!"

The chief electrician whistled and shouted to a detachment of station guards that came running up:

"A madman or a criminal! Put him in the station prison!"

They grabbed the young man under the arms and although he made incessant attempts to bite and spit, they immediately installed him in the communal cell of the station prison.

A half-hour later, the detachment of guards standing by the entrance to the station were relieved by a fresh detachment. They exchanged salutes with the new arrivals, shouldered their rifles and marched off in order to the barracks.

"Cough-cough!" came the sound of a fawning cough and up to the new detachment came a man who was proudly sticking his stomach out. He was in a marvellous suit jacket, and any observer would involuntarily let their gaze come to rest on this imposing figure of a gentleman—something which afforded him the chance to keep both feet in their tattered boots far behind all of the rest of his body.

"Comrades! I'm the communist Vasilov. Here's my document. Take me to thee chief electrician!" The suit jacket pronounced in an important and measured voice.

The gates were opened and the gentleman pressed forward with the front part of his body so speedily that both of his feet were practically left behind on the other side of the gates that slammed quickly shut.

The grey-haired chief electrician came out to greet the second visitor with a certain amount of annoyance. He gave a shudder when he caught sight of the striking resemblance to the first visitor. But his amazement was transformed into dumbfoundedness when the visitor beckoned to him with his crooked finger and said in a mysterious voice:

"Mr. Electrician, come over here! Come on, fellow! I've come to see you on important business. For a good million dollars couldn't you maybe unscrew a couple or more of the transmitters for me? A friendly power and I are getting ready to toss a bomb in here... Eh?"

Ten minutes later he was cooling his heels in the communal cell of the station prison, frightening the guards with his thunderous cackling that resembled something between a roaring and a laughing sound.

Meanwhile, a young man in magnificent ballroom trousers, with his legs bowed in a circular shape and his head bent off to one side as though it were some kind of secret package containing a bribe, stood before the new platoon of guards. He was flaunting his trousers in front of an older guard with a great deal of distinction, pronouncing his name with a nasal tone:

"I am the com-mu-nist Vasilov, here's my document. I must see the chief electrician on government business!"

Receiving his pass, he spun around on his axis and slowly passed through the gates, keeping his feet close together and widening the diameter of the bow of his legs insofar as the anatomy of the human body would allow.

"Strange," muttered the chief electrician, when he caught sight of the third visitor.

"My friend," the young man in the trousers said to him. "Suppose that you have a wife and children. On the one hand, a wife, children and a trillion dollars, not just any old kind, but Washington dollars, take note. On the other hand, what a miserable bit of electrification. Come to your senses, old buddy!"

After locking him up in the communal cell, the chief electrician called the duty officer on the telephone.

"Hello!" he said curtly. "A psychiatric epidemic has appeared in the city, that is, if it isn't a conspiracy. Don't change the guard until evening. If any new Vasilovs show up, seize them without a word, search them and conduct them under armed guard to the station prison."

The duty officer did not even manage to hang up the receiver when a service automobile from the Putilov works pulled up in front of the platoon of guards and an impressive man in a complete two-piece suit together with all the other paraphenalia of attire jumped out.

"I'm the communist Vasilov," he declared politely, going up to the duty-officer and raising two fingers to his cap. "Here is the requisition from the director of the Works..."

He did not manage to finish before several dozen Red Army soldiers pounced on him, tied him up hand and foot and searched him from head to toe.

"Lock this up in the guard-hut," one of them said, handing the duty officer a strange piece of glass, some master keys, a bottle with pale blue pellets and a monstrous steel instrument.

The arrested man was taken by the collar and under armed guard to the communal cell in the station prison where he suddenly gave a shudder and stared fiercely at the three cheerful lads who were so terribly similar to him and who were dissolving in frenzied fits of laughter at the sight of him.

CHAPTER 46
THE NEIGHBOR'S GRATEFUL DONKEY

A hot midday in the state of Illinois, a familiar occurrence mainly because it is typical of a Northern Central region, resembling the hot middays of any other country that is of the same longitude.

On the veranda of a country home, beneath a canvas awning, sat a serene old man stricken with paralysis. This was the Attorney General of the state of Illinois who had vainly been seeking retirement. Two old negroes on his right and left were brushing flies away from him. A pink parrot sat on his shoulder. On his knees lay a cat, at his feet, an Irish setter with four pups. The old man's gaze was fixed on a marvellous aquarium not far from his armchair that was filled with all manner of Chinese hydropods—a superfluous feature for fish who dwell in moist places in any event.

The old man's tongue, twisting with difficulty, came into motion:

"H-h-how are my p-p-piglets?" he asked one of the negroes.

"They're eating, Massah Milky, praise be to the Lord."

"And m-my f-f-frog?"

"Let down the well, Massah Milky."

"And m-my daughter?"

But the latter did not afford the negro an opportunity to reply since she appeared on the veranda in the company of a guest, the representative Pirouette who had come visiting.

"Wipe papa's nose!" she said angrily to the negroes and seated herself in an armchair, crossing her legs. The representative sat down beside her.

The youthful Miss Milky was a spinster of fifty-three years of age. Her short lawn-tennis skirt showed off her figure to advantage, and her curly red wig lent her pert little face an even greater piquancy.

"Don't try and console me, dear Mr. Pirouette! I am convinced that I shall go mad! And the sooner, the better!" she blurted in a long-suffering whisper.

"But your dear papa..." Pirouette noted anxiously.

"Oh! They won't let him retire for anything! After this famous business they latched onto him as though with tongs! And try to understand, dear Mister Pirouette, all his correspondence, all these letters, complaints, appeals and counterappeals, I have to read all of this myself. During the best years of my life, while others are dancing, cavorting and... alas!... meeting other people like themselves, but I have to sit over these papers!" A moan escaped from Miss Milky's abundant bosom.

"But why don't you hire a secretary?"

Miss Milky fixed an amazed look on the representative.

"Hire a secretary, in Illinois! Dear Mister Pirouette, you ought to know that it's easier for us to buy a railroad than to hire a secretary! We don't have a single workhand here!"

The representative Pirouette looked at her in horror.

"Not a single one!" she repeated energetically. "And whenever any old wretched émigré comes our way—you do know that there was a time when they did reach Illinois—then they're snatched up immediately by that dog, that monster, that madman, that young Nero, that *Apache Indian*, Mister Dot!"

With these words, Miss Milky collapsed against the back of her chair and her body began to tremble all over with a nervous convulsion.

"Tell me, who is this Mister Dot?" the representative inquired tenderly, placing his hand on the trembling fingers of the wretched Miss.

The answer was a long silence. Finally, gathering her strength, she opened her eyes and pronounced hoarsely:

"Dot—he's a fatal man, Mister Pirouette. He's the perpetrator of all our misfortunes... Sometime, when there's a spare moment..."

"But I'm leaving today!" the representative exclaimed fearfully.

"In a spare moment, I'll tell you the terrifying drama of our lives. But for the time being, just a single word: Dot's an author! He's the author of the vile article about the detective talents of my father. He's the author of the interview that caused such an uproar and in which my daddy..." Miss Milky sobbed... "my daddy was described in such... such words as though Sherlock Holmes and Nat Pinkerton were no better than chimneysweeps next to him!"

Without the strength to continue the conversation, Miss Milky covered her face with a lace handkerchief, just in the nick of time to catch a piece of make-up that had fallen from underneath her left eye.

Mister Pirouette was moved with interest. He was already on the verge of telling Miss Milky that he would agree to delay his departure, when from the direction of the driveway that curved around the summer home, frenzied cries broke forth.

"Stop! Stop! Stop!" someone wailed in a fury, flourishing a club and dashing as fast as his legs would carry him after a small grey donkey that was dragging a strange burden along the road.

But the donkey, as more often tends to be the case with donkeys, expressed a completely contrary intention, and, kicking its pursuer, dashed on ahead at a gallop.

Miss Milky's fingers dug into the representative's arm. Miss Milky's eyes fastened on the donkey's pursuer.

"Dot!" she whispered feverishly. "Look at that, that horrible Dot is persecuting his donkey... And the donkey... Good Lord, what's he dragging?! Dear Pirouette, hold me by the waist, I'm fainting, I'm dying! He's dragging an émigré!"

The spectacle which was unravelling on the driveway became more and more catastrophic. Dot, a black-moustached man in a straw hat and the unkempt dress of a farmer, dashed to cut off the donkey, trying to chase it back into his yard and heaping abuse on it. But the donkey, braying frenziedly, slipped past him, made two or three zig-zags, flicked its tail up and, quite unexpectedly to everyone's surprise, suddenly flew into the yard of Mister Milky's home. It dashed right up to the armchair where the paralytic old man lay and shook its head, trying to throw the halter off its neck that the strange burden was clutching onto.

"Nice d-donkey!" whispered Mister Milky, smiling blissfully. "C-come h-here, nice donkey! My grateful friend! My donkey-g-gentleman!"

While these phrases were being forced from the old man's tongue, Miss Milky and the representative were energetically disentangling the donkey's burden. It was an older, poorly dressed and terribly wasted man. The stamp of profound suffering lay on his face.

"You're hired! Sign the contract!" Miss Milky shrilled at the same time as Mister Dot was demanding his donkey back amid curses, promising to tear the hide off it and stick a hot branding-iron under its tail.

"I'm an émigré," the wretched fellow muttered, hanging his head. "I didn't have the strength to go on foot and attached myself to this kind animal that was grazing in the meadow, in the hope that it would lead me to some dwelling."

"You're hired on the spot!" Miss Milky rapped out. "The building you see here is the ancestral residence of my father, the Attorney General of the State of Illinois."

"For an émigré you have excellent command of the language," the representative butted in. "What's your name, my dear fellow?"

The wretched man passed a hand over his face.

"My name is Pavel Tusk."

CHAPTER 47
CONCERNING THE REASONS
FOR THE DONKEY'S GRATITUDE

"Now that you have a secretary and I've stayed over for an extra day," the representative Pirouette began tenderly as he sat with Miss Milky under the moonlight on a garden bench, "now I want to learn from you all about these secrets! Why they won't let your papa retire, why this Dot has sung his praises all over America, and why Mister Milky called the donkey a grateful animal?"

"Ah," sighed Miss Milky. "You want to peer into the depths of my heart... I agree. Listen to me, dear Mister Pirouette, listen and cry your eyes out!"

She bowed her head, gathered courage and began the following tale which was interrupted by the frequent croaking of a frog, the oinking of piglets and the nocturnal screech of bats.

"We moved here when daddy was stricken with paralysis, about two years ago, sir. This place was deserted and gloomy, particularly for a youthful creature. Daddy felt wonderful because he adores animals, but I had to look after the farming day and night, at the same time that the melodies of Schopenhauer were singing in my breast."

"You mean, Chopin?" the representative asked.

"Of course, Chopin Hauer," Miss Milky corrected herself. "My father applied for retirement and they were willing to accept it. They were merely waiting for a suitable workhand to take his place—something which is devilishly difficult in Illinois, as I've already told you. And then, one fine day, they came running up to us and told us that the neighboring farm had been bought and that we would shortly have a neighbor, a certain Mister Dot from Arkansas. I immediately took my geography text, sir, and started an inquiry. I learned that Arkansas lay in the south and that natives from there possessed a fiery temperament. Alas, sir, an anguishing presentiment seized hold of me!.. The neighbor arrived and not three days passed before he paid us a visit."

Miss Milky broke off her tale, pressed her hand to her heart. The representative put his arm encouragingly around her waist.

"Just imagine, sir, a tall, handsome man with a black moustache. Imagine, on the one hand, this desolate, agricultural place and a young, helpless girl, and on the other hand, a tall man with a black moustache and a fiery Arkansas temperament. What I feared, came to pass: Mister Dot fell in love with me from the first glance. True, he did not admit it to me. But his looks, his gestures, were more eloquent than words. I only had to move closer to him and he would shudderingly push me away from himself. I would barely manage to enter the room and he would interrupt his conversation with Daddy and grab his hat. If I looked at him at the table, he wouldn't eat; if I fell ill and remained in my room, he would come to visit daddy for the whole day, obviously concerned about my health. This couldn't go on like that, sir. I know how to be firm despite all my youthfulness. I wrote Mister Dot a letter requesting a mutual clarification and the termination of needless sufferings which had put both me and him in an untenable position...

"Mister Dot did not reply. Moreover, he ceased to visit us and hid out on his farm for the course of two weeks. The negroes were saying that during that time he carried on Nero's style of life. He only drank alcohol, sir, he burned entire heaps of rubbish in his yard and he would go off to bathe in the pond. I understood my female duty. For fear that he might commit suicide, I put on a light scarf and at sunset I went to him, ignoring all meaningless prejudice.

"At the sight of me, Mister Dot gave a shriek, leapt up from his place, took two steps and as though mown down, he fell at my feet. I hid my triumph and placed both hands on the head of this frenzied man. I whispered:

"No explanations are necessary! Let's go along to daddy!"

"But Mister Dot's pride proved to be so pathological that he began to refute the obvious fact and, like a child, he insisted that he had wanted to run out of the room and had fallen as the result of a broken heel. And he even contrived to show me that heel which had been broken in some accidental fashion. Knut Hamsun, sir, if you've at least read that writer, specialized in portraying that kind of pride in his love novels. I remembered them and wouldn't let myself be drawn into deception. Smiling tenderly, I threatened Mister Dot with my finger and called him a 'madman in love'. Ah, sir, I never suspected what the result of that would be. Mister Dot seized his hat and ran off into the plains. He hid out in the plains for three days, spending the night out in the open and sustaining himself on green peas. On the fourth day he showed up, bringing a small grey donkey with him."

Miss Milky sighed and wiped her eyes.

"I should tell you, sir, that I was named Eunice in honor of my grandmother. And then that insane man from Arkansas ceased to be on speaking terms with me and my daddy, finding a perverted satisfaction for his passions. He named his donkey Eunice and the whole day long he would beat this animal with a club right in front of our veranda, smiling like the Marquis de Sade. My father, as you must have noticed, nourishes a positively tender feeling for animals of both sexes and of any species. I barely had time to recover when he started to rock on his chair and demanded that I initiate legal proceedings against Mister Dot for tormenting the donkey. As though that wasn't enough, sir, daddy rocked himself into such a state that he ordered himself to be carried to the trial hearing and he himself delivered the speech for the prosecution. If only you had seen the way it was! The entire room cried rivers. Daddy was all covered in tears and couldn't wipe himself dry. Mister Dot was sentenced to pay the most enormous fine. Since then, sir, I have been living under the threat of his vengeance. For a while everything was quiet, he had gone off somewhere. Then suddenly lightning struck. Dot placed an article in the newspapers about the famous detective abilities of my daddy. Poor daddy's retirement was postponed, and from that day forth, sir, we have been receiving daily hundreds of letters about various criminal acts with requests to solve them... What I've been going through because of these letters which insult my innocence, no description would do it justice!"

Miss Eunice Milky sighed and leaned her head on the representative's head. Then she shrieked as though she had been stung, kissed him directly on the lips and like a delicate doe she dashed off into the house.

Mister Pirouette quickly pulled a piece of make-up out of his mouth which had fallen there, looked around on all sides and, like a thief, made his way to the stables.

"Saddle up my horse!" he whispered to a negro, giving him an energetic kick with his foot. "I have to get back to Michigan by first light and I don't want to bother my hosts."

Now astride his horse and having put twelve miles between himself and the cottage, the representative finally found the courage himself to turn around and direct a farewell speech Eunice's way.

"The way things were turning out," he muttered, "she would have walled me up with her make-up plaster after five or six meetings. A fine sight I would have been turning up before my constituents, solidly plastered over like some kind of door! And then I'd like to know how I would have been able to campaign against the trade agreement with Russia."

CHAPTER 48
A WALRUS FROM SAN FRANCISCO

The morning frogs had barely enough time to croak out their hymn to the sun when Mr. Milky's new secretary appeared on the veranda and set about fulfilling his responsibilities. On the table lay a stack of correspondence which had just been delivered to the address of the Attorney General.

He mechanically opened several envelopes, ran through them and began to make notes in his notebook. Pavel Tusk was a precise person. Despite the strange stamp of lifelessness and numbness covering his entire exterior, Tusk's eyes manifested a high level of intelligence. He had completed half of his work when a small, filthy envelope saturated with tobacco smoke turned up in his hands. With exactly the same methodicalness, he opened this envelope as well and was about to immerse himself in reading it when suddenly color spread throughout his face and his eyes began to flash like a madman's. Mister Tusk leapt up from his place and his eyes began to search for the bell. To tell the truth, his actions did not in the least resemble those of an official person from an emigrant background. The negro who appeared in response to his ring, halted in the doorway as though riveted to the spot.

"Hey, listen!" the secretary announced in an authoritative voice, holding the envelope in his hands. "Who's been reading Mr. Milky's correspondence up untill now?"

"Miss Eunice," babbled the negro, his eyes bulging out at Tusk.

"Call her here!"

"Miss Eunice is taking a milk bath," the negro dared to report.

"Call her here when she's finished!" the secretary said and once more buried himself in the letter.

"Nolla," said the negro to a fat negress who was in charge of Miss Eunice's maids. "Tell the young missy that she's to crawl out of the milk. The new secretary can hardly wait to see her, tell her that."

"Fool," replied the negress. "It'd be easier to call that salt pork fresh that she's been giving us for dinner!"

And, tying up her mobcap, she went into the bathroom where Miss Eunice Milky was peacefully lingering in milk to doubtful purpose for herself, but to the immense good fortune of those close to her, because milk, as is well known, is not distinguished for its transparency.

Miss Eunice was definitely out of sorts, but the basic feature of her staunch nature was the ability not to surrender dead or alive to fate.

"You say that he left late at night without telling anyone to be awoken?" she questioned yet again her maid who was preparing a balsam concoction out of dried heliotropes, powder and various creams in a mortar.

"That's the way it was Missy," the maid replied in a talkative mood. "The stablehand said it looked as though he were prancing around like a hot mare waiting for his horse, and then he jumped into the saddle and disappeared."

"That's what the meaning of jealousy is," Miss Eunice declared thoughtfully, her joints creaking in the milk like castanets. "Dorothy, I advise you never to tell a new admirer about your other worshippers. It has a terrible effect on their pride." She fell silent for a few moments, gazing at the ceiling: "And I shouldn't have rejoiced at the appearance of Mr. Tusk in his presence, no, I definitely shouldn't have!"

"Mister Tusk begs Miss Milky to come out and see him as soon as possible," Nolla announced, catching her breath, as she stuck her black head through the door. "He told Sam and Sam told me and I..."

Miss Milky did not allow her to finish. Tossing a triumphant look Dorothy's way, she parted the milky waves and arose out of them to her full stature in the likeness of Aphrodite.

A half-hour later, a red-haired girl in a short dress ran pertly out onto the veranda.

"Let's go and have breakfast, dear Mr. Tusk! Business can wait!" she cried with captivating naiveté and clung to the arm of the secretary.

But the secretary displayed an extraordinary tenacity. He gave her a piercing look, held out the envelope to her and said:

"Read the letter and try to remember what you did with the preceding letter that the writer alludes to."

Miss Milky submitted to the secretary's order despite herself. She read the following:

> Of unknown origin, delivered by a dog who arrived from America in Kronstadt, and sent on to the addressed by the captain of the vessel *Amelia*, MacKinley, the Irishman.

Following these oversized curlicues that were utterly saturated with tobacco smoke, ran the letter:

> To the Attorney General of the State of Illinois,
>
> Esteemed Sir,
>
> If you have received my preceding letter and have recovered the packet from my secret hiding-place you will not be uninterested to

learn about the sequel to the Morlender affair. In my hands I hold all of its threads. I have been placed in an insane asylum where there is no better place to follow the principal criminal. You will understand what I mean if you demand the release from cell No. 132 of the madman,

Robert Druck

Miss Milky shrugged her shoulders impatiently:
"Dear Mr. Tusk, he does not in the least conceal the fact that he is a madman. I cannot comprehend whether it's even possible to attach any significance to the letters of madmen."
"But you received his first letter?"
"Alas, how implacable you are! Over there in that trunk are definitely all the letters which have been received in my daddy's name! If you wish, take them and sort through them to the very bottom."
Pavel Tusk did precisely that. Despite a deputation of four negroes who summoned him three times to breakfast, he sat over the trunk and spent the better half of the day with it. All his searching proved to be in vain. Nothing resembling Robert Druck's letter came to light there. Then he manifested an extraordinary energy: he ordered horses to be harnessed up and to have himself driven to the neighboring telegraph station from where he sent a telegram to Chicago in the name of the Attorney General requesting the immediate despatch of a complete list of New York insane asylums. Thereupon he returned to the cottage and began to bind business papers and letters into work folios.
When the serene old man was rolled out onto the veranda after dinner, Tusk sat down beside him with a look of such independence that a horrible presentiment stirred in Miss Eunice's bosom: maybe he was a henchman of that very same Dot.
"My kind sir," he said to the old man in a business-like tone. "You have let things slide badly. If you will permit, you and I will make a trip to a session in the city today and we will begin action on a few of the complaints that have been directed to your attention."
"N-not t-today, sir!" the old man moaned piteously, directing a helpless look at his secretary. "T-today I am d-devilishly busy!"
"Massah Milky is expecting the famous walrus today, sir," the negro Sam interposed as he came to the aid of his master.
"Walrus?"
"From San Francisco, sir. According to the newspaper description!"
"Yes, of course," Eunice added capriciously, standing in opposition to the self-willed secretary. "If we hire people, Mr. Tusk, we always ask

them the questions and they reply, and not the other way around!"

"What kind of a walrus from San Francisco?" the implacable secretary continued to probe in his abrupt tone.

"A walrus!" Eunice cried hysterically. "I read daddy in the newspaper that a marvellous walrus of extraordinary girth crawled up on the shore in San Francisco and started to bark horribly. When they tried to catch him, he dashed on his flippers straight into the city, ran past three streets, crawled into a pharmacy and almost chewed up the pharmacist. Daddy, of course, wanted to buy this walrus and we ordered him from the pharmacist for a fixed price."

"That's a fine way you have of dealing with government affairs, Mr. and Miss Milky," the secretary cut her off sternly as he fastened a reproachful look on both of them. "Right here in my briefcase, waiting in line, is the mysterious murder of a colonel's widow, the theft of diamonds from a Creole lady, the disappearance of a will from an office in Chicago, and two or three more affairs of no less importance. There's a legal charge against a cocaine dealer, eight complaints of torture and rape, four hundred unsolved cases of blackmail and extortion, a denunciation against a joint-stock company for rafting timber down the Mississippi, a notice about the apprehension of a bankrupt fugitive with two billion dollars, and, finally, an anonymous letter concerning the bribing of the representative Pirouette by Prince Feofan Obolonkin, but you've read none of this and have not taken any action. Negro! Give me a pen, ink and paper!"

Sam ran out of the room, his jaw trembling, and returned a second later with all the essentials.

"Miss Milky, write!"

For some unknown reason, Miss Milky timidly took the pen and wrote down the following dictation from the secretary:

> In view of my condition of ill-health, I am transferring all my rights as Attorney General of the State of Illinois to Mr. Pavel Tusk.

"And now sign it for your father!"

Miss Milky's trembling fingers produced the signature.

"Good! And now take care of your walruses and do not allow any correspondence to be unsealed before my return!"

With these words, the secretary grabbed the paper, nodded to Miss Milky and her father and quickly descended from the veranda, heading for the stables.

"Usurper!" Miss Milky shouted shrilly after him, spread her arms out on either side of her body like two oars over a fragile boat, and fainted.

The tranquil old man sat in his chair, gazing at her with childlike sympathy and vainly trying to call to the negroes who had run off in various directions.

"Euny," he uttered with difficulty, "the gentleman is right... Don't cry, Euny!"

After lying there for five minutes, Eunice regained consciousness, looked at her father with a strange, disturbed look and went off to her room.

Pavel Tusk galloped down to the station and rode into the city on the express. He investigated about a dozen criminal cases, delivered two speeches, carried out several sentencings, visited two of three prisoners and promised them a speedy conclusion to their cases, and ended up by pleading for the legal profession to the extreme.

"Now there's a real workhand!" they whispered behind his back while he was conducting business conversations in his abrupt speech.

It was already evening by the time he returned to the country home. A strange picture greeted his eyes.

Before Mr. Milky's chair, in a zinc box full of water, sat an enormous, glistening walrus, peering with its tiny, clever eyes directly into the old man's eyes. Barking sounds were escaping from its half-opened mouth, the flippers were splayed out lifelessly along the walls of the box.

"So it came!" the secretary said without special pleasure as he walked past the walrus onto the veranda.

At that very moment the walrus tossed back its head and the air resounded with such a terrible, such a rending bark, that the negroes fell down on the ground, hiding their faces between their knees while Mr. Tusk felt an unpleasant contraction of his heart.

"The w-walrus is s-suffering!" muttered Mr. Milky... "Help him, sir!"

"Nonsense!" the secretary said abruptly, nonetheless going up to the walrus. He looked it over intently, raised the flippers, passed his hand down its neck and belly, and the walrus bore it all with amazing timidity. Suddenly the secretary's hand dove under the water and he shouted to the negroes:

"Hey! Bring a cup of emetic here!"

Grumbling and sputtering, the frightened negroes brought him what he needed.

"Pour it down the walrus' throat!"

But this time the secretary's magic voice produced no action whatsoever. The negroes backed away one after the other and halted about ten paces away from the walrus. Muttering a curse, Mr. Tusk raised the walrus' snout, and the fierce animal swallowed the medicine without a single protest. Then, rolling up his sleeves, he stuck his hand once more into the water and pressed on something with such force that a shudder passed through the body of the walrus.

"Arf, Arf!" it barked once more and began to writhe in horrible agony. One second, two, three, and something shiny appeared out of the walrus' mouth. Another second—and it came flying out and landed on the floor and shattered with a ringing sound at the feet of Mr. Milky.

"A bottle!" the secretary said, freeing his hand out of the water. "And there's paper rolled up inside!"

With these words he quickly seized the yellowed packet of sheets and carried them off to his room, leaving the walrus and attorney engrossed in pleasant, mutual contemplation.

CHAPTER 49
THE ADVANTAGE OF RAISING RABBITS

Nighttime.

A mysterious light in Miss Eunice's window. She was writing something, reading it through and tearing it up into tiny bits.

A light in the secretary's window as well. He had just finished reading the manuscript with the title of *Bisk's Journal*, and was deep in thought. Then he took out the envelope with Druck's letter, bound both documents together, shook his head and lay down to sleep.

There was a light in the kitchen window as well. The entire black staff had gathered around the table and were busy debating the mysterious personality of Mr. Tusk.

"The president in disguise," Sam whispered in a convinced voice.

"And I think it's the deceased Washington, that's who!" the cook got her word in. "A dead man doesn't fear anything, you know. You can see him, but his body is all like muslin, that's the way he shows up. After all, would a living person start to hang around here if he were in danger of being married off at any moment? Just look at what a man that Mr. Dot was and yet he got scared."

There was a light in Mr. Dot's window as well, but peeking in, we would have seen that nothing particularly mysterious was going on there: the light was beaming down from the ceiling, one Mr. Dot was snoring peacefully on his bed, hidden behind a screen, while the other Mr. Dot was standing in front of the barricaded door, his sleeve raised and the mouth of a gun barrel sticking out of it. The head of this second Mr. Dot had a great deal of resemblance to a broom, and two fireplace pokers were peeking out of his trousers and were shod in high boots.

It was dark only in the serene Mr. Milky's room. He was sleeping, surrounded by a crowd of his animals and if it had not been dark, we would have seen a blissful smile on his lips.

The morning post delivered an official package with a seal on it to the inexhaustible secretary. It contained a list of all the insane asylums in New York.

Mr. Tusk quickly finished his breakfast, unfolded the list and noted two addresses with a red pencil: these were the only homes where the number of cells reached the figure of 132.

Then he folded his napkin precisely, hid all the correspondence in his briefcase, took a notebook and made out a list of business for the current day. That finished, he turned like lightning and grabbed the curious Nolla by the collar right at the very moment where she was about to pinch him from behind.

"What the devil do you want from me?" he shouted threateningly, boring into the wretched negress with his steely eyes.

"Sir, forgive me!" Nolla muttered, shaking all over. "I just wanted to pinch you, sir, to see whether you were a person or a ghost."

Mr. Tusk let her go and not the slightest anger showed on his face. Black Nolla swore later in the kitchen that his face had even become sad, just like that of a real corpse that had been washed and laid out in its shroud.

"Yes, I'm a ghost, if you like, my good woman," he had replied in a very peculiar voice and then had gone off to his own room.

This kind of affirmation of the kitchen hypothesis had filled the negroes' hearts with an utter and panicky terror. They conferred for a long while more, and exchanged winks with one another whenever they met in the corridors, the kitchen and the stairs. But the peculiarity of their behavior remained hidden from the family of Mr. Milky, since Eunice was stubbornly staying in her room and the serene old man was deprived of the means of getting around.

In the city the secretary was told in solemn tones:

"Dear Mr. Tusk, Mr. Milky's retirement has been accepted! You have been named to his place as the Attorney General of Illinois."

"I accept, but on one condition," Tusk replied abruptly, like a man who was accustomed to giving orders and not taking them. "You will give me a month's leave so that I can make a trip somewhere and investigate a crime."

He immediately received everything that he wanted, including a government seal, blank forms for making arrests, plenipotentiary powers and certifications. The new attorney devoted the remainder of the day to a brilliant prosecution of the representative Pirouette who did not appear for the trial, and to a whole series of various pieces of business. Once more he returned home only at sunset.

It was still light when he rode up to the familiar gates. A large cart, filled to the top with baskets, blocked his way. The driver, a grown man tanned like the devil, was bellowing at the top of his voice in a fit of the most unrestrained wrath.

"Why are you bellowing?" Tusk asked, riding up to the cart.

The man turned around to him, red as a beet, and stamped his feet.

"I'm in the public service, you understand! My time is calculated right down to the last fraction of a second! I'm not one of those to stand around for nothing for half an hour straining my public throat!"

"What's the matter?"

"A fine matter! Idleness, sir, genuine idleness! I've been standing here for an hour-and-a-half trying to deliver these rabbits to this address. I've been knocking, calling, shouting, stamping, but it's just like they've gone and died. Some blockhead has been sitting there in a chair, looking right at me, and it never enters his head to unlock the gates, that's what!"

Tusk tied his horse up to a tree. In a flash he had climbed up the gates and carefully avoiding the spikes, had jumped into the garden. He opened the gates himself and admitted the sullen, red-faced man who was bearing an excellently packed cage with a pair of magnificent grey rabbits up to Mr. Milky on the veranda.

"Take them!" he said maliciously. "It's not very considerate of you. I'm a man in public service and because of me the state could suffer some significant losses."

"Th-these aren't my rabbits, sir!" Mr. Milky muttered meekly.

"What do you mean, not yours, sir!" the driver screamed in a fury as he pulled a letter out from under his shirt. "The exhibition commitee for animal husbandry has charged me, sir, with the return shipment of rabbit exhibits for the State of Illinois. Every case is addressed to its proper place, and there is even a whole envelope made out to you, sir. I am a man in the public service, I cannot knowingly make an error!"

He threw the letter on the old man's knees, tossed his head angrily and departed, angrily whipping up his horse fore, aft and on the sides.

Mr. Tusk calmly locked the gates, climbed up on the veranda and was about to ask the old man where the black servants had disappeared to when his eyes fell on the white envelope.

To the Attorney General of the State of Illinois

From Doctor Lepsius, Knight of the Order of the White Banner and esteemed member of Boston University

The highly esteemed Mr. Attorney General,

A short while ago it was printed in the newspaper that you are the national pride of America in the field of solving mysterious crimes. In the notice it was stated that Nat Pinkerton, Nick Carter and Sherlock Holmes were nothing more than ordinary chimneysweeps compared to you. I am addressing you for help in a very bizarre affair. You have heard that Jeremy Morlender was killed in Russia by the Bolsheviks. There is reason to believe that he was not at all killed by those persons who have been officially accused. At the present time, Arthur Morlender, his son, has disappeared, although his relatives are concealing his disappearance. In the name of justice and for the sake of saving the life of the young man, please take this intriguing affair into consideration.

I have the honor, your respected, etc.

Mr. Tusk's steely eyes darkened. In a flash he darted to the table where his papers lay together with the numerous personal effects that he had purchased in the city. Glancing quickly at his watch, he rapidly began to pack, sorting and organizing the packets, binding them up and laying them in his briefcase.

While he's busy with this business, we'll pay a visit to Miss Eunice who is spending the second day in her room without going out.

Miss Eunice Milky had arisen from her bed where she had been lying fully clothed, and looked out the window. Dusk was settling. A strange silence inhabited the garden, the veranda and the house. There were no one's steps to be heard, not a single human voice reached her. Miss Milky shuddered and hunched her shoulders.

No one had come to her room since early morning. The cook had not appeared with the menu for her cooking chores. The stablehand and the gardener had not brought the keys. The maids had all disappeared down to the last one. Nolla had not once poked her mobcap through the door, and Sam had not come to report on the health of the old master.

Miss Milky was hungry. Moreover, she was amazed and frightened. Standing for a moment, she went up to the mirror, tossed a shawl over her shoulders and moved firmly towards the exit.

The serene old man was sitting quietly in his armchair, staring tenderly at the round eyes of the grey rabbits who were poking their noses through the wattling of the cage at him. To tell the truth, he felt rather cold and hungry. Breakfast aside, no one had brought him anything, no one had come to shift him around and to clear up for him, or even to wrap him up in his rug for the evening. He had not managed to complain to Mr. Tusk about this strange order which had established itself in his house, and he was now sitting, consoling himself with the spectacle of his nice little animals.

Suddenly someone's hand touched his shoulder, and a voice which he hardly recognized as that of his daughter declared fearfully:

"Daddy, dear, have you really been sitting here since morning?"

"The whole time, Eunie," the old man replied timidly.

"I understand, daddy, you've been sitting here without any help at all. My God, haven't they even fed you today?"

"I had breakfast this morning, Eunie!"

Miss Milky gave a cry, moved her father's chair herself and wheeled him into the diningroom. Then she dashed headlong into the kitchen, heated up the stove, prepared some warm food and began to feed her father like a tiny baby, talking all the while:

"They've all run away from us, daddy! I saw their rooms, they've taken all their things away. I cannot understand what has happened to them"

Mr. Milky ate, to tell the truth, with an excellent appetite and kept staring wide-eyed at his daughter as though he were seeing her for the first time. They were both so occupied with each other that they heard the steps of the former secretary only when he had halted in the middle of the dining room with his briefcase and suitcase in his hands, and his hat on his head.

"I must leave without delay," he began abruptly and suddenly gave a cry. His eyes had fallen on Miss Milky... but what sort of Miss Milky was this?

Before him stood a tall elderly woman in a housedress with a tortured face and a clump of grey hair gathered at the back of her head. She did not turn her face away from Tusk's gaze and declared simply:

"All our servants have deserted us, Mr. Tusk. Daddy and I are left alone in the whole house."

Mr. Tusk put his suitcase and briefcase on a chair, took off his hat, extended his hand to her and said in a voice that he had never used once before with her:

"Greetings, Miss Milky, we haven't seen each other today. Do not be concerned.. I shall stay here the night, and tomorrow we'll think of something. I fear that they have run off because they were frightened of my person."

CHAPTER 50
A MIGRATION OF CROWS,
OR WHAT CAN BE ACHIEVED
IN A SINGLE PLACE

Early in the morning, Mr. Tusk arose, went downstairs and surveyed the whole household with a critical eye to all the household duties connected with the bare essentials of living in a home. He was far from being a sentimental person and was not at all about to put on coveralls, chop wood, heat the stove, slaughter chickens and so forth, as a gentleman borrowed from some novel would have done in his place. He lit up a cigarette, left the house and with determined steps crossed the distance dividing Mr. Milky's abode from the farm of Dot.

No one responded to his knock. Tusk knocked two or three more times with the same results, and then he raised himself on two hands, leaned them on the top of the fence and vaulted quite dexterously onto the other side of the boundary.

Dot's farm was striking in its deserted and abandoned appearance. Chickens and piglets wandered drowsily about the yard, the garden paths were overgrown with grass, the orchard served as a scratching grounds for a large rooster accompanied by ten hens. The house was completely closed up and apparently plunged into a deep sleep. Tusk tried to go through the door, but when he was unsuccessful, he shrugged his shoulders and achieved his intention by going through the window. He found himself in the front hall where about twenty servants were sleeping on mats, emitting a piercing snore. He barely managed to reach out to touch one of them when all twenty awoke, leapt up and began to wave clubs at him.

"Stop!" Tusk pronounced abruptly, crossing his hands over his chest. "I am the new Attorney General for the State of Illinois. The cowards have run away from Mr. Milky and you brethren know full well where they've gone to. One of you has to chase after them without delay and bring them back. Understand?"

The servants had crowded into a frightened block and were trembling like quail. "Massah Dot will whip us," one of them spoke out in a trembling voice.

"There'll be no whipping, I myself will have a talk with him. Now, off with you, one-two-three!" And when one of the negroes flew headlong out the front hall, Mr. Tusk coldbloodedly made his way towards the farm's principal stronghold: Mr. Dot's own door. Ascertaining that it was locked, he began to pound on it, first with his hands, and then with his feet.

"Who's the impudent fellow who's desperate for a bullet?" Dot thundered. "Just let him show his face to me so I can turn it into a nice omelet with tomatoes!"

"The new Attorney General for the State of Illinois," Tusk replied calmly.

Silence reigned behind the door, then a key grated, bare feet tapped in the depths of the room, and in a feeble voice Dot bade Tusk a "welcome to come in".

Tusk did not bide his time waiting to be asked again and first of all bumped into the picturesque statue of Dot that was pointing a revolver barrel at him out of an empty sleeve. Passing through the room, he caught sight of the second Dot, a black-moustached man with a kind face, underneath a blanket on his bed.

"Sit down, sir," he said politely, "and if you wish to smoke, there are some excellent Havana cigars over there. Don't be surprised by my behavior. When a wretched and weak-willed person like myself is aroused to such a feverish pitch, he exaggerates, sir, all the human devices for self-protection."

"Who has aroused you to such a feverish pitch?" Tusk asked dryly, lighting up a cigar.

"A sixty year old red-headed imp, sir, who has taken it into her head to marry me."

"I don't know anyone resembling that for forty miles, around," Tusk cut him off, emitting aromatic rings with the expression of a regular smoker. "I have come to you, Mr. Dot, on important business. The servants from the neighboring cottage have run away, leaving an old man stricken with paralysis and a respectable, elderly lady, his daughter, to the whims of fate. I have sent one of yours to chase after them, and I am requesting you to send, without delay, one-half of your servants to help them. To tell the truth, if I were in your place, I would go there as well, moreover since my personal stay with this sympathetic family is unfortunately terminating."

Dot listened, his eyes bulging. Color flooded through his face:

"And the red-headed imp didn't try to dupe you, sir?" he blurted out distractedly.

"I repeat," Tusk replied curtly, "I have not met any person answering to your description. The elderly lady, the mistress of the cottage, is worthy of every possible respect. Get dressed!"

Completely stunned, Dot obeyed, just as everyone else had obeyed the stern voice of this unknown gentleman. He put on every part of his attire in order, rinsed his face, had a swig out of a bottle, took his hat and declared sullenly:

"Well, let's get on with it then, may the devil bind me hand and foot!"

This strange request on the part of Mr. Dot did not elicit the slightest protest on the part of the imperturbable Mr. Tusk. In the hallway they bumped into the petrified servants and Dot ordered half of them to follow.

Meanwhile, a return to domestic life had begun in the country residence. Miss Milky had wheeled her father out onto the veranda, boiled him an egg and had just set about his feeding when her hand gave a start and her face turned pale.

Two men, with hats in hand, had approached the veranda with quick steps, and they now measured off a low bow to her.

"Mr. Dot has come to ask you, dear Miss Milky, to accept whatever help he can offer in bringing back your servants," Tusk said good-naturedly, shoving in front of himself the dumbstruck man from Arkansas whose eyes continued to bulge at what was sitting in place of the redheaded imp.

"I thank you, sir," the elderly lady replied with embarrassment. "All the same I'm managing with morning coffee. There is enough brewed for you as well, and if Mr. Dot will not refuse to have breakfast with us, I shall pour him a little cup too."

She nodded with dignity to both men and brought the breakfast from the kitchen with her own hands.

A half-hour later, while his negroes were busy with domestic work in the cottage, Mr. Dot, who had assimilated himself to the new order of things, was expounding his theory about how it would be possible within the shortest period of time to develop a new breed of hens.

"It's time for me to go," Mr. Tusk said, not without regret, as he glanced at hiss watch. "I'm leaving you, my friends, for a month, so that... what is that?" The latter exclamation from Mr. Tusk concerned the morning sky which had suddenly turned dark just as though an eclipse of the sun were about to take place.

Everyone turned their eyes skyward and leapt up from their place. An enormous black cloud was approaching their country home. It crept along, covering the horizon and descending lower and lower. Strange sounds, reminiscent of peals of laughter, soon began to shower down out of the clouds.

"Crows!" Dot shouted. "We're lost! They'll land, they'll cover all our orchards, fields and gardens! Bang, shout, throw stones at them! Come here people, over here!"

He began to scream frenziedly at the crows, throwing a cup, a plate, a hat, chairs, Miss Milky's umbrella at them—anything he could get his hands on.

"It's alright! It's alright! D-don't be afraid, my friends," the serene old man babbled, gazing calmly at the crows. "Nice little birdies!"

"Some nice little birdies!" shrilled Dot. "Don't you understand, you mad man, that this is our ruin! They're thicker than locusts! Don't let them land for anything in the world! Tusk! Damn it, where have you gotten to?"

Mr. Tusk was no longer in their midst.

"He ran off into the cottage," whispered Eunice.

Dot tore off the tablecloth, leapt up on the table and began to wave it furiously in the air. Crouching on their heels, the servants set up a proper concert of catcalls. They wailed, whined, hissed, whistled, beat on improvised drums. The animals of the serene old gent raised a hellish commotion: the bitch howled and leapt into the air with her fur standing on end, the parrot shrieked "good-bye" a hundred times in a row with its shrill voice, the walrus groaned like a frenzied thing. But nothing helped: the crows kept descending lower and lower.

The first of them, separating from the cloud, were already clearly visible. The frightful cawing and the whistle of beating wings filled the air. It was difficult to breathe because of the wind and the smell of feathers; another ten or fifteen minutes, and the terrible black horde would have come crashing down on the cottage.

At that moment Tusk appeared on the veranda. He was holding a gun in his hands, he raised it and fired at the crows.

Bang-bang-bang...

The cloud gave a shudder, the fringes scattered in various directions like black lace. A second later and the horde of crows began to rise once more, maintaining a course in the direction of Chicago, while from up above swirling and white, something began to float downward.

"I used blanks," Tusk announced abruptly. "The good Mr. Milky doesn't have anything in the entire house that resembles a bullet. Aha, what's that falling down?"

Slowly circling in the air, something continued to fall from up above until a solid white envelope came to rest on the old man's knees.

Tusk quickly grabbed it, made an exclamatory sound, and going off to the side, soundlessly opened his find.

He read the following:

To the Attorney General of the State of Illinois.

Dear Mr. Attorney General,

Fearing for my life, I am requesting you to be forewarned. In my hands I hold the threads of a mysterious occurrence. If I am killed or if I disappear, I ask you to fetch without delay the envelope from the secret hiding-place in my room at No. 8 Brooklyn Street, the twelfth parquet slab from the left-hand window, to read it and to commence a legal investigation. I am writing particularly to you and not to anyone else inasmuch as you are distinguished for your love of mystery crimes.

The Clerk, Robert Druck.

"The final link!" muttered Tusk with a strange smile, and pulling a packet of papers out of his briefcase, he quickly went up to the table.

"My friends!" he exclaimed in his authoritative voice. "Before I leave, listen carefully to a few words from me. Hey, you negroes, some of the best bottles from the cellar and some glasses!"

The amazed gathering which had just regained its composure after the threat of the crows, did not object and accepted a glass of fine champagne. Dot poured the serene old gent his portion through a funnel. All eyes were fixed on Tusk.

"My friends!" he repeated, with a glass in his hand. "On the first night of my arrival I chanced to hear in the garden—and we are not about to say from whom and how—the detailed history of a certain prank. It concerned a friendly article about the detective abilities of Mr. Milky who is present here. The prank was intended to be merely a prank. And what came of it? A helpless old gent, bound by a terrible affliction, unable to move from his chair, reading nothing and knowing nothing, has unravelled the most mysterious crime of our age! Yes, my dear friends, right here in this package are collected all the links in a strange affair for the solution of which the name of Mr. Milky will be praised for ages to come. And do you know how he achieved this kind of result? With his love for animals, damn it! Mr. Milky has given his entire heart away to these speechless creatures. He loves them with a tenderness that is worthy of emulation. And what do we see? The first link in this affair is delivered to him on a dog," Mr. Tusk waved an envelope in the air. "The second link is disgorged at his feet from the stomach of a walrus," Mr. Tusk waved a packet of yellowed papers in the air. "The third link arrived to him in a cage with rabbits," Mr. Tusk flourished the second envelop. "And finally, the fourth and final link was delivered to him by a mighty migration of crows!"

Mr. Tusk raised the final envelope and his glass.

"Let us drink, my friends, at this moment of parting, to the health of the worthy Mr. Milky and his speechless admirers, as well as for the triumph of justice which always wins in the end, gentlemen, through the intermediary of everything that is living and dead!"

With these words, Tusk emptied his glass, bowed and with his suitcase and briefcase leapt into the cabriolet awaiting him.

CHAPTER 51
THE ATTORNEY GENERAL OF THE STATE OF ILLINOIS IN SEARCH OF DRUCK

The express delivered Tusk to New York at 8:45 in the morning. A few minutes later he was already at No. 8 Brooklyn Street and was climbing the stairs to the apartment of the former clerk, Robert Druck.

No one answered his knocking for a long while. Finally, a creaking was heard and an old woman in a bonnet opened the door part way.

"Take me to your son's room, " an elderly gentleman declared abruptly, taking his hat off and entering the kitchen. "I intend to stay with you."

"Great Lord, sir!" the old woman exclaimed. "Are you a police agent?"

"I am a friend of your son's," the guest replied, placed his suitcase and hat on a chair and made as if to carry on farther.

"There was someone like that here already," the old woman replied thoughtfully. "Only he was all naked, with the exception of his loins, as they say in the Bible, and smeared from head to toe in tar. 'I'm a good friend of your son,' he said to me, and gobbled up a piece of pudding, the poor boy. 'There's a reason,' he said, 'for looking the way I do.' Maybe you're that same person, in a change of clothing and washed up?"

"I'm the same one," Tusk replied calmly and proceeded to the inside of the apartment.

The old woman led him to Bob's room where everything gleamed with cleanliness and seemed to be awaiting its inhabitant. Along the way she informed him that she had become locked up in her grief ever since the day of the death of her cat, Molly, and if he were agreed, she could unlock herself for him for an hour or two, between heating up the stove and cooking dinner.

"Don't bother to unlock yourself!" Tusk interrupted her. Moreover, you have no reason for grief. Robert Druck is alive, he'll be home in a month's time, perhaps even in a day."

The old woman gave a scream. But Tusk, in turn, locked himself up right before her nose, remained alone in the locked room and immediately set to work. He found the left-hand window, counted off the parquet slabs, and set to work with his penknife. The parquet slab was removed without any difficulty, and underneath lay an envelope on which was written: *The Mystery of Jeremy Morlender.*

Tusk grabbed it, unsealed it and, sitting down in an armchair beside the window, became immersed in reading. The manuscript proved to be fragmentary notes made by the clerk Robert Druck. We are introducing it here, omitting unessential details:

> Today the elder Morlender came to the office. He consulted with Kraft. His face was rather uneasy. After the deliberations, the patron called me into his study and said:
>
> "Bob, you're an honest and clever fellow. I want to put my trust in you. Here is Mr. Morlender's will where he divides all of his property equally between his son and Mrs. Orton, and in the event of her demise, Miss Vivian Orton and any other children of Mrs. Orton should they be born. He has bequeathed his latest discovery to his son in order that his son can use the plans for the good of the American people and all of mankind. I am keeping a copy here. I am entrusting you with the original and you will guard it like your own soul."
>
> I was amazed, but nevertheless I carried out my boss' desire to the letter. After this, Jeremy Morlender left on a business trip for Kressling to Russia. We received a letter from Mrs. Orton in which she expressed her anxiety about the health of Morlender and asked us where he was. The boss wrote a reply.
>
> No news whatsoever.
>
> No news whatsoever other than strange rumors to the effect that Morlender may have married Mrs. Elizabeth Wesson before his departure. The boss brought a pile of Russian newspapers and consulted with a translator about something for a long while. I was not made privy to the business.

Dissatisfied with the boss: he is clearly keeping me in reserve. I decided myself to carry out some investigations. For an entire week I poked around to find out what kind of a person this Elizabeth Wesson was. I learned some strange things: she is Jack Kressling's private secretary. I began my investigations from the other end. Mrs. Orton, who was mentioned in the will, is a typist in the office of that same Kressling.

No news whatsoever.

Shattering news! Mrs. Orton has died suddenly.
Today the boss surprised me with his nervousness. He was twitching, looking all around himself, pale. He complained to me that he was having bad nightmares and had begun to fear death—something which had never happened to him before. I advised him to take a week's vacation and go to Atlantic City. He agreed, but wanted to wait just until Morlender returned.

Sturm und Drang in our office. The older Morlender arrived, but dead, in a zinc coffin. It's simply unbelievable. The Bolsheviks killed him somewhere in Russia. The boss is as gloomy as a rain-cloud.

The boss is dead! His automobile ran into a streetcar: the chauffeur is alive, the boss was crushed. Our office is closed for three days.

Some Italian, a Signor Gregorio has been named liquidator in Kraft's place. He has let all our clerks go and has installed his own. I have been left until matters have been cleared up. A new will by Morlender has been sent, I'll see it tomorrow.

A stunning day! Robert Druck, you are the witness of a crime! Hold your tongue! In order, the business was as follows: I saw the will which has been brought from Russia. It annuls all preceding wills and gives Morlender's capital in its entirety to Mrs. Elizabeth Wesson, and the plans for the invention to the League of Imperialists. Miss Orton, the young Morlender—they're left without a dime. But the fact of the matter is that Morlender's signature has been falsified in the most obvious fashion. I could prove it if I so wished. But I am afraid of starting something against some unknown person. I've hidden the old will in a secret place. I've decided to wait for the appearance of Orton's or Morlender's heirs so as to start an action together with them. Gregorio is busting a gut looking for the old will. I'm behaving like a conscientious blockhead. I don't care for this Signor at all, I don't know for certain, but I believe that he's mixed up in this affair for his own profit.

Today a hunchbacked girl came to the office, calling herself Miss Orton. She looked at me, took off her veil—I've never seen a more beautiful face in my life. She asked for the boss. I slipped her my address. Signor Gregorio met with her and acted rather suspiciously; a clerk telephoned somewhere. I fear that he has guessed that this is the heiress and that she could contest the new will. I'm waiting for her right now.

At this point the manuscript broke off. Mr. Tusk took a deep sigh and sat for a few minutes in complete immobility. Then he opened up his notebook, read two addresses: New Jersey, No. 40, and Riverside Drive, No. 174. He took his briefcase, put the manuscript he had read inside and went out.

"Mrs. Druck," he said to the old woman, "I shall return for dinner. Not a single word about my arrival. Let no one into the apartment."

He went downstairs, hired an automobile and ordered the driver to go to No. 40, New Jersey. Two or three blocks later they stopped at an elegant building with a doorman, elevator and gilded entrance. Tusk entered, made his inquiries and came out again a minute later.

"Riverside Drive, No. 174," he said abruptly to the driver.

Now they were flying away out of the city. The glistening, crowded streets flew past one after the other on the left and the right. A deserted road came into view, with gloomy, infrequent buildings surrounded by gardens, with endless fences and hedges. Passersby became rarer and rarer. Finally the automobile turned off to the side, drove into an asphalted yard and stopped by the gloomy black grating behind which a park stretched away.

"Wait for me here. If I don't come back, raise the alarm. I am the Attorney General of the State of Illinois," he said in an authoritative voice to the driver as he leapt out.

In response to Mr. Tusk's ring, the door was partially opened by a tall man in a white uniform with a face ravaged by smallpox.

"What do you want? There's no reception here!" he shouted rudely, without taking the chain off the door.

Tusk flourished his document in the air;

"Let me in this minute! I am the Attorney General sent here to investigate insane asylums."

"The director isn't in New York, sir," the man replied in confusion.

"I have been ordered not to let anyone in before he returns."

"The government has designated the investigation for precisely when the directors are absent," Tusk replied unperturbed, staring fixedly at the porter. "Let me in before I summon the police."

Turning deathly pale, the porter removed the chain.

Tusk quickly entered, fingered his revolver and allowed the tall man to go on ahead. The latter unwillingly led him along murky, gloomy corridors lined with innumerable doors. From behind the doors came a wild shriek, laughter and the tormented cries of wretched people that would have frozen the blood in the veins of a less composed person. But Tusk walked on as though nothing were out of the ordinary, giving orders to open cells and glancing into them with a cold eye. He saw the tormented, the dying, people contorted in convulsions; he saw those who were frozen still and staring at a single point, he saw people dancing—who seemed, to be sure, even more terrifying than all the others. But the most shocking were the strange, pale, clean-shaven people who were sitting like watchdog, on chains screwed into the wall. One of them had had his tongue cut out.

"I'm healthy," a pale man in chains whispered to Mr. Tusk. "My relatives are keeping me here, investigate my case."

"They all talk like that!" complained the porter, giving the wretched man a crooked look of savage hatred.

Tusk asked the name and surname of the prisoner, entered it into his book, went out into the corridor and fixed his gaze on the porter:

"Have you shown me all the cells?"

"All of them!" the man protested.

"You're lying! Take me to number one hundred and thirty-two!"

"That's a personal relation of the director, we're responsible for him," the porter muttered, turning from pale to red and from red to violet.

Tusk stared at him with a commanding look and the man stumbled on ahead with uncertain steps. They emerged onto a stairway and began to descend. One, two, three stories. The walls became soggy with moisture, there was the repellent odor of mould on the staircase, the bulbs gave a feeble gleam. Deep down below ran yet another corridor with strange alcoves. Silence reigned here. Not a single sound reached them from any direction, other than the quiet trickling of water down the walls. Their steps produced a hollow echo in their ears. The porter rattled his keys and with great difficulty unlocked a heavy iron lock.

Cell No. 132 was a dark, damp cave. Light penetrated there from a window onto the corridor. Hunched up on straw in a corner slept the imprisoned man.

The porter directed the light from his flashlight onto him, the sleeping man stirred, leapt up and turned a bloodless face to Mr. Tusk and screamed wildly.

"Do not be afraid, I am the Attorney General for the State of Illinois!" Mr. Tusk rapped out, going right up to him and peering fixedly at him. "I received your letter. An investigation has been initiated. Get dressed, I am taking you with me."

The porter dropped his keys to the floor.

"The professor will murder me!" he groaned wildly. "I won't let this man go even if you're the president."

"About face, sweetheart!" Tusk cried, directing his grey eyes on him. "What kind of nonsense is this! Give Mr. Druck his clothing, one-two-three!"

Ten minutes later, as though it were perfectly normal, Tusk and Robert Druck walked out the doors of the madhouse.

"Well," Tusk said curtly, when they had gotten underway, "I'm listening to you, Druck."

CHAPTER 52
DOCTOR LEPSIUS IN SEARCH OF PROFESSOR HISERTON

Miss Small was crouching on her heels while the mulatto Toby was on top of her shoulders. An acrobatic trick was the last thing they were trying to demonstrate. Their objective was the keyhole which peeked into Doctor Lepsius' study.

"He's still sitting," muttered Miss Small, shedding tears, "he's been sitting in the same spot since morning, our darling. He doesn't eat, he doesn't ring, he doesn't walk around, he doesn't curse, my Lord, I'm going to burst into tears straight away."

She did not have time to fulfil her threat before Lepsius unexpectedly dashed to the door, flung it wide open and knocked the human pyramid upside down so that Miss Small found herself on Toby's shoulders.

"The automobile," he barked. "Toby! Call the chauffeur!"

Thereupon he hurtled back, grabbed his hat, gloves and walking stick, and practically flew head over heels down the stairs. His face was red. His eyes glittered with determination. He had thought out a plan on how to gain entry to Professor Hiserton.

"The university!" he ordered the chauffeur as he sat down in the automobile.

Ten minutes later he was there. Going into the chancery, he inquired as to which auditorium Hiserton was lecturing in. The clerk looked at Lepsius in amazement.

"Really, sir, don't you know that the professor is being sent to the psychiatrists's convention in Petrograd?"

"Has he already departed?" Lepsius blurted out.

"Probably. In any event, you can inquire at his home: Riverside Drive, No. 174."

Lepsius wrote the address down and again jumped into the automobile.

"Riverside Drive, one-seventy-four!" he cried to the chauffeur.

Again that desolate street. The farther one went, the gloomier and more deserted it became. Again the black ironwork at the gates to the eerie house that was sealed off and silent as though everything living inside had become petrified like preserved exhibits at a museum.

Lepsius gave a sharp jerk to the bell. The pock-marked porter, all pale with fury, stuck his nose out from behind the grating.

"Get the hell out of here!" he bellowed, examining Lepsius. "No one's being received here! Clear off or I'll let the dog loose!"

"My friend," the doctor declared in a whisper, "I must inform Professor Hiserton about an important piece of business. It's a matter of life or death for him."

"Too late," the porter replied sullenly. "The director has left for a convention in Russia, and there was an investigation today. Everything was taken down and from cell number one-thirty-two they took away..."

"But it's still not too late. What I'm talking about is only known to Professor Hiserton. I am his closest friend. He instructed me that in case of anything I should turn to you. If you wish to save your own neck, you'd better think of some way that I can catch up with him."

The porter stared suspiciously at Lepsius.

"What's your name?"

Lepsius gulped.

"Oleumrizini!" he babbled the first thing that came to his tongue.

At that very moment the porter's face cleared up. He removed the chain and declared respectfully:

"Come in, sir, come in! Apparently you too are an Italian?"

"Naturally," Lepsius murmured, following him into the gloomy abode of death. But the pockmarked fellow did not take him where Tusk had just been. He opened a small door and ushered Lepsius into a marvellous doctor's study that gleamed with irreproachable cleanliness.

"Do sit down, sir, sit down, I'll summon our secretary at once. She'll figure out what to do." Lepsius sat down, feeling utterly downcast. He did not know more than a dozen words in Italian. What if the secretary began to speak to him in that language? Not having the strength to sit, he leapt up again and paced several times around the study, wiping the cold sweat from his face. Suddenly his eyes fell on some excellent pictures hanging on the walls, and at that moment he sensed a pair of black eyes were observing him.

"Itoresco, e... e cascaro sagrada!" he muttered without taking his eyes off the pictures. "Roma Acropoli, Multatuli!"

The outpouring of his rapture was interrupted by pure English speech.

"Greetings, sir!"

Standing before Lepsius was an older brunette with a face that was so strangely similar to someone else's whom he knew quite well... but whose? Damn it, no matter how he searched his memory, he could not recall.

"I was admiring the pictures although my heart is in uttar chaos and disarray," he muttered with embarrassment, going up to meet the secretary. "Dear Miss or Mrs..."

"Miss Croce. As an Italian, I understand your ecstasy, sir, but, unfortunately, I do not know my native language. What has brought you to the Professor?"

"Signorina Croce," Lepsius murmured, rolling his eyes practically out of their sockets, and, insofar as it was possible, striving to achieve the maximum effect, "I am his close friend. We are involved in a certain important business together... a very secret business of extreme importance. It has fallen apart. If the Professor does not take measures, he will be eliminated. At all costs I must catch up to him and forewarn him."

Miss Croce grew serious:

"Danger threatens him in Petrograd?"

"Precisely, precisely!"

"In that case, dear sir, I shall immediately prepare all the documents for you and you can board a steamer tomorrow."

"Marvellous," Lepsius exclaimed.

"Ah, pronounce that in Italian!'" Miss Croce murmured dreamily as she closed her eyes. "It's such a delight for me to hear my native language."

"Hiperoksidato!" Lepsius repeated, smiling. He felt like he was in the swim of things now and his anxiety subsided.

"But one thing, sir, before your departure, you mustn't show yourself in the city any more. We'll hide you here right up until tomorrow."

"But an automobile is waiting for me," Lepsius attempted to protest.

"But that's excellent! Tell the chauffeur that you are going away and that you're not to be expected at home."

Lepsius went down to the chauffeur. The trustworthy faces of the porter and Miss Croce peered out from behind the doors.

"Tell Toby and Miss Small that I have gone away for three weeks!" Lepsius ordered the chauffeur and turned to go back.

When the automobile had disappeared, the pockmarked porter locked the door with a bang.

"And now..." Miss Croce declared, turning to the servant, "throw this fat pig into cell one-thirty-two and starve him until he admits what spy outfit sent him here!"

At that same moment, the stunned Lepsius was seized by the collar, and the porter's iron hands dragged him down the frightful corridor. As though in a dream, he heard the shrieking, wailing and moaning, he saw the gloomy wet walls, along which he was being dragged lower and lower until he was stuck into a terrifying semi-dark vault and tossed on some straw.

The porter guffawed diabolically, slammed the iron door shut and his steps died away. Lepsius remained alone.

"Numbskull! Numbskull! Double numbskull!" he whispered to himself, frenziedly clubbing himself on the forehead. "Now go ahead and sit here like a cabbage, a cranberry, a radish, sit until you croak!"

His anger at himself saved Doctor Lepsius from utter despair. Having expended his entire supply of nervous energy on it, he began wanly to consider what he should undertake. As soon as his eyes became accustomed to the gloom, he examined the vile and terrifying vault surrounding him. The walls were soggy from the dampness. It was dry only in one corner, by the straw, and Lepsius, beginning to sneeze and shiver, huddled in that corner. Running his hand over the walls, he felt how it was all notched and grooved. Lepsius dragged out his doctor's electrical penlight, cleared away the straw and bent closer to the wall. Imagine his amazement when he read the magnificently carved letters:

> To my successor. Raise the slab closest to the wall with the knife which I am leaving under the straw. Climb down. Dig a half-yard deeper. You will see an opening. If you are an observer, uncover the secrets. If you are a coward, try to get away. Regardless of which course you take, be grateful for the memory of the renowned Bob Druck.

"Now this is more to my liking!" Lepsius said to himself. "There was apparently a person with very strong nerves here. Let's give it a try!"

He rummaged in the straw and without difficulty found the knife which he carefully used to raise the slab. There was a hole in the ground underneath which had apparently been dug out by his predecessor. He stuck his legs into it with the same kind of bodily movements as though he were crawling into cold water. The bottom was not far away. Lowering himself into the pit, Lepsius began to dig up the earth. He dug like a mole and quickly arrived at an opening that was as wide as a person's head and a yard in length. It was encased in stone and something gleamed feebly through it. Lepsius lowered the slab over his secret hiding-place so that no one would discover him, and huddling in the underground burrow, he set about trying to peek through the glimmering opening.

"Uncover the secrets! A fine occupation for a person who has been condemned to death by starvation. And what is there to uncover other than the fact that the opening leads into a long stone corridor which disappears into the endless distance, is excellently paved and dimly illuminated with lights?"

Lepsius stuck his hand through and waved it in the air. The opening was too heavily walled in for him to be able to escape from there. Despair seized the wretched prisoner once more.

"I'm lost!" he babbled hysterically. "That vile Miss Croce... God! Why didn't I think of that earlier!"

His eyes bulged and his mouth gaped. He remembered who it was that Miss Croce resembled. Despite the color of her hair, her unattractiveness, the thinness, the age, she unmistakably resembled Mrs. Elizabeth Morlender with that terrible kind of similarity that is often to be found in close relatives.

While Doctor Lepsius was sitting in his earthbound pit, events of a different order were taking place upstairs. A detachment of police were arresting the pockmarked porter and Miss Croce, while the legal prosecutor with numerous colleagues was making the rounds of the terrible cells one by one. He glanced into No. 132, but found no one inside it.

"Quite a fellow, that Attorney General from the State of Illinois," he muttered at the conclusion of his survey. "No wonder the newspapers have made such a fuss over him!"

CHAPTER 53
MIKE IN SEARCH OF GREGORIO CICE

"Pfui!" Van Hope said to Tom the chimneysweep with the utmost disdain. "Pfui-pfui-pfui!"

Tom had just confessed to him about his love for the maid Jenny.

"You're just doing that because you're jealous," he grumbled, turning red as a lobster.

"Pfui!" Van Hope repeated even more expressively.

"Brother, you're jealous!" poor Tom cried, dangling his feet in the air.

"Pfui-pfui." Van Hope rapped out curtly.

"We'll just see!" Tom cried, hurling himself at the plumber and pounding him on the back.

Something creaked behind the wall panelling and the imposing figure of Thingsmaster arose before the two brawlers.

"What's the matter, fellows?" he asked curtly, leading Beauty out from behind the wall and closing the panel behind himself.

"He's swearing, Mike!" Tom cried, without ceasing to treat Van Hope to more blows. "The whole day long and all I hear is the same mockery. Not only do you have to sit in the pipe like a werewolf, but on top of it all he abuses you with the worst words."

"Pfui-pfui-pfui!" came from Van Hope's direction.

"You see! You see!" Tom bellowed furiously, jumping on his adversary with redoubled energy.

If Michael Thingsmaster had been a learned fellow, he would immediately have shown that the letters of the alphabet are far from being the most important thing in speech usage, and he might even have written an entire volume in Latin about the languages of birds and dogs. But for the moment he confined himself to a cuff, which knocked Tom off Van Hope, and to a piercing look in the direction of both of them. Tom and Van Hope silently scratched the backs of their heads.

"So, boys," he declared slowly, "this is the way you've gotten spoiled! Looks as though keeping an ear open and an eye out can spoil even our lads. Now give a good listen with both ears. Beauty and I are setting out to hunt for Cice. Our entire union has already been alerted. If anything should happen, you'll hear from me. I'm leaving a receiver here and taking a battery with me."

"Mike!" Tom and Van Hope exclaimed simultaneously. "He'll bump you off.. Don't go!"

Thingsmaster silently extinguished his pipe, set up a small receiver in the niche where Van Hope's guard station was located, and ran off together with Beauty along the walls to the upper floor of the *Patrician*. Broken-hearted, Tom and Van Hope trudged along behind.

Setto from Diarbekir was enjoying utter peace. Not a single fugitive pretender troubled the walls of his hotel in this off-season. Even Prince Feofan Obolonkin had departed on a diplomatic visit to the new Algerian Bey whom he was supposed to encourage in undertaking open aggression against Soviet Russia, translating for this purpose into Algerian the insulting jibes of the Russian writer Gogol. All was quiet and dead calm in the hotel, and Thingsmaster reached the unnumbered room without any bother.

He pressed an invisible strip and the door, which had been locked from the inside, opened without a sound. Tom and Van Hope followed him in. Cice's room seemed even more deserted than earlier. A layer of dust had settled on the furniture no higher than the rate of exchange of the dollar, and the thread from which Mike had torn the stone fabionite a short while ago was still dangling on the curtain.

"Seems to me that no one's been here!" Mike declared, looking all around. Without any difficulty he found the trap door, silently raised the cover and beckoned to Beauty.

"Old girl," he said, "you passed the first trial like a good doggie. Now we have to start the second one. Find me the person that has left his scent here, do you hear?"

Several times he bent Beauty's head towards things and corners where Cice's scent may still have lingered, and then he pushed her towards the opening. But before following her down there, he turned to the chimneysweep and the plumber.

"Mend-mess, fellows!" he said in a serious voice to them. "Don't fool around."

"Mess-mend, Mike!" they both replied with emotion.

Thingsmaster waved a hand to them and disappeared through the trap door. The dog was waiting for him, panting excitedly and letting its tongue hang out. They were in the nether regions of a long, stepped corridor that was paved with flat stone slabs. Thingsmaster lit his flashlight and moved forward, holding Beauty by the collar. The endless passage kept going down lower and lower and finally turned into a tunnel which from time to time would widen out into an alcove. They picked their way forward, without hearing the slightest sound, until Mike's foot stumbled against something and he gave a surprised cry.

It was a rail. A single-track railway ran along the tunnel.

Mike bent down and zealously studied the rail, then he examined the screws, nuts and spikes. The workmanship was old, strong and not from American factories. Then he moved on farther, glancing at his watch from time to time. Damn it! They had been walking for a little less than half-a-day, yet the same maw of the tunnel loomed darkly in front of them as it led off into infinity. And if a mysterious rail car had appeared out of there, both Mike and Beauty would have been smashed to bits.

Running out of strength by the tenth hour of the journey, Thingsmaster crawled into an alcove, got out a piece of bread and set about eating. Beauty, not in the least tired, settled down beside him, wagging her tail and catching pieces of bread from her master's hands.

"We must be already outside the city, Beauty," Mike said thoughtfully. "Thingss like this tunnel simply aren't built for no reason. You and I are hunting for big game."

After eating and resting, they moved on. The monotony of the passage had already begun to exhaust Thingsmaster into a stupor when suddenly he saw that the tunnel made a sharp turn and all of a sudden the track came to a halt. At that moment, Beauty went on ahead, turned her head to him with her clever, beckoning gaze and silently dashed on ahead. He ran after her as fast as his legs could carry him.

Imagine his amazement when around the corner he saw the dog leaping furiously at the wall, whining and flogging its tail back and forth. Going up to her, Thingsmaster felt the convulsive grasp of someone's hand, and a hoarse voice declared right beside him:

"I'm unspeakably happy to see you, sir! A fortunate and salutary encounter!"

Mike's eyes zealously searched for the person who had pronounced these words until he noticed a hidden opening in the wall about a yard long. From the outside it was not at all visible, and if it had not been for Beauty, he would have calmly paused it by. Through the opening could be seen the distracted face and disshevelled head of a fat person, pale and trembling as though in a delirium, and his outstretched hand.

"I am a captive, sir! Locked up in a mad house! I entreat you by all the gods, sir, to free me!"

Thingsmaster silently examined the hole, took a crowbar and worked on the bricks for half-an-hour. After he freed one of them, he began to work the others loose until he had formed a hole big enough for Doctor Lepsius to pass through with all his limbs.

"Oof!" muttered the fat man, tumbling out into the tunnel. "Blessed be that Bob Druck here on earth, and in heaven, if he no longer has need of a physician's aid. Thank you, sir! Thanks to your dog! I am Doctor Lepsius."

"Alright!" Thingsmaster replied, giving his companion a critical once-over. "You speak of Druck. Who is he.?"

"My predecessor in the cell who dug out this opening."

Mike pondered. He understood now how the letter had turned up on the neck of his dog.

"Let's go," he turned to Lepsius resolutely. "We're on the trail of a monstrouss villain. There's nothing else for you to do but to reinforce our side."

Doctor Lepsius cleaned off his suit, smoothed his hair down, donned his gloves and replied philosophically:

"I too am hunting down a criminal. I trust, sir, that this enterprise will proceed more successfully for me."

They once more set off down the tunnel, now and then exchanging monosyllabic words. Beauty cheerfully ran on ahead. The way was apparently well known to her and concealed nothing frightening in itself. Now and then the dog halted and glanced at her master with her clever dark eyes.

After going along for about a hundred steps, they once more ran into the track. This time Thingsmaster pulled out his magnifying glass and assiduously studied both walls to the left and right. But all his searching proved unsuccessful: there were no cracks in the wall, no slots, nothing resembling hidden doors into a depot or garage.

"Where does the railcar disappear to, damn it?" he asked himself. "Sir, while you were sitting in your hole, you didn't notice any trains or cars passing by, did you?"

"Not a sound, not a rustle, not a squeak!" Lepsius exclaimed. "Your dog's bark was the first news of life."

"Strange," Thingsmaster muttered.

Two hours more and their legs were buckling under them. Settling into an alcove, Mike and Lepsius ate some bread and peacefully fell asleep while the faithful Beauty kept watch over them, running back and forth along the tunnel.

Waking up, Thingsmaster leapt up from his place in an instant.

"On the double!" he ordered the doctor, and the fat man, without the least annoyance, walked gingerly off down the endless corridor behind the giant.

The track came to an end once more. This time Mike noticed strange echoing sounds that indicated that the wall was hollow. But his interest in that did not last long.

"We're going down, take a look!" he whispered, pointing to the tunnel. And to be sure, the road was making a sharp turn downward. Water began to trickle down the walls. The tunnel opening became narrower and narrower—until it turned into just a cylindrical hole. As though nothing were amiss, Beauty gave a wag of her tail and crept forward. Thingsmaster began to crawl carefully after her, and behind him, puffing laboriously, Lepsius squeezed himself into the hole.

It was hard to breathe here. The metal walls of the cylinder appeared to be very hot. Strange rhythmic sounds reached their ears. Suddenly the dog seized a metal ring in her teeth, gave a sharp tug on it, and at that very moment Thingsmaster and Lepsius were blown out of their cylinder somewhere down below as though by the force of a pneumatic cannon, and the opening slammed shut behind them with a sliding sound.

As they tumbled on top of one another, a cry of pain echoed out. Thingsmaster felt Doctor Lepsius all over, Lepsius felt Thingsmaster, both felt the dog—everyone was in one piece!

"Who groaned?" they asked each other simultaneously.

"I did!" someone replied from a corner in a voice that was eerily familiar.

It was neither Lepsius, nor Thingsmaster. It was not even Beauty.

At that moment Thingsmaster illuminated his flashlight, dropped it and rushed to the corner with a cry:

"Bisk! old buddy!"

"Mike! Mend-mess!"

A half-hour passed before both friends could regain their wits and finally get down to questions. Meanwhile, Lepsius examined the area with the aid of the flashlight that Mike had dropped, and finding a barrel with dry crusts, set about tranquilly fortifying himself.

"We're on the *Torpedo*," Bisk began in a whisper. "Both my legs and one arm are broken, but, fortunately, they've already begun to knit well. Did you get my report from the bottle?"

"No, I received the nine pigeons all at once," Mike replied. "And I realized that you had had an accident."

Bisk briefly told him about everything that we already know from his journal. And then he completed his story:

"At that moment, buddy, I thought my time was up. I grabbed for the opening, tossed the bottle into the water and then suddenly I was sucked down as though into a funnel, twisted around on cog wheels and had my bones thoroughly broken. If I wasn't Bisk, the Scotsman, it would have made mincemeat out of me. By some miracle I grabbed onto the drive shaft axle and was thrown into this corner with both my legs broken. For about three days I bled. There was never any light here. A couple of times secret openings would slam shut and someone would steal past, fortunately without noticing me. Once a dog jumped out of a secret opening. It licked my wounds, sucked my sores clean, found dry crusts and water, dragged them here to me—the crusts in its teeth, the water on its tongue. If it hadn't been so dark I could have made out who it was. Word of honor, I thought it was Beauty. I tore off a strip from my shirt, and wrote on it in the dark with my blood:

"Bisk. *Torpedo*." and tied it to her paw. From that day I started to get better,, Mike! Then at some point when the swaying stopped and I realized that we had stopped, something began to happen with the funnel, it started to move, twist, and the dog rushed to it and disappeared through the hole. Yes, Mike, I would have gambled my neck away that it had been the captain's dead dog that had been howling beneath the deck during our entire trip."

"It was Beauty, buddy!" Mike exclaimed cheerfully. "It was she who delivered your strip of clothing to us. But now you and I are on the hunt for Cice."

"What do you mean, Cice!" Bisk declared quietly, and his voice trembled. "Mark my word, Mike, the main villain is none other than that red-haired Captain Gregoire!"

"Well, forgive me!" Lepsius said calmly through his teeth, with a crust of bread protruding out of his mouth. "I have been listening to your talk, my friends. I have put all the facts together. The odds are one hundred to one in favor of the fact that the main villain is Professor Hiserton."

He barely had a chance to utter these words when the dog whined convulsively. A rhythmic shudder began underneath them, their entire hiding-place fell into an even motion.

"The *Torpedo* is under way! We've set sail again!" Bisk exclaimed mournfully.

And while all three of them, together with the dog, were setting out on a distant journey without any idea of where they were headed, up above, in one of the cabins of the *Torpedo*, travelling to Kronstadt, was the taciturn and important Attorney General of the State of Illinois, Mr. Tusk, who had left the rescued Druck in the care of an overjoyed mother. He entered his cabin without being noticed by anyone. During the whole sailing he did not once show himself on the deck. And what was all the more amazing—not even Captain Gregoire himself saw him a single time.

CHAPTER 54
THE GIFT CLOCK

"Well, now it's time for me to go and report," Sorrow said to himself after waiting in vain for Laurie, Ned and Willings.

The fever had left him completely, but, as was always the case, it had marked him all over with sores and ulcerations. Pasted up with bandages, but cheerful and content, Sorrow left his abode and began to hobble over to the Petrograd Soviet. The ceremonial session was supposed to take place in the evening and there the trade agreement with America would be announced. And then there would be the presentation of the gift... Sorrow knew that Kressling's cards had been shuffled up, and no direct danger threatened his Russian friends. But where had the gift gotten to? And who was going to present it? And where was young Morlender and Vivian Orton? He had no answers to any of these questions. And he would have to make an effort to get the fellows free.

However, something unexpected awaited him at the doors to the Petrograd Soviet. A tall policeman standing at the entrance curtly announced to him that the session had already taken place.

To the dozen questions tormenting Sorrow were added new ones. When and why had the session been rescheduled? What had happened at it? Had the gift been presented? Wandering in confusion along the streets near the Petrograd Soviet, Sorrow decided at last to take a look in the house on Moika Street where the phony Vasilov had lived. But there too it was deserted and silent. The cheerful shoeshine boy no longer sat by the doors, he met no one on the stairs, the entry to Vasilov's room had a lock hanging on it. Sorrow frowned and slowly went out onto the street. He had no idea where he would have gone if suddenly a cheerful "mend-mess" had not echoed alongside his ear and the smiling mug of Laurie who had put on weight because of prison food and lack of exercise, had not popped up behind his shoulder.

"Mess-mend," Sorrow quickly replied without restraining his joy. "Where did you come from? Where are the others?"

"Old-timer, I've been running after you all over Petrograd. I sensed where you'd go. March faster, they're waiting for us at comrade Rebrov's, and along the way I'll give you all the news, just like a novel with a sequel...."

And while they marched along the streets—Laurie Lane almost at a run and Sorrow skipping along trying to keep up with him—he gave him a serious but elaborate account of what had happened at the Aero-

Electric Station about the mysterious fourth Vasilov...

"We applied a little handiwork to him, Sorrow. Of course, if one were to look at it from the point of view of arithmetic, three of us to his one, perhaps the odds wouldn't seem so bad. But, Sorrow, old man, we saw it quite differently. He could really bite! But still we wrung out of him what side he was on and it wasn't difficult to see. Well, at the interrogation all three of us admitted to the masquerade and so forth. Our Russian comrades, Sorrow, laughed their hearts out together with us. And then, just like in a book, we went to a certain place and there was our little gift in a box and both Miss Orton and Morlender right before our eyes..."

But at this point they had arrived at the spot. And giving Laurie a graphic sign to hold his tongue, Sorrow ran up the stairs like a young man.

Laurie was right. The young Morlender and Vivian, as soon as their numb limbs were capable of movement, had stealthily crawled out a window of their prison, climbed down the roofs to the street and reached Rebrov's apartment in utter exhaustion. After hearing what they had to say, he gave them food and drink, rubbed them down with alcohol and put them to rest. A half-hour later some burly Red Army soldiers, searching the deserted apartment of the phony beggar woman, fetched the box with the clock from there as well. A foremost specialist, following the advice of Ned and Willings, was unpacking the box when Sorrow, accompanied by Laurie, burst into the room.

Rebrov, who already knew him by hearsay, gave a firm handshake to the famous worker-inventor.

"Careful, friends!" Sorrow cried, going up to the box. "To be sure, we did what we could, but still..."

"And what did you do?" the specialist asked, slowly unscrewing the carved case of the clock.

"We used our heads a little," Sorrow replied with embarrassment. "There's an ancient expression concerning watchfulness. So, by means of a phonograph, we coupled it to the gong, and the bomb, of course, we removed."

"You think you removed it?" the specialist said, quickly severing some kind of wire inside the clock with a rubber-gloved hand. "Well, if you took it out, then someone put it back. Bring the bucket of sand here quick!"

From underneath the dial of the clock he withdrew quite a small, compact mechanism with a metalic cover from underneath which a broken wire dangled— and with the greatest care, he lowered it into the sand. "Take it away to our laboratory!"

The same Red Army men who had brought the box, took the bucket with the mechanism buried in the sand and quickly carried it out of the room.

"And now," Rebrov said, "your turn to act, comrade Sorrow. Show us that trick you installed into this nice little present from the capitalists!"

Triumphantly Sorrow went up to the clock. It now stood uncovered, in all the amazing beauty of its carving, gleaming with the deep gloss of the casing of rare Brazilian food. The old master felt around for the winding mechanism, placed the hands at twelve, wound it up several turns, and in the utter silence a clear, distinct, loud voice pronounced in Latin: "Timeo danaos et dona ferentes!"

"Beware of Greeks who come bearing gifts" Rebrov translated as he burst into laughter. "My dear friends, your warning was very appropriate! And the clock, this magnificent clock, a marvellous piece of work, now that it has released its secret, will serve us and work for us just as faithfully as Time Itself works for and with us!"

CHAPTER 55
THE CONVENTION OF PSYCHIATRISTS

Arriving on the *Torpedo* peacefully and without any adventures, Mr. Tusk climbed down the ramp onto Russian soil. Apparently he was familiar with this country, because he found himself a comfortable room in a hotel without any special difficulty.

But the landing was far from being as comfortable for Mike, Lepsius and Bisk. The Scotsman, cheerfully hobbling along on his revived legs, was practicing walking among the empty barrels of the ship's hold when the *Torpedo* began to slow down.

"Into the cyliner!" Bisk exclaimed, and the friends barely managed to plunge into the cylinder before it began to spin like a funnel and with incredible force the air shot them through the widening aperture together with the rubbish, tins, paper, cigarette butts and bread crusts which had collected at the bottom of it. Covered with all of this from head to toe, our travelers found themselves at the bottom of a wooden shaft that was equipped with almost sheer steps. Hanging onto the rungs, they crawled upwards, led on by the clever Beauty. Ten minutes later they leapt out onto the ground.

They found themselves in a furnace in a sparsely built-up area not far from the harbor. Here Doctor Lepsius expressed a firm resolution to clean himself up, while Bisk wanted to determine his latitude and longitude with the aid of his compass.

"Rubbish!" Mike replied. "We're in Petrograd! There's no time to be lost! Take a look at the dog the way she's dancing and getting excited! Let me give her a good sniff and she can lead us to Cice."

With these words he pulled a handkerchief out of his pocket that had been wiped against the floor in the room of the *Patrician* and put it right up to Beauty's nose. The dog snorted, the hair rose on her back and she shot like an arrow along the street.

"Hey!" our travelers shouted, dashing after her and leaving the limping Bisk behind. But it was a bit difficult to catch up to Beauty. She flew along the streets of Petrograd with the speed of lightning, paying no attention to the whistles of the police, and they probably would have collapsed if Beauty had not come to a stop outside the doors of a beautiful building that was decorated with signs ten feet high:

PSYCHIATRISTS' CONVENTION
Inauguration
1. Opening remarks.
2. Lecture by Professor Bechterev
3. Lecture by Professor Hiserton

"Damn it!" Lepsius grumbled, catching up to the dog. "Isn't this some kind of circus and Beauty has led us to her four-legged friends?"

"The dog isn't like that" replied Mike. "We've got to do some thinking about what to do!"

"There's nothing to think about," Lepsius objected, whose linguistic skills appeared to be at their peak on this occasion. He managed to decipher the notice and turned triumphantly to Thingsmaster: "My friend, there are notices here in all languages, even in Italian. The convention of psychiatrists is in this hall! Professor Hiserton will read his lecture here! Let's wait somewhere in a hotel until he reveals himself and I guarantee that we'll get in there!"

Two hours later, having assumed a more respectable appearance and holding Beauty on a chain, they were standing in front of the doors to the hall together with Bisk who had managed to catch up with them.

"Professor Lepsius!" the fat man announced, going up to the porter and poking his documents at him. "Mea mecum. Assistenti!" With these words he pointed to Bisk, Thingsmaster and Beauty.

"The dog isn't allowed in," the porter intercepted him with determination. "Come here, doggie, come on, girl, sit with me in the guard-station."

"This is an experimental dog, a pupil of your learned Pavlov," Lepsius declared with no less determination. "It is essential to have her at the lectures!"

The porter, scratching the back of his head, let the entire company through, and Beauty gave him a friendly wave of her tail.

"You've proven to be a useful person, doctor," Thingsmaster whispered to him with a certain amount of respect. "But just remember that while you'll be hunting for your Hiserton here, I'll have to snare my Cice."

"And I'll have to get my Gregoire!" Bisk interposed.

The psychiatrists' convention was already in full swing when our three travelers mixed in with the crowd and quickly pushed their way through to the stage. Despite the daylight, the hall was flooded with hundreds of electric lights. On both sides of the parterre stretched boxes of smartly dressed diplomatic representatives. The entire pride of Russian science was gathered in the parterre. In the corridors and passageways, the university youth were crowding. Up on the stage, which was richly decorated with greenery and portraits, stood a long table at which Professor Bechterev had just commenced his lecture.

Thingsmaster took in the hall attentively. His pale blue eyes moved from face to face and then suddenly someone whispered to him:

"Mend-mess!"

"Mess-mend!" he replied with a shudder.

The technician Sorrow, all covered with the persistent sores from his swamp fever, emaciated and pale, placed his hand on his shoulder.

"I didn't know whether I'd meet you here, old-timer!" he whispered, excitedly. "Today they defused that nice little bomb of ours that you're familiar with, buddy.. Well, the fascists got nothing for their pains! The fellows and I have given them a rough time as well!"

"Where's Cice, Sorrow?"

"You'll see, Mike,!' Sorrow replied calmly.

Thingsmaster carefully ran his eyes over the public.

In the third row of the parterre, a pale couple sat side by side, arm in arm: Arthur Morlender with a grey strand in his hair, and the emaciated Vivian. Mike's blue eyes slipped over these two faces as well. He wanted to whisper something to Sorrow, but at that very moment the hall began to shake with stormy applause: Bechterev had finished his lecture. He arose, bowed his leonine head before the gathering and left the stage.

The master of ceremonies brought out a fresh glass of tea for the following speaker, pushed the chairs together and then announced in several languages:

"And now we shall have the lecture of Professor Hiserton concerning the regeneration of nerve centers under the influence of hypnosis."

Several moments of anguish passed. Mike Thingsmaster involuntarily glanced sideways at Lepsius. The fat man was standing with his eyes fixed on the stage, oblivious to everything and everyone. His nostrils were flaring, his eyes had narrowed like a bloodhound's. A few seconds more and the soft footsteps of an old man could be heard. Before them appeared the diminutive figure of Professor Hiserton, hoary with age, wearing a fluffy snow-white beard, pink-faced like an infant. A cheerful, sweet, timid old gentleman who peered somewhat absent-mindedly into the hall from beneath bushy eyebrows with the kindhearted gaze of a scholar. Furious waves of applause echoed through the hall.

Bisk snorted and tugged Lepsius by the coattails. The fat man continued nevertheless to peer at the poor professor in hearty despair. He was disappointed, crushed, annihilated.

The professor took in the hall with his eyes and began his lecture in a quiet, rambling voice. But at that moment, opposite to him, in the box for foreign guests, a door was slowly opened. One after the other entered Senator Notabit with his daughter, the banker Westinghouse and several American industrialists who momentarily attracted the attention of the entire hall. It was clear that the foreign guests were upset over something and thrown into confusion. Westinghouse was pale and barely managed to catch his monocle which kept falling out from time to time. He was evidently short of breath and he kept inhaling frequently. There was confusion on the faces of the American industrialists; they were exchanging silent glances.

"Obviously the rumors about the bomb have reached them," Sorrow whispered to Thingsmaster, pointing their way with his eyebrows. But at that moment, the Senator's curly-headed daughter who was peering into the hall with curiosity, suddenly gave a desperate scream:

"The mask! The mask!"

Banker Westinghouse's piping voice rang out after her:

"Vivi! Vivi!"

These cries, which scandalized the learned public, inexplicably shook the pink-faced, kindly old gentleman on the stage. He ceased rambling. His eyes were fastened on the spot where Westinghouse and Grace were looking while leaning out of their box. His eyes widened and fastened unwaveringly on the pale couple. And at that very instant, giving a convulsive jerk with his hands, Professor Hiserton lost consciousness.

The master of ceremonies rushed to him with a glass of water. The professor was raised and placed in an armchair. But all attempts to revive him were futile: he was trembling, his eyes wandered aimlessly, he did not respond to questions and did not manifest the slightest intention of continuing his lecture.

The face of Thingsmaster, who had been following this scene, grew serious. He glanced at Doctor Lepsius. But the latter had already worked out a plan of action.

Unbuttoning his jacked all the way up to his chin and pulling a packet of papers out of his pocket, he made his way with resolute steps to the master of ceremonies and said several words to him in a whisper. The master of ceremonies helped him to climb up onto the stage, entered his name and surname into a notebook and turned to the public:

"Professor Hiserton is indisposed. Unfortunately he is unable to finish his lecture. In his place, the well-known clinician from America, Doctor Lepsius, will deliver a lecture on the *vertebra media sive bestialia* which he has discovered."

At that same moment the fat man rolled out to the front of the stage. He stood beside the chair of Professor Hiserton, let a burning gaze sweep the public and shook a pile of papers in the air.

"Ladies and gentlemen!" he cried in a sonorous voice. "I have been waiting for this moment all my life! I have been waiting for the moment when I would be able to expound my discovery before a gathering of world scholars and demonstrate it with a living specimen. All has come about in the best possible fashion: the gathering, the scholars and even the specimen! Allow me to take my time, ladies and gentlemen! And allow me to advise you to be very attentive, extremely attentive, for what I am going to tell you will shake all of mankind!"

This speech did not resemble a scholarly lecture in the least. But there was such force in Lepsius' voice, his plump face had been so awesomely transformed that the calm and smartly dressed public surged more closely together from an inexplicable excitement. Even Sorrow, Bisk and Thingsmaster fastened their gaze on him. Even Arthur Morlender, gently pressing Vivian's hand, whispered to her:

"Good old Lepsius has turned up here as well!"

Even the steely eyes of the Attorney General of the State of Illinois rested on Lepsius with something resembling amiability. Only Professor Hiserton lay in his chair, breathing heavily and manifesting no sign of interest in anything whatsoever.

"I shall begin in a roundabout fashion," Lepsius continued. "Many years ago, while still a young doctor, I happened to practice medicine in an aristocratic European health resort. There I became familiar with my first patient, a minister who had fled from a revolution. He had been banished by his people a few years beforehand. From that time he had wandered about foreign lands, eaten and drunk food to which he was not accustomed, and had not experienced around himself the kind of milieu that sustains a person the way the tilled and fertilized earth sustains a plant and which is called our native soil. On several occasions he complained of a slight limp and a small pain in his spinal column. I treated him with massages, baths, mineral waters. It did not help. Then I attempted to study his spinal column assiduously. I was struck, ladies and gentlemen, by an insignificant spot, a bump, which could barely be felt, at the base of the spinal column, and a strange protuberance between the third and fourth ribs which caused my patient to let his shoulders droop somewhat. After I lost sight of him, I forgot about this incident. My practice grew. I had to work amost exclusively among the upper classes. I was frequently summoned to the crowned heads of Europe for diagnoses. Aristocrats arriving in America were treated exclusively by me. Among my patients were a multitude of so-called "claimants": people who had found support with the capitalists of America and who sought through their aid to regain their lost positions in their homelands. All these people were seeking power against the will of the majority of their own people. And however strange it may have been, among them I discovered several further cases of the aforementioned swelling and protuberance. The symptoms were all identical. The patients complained of one and the same thing. Treatment did not help. Almost invariably I observed practically undetectable changes in the structure of the spinal column. Finally, I was forced to draw two conclusions: that the indicated symptoms were to be encountered exclusively among the class of people who had lived for a long while far from their customary nourishment and the influence of their own people. As for the symptoms, they manifested themselves as the rarest form of degeneration. But of what kind? From that day forward, my whole life was dedicated to seeking the answer. But I was deprived of the possibility of clinically studying my highly placed patients. Then, ladies and gentlemen, I was fortunate enough to receive a clinical patient. He himself was not from among the banished rulera. He was a capitalist, a person who had appeared as a principal supporter for fugitive claimants, who placed enormous stakes on them and on their restoration to power. And however strange it was, I discovered in him the very same symptoms! With each year his shoulders drooped lower and lower. His head would assume the vertical position with the greatest reluctance, and there were no tricks whereby I could force him to look upwards. At the same time, ladies and gentlemen, the hands of my patient began to change their appearance drastically. At first they were merely badly afflicted with gout in the joints. Then I noticed that the swelling began to exceed the customary human norm. At this point, ladies and gentlemen, I should like to call a halt and illustrate the situation for you with an example. But first of all briefly about one general psychological condition which preceded the beginning of the illness in my patient. It coincided with the general symptoms in the early stages of illness in the claimants as well. This is a powerful, apparently unbearably powerful feeling of terror in the nervous system: a feeling of terror in the face of the inevitability of communism! I now go over to the example."

Doctor Lepsius sighed deeply, threw a burning gaze over the silent hall which was listening to him with bated breath, and almost casually took the lifeless hand of Professor Hiserton. The hand was in a black glove.

He tapped it amicably, raised it up high and began to pull the glove off it. One finger, two, three. Something strange, that was supposed to represent a human hand, was raised above the public from the stage.

CHAPTER 56
DOCTOR LEFSIUS' SECRET

A whisper of terror arose in the hall. Like a single person, everyone stared, without turning their eyes away, at the membranous extremity that was badly swollen in the joints, loathesomely prehensile and deformed.

"This hand," Doctor Lepsius continued, in a voice that trembled badly, and with a face pale as death, "this hand has surpassed all of my expectations. It displays a stage of degeneration that I have never before encountered in nature! Therefore, I am requesting permission from this respected gathering to display this old man in his entirety!"

The master of ceremonies, petrified with terror, did not utter a single word. A few people arose from their places in the hall. Women were close to hysterics.

And precisely at that moment, signs of revival appeared on Professor Hiserton's face. The vacant eyes grew more conscious. They fell on his own hand and horror flashed in them. His teeth grated, the cheekbones grew taut. Tearing his hand out of Lepsius', Hiserton suddenly sprang up and fastened onto his chest.

The fat man gave a scream, a moan went through the hall. Two husky policemen, appearing from behind the stage, dragged Professor Hiserton away from Lepsius. Despite their huskiness and muscles they could only restrain the small man with difficulty.

"Go on!" someone shouted from the hall. "You can't stop in the middle now!"

"I will continue," Lepsius replied with difficulty, wiping the cold sweat from his face. "I will continue and conclude. This professor is not a professor! He is incapable of working with his own mind! He is one of those who is rejected by the earth of his native land, one of those who has served as a specimen for my observations!"

With these words, Lepsius stepped resolutely up to Hiserton, seized him by his snow-white coiffure and—tore it away. The hall screamed. In place of the old man there now struggled in the hands of the policemen a middle-aged man with brilliant red hair.

"Captain Gregoire!" Bisk shrieked, plunging towards the stage. "Murderer! Hold him!"

But Bisk was not allowed up on the stage. The iron fingers of Thingsmaster had clamped on his arm.

"Just watch and listen!" he ordered him in a whisper. "You'll get your chance!"

Meanwhile, Lepsius, throwing the white wig to the floor, fearlessly seized hold of the red hair as well. A moment later—and instead of the red-haired man, there was now a pale, distorted man with brown hair in front of the hall, his lips bloodless and his eyes flashing.

"Gregorio Cice!" It was Mike Thingsmaster who shouted this time.

An eerie silence settled in.

"Ladies, remove yourselves!" Lepsius demanded. "Policemen, undress him."

A translator quickly translated Lepsius' order. But no one wanted to remove themselves, and a minute later the policemen had pulled all of Cice's clothing off, leaving him only in his underwear. Two more policemen now came to their aid. A bag was thrown over Cice's head.

"Turn his back to the public! That's right! Uncover his back down to his waist!"

The policemen began to fiddle over something.

"Ladies and gentlemen," Lepsius continued his lecture, "I must now reveal to you the essence of the degeneration that I have detected. Some of you have probably read the old German philosopher from Goethe's time, a certain Herder. In his lofty writings on humanity he introduces, among other things, the concept of the vertical structure of the human spinal column in contrast to the horizontal structure of an animal's. And thus, the lump which I have discovered has proven to be nothing other than a deformed point in the spine. This is the *vertebra media sine bestialia*. This is the beginning of the growth of the spinal column not in the vertical position, but in the horizontal, just as is to be found in animals. Take a look here..."

He quickly turned around to Cice and suddenly gave a cry:

"What the devil is that?"

"I don't know, sir," muttered the translator standing alongside the policemen who were shaking in terror. "There's something iron on him, sir, you can't get it offf his body."

The back of the stripped man was in a steel case.

Lepsius rushed up to it, looked at it from all sides, found the metalic clasps that were like the ones on ancient folios and feverishly began to unbuckle them. One, two, three...

"Remove the case!"

The policemen ripped it off, letting Cice go free for a moment. At that very second a stunning shriek burst out of thousands of mouths. Onto the table had leapt a beast with a spine that was rounded in a hump like a cat's. He leapt on all fours down from the table into the hall and flew towards the exit barely touching the ground.

"Stop him! Lepsius screamed hysterically. "It's a perfect, one-of-a-kind specimen!"

But not a single soul would have been able to hold Cice. With a shriek the crowd shrank away in terror from him and he dashed towards the unobstructed passage until Thingsmaster's thunderous voice shouted:

"Beauty!"

Then the white figure of a dog appeared across the path of the fleeing Cice. With a growl Beauty had cut off his path, but then something incredible happened. The dog's fur stood on end, her jaws worked piteously, she shuddered and retreated. The passage was free. Cice leapt towards the doors, past the crowd shrinking back in disarray. Another second—and the nocturnal gloom of Petrograd would have devoured him. At at this point a bullet came whistling through the air. A Red Army soldier, standing motionless at the spare exit, calmly lowered the barrel of his rifle to his feet. The half-beast, half-human being had collapsed on the floor short of the door, its skull shattered by a bullet.

For a period of several seconds, no one was in any condition to speak or to move from the spot. Finally the calm voice of Thingsmaster echoed:

"The one whom another beast was too squeamish to touch has ceased to exist. Comrades! But those people are still not dead who have no scruples about using beasts like him!"

"That's right!" someone's steely voiced replied. An elderly man approached the stage. He climbed up on it. He looked around the public with grey eyes, which rested for a moment on the phony Vasilov couple. But Arthur and Vivian could not stand their unbearable sufferings and the terror that had just been experienced. They had both fainted.

"I am the Attorney General of the State of Illinois," the stranger rapped out, pushing aside Lepsius who had dashed up to him. "I have been sent here in order to apprehend a dangerous criminal. But I was among the public just now and I too shrank back together with it, thus allowing him to escape. If it had not been for the accurate bullet of this calm young man, we would hardly have slept peacefully tonight."

In the hall, under the supervision of the distraught Lepsius, they were already quickly clearing away the corpse of Cice.

The stranger continued:

"Before you has appeared one of the greatest criminals of the age. He is of unknown origin. His name is Gregorio Cice. His native country overthrew his power with disgust, he was banished from its borders. And there were people who came forward to champion this man. They gave him power and money; they helped him to change his appearance; they murdered others with his hands. This man had a multitude of addresses. He was a Polish pharmacist, Wesson, from the city of Pultusk, a manufacturer and merchant of the most terrible poisons. He was also the red-haired Captain Gregoire, master of the ship *Torpedo*. He was also the villainous Professor Hiserton who let dozens of healthy, but otherwise undesirable, people rot in his madhouse near New York. In offices, banks, the army, the church, in the best districts of the city and the worst taverns, he had his helpers. His hypnotic power was mighty. His devious tricks were innumerable. He himself spread the rumor about being the descendent of Caliostro. But all the same he was not the master but only the hireling, just as Caliostro once was in the royal courts. And it is only possible to say one thing: those who used him are worse and more terrible than he is."

Having said that, the elderly man slowly climbed down from the stage, with the trembling Lepsius chasing after him. Down below, in the midst of the crowd, the fat man finally grabbed him by the coattails and embraced him with warmth.

"Sh-sh!" the Attorney General said, placing a finger to his lips. "Silence! First of all, let's take care of these two." And he pointed to Arthur Morlender and Vivian who were lying in a deep faint.

Together they carried the two of them out of the hall, summoned an automobile, put the young people on the seat, jumped in themselves, and the Attorney General named one of the Petrograd hotels to the chauffeur.

The people dispersed in silence from the convention. The lodge with the foreigners had long since emptied. Thingsmaster, Sorrow and Bisk wandered off down to the harbor, to the modest abode of Sorrow. Beauty followed slowly after. Her fur was still standing on end and her tail was convulsively pressed between her hind legs.

"The affair had a happy ending, Mike." Sorrow said guietly. "And they've let our boys go after saying thanks. And still it gives your heart a weird feeling to think that the ones who were behind Cice are still in one piece and unharmed."

"Yes," Thingsmaster replied, "but the blow they've received is stronger than a bullet."

CHAPTER 57
THE TRANSFORMED MISOGYNIST

The Attorney General and Lepsius carried the lifeless young couple into the hotel room. The doctor put his professional skills into service and within a few moments Vivian, and Arthur following her, manifested signs of life. The young girl sighed deeply, her lips stirred and she raised her eyelids. Sitting directly opposite her was the Attorney General for the State of Illinois, gazing at her anxiously. At that very moment a weak cry escaped from Vivian:

"Jeremy Morlender!" And once more she fell back on the pillow.

"Father!" Arthur mumured, regaining consciousness. "You're alive!"

"I'm alive, my friends," the Attorney General replied calmly, reaching his hand out to his son. "But before I tell you all of my story, I must make Vivian believe that her mother's death was no less a sorrow to me than to her. I was a victim of her murderers in those days. I had been captured, disarmed, crippled and sent away out of America. I was deprived of my memory and my reason. If it had not been for the iron nerves which you, Arthur, unfortunately, have not inherited from me, I would have been a corpse or a miserable idiot. But I managed to save myself and that was Cice's first failure."

"What about Mrs. Elizabeth?..." Arthur murmured in horror, beginning to suspect the truth.

"She was never my wife! That villainous woman, Arthur, is the henchwoman of the one who killed Vivian's mother, who would have killed me and both of you. She's Jack Kressling's secretary! But that's enough for today. Both of you have to recover properly before returning to New York."

Arthur closed his eyes for a moment.

"Father," he muttered, "I would prefer to stay here!"

The older Morlender raised his eyebrows in amazement. His eyes blazed with a cheerful flame.

"Stay here?" he repeated curtly.

"Yes," Arthur replied and for an instant he began to resemble his father. "I have found myself here. There's something for me to do here!"

"You've been indoctrinated," the old man uttered slowly. "You, the son off America's greatest inventor, have gone over to the side of a foreign power. Lepsius, he's been indoctrinated!" With these words Jeremy Morlender knit his eyebrows, crossed his arms over his chest and gazed threateningly at his son. "Fine, sir. Stay! But just remember that you will never find out a single word about my invention. I am committed to passing it on to my native land and only my native land. I am an enemy of melodramas and do not intend to put a curse on you. But I will say this to you: 'Farewell, sir!' And that will be once and for all."

Arthur leapt up from his place and went up to his father. Both were of the same height, and the young man with a grey strand of hair on his forehead now resembled the old man Morlender as one drop of water resembles another.

"Nothing of the sort, sir!" he exclaimed firmly. "You know quite well that I will discover your secret on my own. You know full well that once it falls into the hands of Kressling, it will never reach the American people! You old conniver, you'll have to admit that fact, and may the devil take me if you don't intend to embrace your own son, sir!"

With these words Arthur fell on the stern old man's neck who immediately responded to Arthur's wise guess.

Following the embrace, Jeremy Morlender grabbed Vivian into his arms without any further words, while Lepsius automatically kissed Arthur. But when finally Vivian came Doctor Lepsius' way and the round robin of embraces was concluded, the young people found themselves facing each other. Old Morlender coughed, winked at the fat man and both of them disappeared out of the room.

"Vivian," Arthur Morlender uttered, going up to the pale girl and stretching out his arms to her...

At this moment someone gave me a sharp tug by the hair and over my shoulder I saw the infuriated face of Jeremy Morlender.

"Sir," he said to me curtly, "as a father and Attorney General, I order you to leave these young people in peace!"

"But I'm the author!" I said indignantly. "It's impossible to end a novel without a single kiss! What will the reading public have to say?"

"They'll say, Jim Dollar, that you're not very good at love scenes!" Jeremy Morlender replied ironically.

He discouraged me completely, my friends, and therefore we will say farewell to all of these people before we bring our business to a conclusion.

CHAPTER 58
SETTO MAKES A PROFIT

Having assembled all the servants of the *Patrician* before her, Mrs. Thindick had just concluded her speech on the vagaries of nature which she had corrected and amplified for the benefit of the new staff of subordinates, when suddenly the window was shattered with a crash and a rotten egg came flying into the room.

Mrs. Thindick raised her eyebrows.

But at the same moment a rotten potato splattered against her nose, and two or three fresh eggs pasted her cheeks.

"Fire!" Mrs. Thindick screamed and fell flat on the floor.

Meanwhile, Setto from Diarbekir came running hastily down the stairs.

"What could it mean?" he asked the staff, frowning. "There's a crowd in front of the hotel. They're forcing their way in through our windows and hurling third-rate groceries!"

"Politics, boss," the cook replied gloomily. "In politics the first thing they do is raise the price of food."

"Go and get a newspaper!"

The cook plopped his hat on unwillingly and went to carry out the patron's order.

Five minutes later Setto unfolded a fresh copy of the *New York Illustrated Gazette* and ran his eyes down the columns.

"Aha! What's this?"

The eyes of the man from Diarbekir narrowed like those of a cat when it's being scratched behind the ear, his cheeks turned pink, his lips went slack. Before him in heavy black print stood:

AMERICANS Read about the discoveries of the famous Doctor Lepsius!!! LADIES Read our newspaper! BILLIONAIRES Who have current accounts!! PATRONS FOR EX-PRESIDENTS Buy today's edition!!!!!!! TAKE A LOOK In the newspaper!!!!!!!!!!!

"We know very well," thus began the article, "that many American families who chase after their forebears completely forget about their offspring. Some of them buy parchment folios in the firm belief that if they own a parchment folio, then they have an ancient ancestor from a famous family. Others affirm that their relatives arrived in America on the first ship. Yet others dash off to Europe in search of lords and viscounts. Finally, there are those—and these are the most dangerous—who harbor a weakness for overthrown politicians who have been banished by their own peoples. Particularly guilty of the latter crime are our native billionaires who prefer to waste American dollars not for the welfare of an American, but for the support of tottering thrones, slipping epaulettes and falling portfolios. Those who have been banished by their native lands promise us anything they feel like, as long as they can fill their pockets with the almighty dollar. But in reality, they are only leading us on and putting America in a ridiculous position. It would not be superfluous to know, ladies and gentlemen, how things stand in medicine with these banished people. Our famous authority, the esteemed member of Boston University, Doctor Lepsius, who has just returned from a scientific congress, has provided us with clarifications on his discovery which was made while treating ex-presidents and ex-generals. Since the discovery is highly technical in its medical nature, it is difficult to understand. But the venerable scholar did not refuse to help us in popularizing it. The matter concerns—as he explained in a conversation with our colleague—"the detection of the *vertebra bestialia* within *processum spinozum* of the creatura humana." In other words, ladies and gentlemen, the henchmen of our billionaires are fated in the near future to jump around on all fours and not to eat while sitting at a table, but, one might say, while lapping it up out of a dish. Moreover, the aforementioned disease is infectious even for the billionaires themselves! But enough about that!! I ask you: is it permissible to waste American dollars on that sort of people? No, a hundred times no, ladies and gentlemen! Down with the ex-beggars! Down with the ex-thrones and ex-titles! And the same with the bishops and cardinals! Remove the parchment from private use and distribute it among the food stores of the United States to be used as wrapping paper for strictly trade purposes! That's the will of millions of voters!"

Setto finished reading the newspaper and got up.

"Wife!" he shouted in a breaking voice. "Wife! Wife! Wife!"

The mistress of the *Patrician* came running out in response to his call just the way she was: in a kitchen apron with a tomato in her hand.

"Wife!" Setto declared in a triumphant voice. "Call the musicians, clap your hands, dance around me with music. Setto from Diarbekir is a great man! He got his full profit: a hundred to fifty!"

EPILOGUE

But in Middletown at the woodworking plant work was seething as though nothing were out of the ordinary. The curly-haired blond giant was wielding his wood-plane skillfully, shaking the drops of sweat off his forehead. His overalls billowed up, the shavings flew in clouds, and the giant's voice cheerfully took up the familiar tune:

> With wooden lathe and plane and glue,
> We promise husbands fine for you.
> From workers' hands and craftsmen's too,
> Are born our daughters—such pretty things.
>
> Go forth on guard where foes do dwell,
> In banks and belle-estages as well,
> Return from there to tattle-tell
> About their regal lords and kings.

"Listen here, Jim Dollar," Michael Thingsmaster said, putting his plane down and looking at me with his wide blue eyes. "You prettied up this story a little bit. The boys are complaining a lot about the fact that you betrayed our secrets ahead of time."

"But what's so bad about that, Mike?" I muttered in reply. "My job is to describe things and yours is to handle things."

Cheerful familiar faces gathered around us in a crowd. There was the grey-eyed Laurie, the staid Willings, and the long-nosed Ned with a cheerful, tail-wagging Beauty. There was the old-timer, Sorrow, with a pipe in his mouth. Bisk, Tom and Van Hope looked in at the workshop for the sake of the occasion. And even Carlo the Jamaican and a few of the boys from the wallpaper factory in Bindorf who had finally joined up with the "Mess-Mend" alliance, stuck their noses in the door.

"Enough, hold your tongue!" they bellowed, giving me a few friendly punches. "Just bite your old woman's tongue about anything more!" And the workshop, in a single voice, took up Mike's tune:

> On kulak's carts so richly laden,
> Upon the general's mighty gun,
> On all the rich man's source of fun,
> Our trademark travels through the land.

For all our father's calloused pains,
For all our want and bitter chains,
Avenge yourselves in labor plain
Creating marvels with a worker's hand.